SEVENTEEN

A SEVENTEEN SERIES NOVEL

BY

SUZANNE LOWE

© SILVERGUM PUBLISHING

First published in 2016
This edition published 2019
Silvergum Publishing Pty Ltd
www.silvergumpublishing.com

National Library of Australia Cataloguing-in-Publication entry:

Lowe, Suzanne, author.
ISBN: 978-0-6483908-4-8
ISBN e-book: 978-0-6483908-5-5

For Young Adults.
Subject: Young Adult Fiction, Science Fiction/Australia

THE SEVENTEEN SERIES

BOOK ONE

"The will to survive can exist in anyone regardless of age, gender or training."

To Steve, Tahlia and Emilie

Many thanks for all your ideas,

the discussions around the dinner table

and your encouragement.

VIRUS

"An infective agent that typically consists of a nucleic acid molecule, is too small to be seen by light microscopy, and is able to multiply only within the living cells of a host."

English Oxford Dictionary

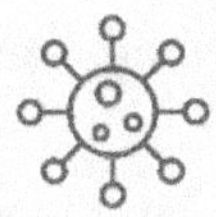

Chapter One

"If you want to survive, you're going to have to learn to be ruthless." It was the last thing he said to Lexi before he left them. What he really meant was, she was going to have to learn to be a total bitch.

That was a few months after the KV17 virus was released on Earth changing every living person's life forever. Lexi and her family were totally unprepared for what was to follow, and they weren't the only ones. The whole world was completely unprepared for the swift and total breakdown of modern society. Within only a few short months' teenagers would rule the Earth. Everything Lexi knew and grew up with would be changed forever, and so would she.

Only six months earlier, the warning signs had started in a little town called Yamagata in the north of Japan. A nasty dispute had been brewing between Japan and North Korea for several months, with threatening words raising resentments in the area. When a small aircraft carrying an illegal biological substance, crashed into Mt. Zoo in Japan, hostilities were heightened even further. The world waited with growing anxiety as it seemed as if war were imminent.

Lexi Valentine was a typical sixteen-year-old Australian teenager who enjoyed going to BBQ's on the weekend and hanging out with her friends at the beach. She wasn't particularly good-looking; she couldn't play a musical instrument or speak several languages. She wasn't even all that skilled at sports. Lexi was completely average. She did, however, have the uncanny ability to read people. She was perceptive about other people's feelings.

So, when Lexi first heard her parents talking about the plane crash in Asia and its suspicious cargo, she could tell by the look on her mother's face that it was serious. Lexi, however, chose to ignore that observation. She assumed that something that was happening on the other side of the world wouldn't affect her and her family and that her mother was just being anxious. All Lexi wanted to do was spend as much time as possible with her friends before the holidays ended, and the new school term started. This year was her final year of school, and it was going to be a tough one. Her parents were expecting her to do well.

"Are you ready for school tomorrow?" asked Lexi's mother preparing dinner. "Year 12, big year."

Lexi looked at her mother and tried not to roll her eyes, knowing it would only cause an argument. "Yes mum, big year. I can't wait," she replied sarcastically.

"At least you'll get to see your friends," interrupted Hadley, Lexi's eleven-year-old sister. "That's if you've still got some!" she said, poking out her tongue.

Lexi turned her back on Hadley and tried to ignore her. She picked up a carrot and started preparing it for a salad. "I wonder if anyone got a tattoo or pierced lip over the holidays?" Lexi ran her tongue over her top lip. "Jessica Buckley told me she was getting a tattoo of a large, redback spider on her neck before term break," she laughed.

"Did she?" asked Mrs Valentine raising her eyebrows. "I wonder what her mother thought of that!" She placed sliced carrots, lettuce, tomatoes and capsicum in a bowl and handed it to Hadley to put on the dinner table.

"Yeah, well that's what she said," Lexi replied nodding. "But I doubt she went ahead with it."

"Did you read that article about the town of Yamagata being placed under strict curfew," inquired Lexi's father as he walked into the kitchen to join the family. "It's plastered all over the front page. Apparently, the town's population has been dying from some new sickness, and the authorities are trying to stop it spreading." He folded the newspaper he was carrying in half and placed it on the kitchen bench. He was frowning.

"That doesn't sound good," said Mrs Valentine as she motioned for Hadley to finish setting the table for dinner. "Do they know what it is?"

Mr Valentine shook his head and sat down at the table. "No. According to the newspaper, they're doing tests at the Centre for Infectious Disease in Tokyo, and I saw on the internet that the sickness had something to do with that plane crash. They think it contained a new biological weapon."

"Well, don't they know?"

Mr Valentine shrugged. "Supposedly, there were containers in the cargo hold of the plane, but the authority's originally thought they were empty." He scratched his nose and glanced at Mrs Valentine. "Guess they'll have to re-test them."

Lexi could see that her parents looked anxious about the Japanese town being quarantined; however, she didn't pay much attention. All she could think about was school tomorrow. Hadley wasn't interested either, and both girls sat down at the table and began discussing the latest episode of the television program, *The Bachelor*.

*

＊　　＊

By the end of the first day back at school, Lexi was feeling worn out; year twelve was tough. Dragging herself wearily out of the school gates, she was relieved to see her mum's red car waiting to take her home. She'd had enough of school for one day and just wanted to get away.

Lexi could see Hadley was already in the car. "Great," Lexi muttered to herself, wanting to have some quiet. She knew she wouldn't get any peace with Hadley there as she loved to talk. Actually, that was pretty much *all* Hadley did. Blah, blah, blah nonstop. No one else could get a word in edgeways, not even the girl's mother.

As soon as Lexi sat in the car, Hadley started chatting straight away. Lexi groaned and rested her head against the car window. She tried to zone Hadley out as much as possible by listening to the music playing on the car radio, but it didn't really work. Hadley kept poking her in the ribs, trying to gain her attention.

Looking at her daughters in the rear vision mirror, Mrs Valentine smiled. "How was your first day back at school, Lexi?" she asked, attempting to rescue her older daughter.

Lexi smiled back at her mum gratefully. "Alright," she replied. "I spent most of the day with my friends Alice and Olivia which was cool, but my history teacher gave me an assignment already," she groaned.

Hadley grinned. "*I* don't have any homework. So, I can watch Game of Thrones tonight!"

"Ah, no you can't," warned Mrs Valentine. "You're too young."

It was Lexi's turn to grin, making Hadley grumble and pout. At least with Hadley sulking she was now silent! Lexi closed her eyes and listened to the radio.

*

* *

The next morning as Lexi was sitting in the Valentine family kitchen contemplating her second day at school, she again overheard her parents talking about the town in Japan. There had now been several deaths, and the sickness had spread to numerous other cities. All of Japan was on high alert.

"Do you think it will spread to Australia?" her mother asked uneasily. She was frantically cleaning the same spot on the kitchen bench over and over again.

Lexi's father put his hand over her mothers, trying to calm her. "I'm sure we will be fine. Australia is a long way away from Japan." He leaned in closer, talking quietly. "The health officials will work out what it is soon and develop a cure. It'll be okay."

Lexi watched her parent's talking about the new sickness. Her mother was frowning and fidgeting with her wedding ring, twisting it around and around her finger.

Surely her father was right, and Australia's distance and isolation from the rest of the world would keep them safe. Nothing would change in their normal, routine lives, would it? Lexi watched her parents for a moment longer, before grabbing her backpack and heading to school. She was anxious to see her friends and see if they had seen anything on the internet about the sickness.

When Lexi got to school, she became immersed in the school day and what the teachers had organised for the rest of the week, forgetting about the *going's on* in Japan. Year twelve was very busy with numerous assignments and tests, not to mention the organisation of the school ball!

Life continued as usual for a few weeks. It wasn't until there was a sudden increase in the number of reported cases of large groups of people dying worldwide, that Lexi realised the sickness had spread from Japan and was now reaching the rest of the globe. Unfortunately, her father had been wrong. Australia, like the rest of the world, was now facing an epidemic.

It was a new sickness the world had not encountered before, and just like viruses such as Ebola and the Bird-flu, it took the world by surprise. As the pathogens made their way into the air, invisible to the naked eye, humanities fate was sealed.

The virus had a very short incubation period and an unusually long lifespan outside the host's body, making it a real threat. Once you came into contact with the virus, you fell sick within 24 hours. There was no escaping it. The sickness had spread worldwide, in tiny droplets of saliva in a cough or sneeze by people unaware they were infected.

The first death occurred in Western Australia from Karvo-virus, or KV17 as the newspapers were now calling it, three weeks before Christmas. Australia had finally caught up with everyone else. Lexi and Hadley's small world which usually revolved around Facebook, texting and the latest YouTube sensation, was about to change dramatically.

People on the girl's street started to fall sick quickly. Schools were shut down and neighbours kept away from each other. Everyone started wearing white, medical face masks and buying copious amounts of hand sanitiser and room deodoriser. None of these things helped. People still got sick, and people continued to die.

The odd thing about it was that only adults were getting sick. Strangely, children seemed to be immune to the disease. There were regular broadcasts on the radio informing people about the virus. KV17 was found to have been produced for warfare by the military. A biological weapon meant to attack the cardiovascular and nervous systems of the human body. Why only adults were falling sick was less clear. Something about areas of the adult brain being more developed than children's making them more susceptible to these particular pathogens.

Lexi didn't really understand it, and it seemed neither did the scientists. What was clear though, was that not one child had died or even become sick from the outbreak. The virus was targeted at killing adults, which made sense if it was initially developed for warfare.

When the virus first hit Perth, some people left town straight away, hoping to run from it. The problem was, there was nowhere to run to. The virulent disease had permeated into the earth's atmosphere and spread worldwide. It was in the air, and you couldn't run from that. Most people decided to stay put in their towns and cities, hoping the government would come to their rescue and find a cure.

They didn't.

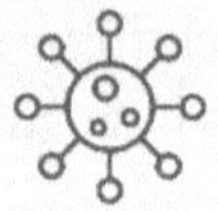

CHAPTER TWO

"**I** think we should stay in Perth," Mr Valentine was advising, tapping his finger on the kitchen counter. "I figure that way we can all sleep in our own beds and be comfortable among our own things." He looked at his family. "What's the use of running when there is nowhere to go?"

Mrs Valentine agreed. If the family had owned a holiday house on some isolated stretch of beach or island away from other people, she might have thought differently. However, they didn't, so she nodded her head and patted his arm, putting on a cheerful face. "Let's stay put."

The Valentine sisters were more than happy to stay in Perth as well. All their friends had remained in Perth, and everything they knew was there. Although the schools had been shut down, their parents stayed in their jobs, and life continued in a strange way.

Lexi tried to stay productive. She used the free time she had at home to read through her school textbooks, just in case school started again, and watch a few old movies she'd wanted to see. Apart from the constant threat of illness all around her, she was actually enjoying being at home. After the continual pressure of year twelve, and all the study that came with it, the lazy days felt like bliss.

Life carried on like that for a few weeks, getting into a strange sort of routine. Getting up, making sure everyone was feeling well, doing chores, listening out for news reports and having free time. Then, Lexi's mother came home with some bad news.

"Well, that's it. I've been laid off!" Mrs Valentine walked into the kitchen and dumped a box of her possessions on the bench.

"What! Why?" asked Lexi getting up from the table where she'd been reading. 'I thought they loved you there?"

Mrs Valentine rummaged through the box and pulled out a plaque saying, "worker of the month". She frowned as she stared at it. "It's not their fault. The whole place has closed down. People just aren't buying plants and gardening products."

Lexi nodded her head. "Yeah, there's so many places closing down. It seems like a new place is shutting every second day."

Mrs Valentine threw the award back into the box. "There's not enough workers to keep things going. You might as well put those school books away. I don't think they're going to be reopening the schools any time soon," she frowned. "I think we should start stockpiling some more food."

Lexi looked at the apple she had been eating and placed it on the bench. "Haven't we got enough? You've already stored a lot in the spare room."

"Hmmm. Still, we don't know how long this epidemic is going to last." Lexi's mother looked grim. "I think I had better head to the supermarket and stock up. I want some more candles, dried beans and rice. I hope they're still open." Her frown grew deeper. Once the supermarkets started closing, it wouldn't be long before looting and violence broke out.

"I'll come and help," offered Lexi closing her school book and shoving it away. She was tempted to throw it in the bin but restrained herself knowing it would annoy her mother. "We should purchase some more medical supplies and vitamins too."

Lexi followed her mum to the front door. *If her mother, who was already a bit of a prepper wanted to buy more food, things must be even more severe than she thought.* Lexi decided once she had finished helping, she would pay a visit to her friends and see what they knew.

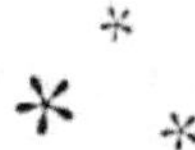

Later that afternoon Lexi convinced her friends to meet her at the local park. Being only a few streets away from where they lived, the girls could walk there easily. Lexi hummed as she walked. She hadn't seen either of her friends for a couple of weeks and was looking forward to catching up with them. Since the schools and many of the businesses had closed, people didn't leave their homes much anymore unless it was to buy food or try to see a doctor. Her friends were the same. Lexi had only been able to talk on the telephone or text with them.

Once Lexi reached the playground, she sat on one of the swings and waited for them. She couldn't wait to hang out with her friends and do stupid things that only friends would laugh at. After being cooped up at home for a month, Lexi needed some *friends* time.

Olivia was the first to arrive, followed soon after by Alice.

"Isn't it weird no one is here?" said Alice looking around the playground. It was usually bursting with kids running around enjoying themselves.

"I know," agreed Lexi. "It's kind of nice though, having the place to ourselves," she smiled. "Even if it's not exactly how I remember it." She nodded towards the overflowing bins and smashed glass bottles on the ground.

"I can't believe everything around here has gone downhill so quickly just because of a stupid virus!" exclaimed Olivia.

"It's crazy," agreed Lexi shaking her head. She walked over to the monkey bars and reached up to the metal rungs. She lifted her feet from the ground and swung for a moment. "My mum got laid off work today. It probably won't be long until Dad is too."

"Geeze," muttered Olivia. "That sucks. My mum and dad got the sack a couple of weeks ago, not long after the school closed. Don't suppose there was any point having them there without any kids to teach," she shrugged. "It's been difficult since then. I think Mum's a bit depressed."

Lexi climbed down from the monkey bars and went to hug her friend.

"What do you think you are doing Olivia!" bellowed a loud, angry voice, making the girls jump.

"Shit!" exclaimed Olivia, glancing at Lexi. "Dad's here."

Olivia's father stormed up to the girls and started ranting about germs and infection. He yelled at them to go home and wash their hands thoroughly with some disinfectant. Olivia's father spoke animatedly, waving his arms around over his head. His face had been like a red balloon, and the girls were worried he was going to have a heart attack.

Lexi looked at her friend and gave her a small smile. She could see Olivia was immensely embarrassed. Her face was bright pink, and there were tears in her eyes. No one likes to be yelled at by their father in front of their friends. "It's okay, Olivia. I'll talk to you later. Lexi managed to say before Olivia's father grabbed his daughter by the arm and pulled her down the street away from her friends.

"I suppose we should go home too," suggested Alice, not long after Olivia had left. The joyous mood of the afternoon had been lost.

Lexi hugged Alice goodbye and started to walk home; she kicked her feet along the ground as she went. *Olivia's father was probably right. They shouldn't have been out of their homes, but there hadn't been anyone else around, and they had just wanted to spend some time together. It just wasn't the same when all you could do was Skype or talk on the phone.*

After the park "*incident*" Lexi didn't hear from Olivia for a few days, and neither did Alice. They figured that she was still feeling embarrassed about her dad yelling at them, so they gave her some space and didn't call her.

A few days later, Lexi's dad came to her bedroom early in the morning and knocked on her door, waking her up. She could tell something was wrong by the serious look on his face, not to mention that it was five in the morning.

"It's for you," her father said bleary-eyed as he held out the family's home phone to her.

Lexi quickly grabbed the phone immediately expecting trouble. It was Olivia on the phone. "My parents have decided to leave Perth," she mumbled. Her voice sounded thick and hoarse as if she'd been crying. "We're going to Merredin to stay with my Uncle Peter, he's got a small wheat farm," she exclaimed tearfully.

"Can I come over and see you before you go?" Lexi asked quietly gripping the phone tightly. She could hear Olivia's dad yelling in the background.

"No, we're leaving this morning," Olivia sobbed. "Dad says I can't see anyone!" Olivia's voice faded away.

Lexi stared at her bedroom wall trying not to break down. Her bottom lip quivered. She wanted to ask her friend so many questions, and Lexi didn't know how long they would be able to talk. She could hear Olivia's parents arguing loudly.

"Are you coming back?"

"I don't think so" replied Olivia her voice getting quieter and quieter.

Lexi didn't know what to say. Her friend sounded so sad, and she wanted to try and cheer her up. "Well, at least we can still talk on the phone and Skype," she suggested trying to be cheerful even though her stomach was in knots and she felt as though she were going to throw up.

"There's no internet or phone coverage where we are going," wailed Olivia her voice suddenly loud. "I wish I didn't have to go!"

It was right about then that Olivia's father grabbed the phone. "I'm sorry, but Olivia has to go now," he stated gruffly before hanging up.

Lexi felt stunned. She sat on the edge of her bed with the phone dangling from her hand like an unwanted toy. She was shocked and numb. *What the hell had just happened? Why was Olivia's dad acting this way? He was usually so calm.*

That was the last Lexi or any of her friends ever heard from Olivia. It was as though she had vanished from the face of the earth. Lexi thought about her all the time, wondering what she was doing and if her family were alright. She sat in her room and tried to write Olivia a letter.

"What's the point," she yelled angrily, screwing up the paper and throwing it at the wall. "I don't know her new address, and there's no postal service working anymore anyway!" Hot angry tears rolled down her face as she stared out the window. It was difficult to just forget about someone who has been a part of your life daily for close to five years. Hearing a timid knock at her bedroom door, Lexi wiped her eyes and went to see who it was.

"You okay?" her mother asked poking her head into the room. Her brow was furrowed.

Lexi nodded slightly. "I'm just feeling sad today. I miss Olivia, and I haven't been able to get hold of Alice for the last two days." Lexi scratched her head and shrugged. "She's not answering her phone."

Her mother blinked slowly as if she wanted to say something. She rubbed her eyes.

"What's wrong?" Lexi put her hand on her mother's shoulder. "Is it Dad?' her voice rose.

Mrs Valentine took her daughter's hand in hers. "No, it's not Dad. It's Alice and her family."

Lexi stared at her mum. "What is it?" she said her voice trembling.

"They've left the city." Mrs Valentine's tone was flat as though she was disappointed.

"What! No, that can't be right. She would have told me!" Lexi grabbed her phone and frantically dialled Alice's number. There was no answer. Lexi peered at the phone, her eyebrows coming together in concentration. *Why didn't Alice call her?*

Mrs Valentine placed her hand gently on Lexi's arm. "Dad spoke to their neighbours, the Melsoms. Apparently, they left yesterday, just driving away in the middle of the night."

Lexi looked at her mother for a moment before her face crumpled. "But I didn't even get to say goodbye to her! Why would they just leave like that?" Tears formed in her already red eyes.

"I don't know, Lexi. I guess some people can't handle goodbyes." She put her arm around Lexi's shoulders and hugged her daughter to her. "Why don't you try texting her or leaving her a message," she suggested.

Lexi nodded, hugging her mother for a long while. She felt devastated. Both her friends had now left the city, and even though her own family was with her, she felt abandoned. A few months ago, they had been excitedly planning what they were going to wear to the school ball, their thoughts filled with gowns, hairstyles and limousines, and what they were going to do when school ended. Travel, university, work? Lexi hadn't decided what she was going to do with her future, and now all of that suddenly didn't even matter. That way of life was gone. Everything she had known and grown up with was slowly disappearing. Now, even Lexi's friends were no longer part of her life, and it felt so strange. She was struggling to adapt to the changes.

Mr Valentine came into Lexi's room to join her. She looked at him and shook her head. "Why is everyone moving away?" she asked as she stared out the window at another family loading belongings into their car. The vehicle was already crammed with overflowing boxes and suitcases. "Unless they're leaving to be with family, I don't understand it."

Lexi's father stood by his daughter and pulled back the curtains. He too peered outside at their neighbours. "I don't understand it either, Lexi," he said frowning. "Surely the situation won't be any better elsewhere? Alice's family didn't even know where they were driving to! It's insane."

They both stared at the family outside as they hurriedly drove away as if they had somewhere important to be.

"The government and health officials have said to remain in your house, and try to stay healthy," Mr Valentine stated, closing the curtains. "And that's what we are going to do." He went to stand by Mrs Valentine. "That was our initial plan, and we're sticking to it. It doesn't matter what everyone else does."

Lexi gave her parents a sad smile before flinging herself onto her bed and picking up her phone to text Alice. She hoped her father was right because at this moment she felt very much alone.

Lexi's family decided to stay in their home, hoping to wait things out until the virus died out like the plague eventually did, or the scientists and doctors finally developed a vaccine. That was her father's plan, and everything was going alright until nature decided to throw a curveball. Then everything suddenly changed.

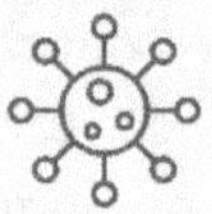

CHAPTER THREE

It had started as a normal day for Lexi, well, normal for this *new life* they had been so suddenly thrust into. Lexi and Hadley's parents had been out to the local supermarket trying to buy fresh food, of which there was now a minimal supply and had come home feeling unusually exhausted. Nobody thought anything of it and put it down to the fact that they'd walked quite a distance to and from the supermarket rather than driving. Petrol was now being rationed by the government to conserve supplies. Hadley and Lexi had made dinner of 'chilli and rice', and after clearing up and chatting for a while, the family had gone to bed as usual.

The next day was different. Lexi remembered it vividly. Around 11 o'clock Lexi awoke to find the house abnormally silent. Hadley was apparently still asleep, which was not unusual, however, so were her parents. Climbing out of bed, Lexi stumbled to her parent's room. *Why was it so quiet?*

"How come you guys are still in bed? Are you feeling alright?" The lights were off in their room, and the curtains were still drawn. Lexi immediately felt worried and went farther into the room. The first thing she noticed, was the blue and white covers of her parent's bed lay in disarray around their feet as if they had been tossing and turning in the night. Then, she noticed how terrible they looked.

Lexi breathed in sharply and rushed to their bedside. Her mother's face was an ashen grey colour, and her hair was plastered to her forehead, slick with sweat. Her father looked the same.

"Mum, what's wrong? You don't look so good."

"I'm fine," mumbled her mother. "I think we just have a bout of the flu. We just needed to rest." Her voice sounded stuffy as though her nose were blocked, and her throat inflamed.

Lexi looked at her mum's face, and just for a moment, she saw her cheerful façade fail. Lexi could see in her eyes that her mother knew it wasn't just the common flu. Leaning forward, Lexi had peered closely at her parent's faces. Their eyes were blood red-coloured and swollen, and their hands were covered in a red, inflamed rash. It was the KV17 virus!

Lexi's hands flew to her mouth in realisation and horror. She closed her eyes and sat on the edge of the bed, placing her head in her hands. No one ever got better from this virus. No one she knew of anyway. Every adult who developed this sickness had died. The latest news reports had said that the government was still putting every available resource into trying to create a vaccine against the virus, but so far everything they tried had failed. Lexi looked up to the ceiling and prayed that they would find one soon. Soon enough to help her parents.

Mrs Valentine seemed to get it the worst. She quickly developed a blistering fever that turned her body into a burning hothouse. Each cold cloth Lexi and Hadley laid on her hot forehead became warm within minutes. She was wracked with a persistent hacking cough, weakening her already ravaged body quickly sapping her energy. Every morning, Lexi would pull open the rose-coloured curtains blocking the sun's harsh light and open the windows. She hoped to cool the stifling room with a little breeze in the intense summer heat. The Government had now rationed electricity to a few hours a day per suburb, and even then, the limited supply would only power small appliances. Anything like an air-conditioner would not work as it drew too much power.

In the evening, Hadley and Lexi made her vegetable soup, and although she didn't have an appetite, she tried to eat some anyway. With only a limited supply of fresh food left, their mother had not wanted to waste it. Sitting on their parent's bed which had always seemed so big to the girls when they were young, the family had noisily slurped their soup. It was a good way for them all to be close to her and this way, she didn't have to expend her limited energy and walk to the kitchen.

A couple of days later Lexi and Hadley heard their father arguing on the telephone with their local doctor. He sounded furious; his voice loud and gruff as he started to yell and swear. Lexi could see his fists clenched in tight balls of fury.

Hadley looked at Lexi in alarm. "What's going on?" she whispered, her eyes growing wide.

Their father rarely got angry; it was their mother who had a short fuse and quick temper.

"I don't know," said Lexi quietly. "Let's go and check on Mum." She turned to run to her parent's room with Hadley close behind her. Their mother was propped up on pillows with her body slumped slightly to one side. Her eyes were closed, and she looked worse. "Mum," whispered Lexi, as she quickly took her mum's hand in hers. It felt hot and clammy, and Lexi felt an immediate sense of dread.

Lexi's eyes flicked to Hadley who was staring bleakly at them, her gaze wide and unsure. "Go and fetch some water," Lexi suggested in a hushed tone not wanting to disturb their mother.

"Okay," said Hadley, her voice barely a whisper.

Lexi placed her mother's hand back on the bed and noticed she was now awake. Her eyes were puffy from sleep, but she was smiling and seemed happy. Lexi threw her arms around her mother giving her a big hug. *Maybe things weren't going to be so bad, after all.*

The family sat together all morning. Hadley and Lexi snuggled up on the bed as though they were five years old reading to their mother from one of her favourite books; *Chocolat* by Joanne Harris.

Even though the girls tried to make her comfortable, their mother quickly tired and soon fell back into a restless sleep. She mumbled while she slept as if her dreams were tormenting her, and the fever returned with a vengeance, making her head burn as though there were hot coals buried under her skin.

Neither Lexi nor Hadley wanted to move from their quiet vigil. They sat quietly by her side, not quite sure what to do, but at the same time not wanting to leave. Just sitting and watching her. All the time hoping the fever would break, and she would wake up feeling better. Their dad came and sat too, bringing fresh cold flannels to wipe her feverish face. She would moan quietly when the cool cloth touched her brow, and Lexi hoped it gave her some relief from the persistent fever.

By the time the afternoon rolled on, the girls could see their mother was losing her fight with the virus. She no longer opened her eyes when they spoke, and sometime around three o'clock, she took her last laboured breath.

"Mum!" Lexi laid face down on the bed next to her mother and cried. Big uncontrollable sobs wracked her body. The shock of her mum's death, along with the emotion she felt at losing her two best friends only days earlier completely floored her. She let her sadness gush out of her like a dam breaking its banks.

"It's okay, Lexi." Her father said emotionally as he tried to comfort her, placing his arm loosely around her back.

Lexi rudely shoved him away. "Leave me alone!" she yelled, before running to her bedroom. She could hear him calling plaintively after her, his voice hoarse and raspy with grief. Lexi knew it wasn't his fault that her mother had died, but she couldn't help feeling angry at him. She was angry at him, angry at the government, angry at the world for letting this happen. All her friends had gone, and now her mother had died, and she hadn't been able to do anything about any of it! Lexi felt helpless, with no control over anything and she loathed the feeling. She hated feeling so utterly at the mercy of nature. Lexi wasn't used to it. None of them were. *Humans ruled the world, didn't they?* We'd conquered the oceans, the land, even space and now a microscopic bug was conquering us!

Staring wretchedly out of her bedroom window, Lexi glared at the crows sitting on the fence. They were making an ugly cawing noise. Caw, caw caw…

They wouldn't shut up! She wanted to run outside and throw something at them.

What reason had they to be so happy? Instead, feeling defeated, she lay down on her bed and cried, covering her ears with her hands.

After a while, Hadley and her father knocked tentatively on the closed door. Lexi sheepishly invited them in. Her father carried a cup of tea in his hand, which he placed on her bedside table before giving Lexi a small smile, his eyes remaining sad. Hadley hovered by the doorway uncertainly, her face and eyes red and puffy from crying. Lexi felt terrible for having yelled at her dad as she knew he and Hadley were hurting just as much as she was.

Pushing herself up from her bed with one great heave, Lexi threw her arms around her dad's waist and gave him a hug. "I'm sorry," she said tearfully.

After a while, Lexi's father gently pulled her away and looked into her eyes. His face was serious and grave. "It's okay to be upset, Lexi. We all are. But we have to stick together as a family and look after each other." Lexi's father nodded his head towards Hadley before a coughing fit made him bend over double. His words silenced by the spasms.

Lexi glanced at Hadley in concern. She was staring at their dad with a look of horror in her eyes. The girls had momentarily forgotten that their father was sick too. He had been so brave looking after their mother, always putting her needs first, often ignoring his own.

Suddenly, Lexi knew why her dad had nodded towards Hadley. He meant for her to look after Hadley if something happened to him! She stared at him in shock. *He couldn't die too!* Lexi quickly led him into the lounge room and eased him into one of the comfy armchairs. The coughing had stopped for now, but his face was hot and red from the exertion, and he looked agitated. Hadley brought him a drink of water, and Lexi turned off the main light and lit a couple of candles. With the light off, they had enough electricity to power the radio. However, the signal was weak, and the broadcaster only repeated information about the virus over and over again. In exasperation, Lexi tried to change the channel, but they were all the same. In the end, Lexi put on a CD of mixed music from the eighties which her father loved. Hadley sat next to him, her head resting on his shoulder.

Once their father was settled, Lexi made her way back to her parent's room. Her father and Hadley had pulled a blanket up to her mother's chin and placed a yellow rose on her chest. After days of fighting the virus and trying to stay strong, she looked peaceful at last. Walking closer to the bed, Lexi brushed a stray strand of hair from her mother's forehead. She gently took her mother's hand, her eyes widening a little in surprise at how cold and stiff her mum's fingers were.

"Oh, Mum," she cried. The site of her mother lying cold and lifeless brought a fresh bought of tears to Lexi's eyes. She wanted to be as strong as her mother had been but instead found herself bawling again. She gently laid her head on her mother's chest. *How much more could this virus take?*

About half an hour later, Lexi's father quietly walked into the room to join his oldest daughter. He gently laid his hand on her shoulder. "I have to phone the Health Department hotline," he said with a broken voice. "I'm supposed to let them know she died."

"Who?" Lexi asked.

"The government. They've got a *hotline* you're supposed to ring," he muttered sadly. His face was creased and strained as if he had suddenly aged in the last 24 hours.

"Apparently it's now standard procedure for anyone dying of, or suspected of dying of the virus, to be taken away by government officials." He ran his hand over his face. "It's now illegal to hold funerals at funeral parlours, or burials at cemeteries."

"What! Why?" asked Lexi her voice rising.

Her father shook his head. "I guess it's because the government is trying everything to stem the spread of infection."

While Lexi knew the government was trying to contain the virus and find a cure, it all seemed very cruel and harsh. *Weren't we all still human and entitled to our right to say goodbye to our loved ones and hold a funeral for them? It seemed to be an important human ritual that people shouldn't just be forced to give up.*

"So, are you saying we can't hold a funeral for Mum?" Lexi asked her father. She slammed her fist on her mother's bedside table making the half-empty glass of water sitting there, wobble. "It just doesn't seem right!" Her face had turned red and blotchy.

"I know Lexi," her dad replied unhappily. "We can't do anything about it. The authorities must take your mum away. None of the funeral homes are holding funerals anymore." He stared out the window into their back yard deep in thought.

"We could hold our own ceremony here at the house?" he suggested pointing to the backyard. "We can plant some flowers or something for her. She would like that."

Walking over to where her dad stood, Lexi glanced out the window. She nodded in agreement. *They could hold their own funeral.* At least it would be something.

About an hour after Mr Valentine made his phone call to the authorities, officials dressed in khaki green clothes, face masks and gloves barged into the Valentine family home and took Mrs Valentine. It was all clinical and abrupt with barely a word spoken to the family.

Lexi watched as her dad signed a clipboard thrust at him by some nameless official as if he were signing for a delivery from Australia Post. She felt devastated. It was as though their home was being violated and a vital part taken away. It was such a shock. Even though she knew her mother was sick, she had always thought her mum would somehow get better or a cure found in time. Lexi had seen it happening to families all around her; however, she never thought it would happen to hers. Both Hadley and their father were utterly shattered as well.

After the men had taken the girl's mother away, the two sisters had ridden their bikes down to the local nursery where their mum used to work to buy a plant. Wandering inside, they were surprised at how unkempt the whole place looked. It was obvious that no one had worked there for many weeks. Someone had spray painted blue graffiti on one of the walls, and the gates were swinging wide open making a loud metallic clanging noise.

"How about this one?" said Hadley pointing to a cute little tree full of blossoms that was perfect for their mum. *Cherries had been Mrs Valentine's favourite fruit.*

"Perfect!" agreed Lexi picking up the plant ready to carry back to their bikes. She felt guilty at taking the tree without paying, however; she didn't think anyone really cared anymore, and there wasn't anyone around to take their money anyway. There were bits of paper and rubbish blowing around in the yard, and all the lights were off in the office.

"Everything looks so dead!" exclaimed Hadley pointing to a row of plants that had fallen over. Their pots were smashed, and soil was seeping onto the ground. The whole place looked abandoned.

Feeling a little unnerved at the ruin of the once vibrant shop, Lexi grabbed Hadley's hand and urged her out the gate. "Let's get home. This place is eerie!" Lexi balanced the cherry tree in her bicycle basket. "Plus, I don't want to leave Dad alone for too long."

Hadley agreed, and the two girls left the abandoned store and quickly cycled back to their house. Once they returned home, the family made their way into the back yard where they held their own private funeral of sorts. There weren't any friends or relatives, or even a priest. They planted the little cherry tree with its delicate pink and white blossoms, in the garden over by the back fence and placed small white pebbles around its base.

"I feel a little better now," said Hadley pointing at the cherry tree.

Lexi nodded. "Mum would have loved it," she whispered grabbing Hadley and her father's hands. It all felt so surreal. It was as if her mother was only away at the supermarket or work, not dead!

The family stayed in the garden by that little blossom covered cherry tree until it got quite dark. It had been quite a cool day for once, and when the evening chill started to make Mr Valentine cough, Lexi hurriedly stood and pulled him to his feet.

"Come on Dad, it's time to get you back inside," she urged wrapping her arm around his back.

The girls followed their father inside, feeling strange without their mother but somehow closer together. The KV17 virus had struck their family in the worst way possible, but it had also brought them closer together. It wasn't some scenario from a zombie apocalypse movie. It was real-life, and their family knew they had to stick together. It wasn't going to be easy; real-life rarely was. Somehow, they had to find a way through it, and they would need each other to do it.

The next few days were hard. Lexi watched her father trying to be strong even though she knew inside he must be hurting. No matter what she tried, his sickness continued to get worse.

"I don't know what else to try," complained Lexi, twisting her hair around her finger in frustration. "We've tried medicine, herbs, vitamins, even old-fashioned warm chicken soup. Nothing's working!" she snapped, her voice brittle.

Hadley's eyes widened. "Is he going to…?"

Lexi quietly closed her father's bedroom door, where he was resting. She held her finger to her lips. "I don't know. He just keeps getting worse," her voice shook.

Walking to the bathroom, Lexi grabbed a plastic bowl and washcloth from the counter. "I'll get some cold water to bath his forehead and neck. His temperature is really high."

"Okay," murmured Hadley quietly. "I'll go and sit by his bed in case he needs anything." She opened the door and walked into the bedroom.

As Lexi was making her way to the bathroom, she suddenly heard Hadley call for her in a panic. Running to her father's room, Lexi saw the look on Hadley's face and knew instantly their father was dead.

Lexi let the bowl and washcloth fall from her hands, the water spilling everywhere as the container hit the floor with a loud crash. She stared glibly at the top of the bed head unable to look at her father. Tears streamed down her face.

Hadley threw herself on their parent's bed and moaned.

The Valentine family had just become two.

CHAPTER FOUR

After the death of their parents, all Lexi wanted to do was curl up on her bed under the duvet and let someone else take charge. They had been such a big part of her life, and she didn't know how she was going to cope without them. Sure, she had always complained about her parents to her friends and fantasised about moving out of her home and being independent like most sixteen-year-old teenagers do. But when it came down to it, Lexi wasn't ready for it. She didn't want to *take charge*. However, the problem was there wasn't anyone else. Unless you counted Hadley, who was already on the verge of going into complete meltdown.

Taking a deep breath, Lexi walked into the kitchen and picked up the telephone. It was time to inform the authorities that her father had passed away from the virus. She could hear Hadley throwing things around in her bedroom and was tempted to join her; however, she knew they couldn't just leave their dad lying in the bedroom. So, Lexi picked up the card her father had left by the phone and dialled the number, her fingers trembling.

A few hours after Lexi made the call to the authorities, a dark-haired woman and two men from some government department came around to the Valentine family home. These ones wore plain white starched clothes like doctors and had grim looks on their faces.

"Move out of the way," one of the men said gruffly, as he pushed past Lexi refusing to look at her. Lexi stared at the man feeling invisible. *How can they be so disinterested and unfeeling?*

"Be careful!" yelled Lexi, as she watched the men roughly lift her father's body onto a stretcher. His right arm had fallen out from underneath the sheet and was dangling downwards as they jerkily maneuvered him through the house. Quickly running over to her father, Lexi held his hand for a few moments before the men abruptly shoved her aside and wheeled his body away. They acted as if they were in a hurry, and Mr Valentine was just some *thing* they wanted to be rid of.

Lexi's face fell as she went to stand by her sister on the front porch. She glanced at Hadley. Hadley was crying loudly as she watched the men load their dad into the back of a white van. Her face was red and blotchy, her arms hanging limply by her sides.

As Lexi tried to comfort her, she noticed a dark-haired woman dressed in a grey suit and crisp white shirt standing to one side. She was busily writing on a clipboard. Lexi watched her for a few minutes wondering what she was doing. Like the others, she hadn't introduced herself or said one word to the girls. To Lexi, the woman looked extremely businesslike and formal as she hung back from the house, obviously not wanting to get too close.

As soon as Mr Valentine had been moved into the back of the van, the woman stopped writing and peered at the girls for a few minutes. A brief look of sympathy flashed across her face before she snapped her clipboard shut.

"We will be back in a few days to move you to a children's care facility," the woman stated abruptly, her voice hard and uncompromising. "You had better pack a small bag and leave the rest," she said as she waved her hand towards the Valentine house as if its contents were inconsequential. "You can't stay here any longer, and you won't be coming back." The woman looked as though she wanted to say something further but turned and quickly walked towards the van instead. Her high heels tapped sharply on the path making a loud noise.

Lexi stared at the woman open-mouthed, not able to believe how unfeeling she was. Moments before, she and her men had taken their father, and now she was abruptly informing them they had to leave their family home and all they knew, to go to some child-minding centre!

"Excuse me!" exclaimed Lexi marching up to the van and loudly knocking on the window.

The woman inside sighed loudly and reluctantly looked up. Her eyes had lost any resemblance of warmth and had taken on a hard steel coldness. "Yes?" She looked at Lexi but didn't roll down the car window. Her eyes were a light blue colour, which could be considered pretty, but right now seemed harsh and unfeeling. She narrowed them like a snake, expecting trouble.

"This is our home. Why can't we stay here?" argued Lexi with feeling. "I'm practically an adult! We can look after ourselves." She tried to reason with the woman, but she just stared back at Lexi with an uncaring expression, not even bothering to reply.

Looking at the woman's cold hard face, Lexi clenched her fists by her side in frustration. "We don't need to go to some bloody care facility with a bunch of five-year-old's!" she exploded in frustration.

The woman ignored Lexi and went back to writing on her clipboard.

This upset Lexi even further, and her frustration soon turned to anger. "Why won't you listen to me? Our dad only died this morning! We're not ready to move!" Feeling incredibly upset, Lexi started to yell. "At least let us try and look after ourselves; we have everything we need right here!" She pointed towards their house.

The blue-eyed woman blatantly continued to ignore Lexi, refusing to look at her.

"What the hell!" yelled Lexi glaring at her in annoyance. She rapped her knuckles loudly on the car window trying to get the woman's attention. Stubbornly, the woman didn't react; it was as if Lexi was invisible. Then, with a flick of her red-manicured fingernail, the woman abruptly flicked her hand at the driver motioning him to drive away, and any chance at discussion quickly faded away.

"Hey!" Lexi screamed after her in a fury. "Come back here!" She stamped her foot and glared after the woman in complete indignation. *What a bitch!*

Hadley walked up beside Lexi and took her hand. The two sisters stood side by side for a few moments watching while the white van carrying their father swiftly drove down the street. Dust billowed out behind it, like a storm receding into the distance.

While Hadley stood sadly quietly weeping, Lexi was fuming. She wanted to scream. She absolutely hated being told what to do by a bunch of strangers and then ignored. As she watched the cold woman drive away with the girl's father, she made up her mind then and there that she wasn't going to pack. Not a single thing. If they came back and tried to make the girls move, Lexi wasn't going to make it easy for them. She planned to fight them every step of the way. As far as she was concerned, they were not leaving their family home and no stranger was going to tell her otherwise. Lexi was determined not to get put into a care facility, and she wasn't about to let Hadley get dragged into one either. Hadley totally annoyed her a lot of the time; however, Lexi remembered what her father told them about family sticking together. If the sisters were split up, they would have a great deal of difficulty finding each other again.

*

*   *

Every day since the woman's visit, the sisters expected an official from some Government department to come and drag them away from their home. However, no one ever showed up. The care facility was either full, or it was no longer operating. The girls were left on their own and so far, they were coping alright by themselves.

As Lexi watched Hadley flicking through Cosmo magazines instead of helping with dinner, she sighed feeling frustrated, but at the same time, grateful her sister was there. Although they fought a lot, Lexi would rather have Hadley there with her than be all alone in this new world. That would be frightening.

"What's for dinner?" asked Hadley suddenly looking up from her magazine as though she felt Lexi watching her.

"Baked beans or tinned soup," said Lexi unenthusiastically showing Hadley the cans. Although the girls were lucky enough to have a reasonable supply of food it was becoming a little monotonous. Mrs Valentine had stocked the pantry with tinned food, packaged pasta and dried beans. So, even though it was boring, at least they weren't going hungry. They had long run out of fresh food including fruit, vegetables and meat.

As the electricity was now completely shut off, the girls had resorted to using a small gas camp stove to heat their food. Which was just as well, as eating tinned baked beans cold really sucked!

As Lexi decided to heat their last can of tinned beans, she remembered back to a couple of days ago when they had tried to ride their bikes to the local supermarket. It had looked totally trashed. There were rubbish piles everywhere, some of them on fire, and rotten food lay scattered all over the ground in the car park. The whole place was starting to stink, and the black flies swarming over the rotten food were horrendous. Gangs of older kids were roaming around, and a couple of guys stood in front of the big glass doors to the entrance of the building. They held metal baseball bats in their hands, standing like a couple of bouncers outside a nightclub. It looked as if they were guarding the place. Hadley and Lexi had taken one glance at the situation and decided they had enough food at home for the moment not to risk it.

Since then Lexi had been trying to ration their food. They were still managing to eat two meals a day, but only small ones and that was not easy when you were hungry all the time. She did worry about what they would do when their stash of food ran out. They would either have to think about finding more or moving on. No one really wants to move out of their family home and into the unknown, however sometimes your circumstances change, and you may not have a choice.

Once the food was heated through, Lexi poured the warm beans into two bowls and brought one over to Hadley. "Want to look through a magazine?" she asked holding an old *Woman's Day* magazine out to Lexi.

"Sure," said Lexi taking the magazine. "Why not." As she opened the magazine, the first page contained an advertisement for chocolate coated Magnum ice-creams. She looked down at her luke-warm baked beans in disinterest. *How she missed ice-cream!* Lexi wondered if she would ever eat the cold milky treat ever again.

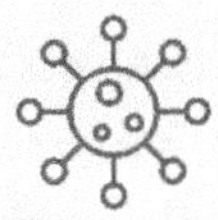

CHAPTER FIVE

Lexi had thought that with nothing much to do, no school or workplace to go to, time would slow down. And after the death of their parents, Lexi half expected the world to come to a complete stop. But it didn't. It just kept ticking along. Days and weeks passed, and before the girls knew it a whole new year had started.

It was early evening, two weeks after Christmas. Though this year, Christmas had been a non-event. Lexi had marked off the days leading up to twenty-fifth on a calendar they had hanging on the wall, and the girls had tried to make the day cheerful. They'd put up the family Christmas tree and sang a few carols without much enthusiasm. Without their parents, it just didn't feel the same. Their mother had bought a couple of Christmas gifts before she had gotten sick and had put them away for the future, thinking that the family would still be together for the celebration. As their parents were no longer alive, the girls had decided to give the presents to each other, sitting in the lounge room, nestled together on cushions by the tree.

Lexi's present had been a series of books she had wanted to read and a little gold necklace with a bright green gemstone that matched her eyes. Hadley helped her to fasten it around her neck before giving her a huge hug. Hadley ripped open the purple wrapping paper on her present, her face breaking into a big smile. Her mother had somehow found the latest PSV gaming console that Hadley had been not so subtly hinting for. Plus, a couple of games to play on it. She immediately started jumping up and down in excitement, her good mood lasting for the rest of the day. The girls lit some candles and opened a tin of ham and some shortbread biscuits for their Christmas feast, wondering if anyone else was bothering to celebrate Christmas that year. It seemed a bit strange to be celebrating when there was so much sadness around them, but it was hard to give up traditions. The sisters talked for a while before blowing out the candles and going to bed. And just like that, Christmas was over.

Two weeks later, Lexi stared at the forlorn Christmas tree standing in the corner of their lounge room, wondering whether she should pack it away. She supposed it didn't really matter anymore. They could leave it up all year if they wanted to. No one was going to be visiting them and asking why they still had their Christmas tree up, in a disapproving voice. Things like that didn't matter anymore.

She watched the dust particles floating in the air as the last of the sun's rays streamed through the open window. The sun was finally starting to set after another scorching hot summer's day, bringing some much-needed relief from the withering heat.

Wiping her hand across her clammy forehead, she gazed out at the orange and reds of the sunset. It looked just like an artist's painting. She sighed wistfully. Just once, Lexi wished it would snow or at least drizzle. Anything to break up this relentless summer heat. She remembered the time a couple of years ago when the Perth summer had been particularly hot and intense. There had been record temperatures that year, of forty-four degrees Celsius. A really blistering summer. She remembered that she had raced outside without any shoes on, and the ground had been so hot that it had actually burnt the soles of her feet. That same day, her friends had come over to her house, and they'd successfully fried an egg on the bonnet of her dads' car. One of them had filmed it on their phone, and they'd posted it on the internet for a laugh. Her dad hadn't been too pleased, and that night when things had cooled off, she'd had to wash and polish his car until it shined. He'd soon forgiven her, and they'd all laughed about it the next day while they watched the upload on the computer.

Smiling at the happy memory, she wandered into the kitchen and contemplated making something for dinner. "I wish we had some eggs now," she grumbled. Her stomach growled in anticipation of food. The girls hadn't had much to eat that day as their dwindling food supply was starting to run short, and Lexi had now cut their meals to once a day.

Hadley was lying around in the next room playing cards and listening for any announcements on their father's battery-operated radio. It was a long-range radio he had bought a few years ago when the family had gone camping in Kalbarri. Each night the girls would pick up a broadcast from someone somewhere in Australia and it felt comforting to know they weren't alone in the world!

As Lexi was opening a tin of stew, she heard Hadley call out from the other room.

"Hey, there's nothing on the radio!" Her voice sounded agitated.

Lexi poked her head into the lounge room. "Have you tried changing the batteries?"

"I tried that," responded Hadley indignantly. "I'm not stupid!" She pulled a face.

"That's debatable," muttered Lexi to herself before turning towards her sister. "Maybe nobody is transmitting any more. I'll take the radio up to the hill tomorrow. Hopefully, I can get a signal up there." She pointed towards the front window of the house.

"That's a good idea," agreed Hadley. She turned to look out the window and suddenly noticed a light moving around in their front yard! "What's that?!"

Lexi moved to the window and peered out through the sheer curtains. Without electricity and street lights, the yard should be dark. However, she could see lights moving around in their front garden! They were flicking back and forth like someone walking around with a torch. *What were they doing in their front yard?* Lexi had a feeling it couldn't be good.

Pulling back the light, silky curtain material from the window so she could get a better look, Lexi peeked through. As her eyes adjusted to the darkness outside, Lexi noticed two tall figures peering suspiciously into her dad's car window, which was parked in the driveway.

Starting to feel alarmed, Lexi watched them intently. Her eyes narrowed and her fists clenching involuntarily by her sides as she scrutinised them. Her instincts told her they were up to no good.

As if drawn by her gaze, one of the figures suddenly pointed his torch up towards the house, making Lexi quickly duck down out of sight. Her heart was starting to race rapidly, and she felt an acute spike of alarm. *Who were these people and what did they want?*

Hadley crept over to her. "What are you doing? What's going on?" She shook Lexi's arm roughly.

"Shhh," Lexi cautioned, glaring at Hadley. "There are some people out front snooping around Dad's car. I think they're trying to steal it!" Hadley's eyes widened as she quickly scooted behind her sister.

"Stay here and watch them. I'm going to phone the police," Lexi whispered urgently as she crawled over to where the cordless telephone sat nearby on a little wooden table. Quickly dialling *000* on the phone, Lexi waited anxiously for an answer. She glanced from the phone to the window and back. She tried redialling several times, before realising there wasn't any dial tone. The phone was dead. She dropped it uselessly on the floor.

"Hell," she said, her voice tense. Lexi scampered back to Hadley, who was looking at her questioningly.

Lexi held out her hand. "Quick, give me your mobile."

Hadley shook her head vehemently. "Why can't you use yours? "I don't like anyone touching mine," she said stubbornly.

Lexi groaned and glared at her. "Seriously! Mine's in my bedroom," she said through gritted teeth. "Stop being stupid and give it to me. I don't trust those people out the front." Lexi pointed meaningfully towards the window. "I don't think they're just having an evening walk! We need to get some help in case there's trouble."

Hadley stuck her head up to the window. Her eyes flickered fearfully to the strangers outside; they were now standing and talking in hushed tones next to her dad's car. Hadley pulled her mobile phone out of her jeans pocket and hurriedly handed it over to her sister. Her hand was trembling.

Lexi grabbed the phone, annoyed at not being given it sooner. She quickly tried to punch in the emergency number.

"Oh hell! Yours is not working either!" She looked at the phone's battery level; it was full. Lexi fretfully twisted her hair around her finger. "Damn it! Looks like none of the phones are working, so no police. I guess we are on our own." She bit on her top lip.

Hadley was looking at Lexi wide-eyed in fear. They'd never had to deal with anything like this before. "What! What do you mean the phones aren't working? They've got to be working!" She snatched her phone from her sister. "Let me try.

You're probably doing it wrong."

There was no signal. Hadley stared glumly at the phone before letting it drop from her fingers onto the carpet. No telephones meant no internet either. The girls had no way to contact any of the emergency services. They looked at each other in dismay. No one would be coming to help them tonight.

A ripple of panic shot through Hadley's body. "What shall we do!?" Her voice was high pitched and strained, her breath coming in little rapid gasps. She looked over at her sister for reassurance.

Lexi looked just as scared as she did, crouching down under the window and chewing on her nails nervously. "I don't know! I wish Mum and Dad were here; they'd know what to do."

Hadley searched wildly around the room. "There must be something we can do?" Her eyes fixed on a solid object sitting on the table across the room. Quickly scampering over to it, she grabbed her mother's vase and hugged it tightly to her chest. A look of satisfaction spread across her face.

"What's that for?" Lexi whispered.

"Self-defence. I'm going to throw it at them in case they come inside," she nodded her head determinedly.

"Good idea," said Lexi. "Get me one too. I can hit them over the head with it!"

Hadley grabbed another vase for Lexi and then scampered back to where Lexi knelt by the window watching the men. The two girls huddled together trying to hear what was going on outside. Hadley had the vase by her side ready to use. She held on tightly to Lexi's hand.

The girls could see the people outside talking to each other, their hands gesturing wildly as if they were arguing. Lexi scanned the darkness. One of the figures had now moved closer to the house and was walking around looking under rocks and bushes.

"What's he doing?" asked Hadley in alarm.

"I think he's looking for a spare key," whispered Lexi. "Luckily we don't have one."

There wasn't any moon that night, and in the inky blackness, the roaming figure suddenly tripped over some flowerpots that were nestled by the family's pathway, causing one of the pots to smash. The stranger fell heavily on their knee, swearing angrily. Lexi thought the voice sounded deep, like a man's.

Picking up the broken flowerpot the guy suddenly threw it violently against the fence. The pot smashed into several pieces and fell to the ground with a loud crash. In the stillness of the night, the sound rang out loudly, breaking the silence.

"Jesus, John! Could you be any louder?" said the other figure as coughs racked his chest and he suddenly doubled over, trying to catch his breath.

Hadley looked at Lexi and mouthed. "They're infected." Lexi nodded grimly.

The neighbour's dog, Polo, heard the commotion and started running up and down the fence line, barking persistently, like a machine gun on rapid fire. One of the intruders swore loudly again and kicked the fence where the dog continued to bark frantically.

Lexi cautiously poked her head up again, trying to see. She watched the men standing with their hands on their hips staring at the neighbour's dog, as it continued to growl and bark at them through the picket fence. Lexi took the opportunity of the thieves' distraction to stand and shine her torch out at the intruders. She didn't know why she hadn't thought of it before. "Get off our property, or I'll let our Doberman dog out on you!" Lexi said in a loud, steady voice. She crossed her fingers and hoped the men didn't realise they didn't have a dog.

At the same time, the neighbour's dog, Polo continued to bark loudly.

Lexi peered out of the window at the men, waiting to see what they would do. Her heart was hammering in her chest as she silently willed them to go away. If they didn't leave, Lexi wasn't sure what she could do.

The men spun on their heels in surprise and looked up at the house. They obviously hadn't realised anyone was living on the property.

"Come on," muttered one of the men as he glanced between the house and the neighbour's dog. "Let's find somewhere easier. Somewhere where nobody's home." He took one last look at the car, before staggering down the street to look for an easier target.

Watching the men finally leave, Lexi breathed out in relief, not realising that she'd been holding her breath all this time. She cupped her hands over her face and shook her head. *That was close*, she thought nervously. Much too close for her liking.

"Are they gone?" whispered Hadley, tapping her sister's shoulder with her finger. Her eyes glanced fearfully up at the window.

Lexi hugged her reassuringly. "Yeah, I think so. I think the dog scared them off." They could still hear him barking crazily next door. "Remind me to go and give him a hug tomorrow. I hope the Robinsons are alright." Neither of the girls had seen any sight of their neighbours for a few days.

The girls sat crouched under the window for a long while, not wanting to move in case the intruders came back. Eventually, the dog stopped barking, and it was quiet outside. Nothing moved in the garden, but Lexi still felt nervous; her stomach churning. She bit her bottom lip and continued to listen for any sign of movement outside.

Hadley glanced at her sister uncertainly. Seeing someone creeping around their front yard had been frightening. "Are you okay?"

"Yeah, just a bit freaked out. But it's okay now. Everything's going to be fine," she tried to look reassuring. "I suppose we should have expected thieves to come around at some point."

Hadley agreed. She held on tightly to her mother's vase and glanced fretfully through the window. Her face was pale.

"Come on, let's have a game of Uno," suggested Lexi pulling her sister away. She could see that Hadley was on the verge of freaking out. "Those guys won't be back tonight." *At least she hoped they wouldn't!* Lexi made a mental note to herself to lock her dad's car in the garage the next day. They should have done it weeks ago. She had a bad feeling that those strangers weren't the last intruders they were going to see. As people became more desperate, Lexi was sure others would come.

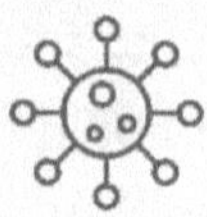

CHAPTER SIX

The next morning, Lexi woke up feeling stiff and sore after having fallen asleep on the couch. Her neck felt like it was permanently bent to the left side and her shoulder ached. She stretched and yawned. Last night's emotional encounter had left her feeling raw, and she could do with some comfort food to make herself feel better.

"Wanna make pancakes this morning?" she suggested to Hadley. "We haven't got any milk or eggs though, so we'll just have to use water."

Hadley, who was still curled up in a ball on the couch, smiled dreamily at her sister. She was only half awake. "Good idea," she mumbled sitting and rubbing her eyes. "And, we can take some over to Polo to say thanks for last night!"

Lexi laughed. "Hmm, yeah he'd probably love that. But only one, we barely have enough for ourselves. We should warn the Robinsons about those guys too." She wandered from the lounge room into the kitchen. The sun was already streaming through the kitchen window, and she wondered if it was going to be another hot day. Her stomach gurgled loudly, and she quickly got out the frypan and mixing bowl and put them on the counter. "I hope we still have enough gas for our camp stove," she wondered, lighting a match. The little portable stove didn't cook very evenly, but at least they could heat food and cook simple meals. She silently thanked her father for being a camper.

Without any milk or eggs to make the batter, the pancakes didn't taste that great, but at least they were filling, and the girls smothered them in runny golden syrup. The syrup was sticky and sweet, just what they needed after last night's scare. They hungrily ate all of them, apart from one, which they left for the little dog, Polo. Rewarding him seemed the right thing to do. After all, he did scare the men away and, things could have ended a lot differently if he hadn't.

"I remember when the Robinsons showed Polo to us a couple of years ago after they had first brought him home," said Hadley as she crammed pancakes into her mouth. "They said they had just picked him up from a local dog shelter, remember. He was even tinier then."

Lexi nodded. "I remember him being so shy and quiet when they first brought him home. Didn't take him long to adjust though," she laughed. "He's like a little rubber ball now, bouncing all over the place!" Lexi made energetic bouncing movements with her hands sending Hadley into fits of laughter.

"Let's go and give him his reward while it's still warm," suggested Hadley, holding the spare pancake between her finger and thumb and wiggling it around. "He's gonna love it," she grinned.

After they cleared the breakfast dishes, the girls wandered over to the neighbour's house to see if they were allowed to feed Polo the pancake.

Hadley found the little brown and white Jack Russell Terrier gazing out his gate looking pitiful. His head hung down toward the ground, and he whined at her sadly. "What's wrong with you, boy?" Hadley asked quizzically, bending down and letting him lick her hand. "Why so sad?"

Seeing the girls, Polo suddenly perked up and started wagging his tail like a windscreen wiper on fast speed. His brown tail had a little tuft of white fur at the end, and the girls thought he was rather cute.

Hadley laughed. "Wow! It didn't take much to get him excited. I think he can smell the pancake!" Hadley peeled the plastic lid off the container holding the warm food.

"Hang on, Hadley," cautioned Lexi turning to face the house. "We'd better ask the Robinsons if it's okay to give him that."

Hadley reluctantly replaced the lid on the container.

Polo immediately stopped wagging his tail, letting it droop. He whined in frustration.

"Oh, look at him," Hadley murmured as she bent down towards the dog. "I think he's starving." She scratched his head, and he started wagging his tail again.

"Well, he can wait just a minute," replied Lexi, going up to the front door and ringing the doorbell. "We can't just give him food without asking first."

There was no answer, so she pressed the doorbell again. Lexi waited for a moment, then knocked loudly on the door. Silence. She looked around. The Robinson's car was still in the driveway. *I suppose they could have gone for a walk?* Lexi looked over at Polo, who was now trying to dig under the fence to get out. He really wanted the food.

"Oh, fine," relented Lexi, smiling. "Just give it to him, Hadley. "I'm sure the Robinsons won't mind."

Lexi watched Hadley break the pancake up into small pieces and feed it through the fence to Polo, who hungrily guzzled it down. "I don't think he can even taste it he's eating it so fast!" She laughed.

Hadley laughed too. "Uh huh. Maybe we should make him some more. Looks like he really loves them."

Lexi nodded in agreement. "Hmm. Well, we'd better ask the Robinsons before we do that." She walked back up the porch steps, deciding to have a look through the front window into the house to see if she could see anything. *Maybe the Robinsons had gone away. Strange that they hadn't taken their car though, or Polo?*

Shielding her eyes from the light of the day, Lexi wandered up to the window and tried to peer through. It wasn't easy. The window had streaks of dust and dirt smeared down the glass as though it hadn't been cleaned for quite a while, making it difficult to see through. Using her hand, Lexi tried to wipe a clean patch and pressed her nose up to the glass. She wasn't sure what she was looking for. Just any sign that the Robinsons were still living there, she supposed. Cupping her hands around her face, she tried to shield her eyes from the sun's glare.

As her eyes slowly adjusted to the light, she could see past the flimsy sheer curtains that were partially blocking her view. There was a TV in one corner with a tall beige lamp standing next to it. One flowery double lounge seat over on one side and on the other side, two single seater armchairs made of the same material with… Lexi's eyes widened in shock, and she gasped in horror at what she'd just seen. Stepping back quickly, she unconsciously tried to distance herself from what was inside the house. Bile rose in her throat, leaving a burning acid taste in her mouth.

It was so awful.

Taking a few shallow gulps of air, Lexi tried to ease her revulsion. She felt stunned at what she'd just seen. *How could the Robinsons have been left sitting in their front room like that?* The thought of them instantly brought up a fresh bought of vomit, sending Lexi stumbling awkwardly over to the Robinson's flowerbed. She quickly bent forward, her hands resting on her knees for balance, and promptly threw up.

Hadley turned around in surprise, "Lexi?" She scrambled up the porch steps towards her sister, a look of concern on her face. "Are you sick?"

"No! Stay there," yelled Lexi her hand outstretched to stop Hadley from coming any farther.

"All right!" complained Hadley loudly stopping where she was. "No need to yell!"

"Sorry," muttered Lexi as she sat down on the front porch steps, wiping the back of her hand across her mouth in disgust. "I'm fine, but you do not want to look in there," she warned, looking like she was going to throw up again. Her face had turned a pasty white colour.

"I was just coming over to see if you were alright?"

"It's okay. I'm fine, but the Robinsons are dead." Lexi looked peaky.

"And it looks like they've been like that for a few days!"

"Oh." Hadley's eyes widened in alarm. They still hadn't got used to people dying. "Do you think it was from the virus?"

Lexi stood up, nodding her head slightly. "Probably. They were pretty old.

At least they died together."

Hadley frowned. "Hmmm, I suppose so. It's still really sad; they were nice people." She gazed off into the distance "But why hasn't anyone come and taken them away like they did Mum and Dad?" she asked, her face troubled. Hadley sat on the porch step next to Lexi.

"Dunno?" Lexi replied grimly, shrugging. "Maybe it's like the telephones. Maybe the hospitals aren't working anymore either, and maybe the police too." She absentmindedly wound her finger around a strand of her hair. "There hasn't been any Internet for a while either. If they don't fix it, I think we're definitely on our own. I don't even know if the government is still operating?"

"That's great! I thought the government were supposed to help people?" Hadley moaned sarcastically, standing and brushing the dust off her pants.

Lexi shrugged. "Well, I don't know how many adults are still alive to run stuff like that," her voice sounded worried. "Unless they can find a cure for the KV17 virus soon, I think we are on our own." She peered down the street at the abandoned houses.

Hadley frowned. "What about Polo?" she pointed towards the dog locked in the Robinson's back yard. "We can't just leave him here by himself!"

Lexi glanced over at the dog. His head hung down piteously, and he whined at them like a child wanting attention. She felt sorry for him, all on his own. He would certainly die without their help.

"Hmmm…well, I guess we can't leave him locked up in their yard. He's probably starving; we'd better take him with us. I suppose he can be our miniature guard dog." Lexi thought about the figures in the garden last night. Although Polo was another mouth to feed, it might be nice to have him around. He could warn them of intruders. Anything they could use for security would be good.

Things weren't looking all that safe around the neighbour-hood anymore, and Lexi was starting to worry about the safety of the house with just the two of them there. *Maybe they could try putting some boards up on the windows so that they couldn't be smashed. Or some more locks on the doors. People always did that in apocalypse movies, didn't they?* The problem was, Lexi didn't know how to use her father's battery-operated drill. She had never had to before. It was a skill she was going to have to learn.

Hadley clapped her hands and released Polo from behind the garden fence. The dog happily followed the girls back to their house, trotting along next to them with his tail wagging vigorously in a delighted manner. Hadley gave him some tinned beef and vegetable stew that neither of the girls particularly liked, then found an old blanket and a place for him to sleep on their back porch. He wolfed the food down quickly, wanting more.

"Sorry, Polo, that's all we can spare for the moment," smiled Hadley. "I'll get you something else later."

Polo settled on the rug and stretched out his legs in front of him like a sphinx. He seemed happy enough, even though he didn't know the girls all that well.

"You must have been pretty lonely and confused on your own, hey boy?" whispered Hadley, leaning down and rubbing the top of the little dog's head.

Polo looked up at her with his big brown eyes, as if to say thanks. He would have surely died without the girl's help.

Grabbing a book, she had been reading earlier, Hadley settled down next to the little dog wanting to keep him company. Polo immediately rested his head on his two front paws and fell straight to sleep.

Unlike Hadley, Lexi couldn't relax. She didn't go inside straight away; instead, she stood on their front porch for a while gazing down the street. She couldn't believe how quickly things had changed. Everything looked so run down and overgrown. Tall weeds had sprung up in their front yard and all along the footpath, running down the side of the road. The vines from their neighbour's garden, once so neat and tidy, had started to creep over their fence like some strange creature from the deep. There were broken bottles smashed on the road, and several houses had graffiti sprayed across their front walls. It looked like a scene from a zombie apocalypse movie, and Lexi couldn't believe how quickly fiction had become a reality.

Another thing she noticed was that the street was silent. There weren't any children playing in their front yards or radios blaring out the latest top ten songs. The whole place looked deserted, and Lexi wondered if there was anyone else still living in their street. It gave her an eerie feeling, and she shivered. She knew that the Robinson's had obviously stayed in their home, not having anywhere else to go and her own family had decided to stay, hoping that a cure would be found.

However, a lot of families, including most of their friends, had packed up their belongings in their cars and driven away. Trying to escape the sickness and inevitable sadness that followed it. The problem was, the more people left the city, the less things like hospitals and police departments were able to work. There just weren't enough healthy adults left to run them. And the more things stopped working, the more difficult it became to stay in the city, and even more people left. It was a vicious cycle.

After a while, Lexi wandered inside. She spent her time going around the house, closing the windows and making sure that they were all locked. She had a worried feeling like a black pit in her stomach. No matter how hard she tried to distract herself by listening to music or flicking through the pages of one of her books, the feeling would not go away. It felt strange not having people around them, and it made her feel unsettled. She wondered again whether just the two of them in the house was safe enough, even with the new addition of little Polo.

Lexi was right to be worried. Later that night after the girls had gone to bed and settled into sleep. Someone broke in.

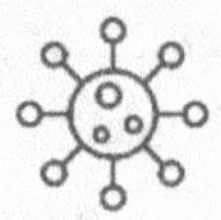

CHAPTER SEVEN

Lexi was having a wonderful dream. It was a beautiful sunny day with only a few white fluffy clouds scattered across the sky. Being the beginning of summer, the weather was not too hot and unbearable yet; the perfect day for being outside. She was down at the beach with her friends, chatting about the latest television show they'd all been watching. They were laughing and having a great time when suddenly one of Lexi's friends started roughly shaking her by the shoulder. She could feel their fingers digging into her in their urgency. Lexi abruptly turned around to face her friend, wondering what was so important. As she turned over, she awoke from her sleep and realised with annoyance that the person shaking her was not her friend at all but her sister in real-life.

"Go away," Lexi mumbled grumpily, pulling the bed sheets tightly around her shoulders. She kept her eyes tightly closed hoping Hadley would leave.

"Lexi! Lexi!" Hadley whispered in a frightened voice, close to Lexi's ear. She shook Lexi's arm trying to force her to wake up.

Lexi mumbled something insulting and rolled over. She wasn't ready to get out of bed.

Unhappy at being ignored, Hadley ripped the bedsheet from the bed. "Lexi, will you wake up," she said through gritted teeth glancing around the room nervously.

Lexi rolled back over to face her sister and sat up feeling foggy brained. She glanced angrily at the clock on her bedroom wall. It showed half past two in the morning. "Hadley, what are you doing? It's too early. Go away! I want to sleep," she moaned loudly, shoving her roughly away. Hadley stumbled backwards.

"Shhh," Hadley whispered urgently, her eyes wide with fear. She pointed towards the bedroom door. "There's someone in the house!"

"What?! Are you serious?" Lexi sat bolt upright, suddenly wide awake.

"Yes, I'm serious!" Hadley hissed indignantly.

Lexi forgot about wanting to sleep and quickly scrambled out of bed, painfully hitting her knee on her bedside table in her haste. Putting one hand over her mouth and the other on her throbbing knee, she tried to stifle a yelp.

Hobbling to her bedroom door, Lexi cocked her head and listened carefully. Hadley stood behind her, trembling.

Instinctively holding her breath, Lexi tried to hear any sounds of an intruder in the house. She couldn't hear anything suspicious except someone's dog barking in the distance. Her brow furrowed in frustration. Slowly opening the bedroom door wider, she stepped out into the hallway. Lexi listened for a couple more minutes before turning to Hadley in annoyance. She was just about to tell her that she had imagined it when she heard a noise like bottles and jars clinking. It sounded like it had come from down the hallway in the kitchen. Someone had just opened a cupboard door.

Lexi swore and slowly crept back into her bedroom. "Okay," she whispered to Hadley, her face up close to hers. "You stay here." She pointed to the ground in her bedroom before turning to quietly walk back out to the passage.

Hadley grabbed her arm and pulled her back. "Wait. What are you going to do?" The worried expression had not left her face.

Lexi looked worried too. "I'm not sure. I'll try to see how many people are down there."

Hadley wouldn't let go of her sister's arm. "Should I come?"

Pulling her arm away Lexi replied firmly. "No. You stay here and hide." The last thing she needed was her little sister trailing after her. She paused at the doorway and listened again. She could definitely hear noise coming from the kitchen, but nowhere else. Taking one last look at Hadley, Lexi crouched down and crept along the passageway until she got closer to the kitchen. Her heart was thumping in her chest, and she had the sudden urge to pee. When she was ready, she made herself peep around the wall so she could see directly into the room where the intruder was.

An older boy, he looked about eighteen or nineteen, was silhouetted in the moonlight coming through the window. He was busy rifling through the cupboard, pulling out food and putting it on the counter. There wasn't much in the cupboard for him to take. Mostly jars of pickles, olives and sauces. Almost all the girl's food was stashed in a cupboard in their spare room, hidden in case they were robbed.

The boy stopped his pillaging for a moment and sat back scratching his nose. Lexi duck back quickly thinking he might see her. *Just one guy.* She held her breath and tried to listen to see if she could hear anyone else. *Maybe they were in the lounge room or her parent's bedroom?* Her lungs started to burn, and she let her breath out slowly. She didn't want to be heard.

After listening for a few minutes, Lexi was sure she could only hear the one guy in the house. She couldn't hear anyone else, just him clanking around in the kitchen. She tried to breathe quietly, not wanting him to notice her. He was making a lot of noise for a burglar. *Maybe like the guys the other night, he didn't think anyone was living here?*

Pinching the top of her nose with her thumb and finger, Lexi tried to make herself think clearly. *What could they do to get rid of this guy? Could they force him to leave? There were two of them and only one of him. Would Hadley be able to do it?* Lexi listened again. She could hear the wind blowing relentlessly outside.

Cautiously peering around the wall again, Lexi saw that the guy had now moved to open drawers. *He would soon run out of cupboards to look in and move to another room. Maybe the bedroom where Hadley was hiding. She couldn't let that happen.* Lexi was going to have to hurry up and think of a plan.

Above the sound of the wind, Lexi could hear a strange noise coming from the back door. It sounded like scratching. She stared into the blackness towards the back of the house feeling uneasy. *Was someone else trying to get in?* Two men or even a man and a woman together would be too difficult for them to fight off. She swallowed hard, unsure of what to do.

Suddenly from the corner of her eye, Lexi saw movement. She quickly crouched down low, trying to look as small as possible, hoping not to be noticed in the dark. There was nowhere to hide in this damn passageway. *At least it was dark; maybe they wouldn't notice her? Had she been wrong? Was there more than one person inside? Perhaps she hadn't heard them?* She peered into the darkness willing her eyes to adjust to the inky blackness of the night. The figure coming towards her looked small, maybe it was a woman or child, definitely not a man. *Good, I can handle a kid,* Lexi thought bravely. She got herself into a position ready to fight and was just about to make a grab for them when they too crouched down. They started crawling towards her on their hands and knees. Lexi was confused. *What were they doing?* Crawling on all fours wasn't exactly a great way to attack someone. *Maybe they couldn't see her?* Lexi squinted her eyes trying to get a better view.

As they adjusted to the dim light of the passageway, she looked at the figure crawling towards her more closely. She realised with both relief and anxiety that it was her sister.

"What are you doing?" hissed Lexi, feeling a mixture of happiness and annoyance. "I told you to wait in the bedroom!"

"I know," whispered Hadley anxiously grabbing her sister's arm. "But listen, can't you hear Polo making all that noise outside?"

Lexi listened intently and realised Hadley was right. The scratching noise she had heard was Polo scraping at the back door and whining loudly. She snuck a look at the guy in the kitchen again. He didn't look like he cared about the dog. Lexi glanced back at Hadley. "Maybe we can use him?"

"What?" asked Hadley confused.

"The dog," Lexi whispered, pointing to the back door. "Maybe we can use him?"

Hadley still looked unsure her face screwed up.

"Look, I'm going to sneak to the back door and let Polo in," advised Lexi, her voice barely a whisper. "You go and get Dad's old baseball bat. It's in his study. Make sure you're quiet," she warned. "When you hear me come inside with Polo, run into the kitchen screaming."

Hadley looked doubtful, and she stared at her sister with a fearful expression, biting her lower lip. "What? I…I don't think I can…" she stammered.

Lexi angrily interrupted her. "Look, all you have to do is yell," she looked into her sister's eyes and squeezed her hands reassuringly. "We just need to scare him. We have to make him leave. Okay?"

"Okay," said Hadley in a small unsure voice as she turned away. Her eyebrows were pulled together in a grimace, and her eyes were large and round like a frightened rabbit.

Lexi grabbed at her sleeve. "Hadley. I know you're scared. I am too. But we need to do this; we don't have a choice. We've got to get this guy out of our house, and it has to be now before he starts creeping around."

Hadley took a deep breath and stared at Lexi with a determined look on her face. She nodded grimly and then was gone. Lexi was alone again; she took a deep breath too. She was going to have to dig deep and find some courage to pull this off. First, she had to get to the back door and outside. That meant crossing the doorway to the kitchen. She snuck another quick look at the intruder. He had his back to her and was rummaging through a drawer. She would have to chance it and hope he didn't turn around.

Standing up, Lexi quickly crept across the door opening and as quietly as she could, made her way to the back. Her heart was pounding in her chest like a bass drum. Polo was still scratching at the door trying to get in. She was amazed the guy hadn't heard him. Or maybe he had and didn't care?

Lexi took a quick look behind her. Then opening the back door, praying it wouldn't squeak, she slipped outside. She had to hold Polo back, who was now growling, a deep rumbling noise coming from his throat. He was desperately trying to get inside, but Lexi wasn't quite ready yet. She wanted to find something she could use as a weapon first. Got to be quick she thought. Don't want that guy leaving the kitchen and roaming the house with Hadley still inside.

Running to the garden shed as quickly as she could, Lexi opened the door and peered into the darkness. She could imagine all the spiders and cockroaches scuttling in the corners, their legs and antennae making little scratching noises as they moved about in the dark. Lexi shivered wishing she had thought to bring a torch with her. She ran her fingers along the wall, trying to feel for anything that could be used as a weapon. It was so dark in the shed, even with the door open, that all Lexi could see where dim shapes of objects.

As her hands ran along the smooth metal of the shed wall, her fingers brushed on a solid shape leaning up against the wall. It felt like a long handle. She paused for a moment, turning her head towards the door. Outside Polo was starting to bark loudly, creating a lot of noise. She needed to calm him down in case the robber decided to come and investigate. Besides, she didn't want to be in their dusty dark shed with all its spiders and insects, any longer than she had to.

"Time to get out of here!" Lexi grabbed the object and quickly ran out of the cramped enclosure. Once outside in the moonlight where she could see more clearly, Lexi looked down at the heavy object in her hands. It was her father's old wood chopping axe from the days when they used to have a wood heater.

"Okay. Well, that's not exactly what I had in mind as a weapon, but it will have to do." Her fingers closed around the handle getting used to the weight. "I don't have time to look for anything else, and I don't have to actually use it on him," Lexi told herself dragging the axe across the lawn towards the house. "Anyway, it looks pretty badass!" she smiled.

When Lexi reached the house, Polo was still scratching and barking loudly at the back door, so she called softly to him trying to calm him down. He turned his head to look at her as if to ask, *what's going on, are you ready for this?* Lexi wasn't sure if she was, but with Hadley still inside with the intruder, she didn't really have much choice. She had to go back inside and do whatever it took to make him leave. Lexi only hoped it wasn't going to end up in violence. She wasn't sure if she was up for that.

It was quite refreshing after such a hot day, and the breeze that was blowing felt good on her face. She breathed it in for a few moments to settle her nerves and prepare herself. Grunting as she heaved the heavy axe onto her shoulder, Lexi could feel the hard, smooth wood. She opened and closed her hand around the axe handle and took a deep breath. Polo was now sitting quietly waiting for her, his black eyes following her every move. Then, before she could change her mind, Lexi quickly dashed inside the house.

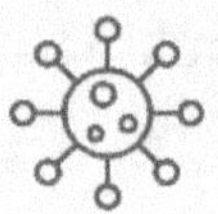

CHAPTER EIGHT

"**G**ET OUT OF OUR HOUSE!!" Lexi ran into the kitchen yelling as loudly as she could. With her axe held high above her head, she looked like a crazy person from a horror movie. At the same time, Hadley came running in from the other direction, screaming in a high-pitched wail. She had her father's metal baseball bat gripped firmly in her hands, her knuckles white from the tension. Polo, who had raced into the house with Lexi, shot between the two girls, almost tripping Lexi up. He was growling and barking with his teeth bared in an angry, aggressive snarl. Lexi had never seen him looking so vicious, and she was glad he was there. Lexi's plan had started well, and the trio converged on the unsuspecting robber all at the same time.

"What the Hell!" he yelled in shock, turning around quickly to face his foes. Polo ran straight towards the intruder snapping at him as if to bite him. Lexi slowly moved forward menacingly. "I said get out of our house," she threatened coldly. Her face looked mean in the dim light. Hadley continued to scream.

The guy stared at them dumbfounded but didn't move. Polo lunged forward at him, viciously biting his leg.

"Owww, you mongrel!" he yelled, throwing the bag of food he was holding at the dog. "Jeezus. Alright, I'm going. I didn't know anyone was here!"

Polo yelped when the bag hit him on the haunches but immediately went for the guy again, teeth bared. The robber swore and backed away. "Get your bloody dog off me! I'm going, back off." He raised his fist in anger.

Lexi went to Polo and put her hand reassuringly on his head. He stopped growling, but his eyes remained fixed on the intruder. "Just get out of here," Lexi said in a steady low voice, raising the axe above her head, trying to look threatening.

Hadley was still screaming, the baseball bat trembling slightly in her hands.

The intruder looked at Hadley and her baseball bat. He looked at Lexi standing threateningly with her axe raised. He looked at Polo, still growling menacingly.

Shaking his head, the guy quickly grabbed a jar of pickles and a bottle of tomato sauce he'd stacked on the kitchen counter.

"Alright, I'm going. Just chill," he said taking the hint and backing away to the front door.

Polo and Lexi followed him all the way and watched him back out onto the porch. The little dog gave a few sharp barks as if to say don't come back, then promptly sat down on the rug and wagged his tail.

Lexi looked over at her sister, her breathing slowing. "Hadley, he's gone. You can stop yelling." She slammed the front door shut and looked out of the peephole. There was nobody there. It seemed as though the guy had left.

Hadley abruptly stopped screaming and gulped. Polo got up and ran over to her, his tail still wagging happily. "Good boy, Polo." She rubbed his neck enthusiastically. "You're a good boy."

Lexi rested the axe against the wall by the front door, her hands shaking.

She was astounded at what just happened.

"Hey, help me move this sofa across the door, looks like the lock has been damaged and it won't close properly. He must have broken it to get in." She held the door shut. "We don't want anyone else getting through."

Polo jumped up onto the sofa as the girls pushed it across the doorway. It was cumbersome and heavy, but they managed to drag it far enough across the floor to keep the door closed. Both girls flopped down heavily onto the sofa feeling emotionally exhausted. Polo immediately jumped up onto Hadley's lap, his nails digging into her skin. She rubbed the little dog's head with her hand and hugged him. He returned the love by trying to lick her face.

"Jeez, that was scary." Hadley's eyes widened as she spoke. "He was great though, wasn't he Lex?" praised Hadley rubbing Polo's belly which he seemed to like. The little dog had managed to stretch out onto his back like a long sausage waiting for his stomach to be rubbed.

"Yeah, he sure was." Lexi smiled slightly, though she still looked worried.

"But you were the total badass!" Hadley taunted cheekily, poking her sister in the arm with her finger. "You and that axe!"

"Ha-ha. Yeah, well just call me *Battle Axe* from now on," Lexi's voice sounded strained. She pinched her sister playfully on the arm, before squinting through the peephole in the front door again. *Was the guy really gone?*

Lexi couldn't see much through the little hole, so she made her way over to the window. She chewed on the skin around her thumbnail as she walked. Brushing the curtains across and looking outside, Lexi peered out into the dark front garden. Each bush looked like a person crouching down or hiding.

After a few minutes, she turned back to Hadley, who was watching her intently and shrugged. "I can't see anything out there."

Hadley hugged Polo again and kissed the top of his head. Her face started to relax.

"We'd better just keep an eye…" Lexi started to say before a loud sound made both girls flinch.

Hadley let out a scream and Polo jumped at the front door, barking and scratching at the wood, wanting to go out.

"That was outside," warned Lexi.

Both girls rushed to look out the window, hearts pounding. Lexi instinctively grabbed her father's axe, dragging the heavy weapon across the floor.

"He's at Dad's car!" Hadley pointed to a dark shape standing by her father's vehicle. "What are we going to do? Is he trying to steal it?" Her voice sounded upset, and her eyes were wide with fear. "You said you were going to put it in the garage!" she said accusingly.

"Oh shit, I forgot." Lexi looked guiltily at her sister.

"You idiot, you said you were going to!" Hadley glared at her.

Lexi looked devastated. "I know. I'm sorry. I just forgot." She stared out the window at the guy.

"Well, what do we do now?" Hadley gestured outside.

Lexi felt dismayed. "I don't know! I don't think there's anything we *can* do. At least he's not in here anymore, and if he steals Dad's car, maybe he'll go away." She felt terrible, but with just the two of them, what else could they do? They couldn't exactly fight the guy. He looked older than they were, was taller, and probably stronger. If one of them got injured, it would be bad news. They didn't know if the hospitals or even the doctors for that matter, were still in operation. The girls watched helplessly as the intruder opened the car door and climbed inside.

How the hell did he do that so easily? Lexi knew her father always locked his car so it couldn't have been left open. She glanced furtively at the little wooden key holder by the front door.

Their father always hung his car keys on one of the brass hooks when he came inside. No keys were hanging there now. "Shit," she exclaimed in anger. "He must have taken Dad's car keys when he broke in the house. I should have hidden them."

Hadley frowned. "Well, there's nothing to stop him taking Dad's car now." She peered outside in dismay.

"I was hoping he wouldn't be able to start it, but there's no chance of that now." Lexi glared out of the window with fury in her eyes. Her fingers tightened around the axe handle, ready to use if she needed it. The wood felt smooth under her fingers, and she was tempted to run outside and confront the guy again. Her skin was tingling with adrenaline, and her heart was pounding like a workman's hammer.

The deep sound of the car's engine rumbling to life made both girls jump again. Lexi glanced over at Hadley, who was clinging onto Polo with her face buried in his fur. She reluctantly unwound her fingers from the handle of the axe. As much as she might want to, Lexi wasn't ready to get into a fight, and she couldn't risk getting hurt. Not when there was no one else here to look after Hadley.

The guy roared out of the driveway at a fast speed, almost hitting their letterbox as he went. Both girls watched their father's car drive away down the street, their eyes following its red tail lights until it receded into the distance. It was the first time that their father wouldn't be in it, and their hearts felt as heavy as stone.

Hadley sighed and put her head on her sister's shoulder. "I hate this," she whispered, tears forming in her eyes.

"Me too." Lexi frowned, her eyes filled with sorrow. "Me too Hadley."

Later that morning, while Hadley and Polo dozed fitfully on the couch, Lexi stayed awake worrying and on high alert. She was still feeling terribly shaken up by the whole intruder experience. She also knew that no one was going to come and help them. Not the police, not the government. Lexi didn't even know how many adults were still in the city, let alone running things. It was evident that they were on their own and going to have to look out for themselves. By the time the sun had fully risen, she had made a decision, and Hadley was not going to like it.

While Hadley slept, Lexi forced herself to get up and wander into the kitchen. She decided to make a drink of Milo. It tasted bland without milk, but at least it was hot. Lexi plopped two marshmallows into the steamy hot drink to sweeten it and breathed in the lovely chocolate smell. Chocolate always made her feel better.

She sat down at the kitchen table and started to make a list of all the things they would need.

Water
Tinned food and can opener
Packaged food
Sleeping bags and pillows
Torches and spare batteries
Clothes
Cooking pot and frypan
Two cups, bowls and plates
Matches
Chocolate!
Coffee and Milo
Vegemite and honey
Pocket knife
Dad's baseball bat

"Mmm, I smell hot Milo." Hadley put an arm around her sister's shoulders; she still looked shaken from the night before. "Are you alright? You're up early." She grabbed Lexi's drink and took a few nervous gulps "Are we safe?" Hadley glanced around the kitchen, her eyes darting everywhere.

"Well, Hadley," sighed Lexi, turning to face her sister. "I'm not so sure we *are* safe."

Hadley choked on the drink and ran to look out of the kitchen window, her anxiety quickly escalating.

"It's alright," said Lexi in a calm voice, quickly trying to settle her. "We're okay for now, but look, Hadley…" she glanced at her sister again and sighed. She seemed to be doing that a lot lately. "Sit down sis. I need to talk to you about something."

Hadley took another quick look outside to reassure herself that no one was around before reluctantly sitting next to Lexi. Her face was grim.

"Things are getting a little dangerous around here," said Lexi, her voice a little shaky. "You saw what happened last night. I know this is our house, and I said I didn't want to ever leave, but I don't feel safe here anymore." Lexi's eyes felt gritty from lack of sleep, and she rubbed them with her fingers. "If that guy hadn't left last night, we could have been in trouble. And what if more than one guy comes around? I don't think we could fight them off."

Hadley looked at her and nodded. "Yes, I know. I think you're right, but what shall we do? We can't just leave!" She looked miserable. "All our stuff is here, plus, Mum and Dads stuff!" Hadley started to cry. Tears welled up in her eyes, her face turning a deep red. Shaking her head, Hadley covered her face with her hands.

"Aww Hadley, I know," soothed Lexi taking her sister's hand. "Maybe we can lock everything up and come back later. When things have calmed down and gone back to normal." In her heart, Lexi hoped this was true, but in her head, she knew it probably wasn't. Once they left, there would be no coming back.

Hadley nodded, her face glum. The two sisters reached over and hugged each other for comfort. It would be hard to leave the family home with all their memories of their mum and dad.

From over Hadley's shoulder, Lexi stared at the kitchen counter. Her father's favourite football trophy was sitting on the bench where he had left it last. Lexi knew it was only an object, but it reminded her of him. The thought of leaving it and everything else that belonged to her parent's behind, made tears glimmer in her eyes. She tried not to cry, knowing that if she started Hadley would lose it completely, and she needed her to be alright with the idea of leaving.

Lexi took a deep breath and let go of Hadley, who was still hugging her fiercely. She took a sip of her hot Milo, the warm cup feeling nice in her hands. She wouldn't look at her father's trophy; it would only make things harder.

After a while, Hadley stood up and let Polo outside. She peered out the back door, her eyes alert. "Where can we go, then? Where will we be safe?"

Lexi put her cup down on the table. "Well, I've been thinking about that all morning. I think we should get out of the city, go somewhere smaller. Like a small town. That's bound to be safer, don't you think? We need to find somewhere where there are people who can help us. Somewhere we can wait this thing out, maybe find some other kids like us."

Hadley nodded, "That sounds like a good idea. Our whole street seems completely deserted. I think we're the only ones left living here!"

"Yes, and that's not a good thing. It won't be long before more looters come around, and I don't want to be the only ones left here when they do!"

Lexi hoped that the people in the new town would be friendly and let them stay. There was no guarantee. Not everyone would be happy to let strangers move in, especially if there was a shortage of food and water. She pushed the thought away. First, they had to get to a town. She would deal with the people later if need be.

"Let's get Dad's country road map and have a look at what towns aren't too far away, that's a start. Then we'd better make a list of what to take. I've already written a few things down." She handed the list to Hadley to add to.

Hadley looked at it sadly. "I know it's a good idea, but can't we stay for a few more weeks and then go?" she asked trying to delay the inevitable. "I've only ever lived here in Perth."

Lexi looked at her sister and spoke firmly. "Hadley, I think we should plan on leaving tomorrow, while the shock from last night is still fresh in our minds. Otherwise, it's just going to get harder and harder to leave. Believe me, I'm not exactly thrilled with the idea of going somewhere we've never been to before either, but I know it's the right thing for us to do, so we've just got to do it. No matter how hard it is." She gave her sister a little smile before going to look for her dad's map book. Lexi knew it was a hard thing for Hadley to accept, but she didn't want to waste time arguing about it, and she knew Hadley could argue all day if she wanted to. If they were going to look for somewhere else to live, they had a lot of things to organise before they could leave. Delaying the inevitable would just make it more stressful and difficult. Better not to think about it too much, and just get on with it.

Hadley stared into space. The heat of the morning was already warming up the kitchen. "I wish we could turn back time. I'd love to spend a day like this at the beach with my friends. You know, relaxing on the white sand and floating about in the cool seawater." She sighed. "Guess that's not going to happen ever again.". She stared down at the list of items Lexi had given her, thinking about what else they should take. She started writing on the piece of paper.

"How about my PSV, I can take that, right?" She called out smiling hopefully. It was the last gift Hadley had received from her parents, and she really didn't want to leave it behind. "The battery is still charged."

"Yeah sure," Lexi replied from the other room. "We just can't take anything too big, we haven't got a lot of room in the car, plus, we need to take food and…oh crap!"

"What's wrong?" Hadley quickly dropped the list and ran into the study expecting trouble.

Lexi had her head in her hands. "The car…" She moaned.

"Huh?" Hadley was confused.

Lexi replied in a frustrated voice. "That guy stole Dad's car last night, right?" Hadley nodded her head.

"Mum's car isn't here either!" continued Lexi. "Remember, Dad leant it to his friend Peter, and we haven't heard from him since. He probably left town with everyone else and took our car with him!" Lexi rubbed her hand across her face in annoyance and started pacing back and forth across her father's study.

Hadley just stared at her.

Lexi looked at her sister and groaned, raising her hands in the air. "My plan involved using Mum's car. I completely forgot that we don't have it anymore. How are we going to get out of here now?" She dropped her hands to her sides. "We can't exactly walk with all our stuff!"

"Oh, right," said Hadley in frustration. "Seems like you forget a lot of things lately," she muttered under her breath.

Lexi heard her and shot her a dirty look. *Hadley could be so annoying sometimes.* Feeling defeated, she flopped down on her father's office chair and ran her long fingers through her hair. Polo looked at her quizzically. Lexi stared back at him. "Don't s'pose we can hook you up like a husky sled dog?" She asked the little dog.

Polo just stared at her blankly, his red tongue lolling out of his mouth, dripping drool on the carpet. "Yeah. That's what I thought," she sighed, gently patting the dog's head. They'd have to come up with an alternative plan. "Looks like we're not leaving tomorrow, after all."

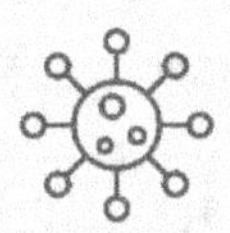

CHAPTER NINE

The girls walked outside and stood at the end of their driveway.

"Come on," said Lexi looking down the street. "Let's walk along the road and see if we can find a car." She didn't wait for Hadley, who had started playing with Polo on the front lawn and started to walk down the street in search of a car they could use to leave the city.

Hadley ran to join her. "This is a lame idea," she whined, kicking the ground with her feet as she walked along. "No one is going to leave their keys in their car like they do in the movies. How are we going to start the car without any keys?"

Lexi walked to the end of the street, looking into people's yards as she went. She stopped and rubbed her eyes; they felt gritty and sore. Peering down the road, Lexi squinted into the bright morning sun. She really needed some sleep.

"Yeah, I suppose you're right. I can't even see any cars anyway. Either they're all locked up in people's garages, or they've already been driven away."

"Or already stolen."

Lexi looked at Hadley grimly. "Yeah, or already stolen. Come on, let's go home. We'll have to think of something else." She swivelled on her heels and turned around to face back down the street. Lexi sighed. "You know, you can always come up with a few ideas," she said back over her shoulder at her sister. "You don't have to leave everything up to me!" Her voice was snippy, and she sounded pissed off.

Hadley stared at Lexi's back and rolled her eyes.

Feeling defeated, the girls started to wander back to their house. It was getting hot already, even though it was barely ten o'clock. The cooling sea breeze from the Fremantle Doctor was yet to arrive, so as yet, there was no relief from the endless summer heat. Lexi pulled her hair up off the nape of her neck into a high ponytail, tying it with a purple elastic hair band she wore around her wrist. Polo, who had joined the girls as they wandered down the street on their mission to find a car, walked along beside her. Every so often he would sneeze loudly at the dust that had settled on the road. With very few cars driving along the streets now, it hadn't taken long for dust and sand to cover the surface of the bitumen like a thin blanket.

"Hey look!" Yelled Hadley suddenly as she ran towards their house. She stopped outside their neighbour's home and pointed. "Look! The Robinson's car is still there. We can take that!" She started bouncing up and down. "I know it seems mean, but they won't be needing it anymore, will they?"

Lexi looked toward the spot where Hadley was pointing. Half hidden in the shade of a large old Hibiscus bush, its branches twisted and bent over like an umbrella, was the Robinson's light blue car. The girls hadn't seen it from the other direction. Lexi nodded her head in agreement and smiled. *Maybe this would work out okay.*

Hadley ran over to the car and pulled off a few branches and twigs that had fallen onto the windshield. She systematically wound her way around the car, looking through every window and trying to open every door. It was no good. They were all locked, and the windows were wound up. They couldn't get inside without breaking a window, and they didn't want to do that unless there were no other way because once it was broken, there was no way they'd be able to fix it.

Hadley walked around and around the car, trying to find a way in. She kicked the car's tyre looking frustrated.

Lexi pulled at her sister's arm. "Come on, Hadley. The car's not going anywhere," she said peering in through the windscreen. "Let's go home and have some breakfast first, I'm starving. We can come up with a plan while we eat. At least we know the car's here. Now we just have to work out how to get inside and start it."

Hadley looked at her and nodded. "Yeah, alright. I'm hungry too. I always think better after I've eaten, anyway!"

The girls laughed as they wandered into their house, discussing their plans for leaving the city, and how they were going to get into the Robinson's car without breaking a window. They decided the easiest option was to look for the car keys.

"I think we should try Jasper's Bay," suggested Lexi pointing to the small town on her father's road map of the Western Australian countryside. The girls were sitting in the kitchen, peering closely at the map.

"It looks as though it's only about four hour's drive from here." Lexi screwed up her nose. "I think I can drive that far."

"Why don't we just drive to Albany? That town is a lot bigger, and it's only a few more hours' drive," argued Hadley tapping her finger on the map.

"Yeah, well don't forget I don't actually have my driver's licence yet," Lexi reminded her.

Hadley rolled her eyes. "What does that matter anymore? It's not as though the police are going to stop you!" she giggled.

Lexi gave her a dirty look. "I know that," she muttered folding the map in half. "I just don't think I can drive for more than four hours. It's not like you can help," she raised her eyebrows and stared meaningfully at her sister. Lexi had only been learning to drive for a few months, and the longest distance she'd driven had been to Mandurah, which was only about an hour out of Perth.

"Besides," Lexi added. "I remember seeing a program on the television about Jasper's Bay last year. It was all about solar power and energy conservation. I'm sure the report said Jasper's Bay was using solar energy to power most of the town." Lexi folded her arms across her chest. "So, that's gotta be good, right? Maybe they still have power on there."

In the end, Hadley gave in, and the girls settled on Jasper's Bay as their destination. With Lexi doing all the driving it seemed only fair that she got to choose, and besides if it didn't work out, they could always move on to Albany later.

So, with their destination settled, now all they had to do was find the Robinson's car keys, and that meant going into their neighbour's house.

Lexi was standing in the kitchen peering out at the neighbour's rundown garden. Her mouth turned down at the sight of the dead roses and azaleas. Mrs Robinson was a keen gardener and would have hated the state her garden was in now. It made Lexi feel sad that everything had gone to ruin so quickly. Even their own backyard was full of waist-high weeds and dead plants.

"Why won't you let me do it?" argued Hadley heatedly. "It was my idea you know." She stood with her hands on her hips and her chin jutting forward.

"Yes, I know Hadley, and it's a good one," replied Lexi tensely, trying to be patient. "But look seriously, you don't want to go into the Robinson's house. Hell, *I* don't want to go in there." She fiddled with the blue gem on her necklace and sighed. "You do realise there are dead people inside, right? And, who knows how long those bodies have been sitting in that room. It's not going to be nice." Lexi looked at her meaningfully.

"Oh. Right. Guess I didn't think of that." Hadley wrinkled her nose in disgust. "Well, you'd better take this then. You're going to need it." She handed her sister a tea towel from the kitchen sink. "You can put it over your nose and mouth. It might help with the smell."

Lexi stared at the red checked cloth unenthusiastically. "Gee, thanks." Now that Lexi thought about actually going into their neighbour's house to find the car keys, she wasn't so keen. It had seemed like a good idea an hour ago. Now that she'd had time to think about it, going into a house with dead bodies inside gave her the creeps. "Maybe we should look for another car. There's probably one in someone's garage?"

Hadley dropped the tea towel onto the bench. "Well, maybe, but we would have to break into all the garages to see, and then we'd have to break into that house to find *those* keys. It's gonna take all day to do that. Anyway, I don't even know how to break into a garage. Do you?"

Lexi looked at her sister in frustration knowing she was right. "No, I don't. And there might be dead people in those houses too, or thugs or druggies." She reluctantly picked up the tea towel Hadley had dropped on the bench and twisted it uncertainly in her hands. "Well, I guess I don't have a choice."

Hadley gave her a half-smile. She looked relieved that Lexi was going into the Robinson's house instead of her. "I'm glad I don't have to see dead bodies!" She whispered crouching down to pat Polo. "Just talking about it is freaking me out!"

Hearing her, Lexi groaned. "Come on then. Let's get this over before I change my mind." Lexi straightened her shoulders and walked out the back door towards the neighbour's garden. *It was best just to get this over with without thinking about it too much.*

*

Slipping through the neighbours' side gate, Lexi went around the back looking for a way into the house. Hadley followed her, with Polo trotting along behind, his tail wagging happily.

Ever since the intruder had broken into their house, the little dog had rarely left Hadley's side. "I don't suppose their back door will be open?" she asked hopefully, pointing to the red wooden door at the back of the house.

The Robinsons lived in an older style home with cream-coloured bricks and a red wooden back door. They had a cottage garden with lavender, miniature roses, and daisies framing the lawn which was now looking extremely overgrown and unkempt. One of the flower beds had an empty blue ceramic birdfeeder in its centre, and a few bright coloured finches flitted around it looking for food. It was rather cute.

Lexi walked up to the back of the house and tried to open the back door. "Nope," she grimaced. "It's locked, of course."

She looked up and spotted a small window in a room that looked like the laundry. Examining the size of the small window, Lexi thought she could probably squeeze through it without too much difficulty. She was going to have to break it though, as it was also locked.

Lexi surveyed the Robinson's backyard for something to break the window with and quickly spotted several large rocks surrounding a small flowerbed over by the back fence. "One of these will do perfectly," she smiled. As she bent down to pick up one of the rocks, Lexi noticed the dying red and yellow flowers in the garden bed and the abundance of weeds springing up around them. Her smile fell, and she quickly grabbed the rock and strode determinedly towards the house. *It was definitely time to move on to a happier place. A place with life and a hope for the future.*

As Lexi stood facing the window, rock in hand, she felt quite rebellious. She had never done anything like this before. Her fingers twitched in anticipation, and her eyes took on an excited gleam. Raising the rock above her head, she glanced back at Hadley who gave her the thumbs up. Lexi grinned and threw the rock straight at the window as hard as she could. It shattered with a loud crash and glass went everywhere. She instinctively flinched even though the glass flew inwards away from her. Up at the window, she noticed that shards of the glass were stuck in the wooden frame just like shark's teeth, waiting to rip her to shreds.

Looking around the garden, Lexi noticed a small gardening trowel in one of the flower beds. She picked it up and strode determinedly towards the broken window. "Those shards of glass look savage," she said raising her eyebrows.

Using the garden trowel, Lexi managed to chip away most of the larger shards and flick them onto the floor. Some of the smaller pieces of glass remained, so she would have to be careful climbing in. Carefully laying the folded tea towel Hadley had given her on the bottom of the window frame, Lexi placed her hands cautiously on top of the towel, raised herself up and got ready to climb in. Her heart was pounding, and a thin layer of sweat was forming on her upper lip.

Lexi was halfway through the window when a foul smell suddenly assaulted her. She fell back coughing, her hands flying to her mouth and nose trying to block out the rancid smell coming from inside the house.

"Oh God," she mumbled, stepping away from the window. "This is going to be difficult."

"What's wrong?" asked Hadley running to her. She promptly screwed up her face. "Oh, geez, what's that gross smell? Smells like something's rotten!"

"I think maybe it's coming from the Robinsons," Lexi replied grimly, feeling a mixture of sorrow and disgust. It made her think about her own parent's deaths and how it had been entirely different for them. At least her parents had died with their family. The Robinsons had been left to rot with no one to take care of them.

"Oh," Hadley murmured sadly looking down at the ground. "That's horrible."

Hadley's voice brought Lexi back to the present. She blinked her eyes rapidly. "Yeah, and it makes my job a lot harder too. I still have to go in there. I just hope the keys aren't in their pocket or something. I do *not* want to have to touch a dead body." Lexi grimaced at the thought.

Hadley pulled a face of disgust too. "I hope they're not like those decomposing bodies of zombies on the TV!" She patted her sister on the back and scuttled back to stand by Polo, away from the smell seeping out of the house. The dog was stretched out quite happily on his stomach under a bush near the fence. He seemed quite pleased to be back in his own yard. "I'll just sit over here and look after Polo," she suggested, rubbing the dog's side with her hand. "He needs emotional support."

Lexi frowned at her. "Uh huh, right. More like so you don't have to be near this gross smell," she muttered to herself as she held her hand over her mouth and nose and headed back towards the window. *Better get this done.* Lexi grimaced again at the smell and hoped she wouldn't vomit. Turning her head to the side, she took a deep breath of fresh air before hoisting herself carefully up onto the windowsill again. Her sneakers slipped a little on the towel as she jumped awkwardly into the laundry. Nearly falling, Lexi reached her hand out to the wall to steady herself.

"Thank goodness Hadley's over by the tree," she muttered, thankful her sister hadn't seen her almost fall on her butt. Lexi took the towel from the windowsill, shaking out any small pieces of glass before holding it to her nose. She cautiously stepped over the broken pieces of glass on the floor, being careful not to cut herself. The last thing they needed was for her to get cut and need stitches.

Now, she thought to herself looking around. *Where would someone put their car keys?* "Please don't be in your pocket," she said to herself. "Not in your pocket," Lexi repeated as she walked into the Robinson's hallway. "Not in your pocket." Hoping, that if she said it enough times, it would make it true.

The house was dark, gloomy, and had an eerie feel. Lexi was creeped out by it and felt like she was invading someone's personal space, which she was. The thought of being alone in a dark house with a couple of dead bodies was giving her the jitters, and she couldn't wait to get the hell out of there.

"I should have brought a torch!" She fumed slapping her leg. "What an idiot!" Lexi had not gotten used to living without electricity.

Squinting her eyes and peering to the right, she quickly headed towards a room she guessed would be the kitchen, not wanting to spend any more time in the gloomy house than she had to. The problem was, as Lexi had only been inside the Robinson's house once, she didn't know the layout or where anything was. She kept walking in the direction she thought the kitchen might be. There seemed to be light coming from that direction, so at least she would be able to see.

Once Lexi reached the room, which was indeed the kitchen, the smell immediately became a lot worse. There was an odour of rotting food mixed with all the other odours. A bowl of formerly red apples sat on the bench. Their skins were turning a dark brown colour as their flesh became putrid and rotten. A few bananas lay nearby, black and covered in a white mould. A lone large black blowfly was crawling on the rotting fruit looking for somewhere to lay its eggs.

"God! This is going to make me puke!" Lexi blocked her nose and breathed through her mouth trying not to think about where the smell was coming from. She really wanted to get out of this house; it felt creepy being in there with festering food and dead people. Her heartbeat was starting to rise, and her palms were sweating.

"Come on, come on," she said to herself as she scanned the kitchen. *Where are you?* The window blinds were open in this room and the morning sun was streaming through the glass, making it easy for Lexi to see. She quickly scanned the benchtops. Nothing. No keys in here, unless they'd put them in a drawer or cupboard, and she didn't think that was likely. *Where else could they be?* Probably not in the bedroom. *Maybe in the front hallway,* she thought. That's where her dad always kept *his* keys, on a little red and yellow hook she had made for Father's Day when she was in primary school. She smiled a little in remembrance.

Looking around again to get her bearings, Lexi noticed that to her right was a door half-open leading to what must be the front living room. Walking closer, she could just see into the area. Gasping, her eyes wide in horror, Lexi immediately took a step back. There was an arm dangling down from a lounge chair. It was the room she had seen into earlier from outside. It was where the Robinsons had obviously died!

Lexi ran both her hands through her hair and shook her head. The last thing she wanted to do was go into a room with dead people sitting in it.

"Shit!" Lexi exclaimed loudly. She knew she had to search the room for keys or what was the point of coming into the house. As she again took a step towards the area, Lexi distinctly heard a strange sound, a bit like bees, coming from the room. It was an incessant droning sound like a blender on high speed. *Why would bees be in the Robinson's living room?*

Lexi cautiously walked into the room not wanting to get stung. As she peered farther into the gloomy area, she felt her legs go weak and start to shake. It wasn't bees making the horrible buzzing noise. They were flies! Hundreds of big black disgusting flies. They were swarming all around the room banging into the walls and furniture as they flew. Almost in a kind of frenzy.

Lexi stood for a moment frozen in place, staring at the macabre scene before her. She had never witnessed anything like it before, and it made her stomach turn in revulsion. Feeling the disgust rise inside of her, she quickly turned away from the room and ran back to the kitchen, dry retching into the sink. How awful. She thought of the Robinsons and how they had always been friendly to Hadley and herself. The sound of the flies was still buzzing in her mind. It was not how she would want to be left when she died.

Lexi wiped the back of her hand across her mouth. *She needed to find those keys and get out!* Lexi knew she would be having nightmares tonight.

Looking around her, Lexi's face fell in dismay. The only way she could see into the front hall where she hoped the keys would be, was through that living room! *Fantastic!*

Lexi dabbed the tea towel across her brow; it was slick with sweat. It was so hot in the house.

"I don't think I can do this," she whispered doubtfully, as she leant over the kitchen sink. Turning the tap on, Lexi watched the water flow down the drain; the sound was calming and gradually the wave of sickness passed.

"Shit!" Lexi exclaimed. "Shit, shit, shit." *You know you don't have a choice,* she thought to herself. *You can't make Hadley do this, and there's no one else. You're going to have to do it.* Lexi turned the tap back on and let the lukewarm water run over her hands and through her fingers for a moment.

"Okay, Let's do it!" Before she could change her mind, Lexi quickly splashed her face and neck with water, before charging determinedly towards the lounge room. As she paused on the brink of entering the room, her heart hammered fiercely in her chest, and her feet felt heavy like lead. They didn't want to move. Slowly, with great effort, she forced herself to take one step at a time and crossed over the breach. *Just walk straight through and pretend they're asleep,* she thought to herself. *Don't look, just walk straight through. You don't need to look.* But, of course, she did look, and it was a shock. Even though she had known that the Robinsons were dead, the reality of seeing their bodies in the flesh was not what she had expected. They didn't look anything like they were asleep, and neither of them looked peaceful. In fact, they looked as though they had died horribly. Their bodies were all swollen and gross.

Lexi saw that both the Robinsons were dead. *At least they'd died together,* she thought briefly, but it was not a sight she ever wanted to see again in a hurry. Mr Robinson's arm was dangling down from the chair where he had been sitting when he died. He was wearing a red-checked cowboy-type shirt, and his hand lay resting palm-up. The skin was white and swollen as if it had been sitting in water for a long time. The fingers were slightly curved, and his wedding ring was straining against the skin of his bulbous finger. Mrs Robinson was sitting next to him in her nightgown. One of her slippers had come off, exposing her red coloured toe-nails that were now swollen and misshapen. Flies were crawling all over their bodies, inside their noses, ears and mouths.

Lexi felt queasy. Her skin turned white and clammy as her hands flew to her mouth and she started to gag. All around her, the room began to spin, and she suddenly had the odd sensation that she was going to pass out. The smell was intense, and the sight of those two bodies just made it worse. The black flies kept slamming into her like kamikaze pilots as they flew around the room, making her cover her head with her arms. The smell of decay invaded her nostrils like a thick fog. Lexi had to get out of there. She did not want to pass out in that room.

Stumbling from the room with her arms still protecting her head, she entered another area. Thankfully, it was the front passageway of the house. There were only a couple of flies in here, and the smell was less intense. She quickly shut the door leading from the passageway to the lounge room, trying to block out the smell of death and the relentless droning noise of the flies. Closing her eyes thankfully, she leant her back against the wall. Bending over and resting her hands on her knees, she waited until the waves of nausea dissipated and she no longer had the feeling of vertigo.

Lexi made a quick decision; she was not going back into that awful room, keys or no keys. If the keys weren't in this front hall, they would have to think of something else. *Maybe they could try hotwiring the car like they did in the movies?* It always looked so easy in the films, and she was sure they could work it out. One thing was for sure, that front room was now definitely out of bounds. Nothing would make her go back in there, and she knew that Hadley wouldn't venture in either. The image of the Robinsons and the flies were going to stay with her for a long time. She did *not* want to see it ever again.

With the door closed, it was dark in the front hallway as there were no windows to let in any natural light. The tight space was very claustrophobic. Lexi ran her hand along the smooth wall with her fingers splayed out searching for the front door to the house. She could feel perspiration running down her spine.

Eventually, Lexi's fingertips felt the unmistakable edge of the wooden door frame, and she quickly ran her hands over the door until she found the handle. Flicking the latch open, Lexi flung the door wide, hitting the door against the wall in her haste. She stepped outside onto the porch for a moment, breathing deeply through her nose. The fresh air smelt so good!

After a few moments, Lexi forced herself to step back into the house. At least with the front door open now, the hallway was less claustrophobic, and she could see. Lexi hastily hunted around, desperately wanting to find the keys. She didn't want to have to go further into the home.

In the corner of the hallway, Lexi noticed a wooden hat stand with all manner of hats, scarves and umbrellas hanging from it. There was also a worn orange-patterned rug with frayed edges partially covering the floor, but not much else. No hooks on the wall and no keys.

Lexi massaged her temples as beads of sweat started to form in little droplets on her forehead. "Where the hell are, they?" she said through gritted teeth. Her fingers were beginning to twitch. Lexi had been in this house for over an hour now, and she didn't want to be in here any longer. Back in the hallway, she could again smell the Robinsons.

"Come on, get a grip," she said out loud to herself, knowing that she would never find the keys if she let the panic take hold of her. Looking around again, Lexi noticed coats hanging on the hat stand. *Maybe the keys were in one of the pockets?*

Quickly striding over to them and pulling each one from its hanging spot she thrust her fingers into the pockets hoping to feel the hard metal shape of keys against her fingers. Tissues, bits of paper and an old half eaten dried up apple core were all she found. Not what she was looking for. Only one coat remained. It was a red woolly jacket with fur trim, so it must have belonged to Mrs Robinson. She wasn't sure if Mrs Robinson drove the car or not, but she plunged her hand into one of the pockets anyway. The front pocket didn't contain anything, so she pulled her hand back out. As she plunged her hand into the second pocket, Lexi felt the familiar hardness of a small metal object shaped like a key. Her fingers closed around it in triumph and pulled it free from its confines of the pocket. Lexi's face broke into a happy smile as she gazed at the key with glee, only to rapidly turn into a frown as she realised the key was too small and could not possibly be a car key. It wasn't even a house key and must have belonged to a letterbox or something similar.

Feeling intense disappointment, she let the key slip from her fingers and flung the last coat onto the floor. Irritation crept over her like an itch you couldn't scratch, she rubbed her face with her hands. This was not going to plan. She was supposed to climb in the window, quickly find the car keys and be straight out again. Groaning in frustration, Lexi slapped her hand on her thigh and made herself look again. She wasn't going to give up, even though it seemed hopeless.

Lexi scanned every corner of the hallway. Nothing. No key holders were hanging on the wall, no shelves, no hooks. Nothing. She clenched her teeth, her anger rising. She'd had enough.

About to give up on the search, Lexi flung herself around to face the front door and was ready to march straight through it when something made her glance down. That was when she finally spotted them. Instant relief washed over her. A little bowl sat innocuously by the front door, initially hidden by the jumble of long coats and scarves on the hat stand. It was only when she had pulled them all off and turned to face the front door that the bowl became obvious. Lexi never thought that she would ever be *so* pleased to see a set of silver keys in a little blue ceramic bowl.

"Oh, hell yes!" She yelled in triumph as she strode over to the bowl, closing her hand into a fist around the keys. Lexi had never been so happy in all her life. *She could finally get out of here!*

CHAPTER TEN

Ten am. That was the time the girls had both decided on to make their departure. The time they were supposed to start on their journey into the unknown. It was now eleven am, and they still hadn't left. It wasn't that they weren't organised, in fact, it hadn't taken the girls long to pack the Robinson's car with their supplies and belongings, including their dad's football trophy and mother's jewellery. However, they were finding it difficult to leave. Lexi had already gone around the house twice, making sure all the windows and doors were locked and secure. Although she knew it wouldn't keep anyone out if they really wanted to break in, it made her feel a lot better about leaving the house.

Waiting to depart, Lexi felt jumpy as she sat on the front step of their porch for the last time. She looked down at one of her mother's old rings which she now wore and twisted it around her finger. It felt strange to be leaving their home like this. It was almost as though they were merely going away on holiday or a school camp and would be back in a few weeks. She couldn't quite believe they might never see their home again. It was all very surreal.

Eventually, Lexi couldn't delay leaving any longer, as there was nothing left to be done. The gas on their little portable stove had finally run out, the water in the house was no longer running, the toilet was blocked up, and their food supplies weren't going to last much longer. It was time to leave the city.

Lexi sighed. "Well, we'd better get going. I think we should get out of the city before midday. I don't want to be driving somewhere I haven't been before in the dark." She stood, looking towards the car. "Let's just hope the people of Jasper's Bay are friendly." Lexi knew it was a risk leaving their home for the unknown. However, as their food supplies were running low, and the threat of crime and danger had spread to their own house, it was a risk they had to take. If they wanted to survive, they had to leave.

Hadley ran her hand over the smooth timber balustrade at the front of their porch. "Okay," she sighed wistfully. "I suppose we can't stay?"

"No, Hadley. I really don't think it's safe here. The TV and radio are not broadcasting anymore, so we have no idea what's going on. We don't even know if the police and hospitals are still operating. Look what happened to the Robinsons; no one came to help them, and we've already had two close calls with looters." She held her hands out in front of her pleading with her sister. "No. I think we need to find somewhere out of the city. Some place where people look out for each other. You know, so we're not on our own. A little town with not many people and if we can't stay at Jasper's Bay, then we'll find another small town."

Hadley stared at Lexi, a fierce look in her eyes, "I know you're right, it's just so hard to leave. I miss Mum and Dad."

Lexi hugged her sister. "God, Hadley, I know. I miss them too, and when I think of them, I want to cry, but we must think of the future. I just don't feel safe here anymore," she pointed to the houses around them. "I know this is our home and our neighbourhood, but everything's changed. Maybe if Mum and Dad were still here with us, things would be different, but they're not. I want to find somewhere we can be safe. Someplace where we can go to sleep without having to worry that someone might break into the house and take our stuff or worse. You know Mum and Dad would want that."

Hadley nodded slowly. "I feel so awful leaving our home. Do you think it feels like this for everyone who leaves?" Her eyes glazed over, and she stared off into the distance.

Lexi could tell Hadley was thinking of her friend Amy and her family who had left a few months before. Amy's mother was a doctor and had strongly suggested they'd be better off out of the city. Away from people, where the virus could spread easily and rapidly. Lexi's parents had listened patiently but reassured Amy's mother they would be fine staying where they were and waiting for it all to blow over. Besides they said, the World Health Organisation would come up with a cure soon. They were sure of it. A lot of people had thought the same way her parents had.

Amy's family were lucky; they had relatives in the country who could take them in. Hadley and Lexi's closest relatives were in Sydney and Melbourne, right over the other side of the country. It would take several days to get there, and besides those cities were even bigger than Perth. That meant more people so the problem wouldn't have been any better there, anyway.

Glancing at Hadley, Lexi could see the sad look on her sister's face. She reached over and put her arm comfortingly around her shoulders. "Well, Hadley, come on. We'd better get going. Just think of it as an adventure."

Lexi looked up at the white-bricked house, knowing that she would probably never see it again. She hoped they would be able to find somewhere else to call home. She didn't relish the idea of having to live in the Robinson's old car if they didn't. Trying not to think about it too deeply, she put on a brave face for Hadley's sake and walked briskly to the car. Inside her stomach was churning with fear. She couldn't help worrying about their future, and what was going to happen to them. Swallowing her uncertainty, she quickly opened the car door.

The car was an old Holden that had seen better days. Like them, the Robinsons hadn't been particularly wealthy and didn't own a new car. The outside was a faded shade of light blue, the colour of the sky on a winter's morning and had several patches of rust on the body. Lexi noticed that there was a small crack in the back window and that one of the car's taillights was broken, but she wasn't worried. It wasn't as if the police were going to pull them over for having a busted light. As long as it took them where they wanted to go, she couldn't care less how it looked. The days of worrying about how fancy your car looked were long gone. She was just glad to have a car that had four good tyres and a roof.

After Lexi had settled herself into the driver's seat, she put the precious car key into the ignition and held her breath, praying the car would start. They had no idea how long the vehicle had been sitting in the Robinsons' yard. The battery could be dead flat for all they knew. Or it could be totally out of petrol.

"We probably should have checked this car actually worked before we loaded it up with all our stuff," she shrugged at their oversite and grinned at Hadley. *Oh well, too late to worry about that now.* They'd soon find out either way.

As Lexi turned the key to the start position, she glanced over at Hadley, who was sitting in the passenger seat with Polo on her lap. Her sister had her eyes squeezed shut and her fingers crossed on both hands as if willing the car to life. They needn't have worried. The old car let out a thunderous vroom sound as it started on the first go. Both girls gave a happy cheer making Polo yelp in surprise, making Hadley giggle.

"Come on what are you waiting for?" Said Hadley, turning to face Lexi. "She pointed to the road "Let's go."

Lexi rolled her eyes but didn't say anything in reply. She simply put the car into reverse, and they were on their way. Well almost. Driving the Robinson's car was not as easy as Lexi thought it was going to be. The Robinsons had a manual car. Lexi had only had a few lessons in her Dad's car, and that was an automatic. It took her four goes to make it out of the Robinson's front yard and onto the road without stalling the car.

To make matters worse, each time Lexi tried to change the car's gears, she forgot to use the clutch, and the gears made an awful metallic grinding noise. She could feel herself getting more and more frustrated every time she stalled the car and had to start it up again. She pressed her lips together tightly and gripped the steering wheel.

Hadley wasn't making things any easier, either. She kept laughing and sniggering whenever the car bunny hopped down the road like it was some big game. Just to make things even more challenging for Lexi, whenever the car stalled the air conditioner would switch off, and the inside of the car was starting to heat up like an oven. Lexi could feel her temperature literally rising, and the more Hadley laughed, the worse she felt. Eventually, the irritation became too great, and she blew her top like a cork bursting out of a champagne bottle.

"Would you STOP!" She yelled. "This isn't easy, you know!"

Hadley snickered again. "Woah, sorry. You don't have to be so grouchy. I can't help it that you're such a terrible driver. It's going to take us hours just to get down the road! It would be quicker if I walked."

"Oh, ha-ha! I'm not that bad," Lexi replied indignantly. "And if you don't stop laughing, you might just be walking." Her eyebrows were raised as she gave her sister a meaningful glare. "You couldn't do any better you know. You probably couldn't even see over the steering wheel!"

Hadley laughed, then quickly covered her mouth with her hands. Lexi frowned at her before breaking up into laughter too.

"Oh, come on," said Lexi, starting the car once again. "Let me try this once more." She took a big breath, then slowly released her foot from the clutch while pressing down on the accelerator.

Thankfully, the car took off smoothly for once and didn't stall. Lexi even managed to get into second gear. "Hey, I think I'm finally getting the hang of this," she exclaimed, feeling quite pleased with herself.

Hadley looked at her and suppressed another giggle. "Mmm," she said with a big grin on her face. "You might even be able to get up to fourth gear soon."

Lexi ignored the taunt and focused on driving. She tried to remember which road they needed to take to get out of town. No Google maps to rely on now. The last thing they needed was to get lost and run out of petrol before they'd even left the city. Glancing at the fuel gauge on the car's dashboard, she noticed with relief that there was almost a full tank of petrol in the car. Lexi smiled happily, *thank you Robinsons,* she thought to herself. At least they wouldn't have to find petrol for a while.

Driving through the streets, the girls saw very few people and even fewer adults. Most of the people they did see were children, who were just milling around looking bored. There were piles of rubbish blowing about everywhere like tumbleweed in a desert, and packs of dogs roamed the streets looking for food. Things were starting to look very neglected and run down. It was frightening.

The two girls looked sideways at each other and had the same thought. *Leaving the city was definitely a good idea.* As they drove past their old school, Lexi slowed the car. The school's windows were all smashed, and graffiti covered the walls. It seemed unreal that they had been going to classes there only a few months ago. How things had changed so fast and so much. A group of older boys were smashing bottles up against one of the walls and turned to stare at the light blue car as it slowly drove past. Several of them pointed and started to run towards the girls.

"Oh no!" exclaimed Lexi, her fingers tightening on the steering wheel.

"Drive!" yelled Hadley in a panic, her eyes darting to the boys running towards them.

Lexi immediately put her foot down on the accelerator praying she wouldn't stall, now would not be a good time to stop.

As the car took off quickly, the group of older boys stopped running and watched the little car drive away. They started laughing and calling out rude remarks to the girls. One of them decided to drop his pants and moon them. Lexi didn't care. She watched them in the rear vision mirror, but she didn't slow down, and she made sure she kept her foot firmly on the accelerator. There was no way she was going to let the car stall. Those guys looked like they were trouble, and that was the last thing they needed right now.

It wasn't long before they left the suburbs and drove out onto the highway leading out of Perth. The long straight road stretched on before them, seeming to go on forever.

Once the girls left the city, Lexi finally started to relax and stretched back in her seat. She was faintly surprised to find that she was actually enjoying driving. One thing she did notice was that the Robinson's car had a lingering smell of stale tobacco. She wondered if Mr Robinson liked to smoke the occasional secret cigarette in there while listening to the radio. Lexi chuckled to herself, wondering what Mrs Robinson would say if she knew about his little secret.

As the car was old, it didn't have a USB port for their iPod like their father's, so, the girls improvised and listened to music using Lexi's purple headphones. One earbud each, listening to their favourite music as they drove along. Jason Derulo, Ariana Grande, Katy Perry, made the long drive a lot more bearable. The iPod was only half charged, and without any way of charging it again, the girls decided to make the most of it.

"I only miss you when I'm breathing!" they sang loudly. The windows of the car were wound fully down, and their hair blew out behind them as they drove along the highway. They both laughed happily. It was good to laugh after the stress of the past few days, and Lexi was glad that they were getting along alright. Hadley had volunteered to navigate using their father's road map. This meant that Lexi could concentrate on driving. It made things easier and less stressful only having to focus on one thing at a time. Driving was hard enough without having to work out which road to take as well.

Lexi glanced over at Hadley, who had taken her hairbrush out of her handbag and had started singing into it like a microphone. She flung her short-bobbed hair around dramatically as she sang. Hadley was a terrible singer; her voice high-pitched and off-key, and Lexi winced. *This could be an extremely long drive!*

Luckily for Lexi, Hadley soon became tired of singing and stared listlessly out the car window. They weren't that far out of the city, yet the landscape had already changed dramatically. Gone were the tall office blocks and skyscrapers of the CBD. Gone were the tightly-spaced houses with their lawns and leafy trees. They had reached the outskirts of the suburbs and the homes and developments here had suddenly become spread out and far apart. It didn't look like a lot of people lived out here. Lexi wasn't surprised. The landscape outside was sparse and arid. Vast stretches of land spread out to the horizon. The land was fenced, and someone had tried to grow grass, but it was a soft yellow colour as if it was desperate to be quenched with water. There were a few trees here and there, however; even those were bent over, struggling against the force of the hot wind that blew from the east. *How could anything survive out here?*

With the heat and rumble of the car, Hadley's eyes slowly started to droop, heavy and leaden like the curtains coming down on a stage at the end of a play.

Lexi watched her sister falling asleep. "Thank God," she whispered. *At last some quiet!*

Just then, a shape darted across the road making Lexi swerve and slam on the brakes. The car fishtailed before skidding to a holt. Lexi breathed heavily; her face turned white.

Hadley jolted awake. "What are you doing?!" she cried out as she was yanked forward in her seat. Luckily her seatbelt held her in place.

"Sorry! Something ran across the road," Lexi exclaimed. "I nearly hit it!" Lexi's heart was beating rapidly, and she felt sick. She twisted her body around in her seat so that she could look back over her shoulder. *What was that?!*

Looking back, Lexi couldn't see anything besides the long black skid marks on the road. She looked at Hadley for a moment before deciding to put the car in reverse and back up a bit.

After she reached the spot where the skid marks ended, she stopped the car and turned off the engine. "Should we get out and look?" she asked peering through the window into the bush. Lexi chewed on her fingernails.

"I'm getting out," said Hadley not waiting for Lexi to answer. "I'm sick of being in this car, and I want to see what it was."

"Wait!' called Lexi glaring at Hadley. "We don't know if it's dangerous!"

Hadley ignored her and opened the car door. "You stay here Polo," she said pushing the dog back into the car and shutting the door. Hadley started to creep towards the bush.

Lexi groaned. "For crying out loud, Hadley," she muttered, unfastening her seat belt. She squinted her eyes and peered into the bush again. She still couldn't see anything.

"Hang on," Lexi grumbled. "Wait for me." She wound her window up half-way so Polo couldn't escape and then proceeded to follow Hadley towards the bush.

Lexi watched Hadley disappear behind a clump of Mulga bushes. "Hadley, wait!" Lexi hissed. "There might be Dugites or Tiger snakes!" She gripped the car keys tightly.

Just as Lexi was about to walk forward, Hadley came running back. She was beckoning to her frantically with her hand.

Lexi's eyes grew wide and her body tense. "What is it! What's wrong?"

Hadley's face lit up. "Come and see," she laughed bouncing around on her toes.

Lexi crept forward quietly and poked her head around the bushes. Her eyes widened in surprise and delight too, and she breathed out a sigh of relief not realising she had been holding her breath. There before her was a mob of red kangaroos. They were feeding happily on the scrubby grass growing in the clearing.

"Oh, Lexi, look," exclaimed Hadley, her eyes crinkling at the sides as she smiled. "They've got a little joey with them. How cute." She pointed her finger. "I've never seen a kangaroo in the wild before. Look at the way they're staring straight at us. They don't look in the least bit afraid." The excitement in her voice was contagious.

Lexi couldn't help smiling too. "Well, I suppose there haven't been very many cars going down this road for a while. They're probably enjoying the quiet." She gazed happily at the kangaroos standing up on their back legs, watching them with their big brown peaceful eyes. "They are cute. I wish I could put it on Instagram. Pity there's no internet anymore."

The sisters stood and looked at the kangaroos for a while, animal and human quietly watching each other. Eventually, the girls reluctantly dragged themselves away and continued with their journey. They still had a long way to go before they reached their destination, and Lexi was keen to get there before dark. They hadn't seen any other people around, but that didn't mean she would be happy sleeping in the car on the side of the road. They needed to get to the town of Jasper's Bay before nightfall.

The excitement of seeing the Kangaroos had been a welcome break in their monotonous drive. Lexi's iPod was now flat, and there were only so many games of 'eye spy' that you could play. Especially when there were only the two of them trapped in the car together.

It didn't take too long for things to get boring again. Hadley once again looked out of the car windows. They were now driving past farmland. Wire fences ran along the side of the entire stretch of road, and some of the paddocks had sheep and cows. The sheep hadn't been shorn in a while, and their wool made them look like little white cotton balls, dotted across the landscape. Hadley stared at them as they drove past, huddled together under trees or wherever they could find a patch of shade. The grass out there was even more withered with its shades of brown and yellow as it baked under the harsh Australian sun. With no one about to tend to it, the pasture had quickly dried out.

After only another hour of driving, Lexi decided she needed to stop again. Fatigue was setting in, and her eyes were starting to feel like they had little particles of grit in them. She looked over at Hadley, who had her eyes half closed and her head resting on the window. Her mouth was hanging open, and she had a little bit of drool coming from the corner.

Lexi reached over and nudged her awake. "Hey, Hadley! Let's stop for a break and have something to eat," she suggested, rubbing her face. "I'm not used to driving for more than an hour."

Hadley stretched her arms, wiped her mouth, and yawned. "Good idea, I think Polo needs to pee anyway."

Lexi looked at Polo. He was fast asleep on the back seat. "Um, Polo or you?"

Hadley laughed. "Okay me, but I'm sure he does too!"

"Well, looks like there's a little bridge up ahead, might be a nice creek under it," suggested Lexi pointing out the window. "Let's pull up over there and take a break. I wouldn't mind dipping my feet in the cool water." Lexi started to edge the car off the road and parked under a big white gum tree so that they could have some shade to sit under. Its trunk was as white as beach sand and its branches covered in dark green leaves that looked shiny in the sunlight.

"Back in a minute," Hadley called jumping from the car as soon as it stopped and heading straight for some bushes. "Come on, Polo," she yelled as she ran. Polo obediently followed her, his tail wagging happily. He had taken a real liking to Hadley since they had adopted him, and she was enjoying having a pet to play with.

"Watch out for snakes!" Lexi warned, yelling after her. "Well, I guess she really did need to go," she laughed to herself.

Lexi climbed from the car and stretched her back and neck. She felt stiff and sore from sitting in one position for so long, and her fingers ached from gripping the steering wheel so tightly. "I have to relax more when I drive," she told herself as she opened the car boot.

Leaning into the boot, Lexi started rummaging through the boxes stacked in the back, looking for some food and drink. Fully occupied with what she was doing, she hadn't noticed somebody creep up behind her and was startled when she heard a voice that wasn't Hadley's.

"Hey, hello!" said the unknown and unwelcome voice.

Lexi stood up quickly in surprise hitting her head on the boot of the car.

"Oww!" she exclaimed, clutching the top of her head in pain. *What the hell!* Looking around quickly she tried to locate the voice and determine if it was going to be trouble. From the corner of her eye, she saw Hadley stand from behind the bushes and come running up cheerfully.

"Hi!" Hadley said enthusiastically to the stranger, waving her hand around in greeting.

Lexi turned to her right to see a tall, skinny guy with dark wavy hair standing a couple of metres away from her. He was dressed in blue jeans, a baggy shirt with some sort of icon printed on it, and high top black and white Converse sneakers. He also wore a large dirty blue canvas backpack like the ones you get from a camping store. He looked about the same age as Lexi. The boy started waving his hand about in greeting.

Where the heck had he come from, Lexi wondered. *He must have been sitting up under the bridge in the shade.* She hoped he wasn't going to be a problem; Lexi wasn't in the mood for trouble.

"Hi there," he said again cheerfully coming up close to Lexi. "Where you guys heading?"

Lexi slowly closed the boot of the car, hiding their food and took a few steps backwards feeling cautious about this stranger. After all, they didn't know anything about him or what he was doing out in the middle of the bush for that matter. He might try to steal their belongings, or worse the car. Her mind was telling her to be wary, and that's just what she intended to be. *I'm going to be the one asking the questions thanks very much, not him.* However, before Lexi could say anything at all, Hadley marched right up to the guy and promptly started telling him where they were from and where they were headed.

Lexi quickly stalked up to her sister grabbing her arm and pulling her away. "Hang on a minute, Hadley," she cautioned in a low voice. "We don't know anything about this guy. He could be trouble." She glanced over at the stranger who was staring at her with intense green eyes. "No offence," she added quickly raising her hand, not wanting to start a fight with him.

Luckily, the boy laughed good-naturedly. "None taken. Actually, you're right," he agreed, nodding his head. "You really shouldn't trust people you don't know."

"Like you?" Lexi looked at him; her eyes narrowing. Her body was tense. *What did this guy want?*

The boy laughed again, a nice deep laugh.

"Well, I suppose, 'cause you don't really know me yet," he paused and rubbed his eyebrow. "I'd like to get to know *you* though." He winked at the girls.

Hadley laughed at how corny he sounded.

Lexi snorted, trying not to laugh too. "Well, *that* didn't sound creepy at all," she said sarcastically.

The stranger took a step back and held up his hands in an apology. "Oh no!" He stammered, blushing bright red. "I didn't mean it like that! Sorry, I'm not good at this," he said awkwardly, running his fingers through his hair.

"Not good at what?" Asked Hadley still grinning.

The guy was shuffling his feet in the dirt. "Well, I dunno. Meeting new people, I guess," he replied quietly, scratching his head.

Hadley pulled her arm away from Lexi. "Why don't you like meeting people?" she persisted.

"Um, well. I usually talk to people on my computer, not face to face," the boy admitted. "Actually, apart from school, I basically sit in my room playing games and doing stuff on my laptop. Well, I used to." The boy continued to shuffle his feet in the dirt.

Lexi's shoulders relaxed. She tilted her head to the side scrutinising the boy. He looked very awkward and uncomfortable. "So, what's your name anyway?" she asked wanting to know more about him. *He didn't seem like a threat.*

"Jason," replied the boy looking up. "My name's Jason. I'm sixteen, and as you can see, I'm on my own." He smiled and gestured around with his hands.

"Do you live around here?" asked Hadley peering at Jason's dirty blue duffel bag sitting at his feet.

Jason laughed heartily. "Ah, no. Actually, I'm from Perth." He looked down at his feet. "My parents died from the virus, and I've been by myself ever since."

Lexi and Hadley glanced at each other. "Don't you have any other family?" asked Hadley.

Jason looked at Hadley and shook his head. "No, I don't have any family or close friends in the city. All my friends were on cyberspace, and now that the internet is shut down, I don't have any way of contacting them." Jason pulled at his ear. "I never knew their real addresses, only their internet blog sites, YouTube channels and Facebook pages." He shrugged. "Since then, I've been travelling on my own looking for somewhere to stay. How about you?"

"We're from the city too," replied Lexi. "Where's your car," she asked frowning as she turned her head and looked around.

Jason's face went bright red. "Er, actually I've been walking." He lifted his feet and showed Lexi the bottom of his sneakers. They were almost worn through, the soles smooth.

Lexi's mouth fell open. "You walked *all the way* from Perth?!" her face looked stunned. "That's 200 km!"

"Yeah, it's a long way, but I started on a bike." Jason paused to pull up his cargo pants which were slipping from his hips. A big grin spread across his face. "I think I've lost a bit of weight!"

"You're gonna need a belt," laughed Hadley, her eyes crinkling.

"Yeah, I am." He sat down on his dusty duffle bag and took a drink of water from a flask. Jason peered back up at the girls. "So, anyway, I decided to leave the city. I rode my bicycle south for three days, not really knowing where I was going, south just felt right. I was just trying to find somewhere I could settle that wasn't as violent and feral as the city, you know?"

Lexi and Hadley both nodded their heads adamantly. The city had been too violent for them too.

Jason gave the girls a half-smile. "I'm not very fit, so I had to stop a lot and even though I've got my sleeping bag with me, I had to sleep rough." Jason nudged his bag with his hand. "Two days ago, I cycled over pieces of glass some idiot had carelessly thrown out their car window, and unfortunately, I got two flat tyres." Jason shrugged. "Since then, I've been reduced to walking."

"Geeze that sucks," remarked Hadley as she bent down to stroke Polo.

Jason yawned, shifting his weight on his pack. "I've come to the rapid conclusion that walking is not an effective means of travel. My legs are aching, and I've got big white blisters on the soles of my feet that look like abnormal growths. Want to see them?" Jason started to remove his shoes.

"No!" exclaimed Lexi holding up her hand. "That's okay, Jason. We believe you."

"I really don't think I can walk anymore," said Jason taking a big breath in and looking up at the girls. He had a hopeful, stupid grin on his face. "When I saw your little blue car drive up, I thought it was a miracle!".

Lexi and Hadley were standing with their arms folded across their chests, patiently listening to Jason tell his story. The girls watched him become more animated and emotional as he told of the death of his parents and his decision to leave home. It reminded them of their own sad story with their parents and having to leave their own family home behind. They could feel his desperation and confusion at everything that had happened to him and the world around him, and they could relate. They felt just like him. A bit lost in this new world but determined never-the-less to make things work.

The girls turned away from Jason and discussed their options. "He looks harmless," whispered Lexi behind her hand. "And having three people travelling together is probably safer than just two, plus, it might be nice to have someone else to talk to." Lexi could only take so much of Hadley's constant chatter, not to mention her singing.

Hadley looked at Lexi and nodded. "Yeah, I think he's alright. It's not long until we reach Jasper's Bay now anyway."

Lexi agreed. They would let Jason join them on their way to find a place to settle.

Lexi turned back to face Jason; the sides of her mouth twitched. "Well, looks like Polo likes you," she said, unfolding her arms and pointing to the dog, who had fallen asleep with his head on Jason's shoe. His tongue was lolling out of the side of his mouth, and drool was dripping on the scuffed black canvas.

Jason laughed as he bent down to rub the dog's head. "I always wanted a dog," he smiled. "My family lived in an apartment, so I was never allowed to have one."

Hadley nodded. "Well, technically he's not ours," she grinned. "We rescued him."

Jason scratched Polo behind the ears. "He's a lucky dog."

Lexi watched Jason with Polo for a moment. She felt good about this boy and decided to tell him of their plans. "So, Jason," said Lexi clearing her throat and smiling at him. "We were thinking. If you want to, you can come with us. We're heading for Jasper's Bay. They've got a solar power plant so we're hoping they still have power."

Jason looked at Lexi, his eyes shining. "Wow, that does sound good. How do you know about…?" he paused forgetting the town's name.

"Jasper's Bay," finished Lexi. It's only a couple more hours drive from here," she said looking back towards the car. "It's a small town, and I only know about it because I had to do a school assignment on renewable energy in Western Australia," she laughed. "I guess some things you learn in school *do* come in handy."

"Not very many," muttered Hadley.

"Yeah, not very many," agreed Lexi poking her sister's arm. "So, do you want to join us? We have room in the car." Lexi peered at Jason; her head cocked to one side.

Jason jumped up and punched his fist in the air, rudely waking Polo, who gave a little yelp. "Woohoo!" he shouted excitedly. "Hell yes."

Lexi and Hadley looked at each other again and laughed. Hadley raised her eyebrows. "Excitable, isn't he?"

Lexi smiled. "I think he's been lonely," she whispered to her sister, who nodded in agreement.

Jason saw the girls laughing. "Sorry," he said grinning. "Was that a bit lame?"

"No," said Lexi still smiling. "Fist pump all you want. Who are we to judge? By the way, I don't suppose you can drive, can you?" she asked hopefully, holding up the car keys. "It would be nice to share the driving with someone."

Jason cracked his knuckles. "Ah, no. Sorry. Haven't learnt yet. I'm a bit nervous in cars," he stated glancing towards the car. A thin sheen of perspiration had formed on his upper lip. "I was in a car accident when I was younger, so I put off learning to drive," he explained. "I was going to start taking lessons in the Christmas holidays, you know, but things didn't quite go to plan, eh?" He shrugged.

"Got that right," said Hadley standing with her hands on her hips. "Things all went pretty crappy really quick." They all nodded in agreement.

"Yeah, sucks," agreed Jason grinning.

"Big time," added Hadley dancing around giggling.

"Well, come on then, you two," said Lexi, who wanted to get driving again before it got too late in the day. "Looks like you'll have to put up with my magnificent driving for a bit longer, Hadley." The girls gathered the leftover food and started to walk back towards the car.

Jason looked a bit startled. He called out to Hadley, "Er, what does she mean? She *can* drive, can't she?"

Hadley glanced back over her shoulder at Jason and grinned mischievously. "Oh, yes, she can drive. She just thinks she's playing Mario Kart. You know, going incredibly fast, dodging imaginary penguins and mushrooms. Swerving all over the road like a drunk person."

Jason stood still and wiped his palms on his jeans nervously. His face had turned white.

Lexi turned and looked at Jason standing motionless, his arms dangling loosely at his sides with an anxious look on his face. "Oh, come on, don't worry. I can hardly get out of second gear! I'm not exactly going to be racing and anyway if I were, I wouldn't be Mario, I'd be Princess Peach!" She threw a piece of bark at him, and it bounced off his nose making her laugh.

"Oww!" Jason grinned good-naturedly rubbing his nose. He bent down to pick up his dusty backpack and hobbled after the girls. "Hang on, I'm coming. Don't leave without me!

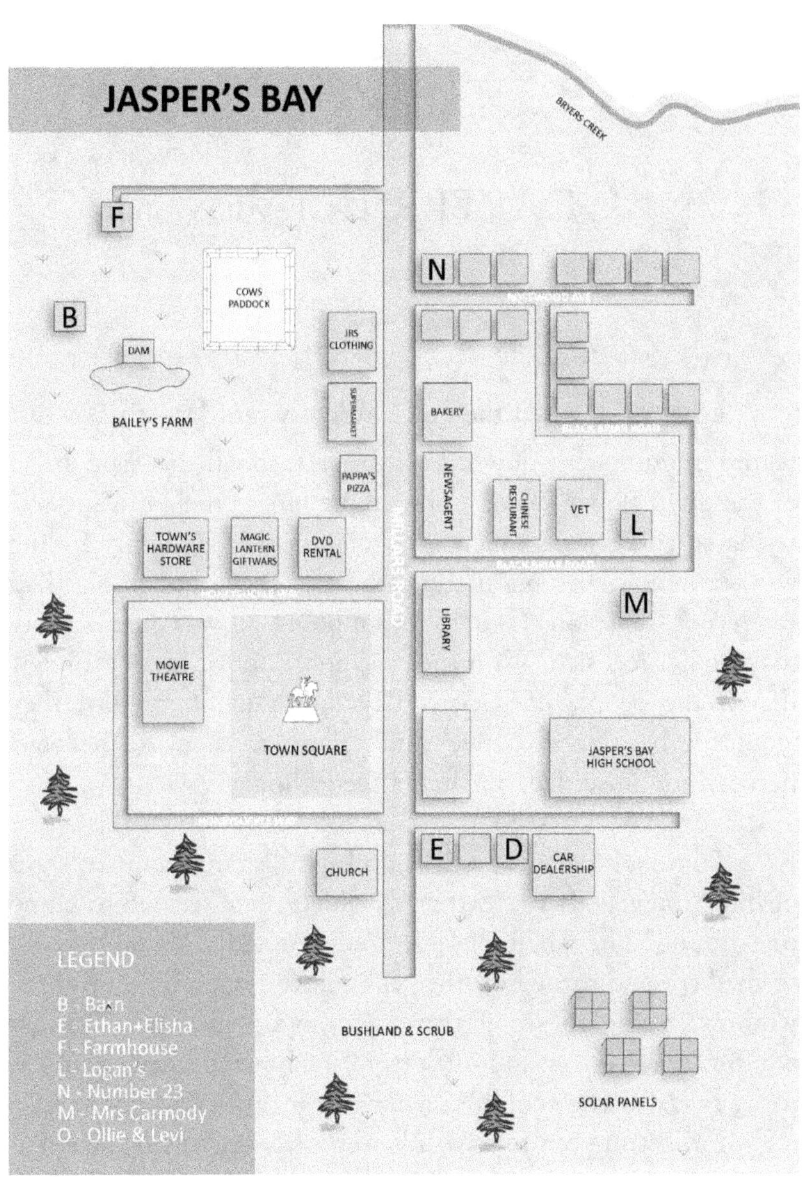

JASPER'S BAY
BRYERS CREEK
F
COWS PADDOCK
B
DAM
BAILEY'S FARM
JRS CLOTHING
SUPERMARKET
PAPPA'S PIZZA
N
BAKERY
NEWSAGENT
CHINESE RESTURANT
VET
L
M
TOWN'S HARDWARE STORE
MAGIC LANTERN GIFTWARS
DVD RENTAL
LIBRARY
MOVIE THEATRE
TOWN SQUARE
JASPER'S BAY HIGH SCHOOL
E
D
CAR DEALERSHIP
CHURCH
BUSHLAND & SCRUB
SOLAR PANELS
LEGEND
B - Barn
E - Ethan+Elisha
F - Farmhouse
L - Logan's
N - Number 23
M - Mrs Carmody
O - Ollie & Levi

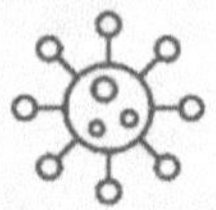

CHAPTER ELEVEN

The trio reached the quiet little town of Jasper's Bay just before the sun went down. Lexi drove through the main street of the town slowly. They were almost out of fuel, and she was trying to conserve as much of it as possible. An empty feeling was settling in the pit of her stomach even though she had eaten not that long ago. She supposed it was just anxiety making her feel sick. With the car almost out of fuel Lexi knew that if the people of Jasper's Bay didn't let them stay, they wouldn't be able to drive much farther. It made her feel nervous and unsettled. She hated the feeling.

Everyone was on high alert as they drove down the street. Even Polo had his ears pricked up high, listening out for signs of life. Strangely, it was extremely quiet; there seemed to be no one around. The whole place looked deserted. Lexi pulled over to the kerb and turned off the car engine. She peered out of the window, trying to see if there was anyone around. The car windows were grimy and dirty from the hours of driving on the dusty roads, so she couldn't see that far into the distance at all.

"I'm getting out to have a better look, my legs are so stiff," said Lexi stepping out onto the side of the road. She looked up and down the street but could not see a single soul. It was as if the whole place had been abandoned. Poking her head back into the car, she looked at the others and shrugged. "Well, I can't see anyone. Maybe we should have a walk around."

The others agreed and slowly untangled their cramped legs and got out of the car, stretching their limbs as they went. The street where they had parked looked like it was the main road in town. There were numerous shops and small businesses on either side of the street. A clothing store called JR's fashion house, a Farmer Jack's supermarket and a Pappas Pizza were among them. Most of the stores looked vacant with their lights off and the doors left swinging wide open.

Lexi noticed that there were a few bikes and scooters scattered in the middle of the street but no people. It felt eerie with no one around, like a ghost town. She was about to wander back to the car when Hadley spied what could be signs of life.

"Hey, guys, look up there!" Hadley was pointing to an old building at the end of the street. It looked like a church. It had big ornately carved wooden doors, which were closed shut and a tall cross on its roof pointing up to the sky. All over the church's front steps were skateboards, bikes and scooters scattered about. There must have been at least twenty of them.

"Good spotting Hadley. *Finally signs of life.* Let's go have a look, shall we?" Lexi suggested smiling at her sister.

"Yeah, come on," agreed Jason. "I'll get my pack. You'd better lock up," he advised, jerking his thumb at the car. "Don't want anyone taking your food and stuff."

"Oh, right. Good idea," agreed Lexi. *She was going to have to learn to be more protective of their food.*

After locking the car, Lexi walked towards the church with a happy bounce in her step. She was feeling confident that whoever was left in this town, would be happy to see them. After all, *Jason* had been pleased to see them.

Jason and Hadley followed behind her, chatting happily as they walked. It felt good to be out of the car and somewhere new. Everyone was in a good mood, even Polo, who trotted closely behind Hadley like her own personal guard dog. He would stop every few seconds to sniff at something on the ground before racing to catch up with the others.

They had just reached the church's steps and were about to walk up when the old building's big double doors opened outwards, and kids of all ages started steaming out laughing and chatting. They looked in good spirits but stopped abruptly as soon as they spotted Lexi and the others. A few of the kids at the back banged into the ones at the front, before stopping as well. They simply stood and stared at the newcomers, their faces frozen in mistrust. Some had their hands planted firmly on their hips, while others had their arms hanging limply by their sides. Hadley, Lexi and Jason all stared back, not sure what to say. Looking over at the motley group, Lexi immediately noticed that every single one of them was a child or teenager. No adults. The virus had obviously hit here too.

Hadley was about to raise her hand to say a friendly hello when two blonde-haired teenagers pushed their way to the front of the crowd to see what the problem was. They looked similar in appearance and might have been twins or at least brother and sister. They didn't look happy.

"Who are you? What do you want?" They asked angrily. Both were frowning, their blue eyes glaring in distrust.

"Jeez, so much for country hospitality," muttered Hadley looking at them crossly. It wasn't the welcome they were hoping for.

"I'll say again. What do you want?" demanded the girl, stepping forward with her hands folded across her chest defensively. She had a fierce look on her face, and her nostrils flared out when she spoke.

The girl looked about the same age as Lexi and seemed to be the more outspoken of the two siblings.

Lexi quickly raised her hand in front of her in a non-threatening gesture. She thought the girl looked like she wanted a fight. "Look, it's okay. We're not trouble. We've just run out of petrol. We've been driving all day and just want somewhere to rest." Lexi pointed back towards their car parked in the street. "That's our car back there."

The girl continued to stare at them. Her eyes were an intense bright blue, the colour of blue jellybeans and her fringe was cut straight across her forehead in a straight blunt line making her face seem harsh. She had an annoyed look on her face, and it was obvious that she didn't want to hear about their troubles.

"We have our own supplies," Lexi added quickly, trying to be friendly. She nervously pushed a stray piece of hair behind her ear and smiled at the girl hoping to break the tension developing between them. She did not want to have to get back in that car and start driving again. Somehow, she had to get these kids to let them stay.

"Yes, we're just tired," whined Hadley, crouching down to pat Polo who was sitting between the two girls wagging his tail happily. "It's been a long drive from the city. We just want to sleep somewhere." She looked up at the gathering of children with the sweetest expression on her face that she could muster. "Please don't make us sleep on the ground again, in the cold with all the bugs." Her bottom lip trembled as if she were going to cry.

Lexi looked down at her and shoved her with her knee. "Stop it," she muttered through clenched teeth.

The brother and sister didn't say anything. They just stood like ridged marble statues, arms folded, faces blank, continuing to stare at the three of them. Lexi cleared her throat uncertainly. *This could get nasty.* She glanced at the other kids standing nearby. They looked to be a mixture of all ages, from a baby in one little girl's arms to others about her own age. They all looked filthy. Their hair was mattered, and their clothes were muddy and torn. She guessed that as there weren't any adults around to tell them what to do, brushing their hair and having showers was low on the children's list of priorities.

The air felt thick with hostility as the motley group continued to stare silently at them. It was kind of freaky, and Lexi wasn't sure what to do next. She bit her bottom lip and glanced at Hadley. *Maybe they shouldn't have left their home after all.*

As it was now late afternoon, Lexi knew they would need to find somewhere to stay for the night. With very little fuel left, they couldn't drive on much further. They were kind of stuck. She rubbed her cheek, wondering what else she could say to these children to let them stay. They weren't exactly giving out the friendly welcoming vibe she was hoping for.

Lexi cleared her throat. She couldn't understand why these kids were so hostile. Sure, they were strangers, but really, a computer geek, two young girls and an annoying dog. How much of a threat did they think they were? Trying to quell the sensation of wanting to yell at them, she took a slow deep breath and looked down at her shoes wondering what approach to take next.

Before she could say another word, Jason, who had been standing in the background, pushed past Lexi and went up to the boy and girl himself. Lexi's eyes narrowed. *What was Jason doing? Didn't he say he wasn't good at talking to people!* She hoped he wasn't going to make things worse. If the three of them, and Polo had to sleep in the car tonight along with all their gear, it was going to be very crowded and uncomfortable. Besides, she wasn't sure that she wanted Jason sleeping in the car with them in such close proximity. He seemed nice enough, but she didn't fully trust him yet. After all, they'd only known him for half a day. How much did you really know about someone after talking to them for only a few hours?

As Lexi watched Jason standing before the siblings, her heart started racing, and her palms became sweaty. She wasn't usually a particularly anxious person; however, the events of the past few days had left her constantly feeling on edge and completely out of her comfort zone. Her eyes bored into Jason's back. *Just chill,* she told herself as she conscientiously unclenched her fists and tried to relax. Maybe Jason would do a better job of talking to them.

"Hi," said Jason, holding out his hand; it was shaking slightly. "I'm Jason, and that's Lexi and Hadley," he said in a friendly tone, his voice rising. "They're sisters," he added smiling. "We've lost our parents and relatives just like you guys." He spread his arms out wide as he talked to the group of kids standing in front of him. "And that's Polo." He pointed at the little dog who was sitting quietly by Hadley's feet. "He was on his own until the girls did what was right and helped him," he said meaningfully. "That's the right thing to do, isn't it? Help people when they need it?"

The brother and sister looked at each other and then back at Jason. No one said a word. It was as silent as a deserted schoolyard after the bell has rung.

"We've just driven all the way from the city," continued Jason, his hands still outstretched. "We heard that the countryside was really friendly and wanted to see what it was like." He smiled again. You could practically see the friendliness radiating off him.

The brother glanced nervously at his sister, then seemed to make a snap decision and quickly took Jason's hand, shaking it warmly. As he smiled, his eyes lit up. The sister, however, frowned deeply, and immediately tried to grab her brother's hand away. He pulled back from her. "Oh, stop it, Elisha. They look all right, don't be so grumpy. We don't have to be unfriendly."

Jason eyed her warily. She looked extremely pissed off.

Finally, the girl looked at her brother and sighed. "Oh, alright," she said in a reluctant tone. "Sorry, didn't mean to be rude," she said turning to Jason. She gave him a small, tense smile. "We've just had some trouble lately with a gang of kids from out of town. We have to be careful."

Jason half-smiled back at her and scratched his nose. "Oh, that's alright. No problem. I hope everything's okay?" The girl didn't answer but instead pushed past him as she strode over to meet Lexi and Hadley. Jason frowned and stared at her back.

"Don't worry about her," the brother said to Jason seeing his annoyance. "We had some problems with kid's pets being stolen last night. She's still furious. I'm Ethan by the way, and my sister's name is Elisha," he said, pointing at the girl. Elisha was in deep conversation with Lexi and Hadley and was starting to look much more relaxed.

Jason relaxed too. He breathed out in a sigh of relief. "Cripes, it is so much easier talking to people by text," he murmured shaking his head.

A few of the other kids had come up behind Ethan to see what was going on. "I'm Logan," said one boy. He was tall with curly black hair and wore a green Minecraft T-shirt with a creeper on it. He looked about fifteen years old. Everyone was a lot friendlier now that Elisha had backed down and the tension had been broken.

"Hey, great game," said Jason pointing at Logan's shirt and smiling happily. He loved talking about computer games. He would have to seek this kid out later and see what other games he was into.

Logan grinned back nodding his head in agreement. "One of my favourites."

"That's Levi and Ollie," said Logan, pointing to two young Aboriginal boys standing over to the side. Jason waved at them, and they waved back.

"And that's Zac. He lives on his family's farm just out of town." Zac was a tall boy with short blonde hair and a friendly-looking face. A smattering of freckles covered his nose from frequently being exposed to the sun, and his arms and legs were quite tanned. The boy was talking to a younger girl who also had blonde hair, probably his sister. She was carrying a baby who looked like a younger version of herself. They were laughing and joking around and didn't seem to be the least bit concerned by the newcomers.

Jason nodded to Ethan. "I think we saw some paddocks on our way into town. That must have been their farm." He shook his head and raised his eyebrows. "All those animals and open spaces must take a lot of looking after." He shivered.

Soon after, Lexi and Hadley came up behind Jason. Lexi put her hand on his shoulder to get his attention, and he flinched in surprise obviously still unnerved by the group's initial reaction to them.

"Hey Jason, Elisha is going to show us a place we can stay for the night. It's an empty house that no one is using." Her voice had a happy note to it, and she looked relieved that they were being allowed to stay.

"Wow, that's great," he said smiling. "Beats sleeping on the ground." He patted his sleeping bag which was still on his back.

"Damn straight," she laughed, nodding her head.

Elisha stepped forward to address the three city kids. "Would you like to pray first before I show you where the house is?" She asked expectantly, her voice serious as she gestured towards the church. Hadley looked at Jason and raised her eyebrows questioningly.

"Um, sure. Lead the way," Lexi said smiling indulgently at Elisha. Then under her breath, she muttered to Hadley, who was staring at her open-mouthed. "We don't want to offend them, Hadley. They just offered us a place to sleep, remember. Unless you'd like to sleep on the ground, in the dark with the bugs?"

Hadley took the hint. "Praise the Lord," she sang, marching straight into the church. Lexi and Jason followed her. Polo had to stay outside. No dogs allowed.

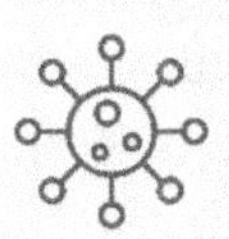

CHAPTER TWELVE

After they left the church and went back to their car, Elisha had shown them to an empty house on a street that looked deserted. Lexi looked at the little cream brick house with interest. The gardens were dying and overgrown with weeds; however, it had a cute little porch out the front, and a pathway made of flat rocks leading to the front gate. The roof was made of tin, and grape vines were growing along a trellis on the side of the house. Lexi noticed some of them were old and rotten, but quite a few looked plump and edible.

"Right, well, welcome to number twenty-three Rosewood Avenue," said Elisha opening the unlocked front door. "No one lives here anymore, so you can stay here for the night."

"I'll be back in the morning," she reminded them. Her face was stern and unrelenting, and her arms were folded tightly across her chest.

"Right," said Lexi, too tired to argue further. *At least they had a roof over their heads for the night.*

"Wow, she was salty," remarked Hadley after Elisha had left them to unpack some of their stuff. She dropped her bag on the floor with a heavy thump.

"Hmm. I don't think she likes us much," agreed Lexi carrying a box of food inside. She stretched her arms above her head trying to work the stiffness out of her shoulders and back. "She's probably just tired. I think Elisha and her brother are basically keeping this town together."

Lexi pulled a can of soup from the box and placed it on the counter. "Plus, I couldn't see any adults here, and most of the kids all look young," Lexi said raising her eyebrows. "It can't be easy. Can you imagine trying to control a bunch of ten-year-old kids? Or even worse twelve-year old's?"

Hadley poked her tongue out at her. "Oh, ha-ha. I'm nearly thirteen by the way."

Lexi smiled and nodded, happy to give her sister a bit of cheek for once. Usually, it was the other way around.

Jason dropped his dusty backpack by the front door and flopped down onto one of the brown fabric sofas in the lounge room. He glanced wistfully at the television. "Yes, plus, I think they've been having some trouble with a gang of kids from out of town," added Jason, stretching his long legs out on the sofa and yawning. "I was talking to the brother Ethan about it. Sounds like the gang is a bunch of real dicks. They've been breaking into houses, stealing kid's stuff, even their pets! What a bunch of losers." He shook his head in irritation.

Lexi nodded her head at him in agreement. Some people could be real idiots, and she hoped that they wouldn't run into this "gang" anytime soon.

"Ethan seems nice," Jason continued talking. "He's a bit stressed out you know, but really chatty. He likes playing COD so he must be alright." Jason started chuckling to himself.

Lexi yawned. "Uh huh, well," she said tiredly. "Don't know about you two, but I'm getting something to eat and finding somewhere to sleep. I'm exhausted. It's been a long day. All that driving has tired me out." The other two nodded their heads in agreement. Food and sleep sounded like a good idea.

"Come on, Jason," said Hadley pulling Jason up from his comfortable spot on the chair and leading him into the kitchen. "You can share some of our food. You did help convince Elisha and Ethan to let us stay here, after all. What do you like to eat? We've got a whole stack of two-minute noodles!"

"Sounds great!" Jason laughed, stumbling into the kitchen after Hadley. "They're one of my favourites!"

Jason looked thoughtfully at the two girls. "Do you think we can convince Elisha to let us stay a bit longer," he asked stroking his fingers across his chin. "We could all build some sort of life here. Obviously, not the same as we had in the city with our parents, but a future."

"I hope so," agreed Lexi crossing her arms. "We're stuffed otherwise. I don't know exactly how far Albany is from here and we've got very little fuel left." She raised her eyebrows at Jason. "We might just have to join you walking!"

"Err, no thanks," said Jason his eyes widening in mock horror. "I'm never walking again," he grinned. "Let's just make sure we convince them," he said, his face turning serious again.

Lexi and Hadley nodded. They would do whatever it took to stay.

The three travelling companions sat down to a quick dinner of noodles, before all three of them crashed out in the lounge room, too tired to be bothered getting up and finding a bed for the night. The lounge chairs were comfortable enough, and even Polo found a rug to sleep on by the front door.

*

* *

The next morning, the trio were sitting in the kitchen when a sharp knocking at the front door interrupted their breakfast of Milo, Cornflakes and long-life milk.

"Jeez, they're here early! Couldn't even give us time to have breakfast," complained Hadley, banging her spoon down on the table and frowning.

"Well, I guess it's true what they say about people getting up early in the country," grinned Jason as he shoved more food into his mouth. Milk dripped out of the corner of his mouth as he laughed.

Lexi looked at them. "I'll get it, shall I?" She asked sarcastically when the other two just sat in their chairs and continued to eat. They grinned, nodding enthusiastically.

Opening the front door, Lexi saw Elisha standing with her hands on her hips, looking irritated. Lexi noticed that her lips were pursed firmly together, and deep frown lines had formed between her eyebrows. She did not look happy. Ethan was the exact opposite of her, his arms hanging loosely by his sides. His face was relaxed with his mouth turned up slightly at the edges in a small smile. He made Lexi feel calm. Elisha did not. Lexi opened the door farther.

Elisha peered past Lexi and saw the others sitting in the kitchen eating.

"Oh. We didn't realise you'd *still* be having breakfast," she said sarcastically. Elisha glanced at her watch, the frown on her face deepening.

"Ah, yes. Well, I guess we slept in," Lexi shrugged. "With all the driving we had to do yesterday, we're all exhausted," she said, starting to feel defensive. Lexi turned slightly so that her back was to Elisha and looked at Hadley and Jason, raising her eyebrows. Elisha made her feel like she was talking to the school principal.

Hadley giggled, then tried to hide it by coughing.

"Well, it doesn't matter," said Ethan good-naturedly as he stepped into the room. "There's no rush. We've come to see if you need any help?"

"Help?" Jason queried looking up from his second bowl of cereal.

"Yes, with packing up your stuff so you can keep going on your travels."

Jason, Lexi and Hadley looked at each other. Now was their chance to convince Ethan and Elisha to let them stay.

Hurriedly rising from his seat, Jason went to join Lexi at the front door. He cleared his throat. "Listen, guys, we know you said yesterday that you want us to leave," he said, his face serious. "But we have a proposition for you."

Elisha stepped forward too and started to reply negatively when her brother held her back. "Wait a minute Elisha. Let's hear what they have to say first. That's only fair." He looked at his sister and smiled encouragingly.

"Yes, alright then," Elisha reluctantly agreed. She stepped back with her arms folded defensively across her chest. She didn't look keen to hear what they had to say.

"Well, like I said. We have a proposition for you," continued Jason, pushing his chest out and standing tall. "We noticed that you don't have too many older kids here. And we know that you've been having trouble with some other kids from out of town."

Jason paused and looked directly at Elisha. She stared back at him, her blue eyes piercing and untrusting.

"Yes," she eventually agreed, her voice sharp. Both of her arms remained folded defensively across her chest like a barrier, and it was apparent that she didn't like talking about the town's problems.

"Right," said Jason, refusing to give up. "Well, Lexi and I are both sixteen and Hadley's twelve. We could help you to protect your town."

"How?"

"What?"

"How? How can you help protect the town?" Demanded Elisha, still being defensive.

Lexi looked at Elisha standing rigid with her mouth stretching into a thin straight line. Her eyes were boring into Jason like a laser and Lexi could tell that she wasn't interested in anything he had to say.

Feeling frustrated at Elisha's negativity towards them, Lexi turned to face Ethan and smiled. "Look," she said, trying to keep her voice calm. "The point is, we've almost run out of fuel which means we can't drive much farther. We've been looking for a little town to move to away from the city, where things are quieter. Like your town." She gestured to the house they stood in. "We can help you protect *your* town in whatever way you've been protecting it so far. We could be of benefit to each other. We need somewhere to stay, and surely you could use some extra help?"

Jason nodded enthusiastically. "Yes. Plus, we might come up with some good ideas that you haven't thought of yet," he suggested, winking. "They do say there's safety in numbers. The greater number of older kids you have here to help the better, right? Besides, the best way to combat bullies is to have friends around you, isn't it?"

Hadley, who had been hovering in the kitchen came up to join the group. "And anyway, isn't it nice to make some new friends?" She smiled as sweetly as she could at Ethan. Her light brown eyes were gazing up at him as she fluttered her eyelashes dramatically. He laughed winking at her and smiling back.

Elisha rolled her eyes and gave in. "Oh, all right. You can stay. I can't be bothered arguing." Elisha gave a half-hearted smile and held out her hand. "Welcome to the town, I guess."

They all shook hands one by one.

"You might as well stay in this house," said Elisha tapping on the front door with her finger. "Obviously, the owners don't live here anymore."

"Great! Thanks so much. You won't regret it," smiled Jason warmly.

Lexi nodded in agreement. "Yes, thanks. We'll start unpacking right away."

"Do you need any help?" Asked Ethan as he looked around the lounge room. His voice was friendly and welcoming.

"Nope we should be good," said Lexi smiling at him. "We haven't got that much stuff, and besides we have this big strong guy here to help us." She grinned at Jason as she punched him lightly on his skinny arm.

Jason flexed his arms in a bodybuilder pose. "Yeah, I'm a real athlete," he grinned. Everyone laughed happily except Elisha. She just stared at them all for a moment before backing out the door.

"Yes, well, I'll probably see you a bit later," she said as she started walking off down the path back to her own house. "Happy unpacking."

Ethan watched his sister stalk off without him. She stamped her feet on the ground as she walked. "I think she's pissed off with me," Ethan sighed. "She likes getting her own way." He shrugged and gave Lexi a sad smile. "You were right though. We need help, and there is safety in numbers."

Ethan turned around to follow his sister. "I'd better catch up with her," he said, running off. "Don't forget if you need anything just come find us. Our house is near the church where you met us yesterday," he called over his shoulder, waving goodbye as he went.

Lexi closed the front door and leant against it in relief. She looked at Hadley, her eyes bright with happiness. "Thank God!" she exclaimed in relief. "No more driving."

"Amen to that!" exclaimed Hadley laughing in glee. "I thought Elisha was never going to let us stay. She is such a grump."

"Hmmm, I don't think we're her favourite people in the world right now. Except maybe for Ethan!" Lexi joked. "Poor kid. Anyway, who cares what she thinks. We're here to stay," Lexi said determinedly. *She was sure Elisha would change her mind about them once she got to know them.*

"Come on you two. Let's get the rest of our stuff from the car. This place won't feel like it's ours until some of our own gear is in here."

Lexi opened the front door, and the three of them trundled out to the little blue car parked in the driveway. "We haven't got much stuff, so it won't take us too long to unpack. Then we can start exploring the town and our new home!" she said, her eyes lighting up with excitement.

Jaspers Bay had just grown by three.

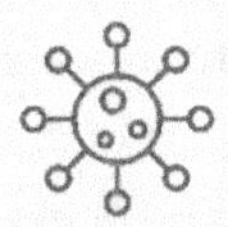

CHAPTER THIRTEEN

Elisha

Elisha Mathews had just turned seventeen. She was quite tall, had ash blonde hair, and pale skin, rather like an albino. Her brother, Ethan, was a couple of years younger. He was fourteen, and, like his sister, was also tall and fair. His hair, though, was a darker blonde, more like the colour of wheat or honey. Apart from their differing hair colour, they looked remarkably similar in appearance and although different in age they were often asked if they were twins. This infuriated Elisha, and she'd recently taken to wearing a lot of make-up to try to make herself look older and not so like her brother.

If you asked anyone about the two siblings, they'd say that they were usually both caring and friendly in nature. Although, over the last few days Elisha had become quite hostile and agitated by those around her.

Elisha sat on her bed staring out of her window. "Why does everyone in this town feel the need to come and discuss their problems with me?" she muttered to herself. "Can't they see I just wanted to be left alone for a little while!" She scratched at her arm making it pink.

As Elisha stared out into the street, she could see several young children playing. The children didn't have to worry about cars or any vehicles anymore and so the road had become a race track for their bicycles and skateboards.

The kids were making an incessant amount of noise as they played and their squealing and laughing was irritating Elisha. She huffed in annoyance. Every little thing seemed to annoy her, as though her skin were raw, and there were a hundred tiny beetles were scurrying about in her flesh. To make things even more uncomfortable, there was a constant throbbing and pounding in her head making conversations absolute torture. Every word spoken hammered into her brain like a red-hot poker jabbing her with pain.

Elisha ran her fingers through her hair. "I can't let Ethan know about these feelings," she murmured not wanting to worry him. Elisha had promised her father that she would look after Ethan, and that was what she was going to do.

Elisha rubbed her eyes. She had managed to keep her troubles to herself so far, and everything had been going along alright. Until last night. Until the newcomers had arrived. Since then, she had noticed Ethan looking at her strangely a couple of times as if he knew something was wrong. *Maybe she had spoken too abruptly, too rudely?* "I couldn't help it," she sighed. "Everything upsets me!" Elisha started to cry. Even the simple task of reading to the younger kids in the church on Sundays, which she used to really enjoy, now irritated her. If they even dared to ask her a question about the story she was reading, she would yell and scream at them.

It couldn't go on this way. Elisha knew that the pressure of running the town was getting to her, but she didn't know how to alleviate it. And so, her grumpiness continued. "I wonder what Dad would think," she murmured bleakly as she lay back on her bed. Elisha put her hands over her eyes and thought about her father.

The Mathews children had grown up in a very religious family. Their father, Michael Mathews, had been the town's Anglican priest and he had liked to give fervent sermons that were cheerful, spiritual and delivered a real message. He often spent many happy hours preparing them, ready to deliver to his congregation on Sundays. Father Mathews took great pride in his church and Elisha was sure he would have been proud to see his two children doing all they could to keep that tradition of a Sunday service alive.

Elisha turned onto her side and traced her finger along a crack in the wall. She thought about how things had been in Jasper's Bay since the last adult, Mrs Pemberton, had died. "I think we've been doing alright since then," she sniffed, staring at the wall, remembering how awful things had been in the beginning.

Without any adults around, kids had run riot. Some of the children began spraying graffiti on any blank wall they could find. Others took to trashing homes and shops, and quite a few started looting. The younger kids who were left on their own were starving with no one to cook for them, and many became sick from food poisoning after eating rotten food.

After a couple of weeks of this mayhem, some of the older kids like Elisha had stepped up and taken control. Trying to instil some sort of order back into the town. No one had particularly wanted *the job*, but after one or two incidents involving knives, and a boy dying after falling from the roof of his house while trying to plank on the balcony, Elisha decided to take charge. She soon put an end to all the reckless and destructive behaviour and managed to get everyone back to some routine. Most of the children had been taking good care of themselves since then and looking out for those who were on their own. She felt proud of the way they had all banded together.

Apart from the boy who had fallen from his house roof, no one else had been seriously hurt or killed, and for the moment everyone had food and water.

Elisha turned onto her back and looked at the ceiling. Although she had been reluctant to the newcomers at first, she was actually hoping they might have an idea or two to contribute to running the town. Elisha hated to admit it but having a few other older kids around was probably going to work out well. She could do with a bit of help. *Maybe I can take a break for a while.* Sighing, Elisha finally closed her eyes and tried to sleep.

CHAPTER FOURTEEN

Ethan Mathews was also hoping the new kids were going to be useful. When he first spotted them standing on the church steps, his initial instinct had been one of alarm and defence. Once the new kids had started talking though, he could see they were just ordinary kids like him. Kids who were trying to adapt to a world that was now vastly different from the one they had all been born into. He knew that Elisha wasn't exactly happy about them staying in Jasper's Bay and that he had practically had to force her into accepting them, but he felt it had been the right thing to do. Ethan knew she would get over it. Hopefully, sooner rather than later.

Over the past few weeks, Ethan could see that his sister was feeling the strain of being the town's unappointed leader. All the other kids in town automatically went to her whenever they had a problem. Even the other older kids. When such and such was fighting with so and so. Or when they started running out of vegemite and peanut butter in their house. Mundane things they should have been sorting out for themselves. He knew Elisha felt it was her duty to take care of them all; however, one person couldn't be expected to shoulder everyone else's problems without a few cracks starting to appear.

Ethan had begun to notice little furrowed lines of stress and worry between Elisha's eyebrows. His once calm sister had started to snap at people at the slightest provocation. Like these new kids. She would never have even considered turning them away in the past.

Ethan stared at his dirty fingernails for a moment, flicking the dirt out underneath the nails with his thumb. He could hear Elisha snoring in her bedroom, so he decided to go and visit the new kids.

Walking determinedly into the kitchen, Ethan began looking around. *Maybe I can take over a small gift to welcome them to the town.* He opened one of the cupboard doors and peered inside. There were a few tins of fruit and some tinned vegetables in the cupboard. "That's pretty boring for a gift," he mumbled, reaching further into the cupboard. His hand grasped a bag of rice and a half packet of dried beans. Ethan looked at the bags unenthusiastically.

"I can't give them this." He shoved the packets back where he found them. Then towards the back of the cupboard sitting under a couple of tins of pea and ham soup, he spotted four plastic tubs of chocolate pudding. "Jackpot!" he laughed. "And there's even one left for me," he grinned.

Ethan grabbed the rich chocolatey desserts and put them in a grey plastic shopping bag. He pulled his shoulders back and stood up a bit straighter. "No need to wake Elisha," he muttered peering in the direction of Elisha's closed bedroom door. He preferred to go alone. He quietly shut the front door and started humming to himself as he walked out of the house.

It was a blisteringly hot day, and the heat hit him as soon as Ethan stepped outside. Apart from a couple of kids playing, no one was around. A few crisp brown dead leaves blew along the pathway outside his house, but nothing else moved. Ethan pulled his shirt away from his hot body, gripping the fabric between his finger and thumb, flapping the sweaty material.

It didn't take him long to reach Rosewood Avenue, and he was soon sitting in the loungeroom with the three newcomers. They were digging into the chocolate dessert Ethan had brought with him.

"Elisha and I run a brief church service in town every Sunday morning," explained Ethan leaning forward in his chair. "One of the other older children, stand at the church podium and read a passage from my father's Bible. Then, we discuss what we think the passage means. Not everyone is religious, but I think everyone likes to join us anyway." Ethan looked up at the three children before him. They were listening to him attentively. "It's a social gathering I suppose," smiled Ethan. "It gives everyone a reason to come together each week, and for the kids still living on their own, that's important. No one wants to feel isolated or left out of the loop."

Lexi smiled back at Ethan. His voice was calm and flowing, and she could see why the other children liked to listen to him.

"We also hold our town meetings in the church. That's what we were doing yesterday when you arrived."

"Do you do that often?" asked Jason.

"Not really," replied Ethan licking his spoon. "It's usually just when something is affecting the whole town, or a major problem needs to be sorted." Ethan sighed. "Our main problem right now isn't the kids who live here. It's a gang of teenagers from out of town. That's why Elisha was so suspicious of you. She thought you might be with them."

"Fair enough," said Lexi adjusting her position in her chair. "Do you know much about the gang? Where are they from?"

Ethan stretched his legs out in front of him. "Well, there's five of them, and they look about my age, fourteen. I'm not sure where they come from, probably Perth," he shrugged.

Ethan went on to tell the group of the gang's escapades in Jasper's Bay. It had started with small things. Like writing graffiti on walls and setting rubbish bins on fire. Destructive and annoying, but nobody had been hurt. This had soon escalated, however, into throwing bricks through kids' windows. Which, with no adults around to fix them was going to make things very wet and cold in the winter.

Ethan explained how in the past few days, things had started to get out of control with the gang stealing other kid's pets. Birds, guinea pigs, even cats and dogs had gone missing. "It's been really stressful, and a lot of kids are devastated. Especially the kids who live on their own with only their pet for company," said Ethan his bottom lip quivering. "Trying to calm a little kid who has just had their pet stolen has been heartbreaking." He shook his head and looked at the floor.

Lexi's mouth dropped open. *Who would want to steal someone else's pet?*

"A lot of the younger children have now decided to move in with some of the older kids. Even though it's meant they've had to leave their family home," added Ethan, his shoulders drooping. "I think the thought of people breaking into your home when you're there by yourself would be terrifying for a young kid. Heck, *I* don't even like the thought of it." Ethan picked at his fingernail and his mouth turned downwards. "We don't know what to do. We've tried talking to them, but they just won't listen."

Jason, Lexi and Hadley all looked at each other.

"It sounds like you've been having a rough time," said Jason, his brow furrowed.

Ethan nodded, his face glum.

"We want to help you," said Lexi moving closer to him. "After all, we are part of your town now. I'm sure we can come up with something. Maybe you should hold another town meeting?" She patted Ethan on the arm.

Ethan looked up and saw the others watching him. Their eyes were bright and their faces eager. *Maybe they would be able to come up with a few new ideas.* "Okay," he said a little more hopefully. "I'll do that. I'll call another town meeting."

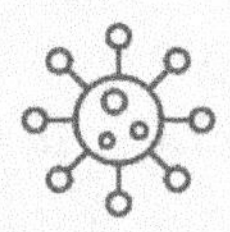

CHAPTER FIFTEEN

Number twenty-three Rosewood Avenue. That was the address of their new home. It was a little way out of the main part of town, but that suited the three newcomers just fine. It felt strange and awkward moving into a new town and into someone else's home. A bit like an intruder in a *Big Brother house* and they didn't want the other kids in town to feel as if they were encroaching on their space.

After Ethan left to go back to his house, Lexi went to stand outside on the back porch. From the back of the little white house, she could see farmland off to one side and down to a small creek on the other. The little creek had a small amount of water in it. Just enough to get your feet and calves wet, and Lexi wondered if it flooded during the winter. Having lived in the city for all their lives, the trio was finding the country environment peaceful and quiet.

Polo especially loved the big garden to run around in, and he didn't seem to have had any problem with the move at all. Lexi supposed that dogs were adaptable, though she did wonder if he missed his owners. She watched him playing for a few moments before wandering back inside. "I'm calling dibs on this first bedroom," shouted Lexi, dumping the box she was carrying onto the bed. "You two can fight over the other two rooms."

Hadley and Jason, who were sorting through boxes in the kitchen, looked at each other for a second before quickly dropping what they were doing and racing down the passageway towards the other two bedrooms. Jason pushed Hadley into the wall as he ran. She laughed and tried to trip him up. They giggled and jostled each other all the way down the passageway, trying to get in front of each other, both determined to get the best bedroom for themselves.

Lexi looked around the bedroom she had chosen. There was a lovely view through the window of the back garden, and she could hear the little blue chested finches chirping as they flew from branch to branch in the bush outside.

It was a cheerful, happy kind of noise, yet, it made her feel a little sad. It seemed odd to be staying in someone else's house and sleeping in someone else's bedroom. She wished she could have brought more things from her own home to place around the room. It would have made the bedroom more comforting and familiar.

Sitting on the bed with its bright red and black geometrical cover jarring her senses, she thought about her bedroom back home. Her own bed cover had been white with embroidered light green leaves and pink cherry blossoms in silk. She had chosen it when her parents had let her upgrade her bed from a single to a double. Smiling she remembered when they had moved the new bed into her room, and she had joyfully flung herself down on it. Stretching out like a starfish her arms and legs flung wide. This bed was a tiny single. *Oh, well, she reminded herself, at least you have a bed; it could have easily been the car.*

Lexi looked at the bare, sanitised white walls of this unfamiliar bedroom and her thoughts drifted again to her old room and the way it had been full of books she had read. There was a whole bookcase full of them. Mainly novels but a few books on other things as well. Like books on the Titanic, how to keep guinea pigs, though she'd never owned any herself, and books on the best horror movies and thrillers of the twentieth century. She'd always been an avid reader and was happy to read anything. Romance, sci-fi, fantasy. Even a few war novels she had been given to read for school assignments. She could devour a book in a day like a hungry lion if she were given a chance. Unfortunately, there had always been someone interrupting her. It was usually Hadley wanting to talk or her mother with some tedious chore that had to be done *right that minute*. It drove Lexi crazy, and she used to wish for one moment of peace, just to be left alone. Now, she realised she could be alone as much as she wanted for as long as she wanted. Only *now*, she didn't really want to be alone anymore. *Now*, she wished her mother and father were there asking her to unload the dishwasher or bring in the laundry. Her face suddenly crumpled, and her eyes filled with tears as she thought about never seeing her parents again. Her chest felt heavy, and it was difficult to breathe.

Wiping her nose on a handkerchief, Lexi walked over to one of the bedroom walls. She ran her hand over the smooth white wall as tears streamed down her face. It wasn't that she was ungrateful for having a place to live. It was just that it had been an emotional few months. Looking at the stark blank walls reminded her that her old life was over. Her old room had been covered with posters of movies and television shows, and Lexi wondered if any of the stars in those Hollywood movies had survived this epidemic. She supposed not. *Even money couldn't buy you protection from something like this.*

After a while, Lexi walked back to the boxes to continue unpacking. Reaching in, she pulled out a *Mr Potato Head* toy. Lexi fondly straightened its pink ears and red nose before quickly putting it away in a chest of drawers by the window.

She knew it was a childish thing to bring with her, however; it reminded her of her childhood, and she just loved its little googly changeable eyes. Lexi left it tucked away in the drawer, though. It wasn't exactly something a sixteen-year-old wanted on display in her room. She giggled to herself feeling a little better. *It was good to have a few secrets.*

Down the hallway, Hadley and Jason had sorted out who was having which bed-room and were now happily unpacking their various belongings. Jason didn't really have many trinkets or possessions with him. Travelling by bike and then by foot, he'd had to pack light. Mostly clothes and toiletries, that sort of thing. He had included a small lightweight laptop computer, and his most prized possession—a limited-edition Assassins Creed figure.

Jason held the figure carefully in his hand. Before he had left home, he had wrapped it securely in bubble wrap to keep it safe in his backpack as he travelled. Unwrapping the figure now, he remembered back to the day he had bought it. There had only been fifty released worldwide, and he and his next-door neighbour, Michael, who was a couple of years older, had decided to try and buy one. They had caught a bus from their neighbourhood into the city centre and camped out overnight. They wanted to be the first in line the next morning when the game shop opened its doors. There had only been two figures released in Perth, and he and Michael had been lucky enough to score both. He smiled happily at the memory. It had been a great day. One he would never forget. He put the figure carefully on the table next to the bed and started to unpack his clothes, humming cheerfully as he worked.

In the next room, Hadley had chosen the bedroom with a big pink fluffy rug and bright purple curtains. Looking around, she wondered what had happened to its previous occupant. Maybe they had moved away when the virus had first hit the town. The room suited her perfectly because Hadley loved everything pink. Pink shoes, pink clothes, pink nail polish, pink mobile phones, so she had been drawn to the bedroom straight away.

She slipped off her shoes and danced around happily on the rug, feeling its soft tufts between her toes. Being a very tactile person, she enjoyed the feel of things. The rough sandpaper in her father's garage, running smooth pebbles between her fingers, water slipping over her body as she lay floating in the local pool.

Like the room Lexi had chosen, Hadley's room was also at the back of the house and had a view of the garden. Gazing wistfully out of her bedroom window, she watched Polo in the yard below leaping around yelping with joy as he tried to catch the butterflies as they flew past him. She sighed happily. Maybe things would be alright here. "This isn't home, but I'm sure we can make it nice," she murmured, opening the window to let some fresh air into the musty room. "And at least I'm with Lexi." She sat on the little wooden chair by the window and listened to Polo playing. The air from outside smelt clean and fresh. Humming a little tune as she smiled, Hadley decided unpacking could wait a while. She threw the jacket she had been holding onto the floor and raced outside to join Polo in the bright sunshine.

CHAPTER SIXTEEN

Elisha

Later that afternoon on the other side of town, Elisha had started to feel dreadful. She was nauseous, and her face felt clammy.

When she woke up that morning, Elisha had felt a little sick and irritated as usual; however, now she felt consumed. It was as though she could actually feel sickness thriving inside of her and if terrified her. The inside of her head felt like it was being ripped apart by two giant hands on either side of her skull, resulting in a massive headache that would not go away. Elisha had tried everything she could think of, from medication, a cold cloth on the back of her neck, to chamomile tea. Nothing alleviated her pain. In fact, it was becoming more intense as the hours wore on. The throbbing was worse when she moved around, so she tried to stay as still as possible.

Peering out of her bedroom window through half-shut eyes, she noticed that the sky was an intense blue colour with not a single cloud to break up the hue. On any other day, she would have thought it looked lovely. Today, it only hurt her eyes, so she quickly reached over and pulled her sheer curtains across the window, trying to block out some of the light. Elisha staggered over to her bed and sat on the edge, resting her aching head in her hands. She felt terrible. Her throat was beginning to burn with hotness as though she had swallowed embers from a fire, and it was becoming increasingly difficult to swallow. *I must have caught some flu*, she thought to herself glumly. *Fantastic.* She couldn't afford to be in bed sick right now; there was still so much to do around town, and the younger kids all needed her.

"Oh, stuff the younger kids," she whimpered. "They can all bloody well starve for all I care." Swallowing hard she rubbed her hand across her bloodshot eyes. A sudden intense wave of anger and aggression washed over Elisha as though she were about to burst open and spew out profanities. It wasn't very Christian and certainly not like her usual self.

Elisha lay back on her white fluffy pillows, her pulse throbbing in her temples, pounding like a hammer. Resting her hands over her eyes, she took a deep breath, trying to calm the turmoil inside her. *Maybe she just needed to sleep?* Her sleep had been troubled lately with weird, violent dreams upsetting her usual peaceful slumber.

"I'll feel a lot better after a little nap," she said in a hoarse whisper.

Slowly removing her hands from her face, Elisha looked up at the ceiling, watching her wind chime of little yellow and black birds swirling around in the breeze that drifted in from the slightly open window. They looked so peaceful, and she felt herself slowly beginning to relax and uncoil. The tension from her jaw started to dissipate and slacken like a pressure cooker releasing its steam. She hadn't realised she'd been clenching her teeth so firmly until her jaw muscles had finally started to relax. Across the room, the sheer curtains fluttered, the soft breeze pleasant on her hot skin. After a while, her eyelids began to feel heavy and eventually she drifted into a restless troubled sleep. Images of blistering fire and burning buildings permeating throughout her dreams.

Ethan

While Elisha was struggling to get some rest. Ethan was outside tending to their small vegetable garden. His mother had planted the garden a few years before, and Ethan had been doing his best to keep it alive. There were tomatoes, carrots, beans, potatoes and a few herbs growing. It sat in the corner of their yard in the sunshine and was easy to look after as long as they remembered to water it every few days and keep the weeds out. It wasn't much, but at least it gave them a few fresh vegetables.

Ethan wiped the sweat from his brow and dug his fingers into the dirt. He hummed to himself as he worked. "Aren't you a beauty!" he exclaimed plucking a ripe red tomato from a bush. "Wish I could use you in a ham and tomato sandwich." Ethan sat back on his heels and thought about all the foods he missed, sandwiches being one of them.

"Maybe I should learn to make bread," he muttered to himself. "It can't be that hard? Wish I could just Google it." He really missed the internet. Maybe the town library had some cookbooks?

Gathering his haul of two tomatoes and three carrots, Ethan wandered inside to store them in the refrigerator. "Thank God the electricity is still working," he said peering into the fridge. It was basically empty, but at least they could keep what little food they had fresh. Luckily for the children of Jasper's Bay, the town's solar panels were still operating at full capacity. Ethan wasn't sure what they would do if they broke down, though. He knew that several of the kids' parents had worked at the solar power station just out of town, but he very much doubted whether the kids would know how to fix the panels if they malfunctioned.

After clearing away his gardening gear, Ethan decided to check in on his friend Nick. Nick lived in the bigger town of Albany just down the coast, and they had known each other since they were six years old. Ethan had met Nick on a scout camp and found they had both liked a lot of the same things. They'd had great fun on that camp, and had stayed friends ever since, even though they lived in different towns. It was amazing how the internet had made it so easy to chat and keep in touch, even from a long distance.

It wasn't so easy now, though, since the telephone and internet service had stopped working and they'd had to improvise. Nick and Ethan had come up with the idea of keeping in contact by talking on a CB radio. Nick's dad had owned an electronics store in Albany that had sold a few CB radios, and Ethan had borrowed his from Logan, the vet's son. Logan's dad had used his to keep in contact with the farmers in the area who were out of internet range and needed treatment for their animals. The CB radio system worked well, and it was good fun too.

After grabbing himself a drink, Ethan sat down again in the kitchen and pressed the transmitter. He hoped his friend would be there.

"Hey, Nikko, you there?" All he heard was static. He tried again.

"Nikko, you there? It's Ethan." He waited patiently. Static again. Then finally a reply came back.

"Hey, Ethan mate, how ya doing? How are those scores on COD going? You beat that guy Zac yet?"

Ethan laughed. Zac was particularly good at playing the video game Call of Duty, and even though he had his farm chores, Zac always found time to play with Ethan. However, much to his annoyance, Zac beat Ethan every time they played.

"No, not yet. I think I'll have to come up with some new moves. Dunno how he's gotten so good. He must sit around playing it all day!"

Nick laughed. "Yeah, probably. Not much else to do now there's no school, or Internet, eh? How's everything going over there? You run out of food yet?"

"No. not yet. Although some things are starting to run out. No more chocolate, Nutella or Doritos in the shop," complained Ethan sadly. They were the first things kids had grabbed from the local supermarket.

Nick laughed again. "Yeah, too bad bro, you'll have to eat the baked beans and tinned peas now! We ran out of the good stuff weeks ago. Our shops are bigger than yours, but we got more kids here. By the way, how's that sister of yours going?"

Ethan sighed; he thought of Elisha passed out on her bed. "Aaaah well, you know. She's pretty stressed out right now and looks like she's sick too."

Nick was quiet for a while, then said, "What's wrong with her, bro? What do you mean sick?"

"Oh, I don't know, probably just the flu or something, I suppose. She'll get over it," Ethan replied. "Why?"

There was a pause at the other end. "Listen, Ethan. There's something I gotta tell you. It may be nothing, but you should know just in case." Nick's voice sounded worried. His tone was serious. "There's been talk around town of the KV17 virus starting to affect kids."

"What!" exclaimed Ethan. "What do you mean effect kids?"

"Well, don't worry, you should be okay. It only seems to happen to older kids. When they turn seventeen, some of them have been getting sick. A sore throat, fever, headache, that kind of stuff," Nick advised. "Similar to when the adults became ill."

Ethan swallowed hard thinking of Elisha's symptoms. "What happens then, do they die?" he asked his friend reluctantly, his voice held a slight tremor.

Nick replied hesitantly. "Err, well no, that's the funny thing. They don't die like the adults did; they just seem to go through a change. You know, go a bit crazy. Really hostile and aggressive. Like their personality is changing or something." He paused as if not sure whether he should go on. "Look, there have been a few problems here. Deaths from fights and stuff. No one I know personally, but I've heard other kids talking, and it sounded bad. They've started nicknaming them *devs*."

"devs?"

"Yes, you know. Short for deviants."

"Oh, right," said Ethan, sounding distracted. He stared blankly at the wall in front of him, his mind was swirling with thoughts and images. He knew that Elisha had been acting differently lately, but he wasn't expecting this.

"It's just what I've heard the other kids calling them. Hey, listen, mate. I'm sure your sister is fine. She's only just turned seventeen, right? It's probably just the flu like you said." Nick tried to comfort his friend. It was never easy when you had to be the bearer of bad news.

"Um, yeah, you're right. Probably just the flu," Ethan muttered to himself. "Well gotta go, keep practising those COD moves, man. We should try to get together somehow and take that Zac down," Ethan promised his friend resting the handset on his lap.

"Definitely, bro, definitely. Hey, Ethan, one more thing. If your sister starts getting an itchy red rash everywhere, especially on her hands and feet, she's definitely got it. She's becoming a dev. That's the last symptom. You know, before they start going all psycho."

Ethan swallowed hard. "Yeah, okay, Nikko, talk soon. Keep safe, man." He turned the CB to standby and ran his fingers through his thick hair.

"Fantastic. Just fantastic," he muttered forlornly, staring into his empty glass. Ethan suddenly felt exhausted. He hadn't noticed any red rashes on Elisha's hands, and she hadn't mentioned anything to him. Still, she had been acting rather aggressively lately. Maybe it was just stress. He remembered back to fourth grade when one of the school teachers had to take stress leave when she was found sitting in her car, physically unable to get out and teach her class. Stress did strange things to people.

Ethan looked at his hands. He decided not to say anything to Elisha, not yet anyway. He didn't want to worry her when it was probably just the flu. At least he hoped it was. So, what if she was seventeen. Seventeen-year-olds got the flu too, didn't they? He was pondering this when there was a sharp knock at the front door.

Ethan reluctantly got up to answer it. It was probably Jason. Should he say something to him about his conversation with Nikko? He decided to wait. Better deal with the gang kids first. *One problem at a time*, he said to himself with a sigh.

The pounding on the door was getting more frantic, and he could hear Jason outside calling his name. "Okay, okay! What's the rush?" Ethan yelled back, feeling slightly annoyed. He opened the door to find Jason standing all red-faced and sweaty. He was bent over with his hands on his knees breathing hard.

"Sorry, not used to running," gasped Jason, sucking in the air. He looked up at Ethan, shaking his head.

"What's wrong?" asked Ethan, in a worried voice. "Why were you running anyway? What's the rush?"

"SHUT UP!" Elisha yelled at them from the other room. Ethan and Jason looked at each other startled.

Jason raised his eyebrows and said, "Someone's a bit grumpy today!"

"Err, yes," said Ethan letting out a tense sigh. "I'd better come outside," he suggested, shutting the front door behind him as he stepped outside to join Jason. "What's up?" He glanced back at the front door nervously.

Jason looked at Ethan with a furrowed brow. "I think there are some buildings on fire!"

"What?" Ethan yelled loudly; he didn't care if Elisha heard them or not.

"You can see smoke from the backyard of the house we're staying in. The smell's really strong too," said Jason talking rapidly. "We're pretty sure it's the farm we saw when we drove into town. You said that kid Zac lives on a farm. Maybe it's his. Looks big too. You'd better get whoever you can to help put it out," advised Jason, waving his arms around animatedly as he spoke.

"Yes, it's probably the Bailey farm. That's close to where you're staying. Now that I'm outside, I can definitely smell the smoke too." Peering towards the horizon, Ethan could see dark black clouds of smoke filling the sky, and the air had an acrid smell to it. "Right, come on, we'd better get some buckets. There's some in the hardware shop. It's down this way, let's go." Ethan pulled Jason in the direction of the main town.

"What about Elisha?"

Ethan glanced back uncertainly at the house. He made a quick decision. "Just leave her, she's feeling sick, and we're wasting time. Come on; let's go!" He started running in the direction of the hardware shop with Jason close behind. *Would they get there in time to help save the farm?*

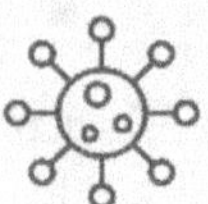

CHAPTER SEVENTEEN

Broc

Broc was sick of smashing windows and setting fire to rubbish bins. While it was cool to see the little kids with their frightened faces peeking out of the broken windows in terror at him, he was getting bored. He needed more entertainment, more excitement.

He wasn't a particularly tall boy, being only fifteen. He was, however, muscular and strong and like his father had a mean streak.

"I'm so bored!" yelled Broc moving his arms up and down as he held onto his baseball bat as though it were a dumbbell. He watched his biceps flexing. At his father's insistence, Broc had been going to the gym with his dad since he was ten-years-old.

"Maybe I should have kept Jessica around, at least I would have had something pretty to look at," Broc smirked, looking at the other members of his gang.

Cindy and Debbie two thirteen-year-old girls gave Broc a dirty look.

Cindy flicked her long black hair, currently adorned with a bright pink streak. "Hmph. I'm glad she's gone. She was always whining," remarked Cindy, shaking her head at her best friend. She took a small mirror from her pocket and started applying mascara to her lashes, turning her face back and forth admiring her efforts.

"Yeah, it was her own fault for getting up the duff," added Debbie. "And besides, Broc was always paying *her* far too much attention," she said more quietly, adjusting her tight-fitting top.

Cindy nodded. "Less competition," she smiled, winking at Broc.

Broc ignored her and looked out to the horizon. He thought about the lovely Jessica Hartley. Broc had known her all throughout high school in the city. She had been a very pretty girl, and Broc had enjoyed her company. That was until Jessica had become pregnant, then things changed.

Her constant whining and moaning at him about what she was supposed to do, gave Broc a headache. She sounded like a goat, bleating on and on. How was he meant to know what to do? Like he said to her, it wasn't his problem.

Broc wondered fleetingly how she was going. He had left her at the last town the gang had been in, he couldn't remember the name of it, but he was sure there had been other people living there. Broc shrugged his shoulders and scratched his nose. *Problem solved.*

"So, Braydon. You got any ideas. Who can we mess with today?" Broc turned to face the tall red-haired boy standing to one side, expecting an answer.

Braydon shook his head and looked at the ground. His heart didn't seem to be totally into this whole terrorising thing.

Broc glared at Braydon and groaned loudly. When Braydon didn't reply, Broc started hitting the ground with his bat. He paced back and forth his feet crunching on the gravel scattered on the ground. "I am sooo bloody bored!" He bellowed and began smashing his stolen VW beetle's headlight with his baseball bat. Bits of shattered glass and plastic flew out in all directions.

Cindy and Debbie looked up from their compact mirrors in alarm. Their lipsticks paused midway to their mouths.

Broc twirled his bat around and around in his hand. He looked at the others, his face menacing. They were all standing around watching him like scared rabbits.

"Someone had better come up with something to do really fast, or I might have to start using this bat on something softer. Like your head!" he smirked and pointed the bat at fourteen-year-old Aaron.

The thin, reedy Aaron took a couple of steps backwards. "Right," he said, his voice trembling. He looked around nervously as though trying to get some inspiration for a suggestion.

The others were now watching Aaron, relieved that Broc had not focused his attention on *them*.

"Um, hey. How about those cows over there?" Aaron suggested in a high-pitched squeaky voice. He pointed to a paddock with about thirty black and white cows.

"Huh?" Broc looked at the direction Aaron was pointing. He had no idea what Aaron was talking about. "Very nice, Aaron, but I don't feel like milking cows right now!" he said sarcastically, shaking his head.

Aaron coughed, his face flushed. "Err, well, we could go and let them out. You know and chase them around, so they run off. Those farm kids won't be too happy about that!" He raised his hands to his mouth and giggled.

Broc stood with one hand on his hip and the other with the baseball bat slung over his shoulder, looking over at the farm in the distance. He peered back at Aaron, with narrowed eyes.

"Yeah, alright." He grinned, opening the car door. "It's a start, I guess. Everyone get in the car. Let's go tip some cows."

The others quickly piled into the car, willing to do whatever Broc wanted as long as he was happy.

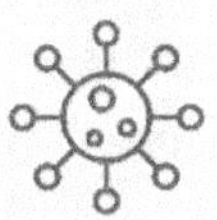

CHAPTER EIGHTEEN

The Bailey's farm had been in their family for six generations. They were mostly wheat farmers with a few cows,
chickens, and goats. Before the virus had hit, both the
grandparents and parents had lived together on the farm with
the children. However, that soon changed when the virus
infected the town, splitting families apart and changing
everyone's way of life as they knew it. The children had to bury
the adults one by one in the garden. They buried them under
the orange trees when no one had come to take them away.
They had murmured a few words from the bible that Elisha had
suggested, said teary goodbyes and then had to get on with the
job of looking after the farm. Caring for all the animals on their
own was a big task, and they didn't have much time to grieve.

The two oldest Bailey children were sixteen-year-old twins,
Zac and Lilly. Both had blonde hair and bright blue eyes and
were always playing practical jokes on each other. Zac's
favourite choice of mischief was a lifelike plastic spider that he
loved to put in strategic places in an attempt to scare his sister.
Like the toilet seat at night or Lilly's pillow while she was
sleeping. Lilly was terrified of spiders, and this one had long
spindly legs with little tiny hairs protruding from them that
tickled your skin when they brushed against you. She would

scream in terror at the sight of it and Zac would crack up laughing hysterically, his blue eyes crinkling up at the sides as he laughed. Zac's joyous laughter would cause Lilly to become furious at him, her face plastered with indignation and rage at being tricked and laughed at. Lilly had a hot temper when provoked and would often let fly with a few swear words, making Zac laugh even harder. Once she had unleashed her rage, the anger would always pass quickly and soon she would be laughing along with him. She could never stay angry at Zac for long. Apart from the odd practical joke and resulting argument, most of the time they got along well for siblings. Right now, they were doing their best to keep the farm running and their younger siblings fed and cared for.

Zac sat on the farm tractor and looked out over the wheat field. The wheat was ripe; however, with both the harvester and tractor out of fuel, the only way to harvest it was by hand. It was a daunting job, nevertheless, being a stubborn person, Zac was determined to try and harvest the field.

Lilly was down in the field examining the crop. "Comfortable up there are you?" she asked, looking up at her brother, her hands on her hips.

Zac leaned back in his seat and whistled. "Yep. I'd rather be here than school, that's for sure," he laughed. School had always been difficult for Zac as he had dyslexia. Being told to stand and read a passage of text in front of the class always made him break out in a cold sweat, and his insides turn to mush. It was something he hated fervently, and he always kept his eyes cast downwards hoping the teacher wouldn't pick him.

He jumped down from the tractor and went to help Lilly. "Give me dirt and cows and crops over school work, any day!" He looked up at the bright blue cloudless sky and smiled. "I would much rather be in the open air."

"Well, come on then," said Lilly glaring at him. "Help me harvest some of this wheat. We need to work out how to make flour with it."

Zac looked back towards the family homestead. "Where is Kevin by the way? He's supposed to be helping!"

Lilly shrugged. She lay a tarp on the ground for the wheat stalks.

Zac groaned. "Let's get started without him then," he grumbled, picking up his machete. "He's never around when there's work to be done."

Kevin was sitting in the shade on the family porch, with his feet up watching his older brother and sister labouring away in the field. He was thirteen years old, had short brown greasy hair and thick eyebrows that shaded his muddy brown eyes, giving him a permanent scowling look. He was short for his age and slightly chubby, having not yet gone through his adolescent growth spurt.

"Aren't you supposed to be out there helping?" enquired Katie, his younger sister. She had baby Sarah balanced on her hip and was scowling at Kevin.

"Nah, I'm good here," replied Kevin puffing out his chest. "Besides, Zac will only start bossing me around if I go out there." He yawned and closed his eyes, getting comfortable in his chair.

Katie stared at Kevin for a moment frowning. "Well, if you're not *too* busy, you can watch Sarah for a minute," she said, thrusting the toddler at Kevin. "I need to wash some nappies for her, plus feed the chickens and goats." Katie ran her fingers through her blonde, curly hair. Now there weren't any adults around to badger her about tying it up, she left it permanently loose. This had given her the slightly alarming appearance of a wild woman, as her hair had become tangled and knotty sticking out at all angles.

Kevin looked at Sarah, his face screwed up in distaste. "Fine," he grumbled. "Just don't be too long."

*

Later that afternoon, all the children were in the front lounge room playing the card game UNO (except for Sarah, who was asleep in her crib) when they heard a commotion in one of the paddocks. It sounded like the cows were going crazy, bellowing loudly in long frightened mooing sounds.

"Hell! I hope it's not dingoes again," complained Zac, picking up a card from the pile. His hands were rough and calloused from doing farm work.

"Or foxes," added Lilly, glancing at her brother.

"Yes, or foxes," agreed Zac, getting up from his chair. "I'll go and have a look. No one touches my cards," he added, pointing his finger at Lilly in particular.

She looked at him innocently and said, "as if."

Lilly watched him walk out the front door, her elbows on the table and her chin resting innocently on her hands. As soon as he stepped outside, she immediately picked up a few extra cards from the pack to add to Zac's pile. "Just to make the game more interesting," she whispered to the others, who all giggled. Lilly held her finger to her lips gesturing them to be quiet in case Zac heard, trying not to laugh herself.

Their merriment was broken by Zac calling loudly from outside. "Lilly! Kevin! You'd better get out here. Katie, you stay with Sarah."

Katie who had stood up with the others abruptly sat back down. Zac sounded serious.

Lilly quickly rushed outside. "Jeez, what's going on?" The cows were all stampeding around the paddock, making the anxious sounds of animals in distress. "I can't see any dingoes or foxes trying to get into the paddock. Though, it's a bit difficult to be sure from this distance. What's scaring them so badly?"

Zac shook his head.

Then, amongst the bellowing of the frightened cows, Lilly heard the distinct sound of laughter. A *lot* of laughter. Squinting her eyes to block out the sunlight, she could see shapes moving about in the paddock. Human shapes.

"I can't believe it!" Lilly exclaimed, her eyes growing wide. "There are people in the paddock chasing the cows around and terrorising them!"

"Come on," yelled Zac, storming off towards the paddock with angry strides. "Let's go see who it is and put a stop to it!"

"Oh, I think I know who it's gonna be," Lilly muttered angrily, looking at Kevin, who nodded in agreement. She stomped after Zac, her fists clenched in anger. Her feet making thumping sounds on the ground as she took big angry strides forward.

Kevin remained at the house. "I'll stay here," he said slouching against the front door. "You two sort it out," he said smirking, before walking back inside and flumping onto the couch. "I never really liked the cows anyway," he mumbled in a low voice, putting his feet up on the coffee table.

Over in the field, Broc looked up and saw the two older bailey children storming towards him. He smiled his top lip curling up in disdain.

"Well, well. What do we have here? *Shark Boy and Lava Girl*, perhaps. Come to save the day?" Broc scoffed.

The other gang members all laughed meanly as they turned to face the twins.

"Oh, you think it's funny, do you, scaring animals?" yelled Zac, running the last ten metres to the paddock fence. Lilly ran with him.

"Nah, not really," sneered Broc who was standing in the middle of the paddock. "Honestly, I'd rather be scaring people, but sometimes you just have to take what you can get." He spread his arms wide, gesturing to the cows.

"Anyway, we're not scaring them, we're setting them free," stated Cindy in a snide voice as she pointed to a section of the paddock fence that had been kicked down. The terrified cows were stampeding towards the opening and running freely into the bush that bordered the farmland.

"No, no, no!" Zac cried in frustration, leaping the fence and running over to the damaged one. They'd have a difficult time getting the cows back into the paddock if they ran too far away. He grabbed onto the fallen fence and tried to pull the heavy wood and wire structure back up. He had to try and stop any more of their cows from getting out and getting lost. The fence was cumbersome and heavy, making him groan with the effort. Zac's feet dug into the dry dirt as he pushed against the fallen fence, trying to force it back upright.

"Grab him!" Broc commanded like an officer in the army, pointing his finger at Zac. Braydon and Aaron immediately marched over to descend on Zac, who was still struggling to hold the damaged fence up. The wire cut painfully into his fingers and his knees bent with the weight of the fence. It was a long piece of fence making it difficult to hold up.

Lilly had run over to help him, trying to stop any more of the cows from escaping the paddock. She stood nervously on the inside of the fence, facing the frightened cows. The animals were all bellowing frantically, and in their agitated state, Lilly was afraid that she was going to get trampled by them. They weren't exactly small animals or particularly smart.

Gritting her teeth, she bravely spread her arms wide, moving slowly towards the frightened animals, one step at a time trying to calm them and herd them back into the centre of the paddock, away from the fallen fence.

The noise and smell of the frightened animals filled the air. In their terror and confusion, the cows were slamming into each other and the fence as they tried to escape.

"I hope they're not going to injure themselves!" exclaimed Lilly watching the cow's panic escalating to hysteria. Her hands were shaking and her eyes wide with alarm.

"Just try and keep them contained," yelled Zac desperately clinging onto the fence, trying to keep the barrier upright. He leaned forward with all his body weight. His knuckles turned white as his hands gripped the wire and forced the fence to stay erect as the cows continued to run blindly into it. Each time a cow would smack into the fence, his body would jolt backward as if he had been hit by an iron fist.

Trying to stop him, Braydon and Aaron roughly grabbed Zac by his arms and pulled him away from the fence. It crashed to the ground with a thud, sending sand and dust flying up in the air from the impact. The two boys held onto him tightly, their fingers digging into his flesh as he struggled against them, trying to break free.

"Get off me, you idiots!" Zac yelled. His face screwed up in anger as he watched more of the cows run through the fallen fence. The boys tightened their grip, pinning his arms to his sides. Zac stopped struggling and glared at them with his eyes ablaze with fury. He was no match for the two of them.

Broc, who had been quietly watching the whole process, sauntered over towards them with an ugly smirk on his face. He looked at Zac and smiled, placing his hand on Zac's head as if to calm him. He stroked Zac's hair with his hand, a big smile on his face. Then, without warning, Broc pulled his fist back, and punched the helpless Zac once in the face and again in the stomach.

As the bigger boy's fist connected hard with Zac's jaw, his teeth clashed together, and his stomach caved in as the second blow hit a soft spot. The air rushed out of Zac, and he bent over, heaving for breath. Cindy and Debbie who were watching closely, stood laughing and smirking at how strong Broc was.

Broc didn't notice them. He had a smug look on his face and started to prance around and crow like a rooster. "How's that feel, farm boy? Didn't take much to shut you up!"

Lilly quickly forgot the cows and came running over to help her brother. "You bloody coward!" she screamed at Broc, throwing herself onto his back and wrapping her arms around his throat. Lilly squeezed hard.

Broc's eyes bulged slightly and his neck tensed as Lilly increased the pressure. "Get this bitch off me," Broc gasped, struggling for air as he tried to reach around and grab Lilly as she hung on. Her feet gripped onto his sides like she was riding a horse in a rodeo.

Broc's face turned red, unable to dislodge Lilly.

Cindy and Debbie quickly came running up to try to pull Lilly off Broc's back. Lilly, however, was not going to make it easy for them. She managed to get a good kick into Debbie's stomach before both girls were able to yank her from Broc's back. Lilly fell hard onto the ground with a thud, the dust billowing out around her.

Out of the corner of her eye, Lilly watched Debbie bend over clutching her stomach and smiled in satisfaction. Cindy, however, was not amused at all. She marched straight up to Lilly and slapped her hard across the face bringing tears to Lilly's eyes. The slap stung, and her face glowed red where Cindy's hand had made an impact.

"You bitch." Lilly glared at Cindy as she held her hand to her stinging cheek.

Broc laughed, his voice sounding raspy. "Good one, Cindy!" and gave her the thumbs-up. Cindy grinned looking very pleased with herself and blew Broc a kiss.

Broc turned his attention back to the twins. "Well now. What shall we do with you two?" Broc had his chest thrust forward and his hands planted on his hips. "It's far too early in the evening to stop all this fun, don't you think? The sun hasn't even begun to set yet," Broc said provokingly. He stroked his chin slowly, smirking.

Broc glanced over at Lilly and noticed that she was glaring at him, looking as if she wanted to scratch his eyes out. And Zac who now had his breath back was again struggling with Braydon and Aaron.

"You two *are* fighters," observed Broc, swaying back and forward on his toes. "That's good. I hate pushovers, always too easy," he said in delight. 'Fighters are always much more fun." Broc casually strolled over to Zac and stood directly in front of him. He turned to smirk at Lilly for a moment, then punched Zac in the stomach again. Only this time much harder. Zac let out a low groan and dropped straight to his knees in pain.

Broc bent over him, putting his face up close to Zac's. "You'd better stop fighting man, or you're gonna end up real hurt," he threatened. He held Zac's chin roughly between his fingers as Zac struggled for breath.

"You really are a bastard!" yelled Lilly standing up. Her eyes glared at him in hate.

Broc sauntered up to her and gave a dramatic bow. "Well, thank you, love. I do try my best" he said, winking at her. Lilly looked at him in disgust and got ready to launch herself at him again.

"Why don't we tie them up in the barn and leave them there overnight?" suggested Braydon quickly. "This is starting to get nasty," he whispered to Aaron.

Broc clapped his hands in delight. "Great idea, mate, let's tie them up. You two bring that one," he ordered, pointing at Zac. "And I'll get her."

Broc pursued Lilly who was trying to back away and grabbed her by the hair. He wound his fingers through the long strands and roughly pulled her towards the barn. "Find some rope," he ordered in a gruff voice pointing at Cindy and Debbie. They nodded before running towards the barn, eager to do as Broc wished.

The barn was old and musty and had been on the family farm for generations. It held the animal's main food supply. There were bales of hay stacked neatly on top of each other at the back and bags of chicken feed all lined up ready to use at the front. The Bailey children were hoping it would be enough feed to last the animals through the winter. Broc had other ideas. He didn't care about the animals, and he didn't care about their farm.

Pulling a sharp pocket knife out of his jeans pocket, Broc held it loosely in his hands. It had been a gift from Broc's father, and he carried it everywhere. Smiling as he opened the blade, Broc looked at the shiny metal, turning it back and forth in the afternoon sunlight, enjoying the way it glinted.

Aaron and Braydon were watching Broc closely, waiting to see what he would do. They stood with their arms hanging by their sides and their jaws slack, as though they were foot soldiers waiting for instruction from their commander.

Broc noticed the other's watching him and cleared his throat. "Well, let's get this party started then, shall we?" crowed Broc with a closed lip smile. He waved his knife at Lilly, then proceeded to slash open the bags of feed, spilling the precious grain onto the ground. He then trampled on the grain with his big Blundstone boots, squashing it and grinding it into the dirt.

Zac swore under his breath, his jaw clenched.

"What did you say?" asked Broc whipping his head around to glare at Zac.

"You heard me," Zac said bravely.

Broc snorted, walking over to him with his fist raised ready to strike. Zac held his breath, clenched his stomach and braced himself, getting ready for another blow and the pain that would follow. Lilly closed her eyes and turned her head.

"We found some," cheered Cindy and Debbie happily skipping up to Broc, unintentionally interrupting the violence that was about to unfold. "We found some rope, Broc!" They smiled sweetly at him holding forth the ominous find.

"Excellent," said Broc lowering his arm and grabbing the rope off the girls. "Now we can have some real fun."

Lilly and Zac glanced nervously at each other. This obviously wasn't going to be a whole lot of "*fun*" for them.

Cindy and Debbie skipped over to stand close to Lilly grabbing her arms, just in case, she tried to make a run for it. They grinned meanly at Lilly, thrusting their faces close to hers. Their strong sweet perfume was intense, and Lilly stared straight ahead, refusing to look at them.

On the other side of the barn, Zac was hurriedly scanning the room looking for a way to escape. There had to be a way out of this mess. He thought he could probably get away from Braydon and Aaron and make a run for it out the door. However, that would leave his sister in the barn on her own to face that thug Broc. Zac shook his head, it wouldn't work. He'd have to come up with something else; he couldn't leave her by herself. Zac didn't like the way Broc kept glaring at Lilly like she was an insect waiting to be squashed under his boot.

Meanwhile, Broc was standing in the doorway untangling the length of rope the girls had brought him. As he cut it into two long pieces, he took his time, enjoying the thought of the fear building in his two captors. His eyes narrowed into mean slits as he smirked at Lilly. He was going to enjoy tormenting her the most.

Watching Broc, Zac started to breathe rapidly. His eyes darted from one side of the barn to the other. Broc was blocking the only way out! Beads of sweat began to form on Zac's upper lip. The air in the barn was hot and oppressing.

Zac's face was red from Broc's earlier blows, and his lip was cut. He began twisting and turning in Braydon and Aaron's arms, struggling in vain as they kept his arms pinned tightly behind his back. Zac raised his head and peered up at the barn roof willing it to open for him and show him a way out.

Too late.

Broc strode over and stood in front of him purposefully showing Zac the rope, a nasty smirk on his face. "You first, farmer Joe."

Zac let his head fall to his chest before glancing over at Lilly, a forlorn look on his face. He had failed her. He had failed them both.

Once Zac was tied up, which was no easy task as he lashed out and struggled at every opportunity, Broc went over to Lilly. He wanted to tie her up against a pole, right in the centre of the barn. She struggled too, but with Broc, Cindy and Debbie all fighting against her she didn't really have a chance. Lilly glared at the other girls hatefully as Broc tied her hands tightly behind her back. The rope cut painfully into her wrists, and the pole felt cold and hard against her back.

Broc chuckled and ran his hand under her chin. His fingers were rough and calloused and smelt of tobacco. "Well, you are a feisty one, aren't you, girly?" He said clearly trying to provoke her. "Not very pretty, though, are you?" He ran his eyes up and down her body slowly, enjoying her embarrassment.

"You're so skinny you're more like a boy than a girl. You *sure* you two aren't brothers?" He stared openly at her chest. "Do you even *need* to wear a bra?"

Broc lifted Lilly's shirt with his dirty fingers and flicked her bra strap. "Well, I guess you are a girl… barely."

Lilly's cheeks flamed red.

Broc noticed Lilly's humiliation and laughed heartily. Cindy and Debbie snickered, whispering to each other behind their hands.

Lilly looked at the girls with a withering stare before dropping her head. Her fingers twitched with frustration, and she pulled at the constricting ropes until her wrists hurt. They wouldn't budge.

Closing her eyes, Lilly breathed in a deep breath. Her hands curled into tight fists, and she raised her head. Her eyes narrowed, and she slowly turned her head to face Broc, who was still laughing and jeering. Lilly's lips curled into a snide smile.

Broc stood and stared at her, his eyebrows drawn together. Lilly stared back at him, her eyes boring into his in hate. Then before he knew what was happening, she pursed her lips and promptly spat straight into Broc's face.

Broc flinched. His jaw dropped open, and he stepped back in complete surprise. The barn grew completely silent.

Lilly smiled at him in glee. "Not laughing now, *are* you?" she said under her breath.

Broc's expression suddenly changed to one of intense fury. His nostrils were flaring, and his hands opened and closed in fists by his side as though he were struggling to control his rage.

Lilly stopped smiling and glanced around nervously, her eyes flicking back and forth. Breathing in sharply, she stood up straight and strong thrusting her shoulders back. Lilly turned her head defiantly and looked Broc straight in the eyes.

Broc stared back at her, his eyes steely and hard. "Well, what *are* we going to do with you?" he said between gritted teeth, wiping the spit from the side of his face with the back of his hand. His hand shook. Broc was obviously having trouble controlling his anger.

Cindy, who had been watching the whole scenario with pure delight, came joyfully skipping up to him. Reaching around to put her arm around Broc's waist, she whispered conspiratorially in his ear. As she leaned in close to Broc's face, she turned her eyes to look at Lilly and grinned.

Lilly glared back and forth between Cindy and Broc, biting her top lip. She swallowed nervously.

Broc's threw his head back and laughed a big belly laugh. "Whoa, that's a great idea," he remarked smiling once more. "I can see you and me, are going to make a fine team," he winked at Cindy.

Cindy blushed and giggled. Debbie, who was also watching, gave her a dirty look. Broc reached into his jeans pocket and pulled out his pocket-knife once more. He looked at it lying in his palm for a moment, before grabbing Lilly by the hair and yanking her head painfully to one side.

"Hey!" yelled Zac alarmed, his fingers clenched into helpless fists behind his back.

Braydon and Aaron both looked alarmed too and glanced at each other as if unsure what to do.

"Don't worry, brother," said Broc reassuringly to Zac. "No one's getting cut today. Well, only a little bit, I'm just going to finish off your sister's boyish look," he laughed meanly as he ran the tip of the cold blade of the knife along her chin. Lilly's body went rigid, and she breathed in sharply.

Zac looked at his sister helplessly. His eyes were full of frustration as he struggled against Braydon and Aarons grip.

"Yeah, he's gonna cut off all her hair. She's gonna look even more like a boy!" laughed Cindy grabbing her crotch. "You're going to be all bald and ugly," she smirked pointing her finger at Lilly.

Broc whistled happily. "Well, no time to waste let's get started," he crowed, getting his blade ready. Cindy and Debbie danced around Lilly jubilantly, clapping their hands in glee and kicking up bits of hay with their feet.

Circling around her poking her arms and back with their long pointy fingernails, they laughed and taunted her. Every now and then, they would bring their faces right up close to hers, so they could fully enjoy her discomfort. Lilly was finding it harder and harder to ignore them as they thrust their smirking faces right up close to hers. She looked sadly at Zac who was fighting against the ropes holding him fast to his pole without success. The afternoon had started so differently. "I hope Katie, Sarah and Kevin are okay," she whispered closing her eyes.

"No going to sleep love," whispered Broc close to Lilly's ear. She flicked her eyes open to see Broc holding his shiny blade up before her eyes. He deliberately turned it back and forth so that the late afternoon light streaming through the barn door reflected off its sharp blade. Lilly's eyes flickered from the blade to Broc's face and back. He had a nasty expression on his face. His eyes were black like a shark's, and his top lip was curled up in a snarl. Lilly's legs began to shake.

Not taking his eyes from her body, Broc walked around to stand directly behind Lilly, right up close to her. His hot breath wafted onto her neck as he leaned in close. His breath smelled putrid as though he hadn't brushed his teeth in a long while. Lilly's nose crinkled and she turned her head away in disgust.

"Are you ready, sweetheart?" He whispered close to her ear so that only she could hear. Lilly leaned forward, away from the pole and away from Broc as much as the binding ropes would allow her. He placed his hand roughly on her stomach and pulled her back towards him. Lilly's toes curled in her sneakers, and her legs trembled.

Grinning, Broc grabbed a fistful of Lilly's long blonde hair and started to roughly saw his blade back and forth, right up close to her scalp. The feeling of her hair being ripped away and the noise of the knife as it cut through the strands made Lilly's eyes widen in panic. It would only take one slip and he would slice her head open with his blade. Lilly strained desperately against the ropes binding her, the rough fibres biting into the soft skin of her wrists making painful indentations. She twisted her hands back and forth to no avail, the bonds held her tight. She couldn't break free.

CHAPTER NINETEEN

Cindy was staring at Lilly intently. Her dark brown eyes piercing into the other girl's skin like a probe trying to worm its way inside her. "I don't like the amount of attention Broc's giving this chic," she complained to Debbie. "He should be focusing on me!"

"You mean focusing on *us*," Debbie said, raising her eyebrows.

Cindy smiled. "Us. Yes, he should be focusing on *us*, not some dumb farm girl," she said pouting. Cindy picked up a handful of old hay and broken sticks from the barn floor. Holding them loosely in her hand, she started flinging pieces at Lilly. Several of the pieces hit Lilly hard on the face making Cindy grin.

"What the hell!" Lilly exclaimed in anger and disbelief as she glared at her tormentor. Cindy just laughed and kept on throwing. Lilly frowned and tried to twist away from the annoying girls.

"Well, that was a lot of fun," laughed Broc, sliding his blade back into his pocket. "I think I'll have a cigarette now," he said, rubbing Lilly's newly shaved head as he stood right up close to her.

Lilly shivered. Broc's face was almost touching hers. The smell of his bad breath and body odour was overpowering. She dropped her head, her chin almost touching her chest she tried to breathe through her mouth to lessen the stench.

Broc saw this as a sign of defeat. "My you do look sexy!" he teased slapping her butt. "If only I had my camera, we could take a selfie together!" He brought his face up close to hers again, pausing for a moment as she tried to lean away from him. Broc stared at her in sudden anger before kissing her hard on the mouth. He let his lips linger on her skin, feeling its softness before sticking out his tongue and licking the side of her face.

Lilly grimaced, which only made Broc laugh meanly before wiping his lips with the back of his hand. He turned and spat on the ground as if he had a bad taste in his mouth.

Lilly's eyes watered, and she dropped her head again refusing to look at Broc. She clenched her hands into fists. "I'll get you back," Lilly whispered under her breath. "When you're least expecting it, I'm going to get you back." Her eyes took on a steely hard look, and her fists remained clenched at her sides. Lilly would not let Broc get the better of her.

On the other side of the barn, Zac's shoulders were hunched as he looked over at his sister with concern. He tried to catch her eye to give her some encouragement, but Lilly refused to look up. Zac noticed that she had a little half-smile on her face and was again trying to loosen her ropes. He tried to do the same.

Broc was looking at Lilly too. However, unlike Lilly, he was having a great time. He began walking around the barn, still smirking in satisfaction at his humiliation of this girl. He tapped his finger on his thigh as though wondering what he could do next. Taking one last drag on his cigarette, Broc flicked the half-smoked butt into the bales of hay scattered around the barn. He started to laugh, "You know, I really should give this habit up," he suggested smugly to Braydon and Aaron, who were still standing near Zac.

Straight away a thin stream of smoke started to rise from the hay, like a gymnast's ribbon twisting gracefully in the air. Lilly and Zac looked at each other in alarm. They knew that a smouldering cigarette end and dry hay were not a good mix.

Within seconds, flames erupted out of the stack of hay and soon rose to a metre high as the dry hay rapidly caught fire. Lilly, who was closest to the fire, desperately struggled against the ropes that held her firmly to the pole.

"What the hell are you doing, you idiot!" She screamed out. "There's no fire service anymore, and there's no way we can put that out!"

Broc, Cindy and Debbie were all laughing mercilessly. "*There's no fire service,*" they mimicked. "*There's no way we can put that out.* Boo-Hoo."

"Well, what a shame. Everything's going to burn then isn't it." Broc replied nastily, his voice cold and hard. He stood with his hands planted on his hips glaring at Lilly, enjoying watching her suffer and squirm in the heat.

Zac turned to Lilly and mouthed, "We have to get out!" She nodded vigorously and resumed her attempt to loosen the ropes as they dug deeply and painfully into her wrists.

Zac turned his head to look over at Braydon and Aaron. The two boys were standing looking at the flames, mesmerised. They weren't moving, they weren't saying anything. They weren't even laughing like the others.

"What the hell is wrong with you!?" yelled Zac through gritted teeth. Sweat rolled down his back as the heat in the barn started to intensify. Taking advantage of Braydon and Aaron's stupor, Zac wriggled his hands back and forth furiously.

The sweat on his wrists made the rope slippery, and the knots started to loosen just a little. If Zac could just get it loose enough, he might be able to slip a hand out and get free. He kept working on the rope.

Meanwhile, Lilly's eyes were watering profusely from the smoke, and she began to cough violently.

"Oh, look, she's crying, poor baby," sneered Cindy in a sarcastic voice, pointing at Lilly. "She wants her mummy."

Debbie and Broc started laughing as if it was all some hilarious joke. Lilly's mouth was set in a hard-thin line. She opened her eyes slightly and peered through the smoky haze. Her eyes were stinging painfully as though she had just cut into an onion, and Lilly struggled to hold them open just a little bit longer. Trying to ignore the stinging sensation, she looked through the smoke and haze. There was a figure standing by the barn door. It looked just like Lilly's sister Katie.

Katie's face was bright red, and she looked furious. She was waving her father's shotgun around threateningly while screaming at Broc, who was laughing at her. Lilly could also see Kevin. He was standing still with his arms straight by his side. He didn't seem to be saying or doing anything. Just watching.

"You leave my brother and sister alone and get off our farm, or I'll blow a hole in your goddam stomach!" Katie yelled threateningly, as she pointed the shotgun straight at Broc.

"Oh, this is too funny! I think I'm going to wet myself. I'm sooo scared," Broc snickered, pretending to tremble in fear. He remarked snidely. "Do you even know how to fire that thing, little girly?" As he put his hands back on his hips, looking at her condescendingly.

Katie smiled wryly as she looked Broc squarely in the eye. Taking a step closer to him, she cocked the shotgun and fired a round straight up into the rafters of the barn. The noise was intense causing everyone to duck and cover their heads with their hands as dust and woodchips came falling down on them like snow.

"I live on a farm you idiot, of course, I know how to use a shotgun. Now get the hell out!" threatened Katie calmly, turning the gun back on Broc, who suddenly didn't look so sure of himself.

"Whoa. Okay, love. We'll leave. It's getting too hot in here anyway." Broc pretended to fan his face with his hands. "Don't think we won't be back, little girly." Broc pointed his finger at Katie. "And sweet dreams to you, sweetheart. I'll be seeing you again *real* soon," he said, winking suggestively at Lilly as he ran out of the barn.

Katie flipped Broc the finger, before rushing over to untie Lilly and Zac. They were both bent over coughing and dry retching from all the smoke they had inhaled. The barn was now full of the thick black choking smoke making it increasingly difficult to breathe.

Once they were finally free of their ropes, the twins rushed outside to breathe some fresh air into their smoke clogged lungs. The cold evening air brought instant relief to their singed skin.

Lilly peered up at the barn with red-rimmed eyes. It was now well and truly on fire. Red and orange flames climbed higher up the barn walls, devouring the wood like a hungry wolf pack with its trapped prey. The family barn with its old wooden structure, its paint faded and chipped, made excellent fodder for the intense fire. The burning wood made loud cracking and popping noises from the blistering heat, filling the air with the frightening sounds of destruction. The children stared solemnly at the barn. The bright orange light from the fire reflected in their eyes. They could feel the heat radiating out from the building as if the fire wanted to devour them too.

"Jesus, the whole thing's gonna come down! I don't think we can save it!" Zac called out. His hands were on his knees as he tried in vain to stop the coughs racking his burnt lungs.

A loud noise erupted as one of the walls started to crumble. Bright orange embers flew through the air singeing anything they landed on. The children quickly backed away from the barn as pieces of burning wood continued to fall from the roof, landing dangerously close to them.

"Well, we have to do something, or it's going to spread to the wheat field and the house!" snapped Lilly in a panicked tone. She wiped her hand across her forehead and winced at the pain. Her face and head were red and inflamed from the heat she had endured in the barn. Blisters were already forming on the delicate skin.

"Let's get the feed buckets and fill them with water," yelled Katie above the roar of the fire.

Zac, Katie and Lilly all looked at each other in dismay for a moment, before sprinting to the farmhouse to find anything they could use to hold water. Anything to try to put out the fire. They had to stop it reaching the house and the animals. The barn was gone, but they could still try to save their home.

"Where's Kevin?" Asked Lilly suddenly, looking around her.

Katie shrugged. "I haven't seen him since I fired the shotgun," she replied raising her voice above the sound of the roaring fire and burning wood.

"Maybe he's back at the house with Sarah," suggested Lilly holding her hands out in front of her.

He wasn't.

Kevin had left with Broc. He had decided to leave his family and join the gang.

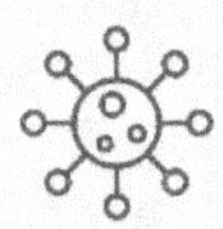

CHAPTER TWENTY

Back at Rosewood Avenue, Hadley and Lexi were getting ready to rush to the farm. They could see the black smoke from the fire billowing into the air from their backyard.

"Do you think their house is on fire?" asked Hadley, her voice shaking. "Will they will be able to put it out without the fire department?"

"I Hope so," said Lexi tilting her head to the side and peering through the back window. "Come on, the quicker we get over there, the better. Jason and Ethan are already there, and it's going to take us a while on foot," Lexi remarked grabbing some towels to beat the fire with. "I'll see if there's a bucket in the laundry we can use."

"Why can't we drive the car there? It would be quicker," asked Hadley as she pulled on her running shoes.

"Well, it's pretty much out of fuel, and I want to keep the last little bit for emergencies."

"Isn't this an emergency?" Hadley raised her eyebrows, her face looking grim.

"Yes. It is, but I mean emergencies for *us*, Hadley." Lexi bit her fingernail. "I know it seems harsh, but we've only been here a couple of days. We should keep the fuel just in case we have to leave. Okay?"

"Yes, s'pose so," agreed Hadley, although she didn't look convinced. "Come on then let's get going. Polo's barking out the back. I'll go get him, and he can come with us." She ran towards the back door.

Lexi frowned slightly. "Actually, you'd better leave him here. He'll only get in the way and…" she stopped mid-sentence, her mouth falling open in surprise.

"*Yeah, he'll only get in the way,*" mimicked an unfamiliar voice.

Hadley turned around to see Broc and Braydon holding Lexi tightly between them. Braydon had her arms pinned behind her back, and Broc held her by the hair.

He had a shining silver knife pressed up against her face.

Lexi grimaced as Broc pressed the edge of the knife into her cheek. It stung as the tip of the blade penetrated her soft skin, causing a single drop of blood to run down her cheek like a tear, leaving a thin trail of red.

Hadley gasped and immediately froze on the spot. Her eyes darted from the knife to Lexi's face.

Aaron, Cindy and Debbie, who had been out on the street, came piling into the house, laughing and shoving each other as they walked. "Did you see that farms girl's face?" smirked Cindy nastily. "Not so pretty now with no hair. Lol!"

The girls pretended to pose like supermodels with their hands under their chins pulling *duck face* expressions. Kevin trailed in behind them shuffling his feet.

Hadley glanced nervously at the mob. She took little steps forward trying to edge closer to her sister. "What… what do you want? Let my sister go. We…we haven't done anything to you," she stammered in a frightened voice, her eyes flicking between the intruders.

Broc grinned. "No, girly, that's right, you haven't, but we might just do some things to you if you don't do what we want!" Broc tapped his foot impatiently. "Let's see. How about you bring us all your food. That's a good start," he pointed towards the kitchen meaningfully.

Hadley didn't move. She stared at Broc angrily, her nostrils flaring. "Are you serious? What are you, the food police?" she said sarcastically, her hands placed firmly on her hips. "I'm not giving you our food. You're just a kid like us, go and get your own food!"

Broc glared at her in amazement, his cheeks puffed out and his eyebrows raised. "I said NOW, girly!" He bellowed loudly, spit flying out of his mouth. "Or I will have to cut your pretty sister's face to shreds. She wouldn't look so lovely then, would she!" His knife pressed deeper into Lexi's cheek, making her grimace in pain.

Hadley's defiance rapidly dissolved, her eyes widening in alarm. Nodding her head, she quickly started to move off towards the kitchen to get the food he wanted.

Lexi quickly yelled out to her. "No, Hadley, stop! We're going to need that." She struggled against the boys holding onto her. "Let me go, you bastards!"

Hadley abruptly stopped where she was, uncertain about what to do next. Her hands trembled as she looked back at her sister. Braydon was forcing Lexi's arm up behind her back painfully, and Broc pulled her head back by her hair. Lexi grimaced and cried out in pain. Her hair felt like it was being ripped out by its roots.

"Stop it!" Hadley screamed at the attackers. "Stop it. I'll get you some food." Running into the kitchen, she grabbed an armful of their precious food from a cardboard box sitting on the table and quickly ran back to the lounge room. "Here, you pigs!" she yelled facing the gang. Hadley threw the food down in front of the bullies, glaring at them in hate. "Now, let Lexi go!"

Cindy and Debbie, who had been enjoying watching the proceedings, laughed delightedly and scrambled to pick up the goodies. Cindy ripped opened a packet of chocolate Tim Tam biscuits, wastefully spilling the contents onto the floor. "Oh, yum. I love these." She slowly bit into a biscuit, smiling gleefully at Hadley. "Oh, these taste really good. You weren't saving them, were you?" She gave Hadley a wink as she grabbed another one and stuffed it into her mouth. Chocolate crumbs covered her lips in an unattractive way, and she licked at them greedily. "Mmm, tasty."

Hadley glared at her, making Cindy laugh even harder. Bits of chocolate flew from her mouth as she laughed. "What a pig," said Hadley in disgust, watching her cram more of the biscuits into her mouth.

Broc looked over Hadley as she stared at Cindy devouring their goodies. "That's pathetic," he shouted, pointing his finger at the food on the ground. "It's not enough," he demanded, his voice low and as hard as flint as he kicked the food with his boots, scattering biscuits across the floor.

Cindy stood up and stepped on them. "Oops, I'm so clumsy." She smiled sweetly crunching the chocolate biscuits under her bright red stiletto shoes, the chocolate mashing into the carpet fibres.

"You didn't have to do that!" Lexi looked at the crushed biscuits lying wasted on the floor.

Cindy blew her a kiss. "Why not, they weren't mine."

"Exactly, you idiot. They weren't *yours*."

Cindy just shrugged and grinned happily, crushing a few more biscuits beneath the toe of her shoe.

"What are you waiting for, little girl? I said to get more!" Broc bellowed at Hadley, roughly pulling Lexi's hair again.

Lexi winced. She could feel some of her hair coming out in his hands.

"Are you enjoying this as much as I am, love?" Broc leaned in close to her and kissed the side of her face. His body pressed hard against hers. She shivered in disgust, being this close to him was making her skin crawl. She had to try to escape his clutches.

Meanwhile, Braydon had loosened his grip on Lexi's arm and was staring at Broc with a look of distaste on his face. He looked as though he badly wanted to say something, as his eyes flittered from Broc to Lexi, and back again. A frown briefly crossed his forehead before his eyes dropped and he looked at the ground instead.

At the same time, Hadley had run back into the kitchen. She looked around frantically trying to find something to help Lexi. Hadley could hear Broc laughing in the other room; his voice was loud and booming. Groaning, she shoved a dinner knife in her pocket and grabbed a couple of oranges before marching back into the lounge room. Facing Broc, Hadley threw the oranges straight at him. "Here!"

Broc didn't have time to react, and one of the oranges hit him on the side of his head, before bouncing off and rolling along the floor.

"Ooh, snap," snickered Kevin, raising his eyebrows in amusement.

Broc turned and gave Kevin a withering glare. "I can take you back to the farm anytime, farm boy." Broc pointed his finger at Kevin. "I'm sure your brother and sister would love to have you back. But right now, you need to be silent."

Kevin quickly shut up and lowered his eyes to the ground.

Lexi and Hadley looked at each other in confusion. "Did he say farm boy?" mouthed Lexi.

Hadley nodded staring at Kevin. "Why aren't you helping with the fire on your farm?" she asked narrowing her eyes.

"Because I hate the farm! I hate the animals, and I hate my family," shouted Kevin, his voice rising. "They can all burn for all I care. I wish they…" he started to say before Broc walked over to him and shoved his arm around Kevin's neck. Kevin was thrust forward, his body bent over.

"Now Kevin," said Broc in a hard voice. "I told you to be quiet. This is your last warning." Broc rubbed his knuckles back and forth on Kevin's head.

Kevin stayed silent.

Satisfied, Broc focused his attention back on Hadley.

"Now, where were we? Oh yes, the oranges" Broc stroked the side of his head with his hand. "Oh, I'm going to have to punish you for that, girly," he said nastily. His eyes narrowed into slits like a snake's ready to strike. Broc walked slowly and dramatically around the room and spotted Hadley's PSV console sitting on the floor by the television.

Hadley's eyes followed where Broc was looking. She breathed in sharply, tears welling in her eyes. The PlayStation portable had been the last present her parents had given her, and she loved playing on it. The game was one of her prized possessions. It helped her to escape from what was going on around her. Let her forget about all the bad things happening in their new world. If only for a little while.

Broc stood in front of the game and looked slyly at her. He could see that she was upset and wanted to take full advantage of her discomfort. His thick black boot prodded the console teasingly.

"This yours, huh?" He bent over and picked up the game waving it around tauntingly in the air." Looks new. Did you get it for Christmas from Santa? Did he put the flower stickers on it or did you?" He threw the game from one hand to the other, pretending to drop it before he caught it again.

Hadley looked up at him; her eyes were no longer defiant. "Please don't," she asked in a small pleading voice as she shifted her weight from one foot to the other anxiously.

Broc brought the PSV up close to his face. He pretended to examine the game with interest, taking his time as if it were the most fascinating thing in the world.

Lexi knew what the game meant to Hadley, and she tried to speak up for her sister. "Hey, listen, why don't you just take the food and ..."

"YOU KEEP OUT OF THIS!" bellowed Broc turning to glare at Lexi. He waved the console at her and lowered his voice. "This is between her and .me." He pointed at Hadley, who was shuffling her feet nervously.

"But don't worry, I haven't forgotten about you, love. I'll be right back to you as soon as I've dealt with this." Broc winked and smiled smugly at Lexi.

Hadley was wringing her hands, looking from Broc to her game console. Broc laughed meanly. "So, your mummy and daddy bought this for you, 'cause you were a good little girl, huh?" Broc held out the game to Hadley offering it to her. He had a big happy smile on his face.

Hadley looked at Broc and cautiously took a step forward, her hand reaching out to take the game from his outstretched hand. *Was he trying to trick her?* She looked up at his face. He was smiling kindly, and he nodded his head gently at her as if encouraging her. She took another step forward, closer to him, closer to her game. She held her breath. She could hear him talking to her.

"Bet you like playing lots of games on it, huh?"

Hadley nodded her head. One more step and she would be able to reach the game. She stretched out her arm, not wanting to be any closer to Broc than she had to be. Her finger-tips brushed on the edge of the black plastic, and she smiled up at Broc in relief as her fingers encircled the game. Within a micro-second, Hadley saw Broc's features change. Just as her fingers were closing around the console, his smile dropped, and he ripped the game from her grasp.

"Well, you won't be playing Angry Birds on it after I do this!" Broc yelled, smashing the PSV brutally hard against the wall. Hadley's treasured game broke into pieces, its damaged parts falling onto the floor. Bits of black plastic, some with butterfly stickers on them, lay in a pile. Broc kicked the mess with his thick black boots, sending the pieces flying.

Hadley let out a moan of anguish, dropped to her knees and started to cry. The pieces of the game lay smashed and scattered across the floor like the Titanic on the sea bed. Never to be resurrected. Her face crumpled in a wave of misery and tears began to run down her face in a torrent as she stared hopelessly at her shattered possession.

Broc looked at Hadley crumbled on the ground and snorted. He sauntered back over to Lexi, who was still being held by Braydon.

"You conceited bastard." Lexi struggled in Braydon's arms, glaring at Broc. She wanted to slap him across his smug face. Broc just laughed and grabbed her roughly by the hair again as she tried to twist away.

"You do have lovely long hair, don't you?" he said, his eyes lighting up gleefully as he wrapped her hair around his fist. "It's a lovely colour."

"Shall I find some scissors?" Crowed Cindy, her eyes were full of mischief. I think we should give all of the girls in this town crew cuts!" Debbie and Broc both laughed.

Braydon looked at the three of them laughing. He looked at Hadley, who was now holding onto several of her broken game pieces, still crying sadly. He looked at Lexi, who was glaring at Broc with her eyes full of fire. His face fell.

"Hey, listen. Why don't we just take the food and leave?" suggested Braydon, who was now only holding Lexi loosely in his arms. "I'm getting hungry."

Broc glared at him, poking a thick finger into Braydon's arm. "I'll tell you when we can leave, not you. I haven't finished having fun yet so just shut up and hold her." Braydon didn't say anything as he watched Broc reach into his jeans pocket to get out his pocket knife.

Braydon looked at Lexi and loosened his grip on her even more, barely holding onto her at all now. His face had a distinct look of distaste on it, as though he wasn't enjoying Broc's antics at all. "This isn't right," he whispered to himself, shaking his head.

When Lexi felt Braydon's grip on her arms loosen, she quickly took her opportunity. She managed to pull one arm free from his grasp and at the same time stamp down hard on Braydon's foot. He yelped in surprise, letting go of her completely. With her arms now totally free, Lexi swung her fist with full force right into Broc's groin.

Broc let out a high-pitched squeal and sunk to his knees in pain. Not stopping there, Lexi ran into the laundry and grabbed her father's wooden baseball bat, thanking God that she'd brought it out of the car earlier that day. She thought about the guy stealing her dad's car a few days ago and how she had stood by and let him take it. Lexi wasn't going to let that happen again. *No way. No one was taking any of their stuff again. Not without a fight!*

"Get out of our house right now!" Lexi screamed as she marched back into the front room; her eyes ablaze with fury.

Cindy snickered and laughed at her. "You can't tell us what to do!" She pointed her finger at Lexi threateningly and tried to look intimidating.

Lexi glared back at her. "I mean it." She raised the bat above her head and straightened her shoulders. It was time to take control.

Cindy just rolled her eyes and sauntered towards Lexi, trying to grab the bat from her. "I said, you can't tell us what to do, bitch," yelled Cindy in a whiney voice. She was apparently used to getting her own way.

"Oh, yeah? Just watch me, bitch!" Lexi yelled back as she swung the bat hard, smashing it straight into Cindy's thigh.

Lexi heard a crunch as the bone gave way. She didn't care; she'd had enough of these bullies and wanted them out of the house.

Cindy screamed in pain. "Aaaa! Are you crazy? Aaaa! You've broken my leg!" She clutched at her thigh with her hands. "Broc, help me," she whimpered, looking in his direction.

Broc couldn't care less about what was happening to Cindy. He was still moaning on the ground with his hands between his thighs. One thing was for sure; he wasn't going anywhere near that baseball bat. He was in enough pain already.

"Come on you lot, time to make our departure." Braydon helped Cindy up off the floor before shoving her out the front door. "It's time to leave."

"Aaah! Be careful, you idiot. I'm injured you know!" Cindy complained loudly, her voice demanding. Debbie ran to help her, dropping most of the food she had collected on the way. Kevin and Aaron were already out on the street. They'd run out of the house as soon as things looked as though they weren't going their way.

Broc gingerly pulled himself up and looked at Braydon. "What the hell is wrong with all the girls in this town!" He limped towards the front door clutching his groin. Before he left, he turned around and glared back at Lexi with piercing eyes full of hate and disdain. "Don't think I won't be back, bitch," he muttered nastily.

Lexi watched Broc limp away. She had a terrible feeling that he would definitely be back to seek his revenge. She'd seen the look in his eyes. It was the mean look of someone who was used to getting what he wanted and didn't care who he hurt to get it. A single bead of nervous sweat rolled down the side of her cheek. Irritated, she wiped it away with the back of her hand. She couldn't afford to lose her courage now. Not until they were all out of the house.

Braydon smiled and walked over to where Lexi stood. He didn't seem at all worried about the threat of the bat she still held firmly in her hands. Bending over, he gathered up some of the trampled food from the floor and carefully placed it on the coffee table next to her. "Sorry," he mumbled sheepishly unable to look her in the eye.

Braydon lingered for a moment looking like he wanted to say something more, before he too retreated out the front door, closing it behind him as he left.

"What was that?" Hadley asked, nodding toward Braydon her eyebrows raised questioningly.

"No idea," responded Lexi with a shrug. She suddenly felt exhausted, now the adrenaline of the moment had passed. Lexi dropped the baseball bat on the floor. Her hands were shaking.

Hadley walked over and picked up the remnants of her PSV. "Bloody shitty bastards," she said angrily, tears once again welling up in her eyes. Lexi glanced at her in surprise. It was the first time she had ever heard her sister swear. Ever. She guessed it was bound to happen. They were all changing and adapting to this new harsh world. One thing was for certain. If the events of this evening were anything to go by, they were going to have to get a lot tougher if they wanted to survive.

There were plenty of kids out there like Broc who would hurt you or take your stuff if they could, just for the hell of it. Without any adults around to control them, it was only going to get worse. They were going to have to learn to protect themselves and their property. And if they couldn't be strong on their own, then they would have to be strong with others.

Lexi quickly locked the front door. She turned and rested her back against it, before slowly sliding her butt to the floor. She blew out a long sigh of relief. "Jeezus, that was intense. Let's hope we don't see them again too soon." She frowned looking at all the food crushed and smeared into the carpet. "What a bunch of asses."

Hadley came and sat down beside her; she still had the pieces of her PSV in her hands. "I'm sorry I gave them our food. I didn't know what to do. She looked agitated.

Lexi put her arm around her sister's shoulders, "Hey, don't worry about it, Hadley. It was bloody scary. I didn't know what to do, either. I was just running off instinct."

"Well, you looked scary with that bat."

"Yeah, well, I think I peed my pants a little!" She joked trying to lighten the tension.

"Do you think they'll come back?"

Lexi shook her head "I don't think so. I think we were too much trouble for them. They'll go somewhere else for their fun." She didn't want to tell Hadley what she really thought. Hadley had been scared enough already. Lexi didn't want her little sister fretting about Broc sneaking back into the house. She didn't know what that guy Braydon's story was. His smiling at her had been strange, but the ring leader Broc and those two girls were definitely trouble. They were the sort of kids who liked to create trouble, especially if there was an audience. Seeing the look in Broc's eyes as he limped out the door gave her the feeling that he wasn't going to let her get away with hitting him. Not in front of his gang. He would seek his revenge somehow. Hadley didn't need to know that though.

"I'm sorry that idiot broke your PlayStation. What a dick. Maybe Jason can have a look at it. He said he's good with electronics." She hugged her sister.

Hadley gave a half-hearted smile. "Hmm maybe." She looked at the shattered pieces of the game console in her hands. She didn't think anyone would be able to fix something so badly damaged. Broc had really destroyed it. "At least neither of us were hurt. It could have been a lot worse." Hadley placed the console pieces back on the ground.

"Come on." Lexi stood and offered her hand to Hadley, pulling her to her feet. "Let's bring Polo inside." Their little protector was barking frantically outside in the garden. "He can warn us if they do come back. Let's break out that last block of chocolate it's hidden in the cupboard behind the cups." They'd been hiding it from Jason, who tended to scoff anything sweet. "I know we were saving it, but I could really do with some comfort food." Lexi looked at her sister hopefully.

"Hell, yes," Hadley agreed, nodding her head vigorously. "Me too."

CHAPTER TWENTY-ONE

Early the next morning, just as the sun was peeking over the horizon, Jason staggered back to the house he was sharing with the girls. His hair, face and clothes were all matted with sweat and ash. He stank intensely of body odour.

Lexi was waiting for him in the front living room. She was perched on the end of the sofa with her knees hugged tight to her chest. Her face held a worried expression, and she looked tired. Polo slept soundly next to her on the sofa, pricking up his ears and giving a low growl when Jason walked in. Lexi rubbed his head gratefully. "Good boy. It's only Jason," she said encouragingly before looking up questioningly at Jason. "How did it go?'

"We finally got it out. We couldn't save the barn though, and half of their wheat crop is gone."

"Are the kids all okay?" Asked Lexi, rubbing her bloodshot eyes with the palms of her hands. She had stayed up all night on watch, just in case, the gang of bullies decided to pay them another visit.

"Yeah. Just tired and dirty like me. They can't find their brother, Kevin, though. Really strange. They said he was there with them earlier. What happened to you by the way? I thought you were coming to help with the fire?" Jason said accusingly, tilting his head slightly to the side and raising his eyebrows at Lexi.

"Yes, I know we were," she said leaning forward. "Something happened here that delayed us. We had a visit from the gang Elisha told us about, and it wasn't fun." Lexi informed Jason of the drama of the night before. He sat quietly listening to her story, his mouth hanging open in disbelief. When she had finished, he got up and started pacing up and down furiously with his hands clenched in tight, angry fists by his side.

Lexi looked at him pacing up and down and thought he was angry at her for not helping him at the farm. She tried to explain her feelings. "I know I said I'd go and help with the fire, but Hadley was terrified last night, and I didn't want to leave her here on her own. I must admit I was pretty shaken up too." She pointed to the front yard. "I didn't want to step out of the house, either, in case they were waiting out there."

Jason stopped his pacing and looked up at Lexi's troubled face. "I'm not angry at you, Lexi! You had every reason not to want to leave the house. I'm just angry about Broc and that lot. What a bunch of dicks." Jason punched his fist into the palm of his hand. "Something's got to be done about them. They were the ones who started the fire at the farm too, you know?"

"What!? I thought that was an accident!?" Her brow furrowed in concern.

Jason shook his head sadly and recounted the whole story as Lilly and Zac had told it to him.

Lexi pushed herself up from the sofa. "Right. Well, you go and have a shower," she suggested, waving her hand in front of her nose. "No offence, but you kind of stink."

Jason laughed.

"While you're doing that, I'll wake up Hadley, and we should all go and talk to Elisha. She's in charge, and I don't think we should do anything without talking to her first. I don't want to give her any excuses for kicking us out of town. But you're right. Something has got to be done about that gang and soon before they cause any more trouble."

Jason nodded in agreement and went off to take a much-needed shower.

On the way to Elisha and Ethan's house, the trio came across what looked like half of the town's kids milling around the town square. Some were crying and looking scared. Most of them look furious. They were leaning in every direction trying to get a better view, peering at something going on in the centre of the square. As Lexi, Jason and Hadley got closer, they could see what the others were all looking at. In the middle of the square, there was a bronze statue of a man on horseback commemorating soldiers from World War Two. Tied to that statue with his arms stretched painfully wide and secured by rope, was Kevin. The missing boy from the farm. Lexi gasped in recognition. He was definitely the same boy who was with the gang the night before. It looked like Broc hadn't taken too kindly to Kevin laughing at him.

"Maybe this will teach you to obey orders, boy," sneered Broc as he threw an empty soft drink can at Kevin. Broc's face held a wolfish grin as he stood with his arms folded across his chest, staring at Kevin.

Aaron, Cindy and Debbie all followed Broc's example and began throwing old food, empty cans and bottles at the unfortunate Kevin. Broc laughed, rubbing his hands together.

Lexi watched as Kevin ducked his head to the left and right trying not to get hit in the face by the onslaught of missiles. Tears were streaming down his face, and he looked miserable. There was a big wet patch at the front of his pants, and Lexi wondered how long he'd been tied up. She noticed that

Braydon wasn't participating in the gruesome little show and was instead standing off to one side. He had his hands in his pockets and was looking from Kevin to Broc uncertainly. He didn't look like he was enjoying the proceedings at all. Lexi also noticed, with some feeling of satisfaction, that Cindy had a large white bandage strapped to her leg and was walking with a limp. *Maybe she'll think twice before threatening me again.*

Pushing themselves to the front of the crowd, Lexi and Jason were just about to step forward to say something when Braydon suddenly emerged through the cluster of children. He walked straight up to Broc, stood in front of him. You need to stop this," he said loudly and firmly.

Everyone fell silent.

Broc leaned his face forward, right up close to Braydon's. "Get out of my way, idiot!" He yelled through gritted teeth as he pushed Braydon backwards with two hands on his chest. Braydon stumbled back, kicking up a flurry of dust with his shoes before losing his balance and falling hard on his butt. Cindy and Debbie snickered behind their hands

Braydon quickly regained his footing. He dusted off his pants, wiped his hands together, and once again walked forward to face Broc. "I said, that's enough, Broc," he said in a calm voice. "I think he's had enough."

Broc stopped and looked at Braydon in astonishment. "How dare you tell me what to do!" He bellowed ramming his forearm into Braydon's chest. Braydon again staggered back. This time, however, he grabbed onto Broc as he fell, sending both of them crumbling to the ground like two stone statues toppling over. They hit the hard pavement stone with a loud thud that sounded like it hurt. Immediately the two boys started rolling back and forth in the dust grabbing and hitting each other.

The crowd remained still and silent, watching the two older boys fighting, wondering what was going to happen next.

Someone from the crowd yelled out with feeling. "You don't belong here! You should take your fight somewhere else." There was a lot of muttering and murmuring of agreement. No one wanted the gang here; they were troublemakers. Neither Broc nor Braydon looked as though they cared one bit what the crowd thought at that moment. Both boys seemed totally focused on each other.

The crowd of onlookers continued to watch.

Braydon was the older and taller of the two boys; however, Broc was the stronger of the two. It didn't take long for him to gain the upper hand and he soon had Braydon in a tight headlock, and no matter how hard Braydon struggled, he couldn't break free.

Lexi watched as bright red blood dripped down onto the soil from a cut above Braydon's left eye, like a tap that had been left on. Drip. Drip. Drip. His shirt was ripped at the shoulder, and his other eye was already swelling shut. He looked like he'd been in a world title boxing match and lost. Broc, Lexi noticed to her dismay, hardly had a scratch on him. His shirt, like Braydon's, was torn and his lip was cut, otherwise; he seemed utterly unscathed.

Braydon continued to struggle vainly as Broc held him down. "See what happens when people get in my way," sneered Broc through gritted teeth. Broc glared at the crowd, his mouth pulling back in a nasty smirk.

As Braydon stopped struggling, Broc let go and slowly stood. He took his time, watching the crowd, turning around in a circle his arms spread wide making sure he had an audience. "Do I have your attention," he yelled pointing his finger at a younger group of children. Then, leaning over the prostrate Braydon, who hadn't moved an inch, Broc swung his leg back and kicked Braydon hard in the stomach with his black thick-soled boots. "How's that feel, traitor?"

As Broc's hard shoe impacted with Braydon's stomach, the air whooshed out of him like a deflated balloon. He curled up into a ball looking miserable, his face lying in the dirt.

The young children watching gasped and clung on to each other. People hissed and whispered to each other; however, no one turned away or left the square. It was if they were drawn to the horror of the spectacle.

Cindy was looking at Broc admiringly. The look of infatuation on her face was plain for all to see. She sauntered over to him swinging her hips provocatively. Unfortunately for her, she didn't look terribly sexy as she limped along. Cindy spoilt her act even further by tripping on her high-heeled shoes. Her right ankle twisted painfully to the side as her heel caught in the gravel. Dramatically waving her arms to regain her balance, Cindy just managed to save herself from falling face-down in the dirt. Regaining her composure, she continued her journey towards Broc and quickly planted a kiss on his lips. He looked highly amused.

Not to be outdone, Debbie hurried over to join them, her big hoop earrings swinging against her cheeks as she walked. Standing in front of Broc, she cocked one of her legs up behind her at the knee like they did in old movies and planted a kiss firmly on Broc's lips, just as Cindy had done. Then, for that extra effect, she leaned over towards Braydon, who had just sat up, and slapped him hard across the cheek.

"That's for being disrespectful, Braydon," Debbie said in a whiny voice. She grinned slyly at Cindy, who glared back at Debbie with her lips pursed angrily.

"You can be so annoying sometimes, Debbie," Cindy remarked, rolling her eyes and flicking her hair over her shoulder.

Broc swaggered back towards Braydon and knocked him back over pushing his face in the dirt with his boot. "I didn't say you could get up," he sneered meanly, his voice flat and hard.

Braydon didn't react; he just lay still. Pieces of rock and sand were stuck to the blood on his cheek like sandpaper, digging into his skin and his right eye had turned purple. He closed his eyes as though he wished he were somewhere else.

"Now, where were we before I was so rudely interrupted?" asked Broc as he picked up another rusty can from the pile the gang had accumulated. He looked at Braydon for a moment, raising his right eyebrow. "Got anything you want to say, Braydon?"

Braydon didn't, so Broc took aim and threw the can at Kevin, who was still tied to the statue. Kevin just managed to duck his head to one side at the last moment, and the can sailed past him barely missing his ear.

Broc laughed. "Ha-ha, this boy's got good reflexes! Let's see how he goes with this." He picked up a rotten tomato, squeezing the flesh between his fingers.

"Don't you bloody throw that!" yelled a female's voice shrill and loud from amongst the silent crowd. Everyone turned in surprise to see who had spoken.

"Oh, what now," groaned Broc, not happy with another disruption to his fun. He reluctantly turned around to see what was going on. Elisha had stepped forward, Ethan, Zac and Lilly were right behind her. Lexi, Hadley and Jason saw them and quickly walked over to join the group.

Broc started laughing again. "God. Not another crazy female. Plus, you've got *Angry Birds girl* and the *extremely* attractive farm girl with you. I *am* honoured." He smirked and raised the tomato in the air, showing it to the crowd, wiggling it around teasingly. Broc began strutting around in front of everyone like the ring leader at a circus, putting on a show.

While Broc's back was turned and he was focused elsewhere, Lilly and Lexi decided to take their chance and sneak back through the crowd toward Kevin. They were planning on trying to get Kevin down from the statue before Broc could stop them. The girls had to duck as they ran as Cindy and Debbie had started throwing rotten food again. They had almost reached Kevin and the statue when Elisha let out a bellowing scream of rage. She had spotted Cindy and Debbie throwing the food.

"Aaaargh! Didn't you hear me? I said no more throwing!" Elisha yelled in a fury, her eyes wide crazy circles and her top lip turned up in a snarl. Turning around slowly in a circle, she glared at everyone, both town kids and gang kids.

People stared back at her in horror, not sure what was going on. As Elisha twisted around, she started emitting a kind of snarling sound from deep inside her body. It was almost animalistic. She was practically foaming at the mouth. One of the younger kids started to cry hysterically in fear and had to be led away from the crowd by an older child.

Ethan looked over at his sister in alarm. "Elisha?" He took a step towards her cautiously, the gravel crunching unevenly beneath his feet. Elisha turned to face him. Her eyes bulged. There were deep creases in her forehead as she frowned, and her teeth were bared in an unnatural grimace. Ethan quickly stepped back away from her, feeling alarmed. A hush had fallen over the group. Everyone was watching Elisha closely, confusion all over their faces. This wasn't the Elisha they all knew. What was happening?

Even Lilly and Lexi, who were untying Kevin from the statue, had stopped what they were doing and were standing there, staring at her. The ropes hung limply from their hands. Unfortunately for her, Debbie did not sense the confusion and alarm that was spreading through the crowd around her. She bent down to pick up a particularly squashy piece of fruit. The sticky juice was dripping between her fingers and running down her forearm. Laughing in glee, she held the rotten purple plum high above her head momentarily before throwing it towards Kevin, who was scampering down from the statue like a rabbit escaping a trap.

The rotten plum sailed through the air like a fly ball in a baseball game heading straight towards its target. Somehow the rotten fruit missed the escaping Kevin and instead hit Lilly square in the face. The fruit pulp matted in her now short hair and the juice ran down her face in clumpy purple streaks. Debbie let out a huge bellowing laugh that sounded like a donkey braying. She jumped up and down on the spot clapping her hands in glee. "Haw, did you see that! Haw."

Just at that moment, everything suddenly seemed to speed up like a movie on fast forward. Elisha let out a blood-curdling scream. Her red lips stretched open in a wide O shape. She hurdled straight over Braydon, who was still lying sprawled in the dust and ran straight for Debbie. Debbie had no idea what was about to happen. She was still standing there, laughing and pointing happily at the juice running down Lilly's face. Elisha, on the other hand, knew exactly what was about to happen. She aimed herself directly at Debbie like a juggernaut on full speed. Smashing into her with the full force of her rather plump body. The impact was sudden and violent. A loud crunching sound could be heard as bone splintered and shattered, followed by a deathly silence as the crowd turned from watching Broc, to watching Elisha and what she had done.

"What the hell's going on?" called someone from the crowd as they all looked on in horror and astonishment. No one quite knew what was happening. That was until someone spotted the bright red pool of blood forming in a puddle under Debbie, as she lay motionless on the ground. In a matter of moments, panic set in. Kids started screaming and running from the scene, shock and terror on their faces. They ran in all directions, banging into each other like balls ricocheting around in a pinball machine, as they fled.

Debbie lay on the ground, clutching her stomach with her hands and moaning loudly. Cindy hovered above her, watching her friend in disbelief. When she saw the blood oozing out between Debbie's fingers, Cindy let out a terrified scream. She tried to pull Debbie to her feet, away from Elisha, who was standing next to the girls with a large kitchen knife in her hand, smiling triumphantly.

"I said, no one throws anything!" Elisha nodded her head up and down as if agreeing with herself. Her eyes widened, as she looked around, glaring at anyone who hadn't fled the scene, daring them to disagree with her.

Broc and Aaron weren't disagreeing. They took one look at Elisha and her knife, turned and fled.

"Hey, don't leave us here!" Cindy wailed at them, as she tried to drag Debbie behind her. She was quite a bit smaller than Debbie and was having trouble lifting her by herself. Eventually, Debbie managed to struggle to her feet on her own. She clutched frantically at her stomach, which was still bleeding profusely. The two girls stumbled awkwardly after the boys.

Braydon, who had been watching the whole incident from his position on the ground, remained where he was and watched them all leave. He wasn't sure whether he should run after them or stay. His eyes followed Broc as he ran down the street that led out of town. No one called for him to come or even looked back once to see if he was following. He stood slowly, like an old man. His body was covered in bruises. Braydon glanced towards Lexi as she stood with Hadley and eyes dropped to the floor. His face and neck flushed a deep pink colour.

Braydon looked back at the gang. They'd now reached Broc's stolen car, which they'd parked at the end of the street and were driving away, screeching the tyres as they went. No one looked or waited for him. They obviously didn't care if he was there or not. Braydon picked the pieces of dirt from his cheek and flung them to the ground.

"Screw you Broc and screw the rest of you!" Braydon yelled at the retreating car, waving his clenched fist in the air.

"You were only using me anyway, I'm better off without you," he murmured quietly to himself, his voice now controlled. "If Broc thinks I'm going to come crawling back after him, he can go and take a flying leap." Braydon glanced once again at Lexi, his eyes lingering for a moment. He smoothed down his crumpled t-shirt and brushed the dust from his dirty pants. "This town looks pretty good anyway. I can always stay and help them."

Meanwhile, Ethan was staring at his sister and her blood-stained knife, feeling mortified. He looked at the drops of blood falling on the ground, making a little puddle as they clumped together. He felt his stomach do a flip as if he was on a rollercoaster ride at a fair. Turning away from her, he bent over and threw up all over the ground.

"Bloody hell, what's happened to your sister?" yelled Zac in confusion. He raced over to join Ethan.

Standing, Ethan wiped his mouth with the back of his sleeve. He looked at Zac dolefully. "I think we've got a problem," his voice was barely a whisper.

"No shit!"

"No, I think we've got a problem with Elisha," repeated Ethan.

Zac nodded. "Ah, yeah. No shit."

"Listen," said Ethan quietly still feeling nauseous. "Help me get her home, and I'll tell you all about it."

Zac frowned and looked at his dirty fingernails. "Err, she's not going to stab us, is she? That's a huge knife she's got there. I mean, I want to help, but I'm not too keen on getting stabbed. I've already had a bloody rough time lately!" Zac rubbed his bruised jaw where Broc had hit him yesterday.

Ethan looked at his friend and nodded. "I don't want to get cut either! Look, let's just try and talk to her." They both looked tentatively at Elisha who was standing slightly hunched over, staring at them with an expressionless look on her face.

Her eyes looked large and unnatural as if the pupils were oversized.

Zac and Ethan took a few hesitant steps towards her. Lilly, Jason and Lexi came rushing over to join them. "What's going on?" Lilly asked in a whisper. "What the bloody hell is wrong with Elisha?"

Ethan turned to them and quickly waved them away. His arms up in front of him as he motioned for them to be quiet. "Too many people around might make her upset again," he cautioned.

So, they all held back waiting to see what would happen. Everyone was feeling anxious and uncomfortable.

Elisha ignored them. She swivelled around and looked over at Braydon who was once again sitting on the ground. He had his head down looking at his feet as if he was contemplating life. Slowly drawing circles in the dust with his finger.

Ethan quickly spoke up. He didn't want any more bloodshed. He knew that Elisha would regret it later when she was more herself.

"Umm. Hi, Elisha, how you?" He slowly and cautiously edged towards her, his face a little green as if he were going to heave again. The noise of his feet crunching on the gravel was loud and obvious in the stillness around them. He held his hands out in front of him in a peaceful gesture.

Elisha stopped staring at Braydon and slowly turned around to look at her brother. She had stopped making the weird snarling noises she'd been making earlier and was now standing completely silent. Staring. Her eyes had a wild, crazy look about them and she was tapping the knife against her thigh.

Ethan turned slightly and glanced back at Zac, who just shrugged. "What's she doing?"

Ethan cleared his throat and tried talking to her again. "Err, Elisha. It's Ethan. You know, your brother?" Maybe she didn't recognise him.

Elisha gave no visible response. She just continued to stare straight at Ethan, her eyes boring into his skin.

Ethan jiggled his right leg nervously and looked around the square. All the younger kids had run back to their homes. The only people left were Lilly, Zac, Lexi, Hadley, Jason and Braydon. They were all watching him.

Ethan turned back to Elisha.

Elisha was still eyeballing Ethan silently. Not a word passed her lips as she glared at him, her eyes hard.

Ethan's hands started to shake as he looked at the bloody knife dangling from her fingers. He took a deep breath to settle himself and tried to talk to her again. "Listen, Elisha. I know something is wrong. This is not like you. I just want to help you. Elisha, you should drop that knife. You're getting blood all over your white shoes." Ethan pointed at the knife Elisha was holding. Droplets of Debbie's blood were still dripping from the end and splashing on her shoes like a modern art painting.

Elisha finally lowered her eyes and looked down at the bloody knife hanging limply from her hand. Drops of blood clung to its blade. She seemed disgusted by it and roughly flung away in distaste. The knife sailed through the air barely missing Braydon, who hadn't moved from his position and was calmly watching what was going on. As the blade flew past his head, he flinched and ducked in alarm. One of his eyes was now completely swollen shut and starting to bruise a deep purple colour. A patch of congealed blood had begun to form over a cut on his other eye. Elisha completely ignored him and looked back at Ethan with her wild, scary eyes.

Ethan smiled at her trying to remain calm. "That's better, Elisha." He started to move towards her with his hand outstretched. "Want to come… oooof."

Elisha had swiftly moved forward towards him and punched her brother roughly in the stomach. Ethan immediately felt the air rush out of him, and he bent over double, winded and gasping for breath. Zac, who had been standing behind him, stepped forward to help. Elisha glared threateningly at him. She swiftly side-stepped her brother so that she could get closer to Zac, clenched her bloody hand back into a fist and punched him hard in the face.

Zac recoiled away from her, clutching his nose in pain. "Owww… what the hell, Elisha!"

Lilly, Jason and Lexi who were all standing watching with their mouths open in disbelief, heard an audible crack as the punch broke Zac's nose. Blood immediately started streaming from his nose and running down his shirt leaving a large red stain.

"Elisha!" yelled Lilly, running to help her brother. "Are you insane. What are you doing?!"

Hearing the voice, Elisha quickly turned towards Lilly, who abruptly skidded to a stop. Her feet kicking up dust around her.

Elisha glared at Lilly menacingly for a moment as if calculating the threat then suddenly, turned and took off running down the road that led back to her house. Lexi and Jason looked at each other, unsure of whether they should chase her or not. They decided not.

Braydon sprang into action. He jumped up from where he was sitting and to everyone's surprise rushed over to help Zac. "Here, hold this on your nose. Sounded like she broke it," he said, offering Zac a dirty rag from his pocket.

Zac looked at Braydon and the rag in distaste. Was this guy for real? One minute he's roughing people up and the next offering to help. "Er, I'm right, thanks." He sounded as though he had a severe cold, as his nose started to swell. "I don't need *your* help."

Braydon dropped his arm and glanced at Lexi hopefully. She gave him a dirty look, and he quickly backed away, wandering over to sit of the base of the horse statue by himself. He looked down at his feet.

"Here, let's have a look. I might be able to help." Lexi turned to see the two boys come running up with a half clean towel and a tray of ice cubes. "Put this on your nose," offered the shorter dark-haired boy, holding out the ice. "It will help stop the swelling and bleeding."

"Wow," remarked Jason smiling. "You're prepared."

Logan laughed, his eyes crinkling attractively. He held out his hand. "I'm Logan. My house is not far away," he said pointing down the street. "My dad was the vet in the area, so I'm used to seeing injuries."

"Well, at least I know who to come to if I need looking after," whispered Jason winking at Logan.

Logan blushed.

"Um, my nose!" said Zac who was leaning back with his fingers pinching the top of his nose.

"Right, sorry," laughed Logan, glancing once again at Jason. "Here, let's get this ice on. It might stop the bleeding."

Lilly helped Logan place the ice in the towel. "I think you can stop being the punching bag for a few days Zac," she grinned giving him the towel. "Unless it's for me," she punched him lightly on the arm.

"Hmm, let's just hope Elisha calms down, and Broc doesn't come back anytime soon," moaned Zac. "I don't think my poor body can take it.

Logan looked at Zac holding the ice pack to his nose. "I think your nose is probably broken. We can't do much for you except try and stop the blood flow," he said looking at the blood seeping into the white towel. "I can try and find you some pain killers, but your nose is going to have to stay broken."

"What the hell is wrong with your sister?" Zac asked Ethan as he leaned forward and removed the towel. The bleeding had now stopped, and dark black bruises were forming around his eyes and nose. "I've never seen her go all psycho like that before!" His broken nose made his voice sound strange, as though he had a bad cold.

"No," said Ethan looking completely bewildered and embarrassed. "Neither have I." Ethan glanced nervously at Lexi and Jason, then to Zac and Lilly. "Listen, guys. I need to talk to you. Can you come over to my house?" He looked like he was on the verge of crying.

"Of course, man, no problem," said Jason. He rubbed his left eyebrow with his index finger. "Umm. Your sister's not going to be there, is she?"

Ethan glanced at Jason uncertainly. "Err, yes, good point. Maybe we'd better meet at your place. You guys come, too." Ethan gestured to Harry and Logan who had hung around to make sure Zac was alright.

Ethan looked over at Braydon, who was standing off to one side. "And what's your story. Why didn't you scamper away with your friends?"

Braydon walked a little closer to the group, looking unsure of himself. "Oh, well. To be honest, they weren't really my friends. I'd rather stay and help you guys than be part of that gang anymore."

Ethan cocked his head to the side slightly and considered Braydon for a moment. "Well, I guess you can come," Ethan said reluctantly. "I suppose you did try to stop Broc."

Ethan looked at Lexi and partially covered his mouth with his hand. "I guess he could tell us some insider info on the gang," he whispered, shrugging.

Lexi nodded slightly. She wasn't sure whether Braydon was telling the truth about wanting to leave the gang or not. Tilting her head to the side, she peered at Braydon trying to read his expression; however, he was looking intently towards Zac.

Zac was staring back at Braydon, his eyes distrustful and his body rigid. After a few moments, Braydon dropped his eyes to the floor. Zac scratched his chin. "Oh, whatever, man. You didn't actually hit Lilly or me *personally*, I guess."

Braydon looked embarrassed and glanced sideways at Lexi. His face was a mixture of blue, purple and red and looked like a bad abstract oil painting.

Zac chuckled, the tension leaving his body. "Anyway, your face looks as bad as mine, and I don't think your leader Broc, is very happy with you."

Braydon shook his head. "He's not my leader. He's my cousin."

Zac raised one eyebrow. "Ouch, that sucks."

Braydon approached Zac, wanting to make peace. He held out his hand. "Listen, mate. I'm really sorry about your farm and everything. Broc definitely took things too far."

Zac looked at Braydon's hand for a moment without saying a word. He nodded slightly.

Braydon dropped his hand and glanced towards Lilly, who was watching him uneasily. Her arms were folded tightly across her chest, and her lips were pursed tightly shut. She was scowling at Braydon, with a look of distaste written all over her face. She rubbed her hand across her shaven head and turned her back to Braydon before he could speak to her.

"I'm sorry about what happened at your house too," Braydon tried to apologise to Lexi. He gave her a sad smile. "Broc was way out of order. I hope your little sister's okay?"

Lexi didn't say anything. She watched Braydon hesitantly for a few moments, then nodded her head slightly. She didn't forgive him yet, but she acknowledged his apology.

"Let's go back to our house then," suggested Lexi facing the main road. "Better keep an eye out for Elisha on the way."

Lexi turned her head towards Ethan and gave him a small smile. She knew he must be in shock having seen his sister react so violently. Lexi wondered what he wanted to tell them all.

As the group moved off towards Rosewood Avenue, Lexi noticed Braydon wasn't following them. "Go," she called to Hadley. "I'll catch you up in a minute."

"You sure?" asked Hadley in concern.

Lexi waved her on before turning to Braydon. "So, Broc is your cousin?"

Braydon nodded. "Yes. He's my cousin on my dad's side. You can't choose your family, huh?" he gave Lexi a small smile and pulled at a thin leather cord he had wrapped around his wrist. "Broc didn't use to be this bad. He just liked messing around and stuff." Braydon's shoulders slumped. "I think he's really enjoying not having any adults around though, because there's nobody to stop him doing whatever he likes now." Braydon shooed away a fly that was trying to crawl on his swollen eye. "Actually, he's become a right bastard. I think he enjoys inflicting pain and misery on people and that's not how I want to be." He looked down at the ground.

Lexi reached out her hand to comfort him, before quickly pulling away. She put her hand in her pocket instead.

Braydon looked back up, his blue eyes meeting Lexi's green ones. He held her gaze for a moment. "Anyway, it was time we parted ways. I know he's not going to be pleased with me, but I was getting sick of being bossed around by him. I don't want to spend my days causing trouble."

Lexi looked at him for a few moments as if trying to judge whether he was telling the truth or just messing with her. After a while, her face softened. She felt a little sorry for him; he looked genuinely remorseful. "Well, come on then," she said. "You can't just stand here all day. You'd better come with us. Maybe you can repair some of the damage your gang has caused. I want to see what Ethan's going to tell us all. I can bet by the look on his face; it's got something to do with Elisha's little outburst."

Braydon just stood there looking a little lost.

"Oh, come on." Lexi grabbed his hand in hers. It felt rough and calloused. "The house is this way. I thought you'd know the way. You were only there last night. Remember?" She looked at him meaningfully and pulled him along as she led the way back to her house. Lexi wasn't going to let him forget the damaged he had help cause in a hurry.

Braydon nodded and trudged sheepishly behind her. The gang had just lost one of its members.

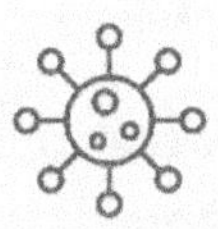

CHAPTER TWENTY-TWO

Jason opened the front door, and everyone piled inside eager to hear what Ethan had to say. Before Lexi went in with the others, she quickly grabbed Braydon's arm and pulled him to one side. She wanted to say something to him privately before they went inside. Being at the house again with Braydon there reminded her of the gang's attack the night before. She remembered how upset Hadley had been, and it made her feel angry all over again.

"You know that was a pretty shitty thing you guys did at our house.!" She pointed her finger at him accusingly. "We didn't do a single thing to you guys. Heck, we'd only just moved to this town the day before." Her voice was riddled with emotion. "You didn't have to break our stuff and mess up our house!"

Braydon stepped towards her, reaching to grab her hand then thinking better of it. He ran his fingers through his curly hair instead. His voice was emotional too. "Yes, I know, and I'm really sorry. I'm not proud of what I did. I just got caught up in it all."

Lexi gave him a filthy look crossing her arms across her chest. "Caught up in all the excitement, you mean!"

Braydon looked her straight in the eye and nodded slightly. "Well, yes, I suppose so. I haven't had an exciting life, so it was kind of fun for a while. You know, racing around the place without anyone to tell you what to do. That was fun. Exploring the towns and places we stopped at. That was fun too. Then a few weeks ago, Broc started hurting people for no reason just because he could, and suddenly it wasn't so much fun anymore." Braydon pulled his shirt away from his body. His perspiration making the fabric stick to his skin.

"He always wants to hit people. I hate it. I've tried to talk to him about it, but he just grins and tells me to piss off. I know we're related, but honestly, I've got absolutely no control over him. He won't listen to a thing I say."

Braydon looked up at the house for a moment. The lights were now on, and he could hear people talking inside. He looked back at Lexi. "Anyway, after his antics at the farm last night and then here at your house. I knew it was time for me to leave. I just didn't want to be part of that crap anymore. For what it's worth, I am *honestly* really sorry."

Lexi's body relaxed a little; she uncrossed her arms and let them drop to her sides. She could see that Braydon was sorry for his part, though she couldn't help continuing to feel negative towards him. Turning her body from him, Lexi moved towards the house.

Braydon grabbed her arm and held her back. "Hey, listen. I'm really glad that Broc and Cindy didn't cut your hair. It would have been a real shame." He gave her a tentative smile.

Lexi's eyes narrowed. She wound a piece of her hair around her finger. *Was he making fun of her?*

Braydon's face remained serious. He dropped Lexi's arm and hooked his thumbs in his jean pockets. Lexi gave him a small smile before starting up the path that led to the house. "Come on, then. Let's go inside and see what Ethan's got to say." She rubbed her hands up and down her arms. "I've got a feeling it's not going to be good."

Going inside, Lexi and Braydon joined the others in the living room. Everyone had already taken all the chairs, including the kitchen ones which they'd dragged into the front room, so the two of them plonked themselves down on the floor.

Ethan stood from his chair and recounted what his friend Nick had told him yesterday about the Kv17 virus spreading to older teenagers in Albany and how it made them emit violent, unpredictable behaviour."

Lexi turned and faced Hadley. "Elisha?" she mouthed silently raising her eyebrow. Hadley's eyes flicked back to Ethan.

"Nick said it only seemed to be happening to the kids who were older than seventeen, he thinks it's some sort of mutation of the original virus," Ethan relayed scratching his head. He gripped the back of his chair with his hands. "Apparently, there has been more and more of the older kids showing symptoms as the weeks go on."

"What *are* the symptoms?" asked Jason who was leaning against a wall over to the side of the group.

Ethan turned to face him. "Well, Nick said it's different from the symptoms the adults showed. Some kids still have the flu-like symptoms of congestion and headaches the adult had, but they've also been showing raised red rashes on their hands and feet."

Ethan paused and turned back to face the rest of the group who were all leaning forward in their chairs listening intently. "They *all* develop the rashes. Every kid who is sick with the mutated virus has the rashes. It's a tell-tale sign they're sick."

Ethan looked at his rash free hands. He turned them back and forth. "After the rashes emerge, the infected kids start having sudden uncontrolled rages, followed by brief periods of normality."

"Does Elisha have these rashes?" asked Lexi interrupting Ethan. She looked at him steadily.

Ethan glanced at the other kids in the room. They had looks of disbelief and shock on their faces. "I don't know, look, to be honest, I haven't noticed." Ethan didn't know what else to say, his shoulders fell, and he sat back down in his chair with a heavy thump. "I don't know for sure if that's what's happened to Elisha. Or even if it's true," he said, his voice trembling with emotion. "All I know is what my friend Nick said. She *was* acting pretty weirdly, right?"

The room was silent as everyone took in the shocking news. *Had the KV17 virus really mutated? Was it now affecting older children?*

"Who is this Nick anyway?" asked Jason when no one else spoke.

"He's a friend of mine; he lives in Albany," explained Ethan lifting his bowed head. "It's a bigger town down the coast a bit, where there are a lot more people. We talk by CB radio."

"Okay. So, what else did he say?" Jason came to sit with the group.

"Not much, like I said. He just told me that Albany was having major problems with some of the older kids. They get sick and then it's as if the virus changes their personality or something. Apparently, they've had a few deaths."

"What do you mean deaths?!" asked Hadley sounding shocked. Everyone was silent waiting to hear his answer. The ominous talk of death made everyone feel anxious. They'd all lost so many people from their lives already.

Ethan looked over at Hadley, not sure what to say. "I don't know, Hadley. Nick just said deaths. I didn't ask him much about it."

Hadley didn't say anything. She just stared at him with wide eyes. After a moment she blinked, before standing and walking to the front door. She peered through the peephole and turned the lock to make sure the door was locked. Hadley stared at the door for a moment, before coming to sit at Jason's feet. He smiled kindly at her reaching down and cheekily messing up her hair with his hand. Hadley retaliated by punching Jason lightly on the leg.

"Ow, that hurt! You're such bully!" laughed Jason feigning injury.

Hadley giggled too, and for the moment the tense feeling in the room was lifted. The children began chatting amongst each other, discussing Ethan's shocking news.

Lexi got up from where she was sitting and went into the kitchen. Opening the cupboards, she briskly smeared a few crackers with Vegemite and then opened a large packet of salt and vinegar chips, emptying it into a big orange fluoro serving bowl that looked like it was left over from the eighties. She carried the food back into the lounge room, and everyone helped themselves to the salty snacks.

After a few mouthfuls, Jason soon became serious again and turned back to face Ethan. "Is your friend sure it's not just some new drug or something making the teenagers go crazy. Maybe it's some new form of Meth or something?" He scratched his head in frustration. "Man, I wish the internet was still up and running. We could Google this thing no problem."

The others nodded in agreement. It was impossible to know what was going on in the rest of the world without the television, internet or radios working. The CB radio was great; however, it wasn't any use long distance, and Australia was a long way from most other countries.

Ethan looked at Jason, his head tilted to the side. "Well, maybe, but then why is it only the older kids who are being affected? I'm sure there'd be some younger kids into the drug too. No, I reckon it's got to be the virus. Something's happened to change it."

"Yeah, that probably makes sense. Albany's a bigger town too, so there'd be more people to infect. This thing, this virus or whatever it is, has probably mutated and spread more quickly among them," agreed Zac, nodding at Ethan.

"Well, whatever it is. Elisha definitely did not look like herself. Unless she's got some strange possessed side, we don't know about. I mean, did you see her eyes! They were wild; she was really flipping out!" Lilly waved her arms around in the air dramatically as she spoke.

Ethan made a little sobbing sound in the back of his throat.

Lilly saw Ethan's face and abruptly stopped waving her arms, dropping them to her sides. "Oh God, sorry Ethan. That was heartless of me. I didn't mean to upset you." She walked over to him and put her arm around his shoulders giving him a hug.

He gave her a small smile in return. "I know. It's alright. It's just that I hated seeing her like that, you know? All wild and violent. It's so unlike her. I could hardly bear to look at her like that. Just for a moment there, I thought that she was going to stab me too." His voice trailed off, and an awkward silence filled the room. No one knew what to say. A clock on the wall ticked loudly, marking each passing second of silence. Some kids looked out the window, others studied their fingernails, and some stared at their feet. Anywhere, but having to look at Ethan who was quietly sobbing to himself. Lilly had her arm gently around him as she looked over at Zac.

Braydon stood up and cleared his throat. "Umm, I know this is a sensitive time right now." He looked around at the others as if trying to gauge their reaction. "And I know you don't trust me, but I think that you really need to come up with a plan."

The others looked at him blankly.

"Well, think about it," continued Braydon tapping his finger on the chair. "If your friend Nick is right and there is a mutation happening with this virus, then isn't it likely that more kids in Jasper's Bay are going to be infected and start changing too?"

"So?" asked Zac, his arms folded across his chest.

"So, if you don't do anything, there's going to be a whole lot of crazy seventeen-year-olds running around fighting each other. Or worse."

"Worse?"

"Yes, fighting us," added Lexi.

Braydon nodded in agreement. "And you said there'd been a few deaths."

"Shit!" Ethan ran his fingers through his hair. He got up from where he was sitting and started pacing around the room. "Maybe she'll change back?"

Braydon looked at him sceptically. "Yeah, maybe. But what if she doesn't?"

"I don't know. What am I supposed to do?" Ethan started yelling as he paced around the room in agitation. "She's my sister. I can't hurt her!"

Zac and Lilly moved towards him. "We know that, Ethan," said Lilly, trying to comfort him again. "We don't want to hurt her, either." Ethan let Lilly put her arm around his shoulder once more.

"The thing is, Ethan, we don't know what she's going to do. She seems unstable right now, and she might start hurting others. You saw what she did to that girl, Debbie." Zac put his hand on Ethan's shoulder. "There are lots of younger kids in town, and it's our job as the older ones to protect them. I don't think she can control it. What if she kills one of the young kids?"

"Oh, God!" Ethan leaned on the edge of his armchair and put his head in his hands.

Jason cleared his throat. "Why don't we exile her?" Jason said tentatively.

"What?"

"Why don't we exile Elisha and anyone else who goes feral, from the town?" suggested Jason reasonably. "Just until we know what's going on."

"But we can't. She'll be on her own!" moaned Ethan.

"I don't think she really cares about that at the moment, Ethan," said Lilly, trying to be rational. "Besides, I think the only alternative would be much worse."

Ethan looked alarmed. "What do you mean? You don't mean death?"

Jason spoke up quickly. "No. she doesn't mean that," he said glaring at Lilly. "I think we should chase Elisha. I mean, encourage her," he paused to glance at Ethan.

"We should *encourage* her to leave town for a while. At least the main part of town. We can leave some food and water for her. And if Elisha gets better, she can return." Jason looked at the others, who were all nodding in agreement all eager for a solution to the problem.

Ethan sighed, his shoulders slumping. He looked utterly dejected, staring at the patterned carpet on the floor. "All right," he said. "Fine. Let's chase her out of town. Just let me try and find her first. I want to explain what's happening to her, and I want to say goodbye."

"Sure, Ethan, just be careful," said Lexi patting him on the back. "Elisha is obviously not herself."

Ethan looked bleakly at Lexi giving her a tired, weak smile before slowly, getting up and leaving to find Elisha. "This day is going from bad to worse," Ethan muttered to himself as he left the house. "We don't even know if she has the virus and they all want to kick her out of town at the first sign of trouble. I should never have told them about the virus!" he cast his eyes back up at the house angrily.

Ethan sighed and started walking home. "I guess I can't blame them; she did stab that girl and break Zac's nose." He kicked a stone along the ground as he walked, he prayed that Elisha had just been having a bad day. A very bad day, and that he wouldn't have to ask her to leave town. Ethan shook his head, his eyes cast downwards. "This is going to be a difficult conversation," he said, turning the corner to towards his house.

After Ethan left, the other teenagers gathered around to discuss tactics. Lexi rested her hand lightly on Jason's shoulder. "That was a good idea Jason, but exactly how are we going to make her leave if she doesn't want to?" She raised her eyebrows questioningly. "Elisha didn't exactly look like she was in the mood for compromising."

"Yes, and how are we going to keep her from coming back?" Lilly wanted to know.

"I just can't believe this has happened. She seemed perfectly fine a few days ago. Maybe a bit grumpy but nothing like today," said Zac, his face showing concern.

"I know. This whole thing is just so scary. Poor Elisha, I feel so bad for her. It's horrible having to exile her, but we can't risk her attacking anyone else. She's going to have to leave. Even if it's for a little while until she calms down." Lilly looked down at her shoes.

"It's not going to be easy to make her leave. We don't want anyone, including Elisha, getting hurt." Zac looked at the others.

No one said anything.

Time passed, and still, no one said a word. The room began to feel slightly claustrophobic with the number of bodies strewn around the room. Everyone seemed involved in his or her own private thoughts.

After a while, Logan stood from where he had been sitting in the corner of the room. "My dad has a cattle prod. It lets off an electric charge," he offered.

"Bloody hell, I'd forgotten you two were here!" Lilly flinched in fright.

Logan grinned. "Sorry, Lilly. I didn't mean to scare you." He winked at her, and she threw a cushion at him. He caught it and hugged it to his chest. "Like I said. My dad has a cattle prod. It lets off a spark and gives out a small shock. Elisha won't like it, but I'm pretty sure it will get her to move, and it won't injure her."

"Jeez. Remind me not to get into a fight with you!" Lilly exclaimed.

"I reckon!" agreed Lexi nodding vigorously. "Medieval or what!"

Logan grinned and shrugged his shoulders. "Just trying to be practical."

Zac nodded. "Okay. Well, good. We'll go with that then unless anyone else has an alternative suggestion?" No one did. "Hopefully, we won't have to use it. What about keeping her out of town until she's better? It's no good chasing her out of town if she keeps coming back again."

"What about some kind of barrier around the town?" suggested Lexi, making a circle shape in the air with her hands.

"What like a force field?" Braydon smirked as he walked over to stand next to her, his hands resting lightly on his hips.

"No," said Lexi, punching him on the arm. "Like a circle of cars or something." It was her turn to smirk at him. "You know, like one of those medieval fortress towns that have a wall around them, ever read about those? They talk about them in history books." Lexi raised her eyebrows at him making Braydon laugh. "Except we'll do it with cars," she added.

"Hmmm, yes. That could work for now." Jason rubbed his hands together; he was getting into this. "We can add barbed wire over them so she can't climb over."

"Yes, and something on the windows so she can't break through," added Lexi.

Jason leaned forward in his chair, his eyes full of excitement.

Lexi looked at him frowning. "Um, Jason, you know this is not one of your computer games, right? People could get hurt."

"I know that," he replied rolling his eyes at her. "It just feels good to be making a plan for the future."

"The future?"

"Yes, you know. The future of the town. I wouldn't mind staying here for a while." He smiled at Logan, who turned a little red.

Lexi glance between Logan and Jason and smiled too. She offered her hand to Jason, giving him a hand up from the couch.

"Well, come on then, game master. Let's go and shift some cars. There's a whole lot down at the car dealership, plus there are plenty left behind at people's homes. We won't have enough cars to encircle the whole town, but we should have enough to protect the main houses and town square. At least it's a start."

Lexi walked over to Hadley. "Also, if we get some plywood from the hardware store, we can seal the outer car windows, so they're harder to smash." She held out her hand to Hadley. "Want to help me find some wood?"

"Sure, I can do that," agreed Hadley looking happier than she had a few hours ago.

Jason pulled on his jacket and grinned at Lexi. "That sounds like a good plan, except I can't drive, remember?" He winked.

Lexi playfully poked him in the ribs. "Ah yes, but you can push, right?" she laughed. "Some of the cars won't have fuel; we'll have to push them."

Jason nodded and smiled. "Touché."

Hadley tapped Lexi on the shoulder. "Do you think the cars will keep Broc out too?" she asked hopefully. Lexi knew Hadley felt petrified of Broc since he'd invaded their house the night before.

"I'm sure it will, Hadley," said Lexi, smiling at her encouragingly. Though inside, she wasn't so sure. Lexi didn't think anything would keep Broc out if he really wanted to get into the town. And unfortunately, the Bailey farm was on the outskirts of town which made it difficult to protect. From what Brydon had already told Lexi about Broc, it seemed as though he was used to getting his way and doing whatever he felt like doing. At least the ring of cars might be a deterrent. After what he did last night, if Lexi could make anything more difficult for that bastard Broc, then she was going to do it!

Lexi watched the others animatedly discussing the plan to create a barrier around the main part of town. They looked encouraged and the room no longer felt claustrophobic. It felt alive and full of energy. This new trouble with Elisha had given them all something to work on. Something to help their town and if it aided in keeping Broc out or at least make him think twice about coming back into Jasper's Bay, then that was a bonus.

"Come on Jason, let's go and move those cars," said Lexi walking to the front door. She opened it wide looking out onto the bright summer's day. It was now mid-morning, and the sky was a brilliant blue, not a cloud in sight.

"Wait, we're coming to help too," piped up Lilly and Zac, eager to help. "We know how to drive!" laughed Zac having a playful dig at Jason.

Lexi smiled as she strode purposely down the path with the others following behind her. Like the others in the group, she felt pleased about doing something productive, something that was her idea. It made her feel good, made her feel useful. She had come to the decision that Jasper's Bay would be a good town for her and Hadley to stay in. Maybe not forever, but for now, it was comforting to have others her own age around her. Others who had a purpose. To protect the town and if it meant getting into a fight with the gang, so be it. There was safety in numbers anyway, right? If Broc moved into the town and started running things, the younger kids would not stand a chance against him. Lexi wasn't exactly used to fighting, but she knew it was the right thing to do. She had to stand up and protect what was theirs and to help the younger and weaker kids. That was going to be vital if they were going to survive in this new world.

Lexi stepped out onto the road and started to walk briskly into town. She had a resolute look on her face. She may not be good at fighting, but she wasn't too bad at driving. The drive down from Perth had increased her confidence, and she was determined to make that barrier around the houses. Even if it meant denting a few cars to do it. Broc was not going to get back into the town easily. Not if she could do something to help stop him.

Meanwhile, Elisha had gone back to her house and Ethan, feeling angry and confused, was walking straight towards her.

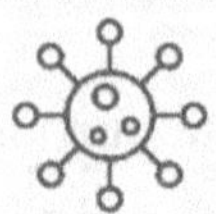

CHAPTER TWENTY-THREE

Ethan and Elisha

Ethan walked slowly back to his house, his hands deep in his pockets and his head hung low. How could this be happening? They didn't deserve this. Elisha had practically run this town singlehandedly, and now she was going to be forced to leave. Kicked out like a stray dog. It just didn't seem fair. He felt hugely let down as though someone had just excluded him from a party. Tears of frustration started to well up in his eyes. He quickly wiped them away with the back of his hand. It wouldn't help to cry.

Stopping for a moment, he looked up at the blue sky. There was not a single cloud in sight. The blue seemed to stretch on forever, and he wondered absently when they would see rain again. He looked across the street at some of the houses where the children of the town were still living. The front lawns looked parched and dry; most of them were starting to turn yellow in the relentless heat of summer. No one could be bothered watering or weeding them anymore. Nicely cut and edged green lawns, once fertilised and mowed every weekend, were now a thing of the past. Along with vacuumed carpets and washed floors. In this new world where necessities like food would soon become scarce, appearances weren't high on the children's list of priorities.

Ethan sighed and ran his fingers through his short wavy hair. After his meeting with the others, he felt confused and unsure of what he should do. If they let Elisha remain in town, she could injure one of the younger kids, but, on the other hand, if they made her leave, he'd be on his own. Good or bad, Elisha was the only family that he had left. Sure, he had friends here, good friends, but it just wasn't the same as having your family with you. Especially when your parents were no longer around. Family meant a lot.

Ethan started walking again, making a slow path towards his house. He continued to think as he ambled along, one foot in front of the other just as if he was walking to school on a Monday morning. He wasn't in a hurry to reach his destination where he knew he'd be one step closer to having to make a difficult and probably emotional decision. He thought again of his sister. They'd both made a good team since their parents had died.

Like all siblings, they hadn't always got along with each other over the years, but when their parents had passed away, and they were left alone, both had made an effort to work together, and for most of the time he thought that they did quite well.

Reaching the path that went past the church, he turned and stepped into his own front yard. He sighed loudly again. He hated making decisions about things; *why couldn't life just continue randomly without anyone having to decide anything?* He started up the little stone path that wound its way like a snake to the front porch of his house. It wasn't a large house, more like a cottage really. The church had provided it for his family to live in when they had moved to the town about six years ago. Before that, they had lived in Perth. It had been strange when they'd first moved to the country, kind of quiet, but it didn't take him long to fit in. His parents had started up a youth group at the church almost straight away, and both he and Elisha had made friends easily. The family had made a couple of alterations to the house over the years, such as a fresh lick of paint and a new kitchen, but other than that the house was essentially the same.

As Ethan reached the front door, he noticed that it was swinging wide open. He hadn't left it like that when he'd gone out earlier. As he got closer and walked up to the stone porch steps, he could hear Elisha singing inside. He smiled to himself; maybe she was alright. She sounded happy enough. Perhaps she didn't have the mutation after all. Perhaps she was just having a terrible day. He suddenly felt relieved and happily stepped inside the house.

The curtains had been pulled back in the front room, and the sun was shining brightly through the open windows. Tiny specks of dust were floating in the air like a thin mist making the room look calm and peaceful. Elisha was busily dusting the family photographs on the TV cabinet. The duster flicked back and forth in a lively manner, and she hummed a cheerful melody as she worked. She looked happy.

When Ethan came through the front door, Elisha abruptly stopped what she was doing and froze on the spot for a few moments before dropping the duster on the floor. She had a queer look on her face as she slowly turned her body around to face him.

Ethan gazed at her suspiciously. He noticed that her dress and hands were still covered in blood from the episode earlier in the afternoon. She hadn't bothered to change or even wash her hands. He frowned a little, feeling concerned.

Elisha stared at him. "Hello, little brother. Where have you been? Why are you looking so serious?"

"Oh, you know, just talking with some of the other kids. How are you feeling, Elisha?"

Elisha ignored his question. "Talking about me, were you?"

Ethan looked closely at his sister, trying to judge her mood. "Er, well, yes," he said awkwardly, his voice on edge. "You did put on quite a show earlier."

"Yes, did you enjoy it?" Elisha asked, her voice cold and hard. A sly grin spread across her face.

"Um no, not really." Ethan's eyes darted around the room. He wasn't sure whether to stay or leave, and his left hand tapped nervously against his thigh.

Elisha stared almost pleadingly at Ethan. Her eyes glittered with an unnatural shine, and she started to make strange panting sounds, a bit like an animal. Raising her hands to her head, she frantically began to claw at her hair with her fingers, pulling out clumps of long blonde hair and dropping them onto the floor.

Ethan could see the tell-tale signs of a red rash covering the backs of Elisha's hands and trailing up her forearms. His mouth dropped open in horror. *She was definitely not okay*. He rushed into the kitchen. "Elisha, let me get you a drink. Don't be upset; everything is fine. People are just worried about you; that's all." He quickly grabbed a glass and opened the fridge, slamming the door against the wall in his haste. Hurriedly pouring orange juice into the glass, Ethan promptly rushed back to the front room. He hoped the cold drink would help calm her down.

Elisha, who had been staring at the clumps of her hair on the floor, slowly raised her eyes to stare at the glass of juice in Ethan's hand. She bent over forwards, resting her hands on her knees, breathing heavily. Her cheeks were puffing in and out as she struggled to maintain control.

Ethan wasn't sure what to say. He cleared his throat uncertainly. "Um, Elisha, maybe you should spend some time away from everyone in town. You know, just until you feel more yourself. You deserve a break." He tried to sound reasonable as he moved towards his sister, offering her the glass. His hand was shaking, and the juice sloshed around in the glass, spilling over the sides.

Without warning Elisha stood straight, her eyes wild like a trapped animal. Lashing out violently she knocked the glass from Ethan's hand, smashing it against the wall where it shattered into jagged pieces. Juice dripped down the wall in rivulets, pooling on the floor in a sticky orange puddle. Ethan stood in complete shock, his arm still outstretched reaching towards his sister.

Elisha was now in a full-blown rage. "You traitor!" She screamed in Ethan's face. Her face was contorted with rage. Droplets of spit flew from her mouth, landing on Ethan's chin. Ethan stared straight ahead. He couldn't move. He stood completely rigid, paralysed, like one of Medusa's statues. He didn't know what to do. Elisha's anger had come out of nowhere, and he didn't have any idea how to calm her down.

Ethan tried to talk to her. "Elisha, I only want what's best for…" he started to say before his sister grabbed onto his shirt collar, pulling him roughly towards her. She raised her knee abruptly and brought it up hard into his stomach. Ethan felt the air forcibly expelled from his body as he let out a whooshing noise before sinking to his knees on the ground in pain.

"Aaaarg." Elisha let out an angry yell of frustration, running to the front door and slamming it hard against the wall. The impact caused chunks of cream plaster to fly from the wall and onto the floor. Elisha didn't notice; she turned and looked at her brother as he knelt on the floor and just for a moment her face lost its rage, and she looked like the old Elisha. Her eyes glistened with tears like tiny crystals. "I can't control it, Ethan. I didn't mean to hurt you. I'm sorry," she managed to cry out in anguish before the anger took control once again.

Her face contorted in fear as she struggled against the madness. Turning abruptly away from her brother, she tore out the front door and raced down the porch steps.

Getting up slowly from the floor, Ethan cautiously made his way to the door. He looked out and saw Elisha running down Millar's road, directly out of town. Maybe through her madness, she had understood him and was leaving the town of her own accord.

Ethan took a deep breath. He hoped so, and he hoped that she didn't meet anyone on the way and cause any more trouble. Elisha really did seem like she was out of control and in that state, who knows what could happen. Ethan felt torn. He didn't want to lose his sister, but maybe the others were right. Maybe it was better if she stayed away from the town for a while. At least until they could work out what was going on. He would try to talk to his friend Nick in Albany again later that day. Maybe he would be able to tell him some more about this new mutation and if he knew of anyone getting better from it.

Suddenly feeling emotionally exhausted, Ethan flopped down on the couch and grabbed a cushion to hug. He started to cry. He felt an overwhelming feeling of hopelessness come over him. The emotion of the day was just too much. He'd just lost the last member of his family.

After a while, Ethan felt calmer and picked up the family photo Elisha had been dusting. The bright morning sunlight was streaming in through the window, creating abstract patterns on the glass frame. Ethan stared at the photograph; sadly, tears clinging to his eyelashes like diamonds glimmering in the light. Ethan blinked them away. The picture was one taken on the beach at a seaside resort the family had visited a couple of years ago, somewhere in Bali. Everyone had been laughing and looking happy. It seemed like a long time ago now. How things could change so quickly. Ethan stared wistfully at the photograph for a few more moments before his emotions took hold of him again and he threw it against the wall in frustration. It shattered and fell to the floor.

"God! Why didn't you help us?" he yelled, shaking his fist and looking up in anger at a golden cross on the wall. Ethan picked up another photo frame glancing at it briefly before throwing that one against the wall too. He watched the glass shatter and drop to the ground, leaving little shards of glass scattered across the floor. He felt so useless and frustrated. Why had this happened? Life wasn't meant to be like this. He was supposed to have a successful life where his family were all together, and everyone was happy. That's how it was on TV, wasn't it? *This new life sucked!*

Passing his hand across his face, he wiped away his tears of anger and sorrow before sinking onto the couch again. His leg joggled up and down as he felt the frustration coursing through him. He peered around the room wondering what to do next when he spotted his father's unopened bottle of bourbon sitting in the glass drinks cabinet. It was dusty and untouched.

His father didn't drink alcohol himself, though he often kept a bottle in the house for visitors. Ethan walked over to the cabinet, opened the door and looked at the bottle, his fingers twitching. He had always done the right thing. Never caused problems, never been any trouble. Right now, though, he didn't care about any of that. Right now, he didn't care about anything. All he desperately wanted to do was to feel numb.

After a brief moment of hesitation, Ethan grabbed the bottle and held it in his palm. He gazed at the glass bottle filled with its golden-brown liquid. It looked a bit like iced tea, though he knew it wouldn't taste like it. Before he could change his mind, he quickly unscrewed the cap from the top of the bottle and flung it across the room. He walked purposefully outside and leaned against the porch railing. Bringing the bottle up to his lips, he could smell the strong liquor inside and took his first drink. The liquid ran down the back of his throat, giving off a burning sensation and making him cough. Ethan didn't care and took another mouthful. Anything to dull the senses. Anything to dull the pain.

Later that evening, Braydon was sitting in the lounge room at Rosewood Avenue with Jason, Lexi and Hadley. Braydon had followed them around all afternoon, trying to help out and make amends for his bad behaviour at the house and the farm. Come evening time, he had followed them back to their home. Lexi had let him in. She still didn't fully trust him, but he looked so lost and unhappy that she had suggested that he could stay with them for a couple of nights until they worked out what to do with him. First, they had to deal with Elisha and then the gang. Braydon was low on the list of problems right now, and he didn't seem much of a problem, anyway. As far as Lexi was concerned, though, he wasn't getting a bed to sleep in. Until they knew him better and he had made up for his role in the attacks, he could sleep on the couch.

"Do you think Ethan's still out looking for Elisha?" asked Hadley as she sat on the floor playing with Polo.

"I don't know," said Braydon. "Let's give him some space. He's had a pretty big shock and probably just wants some time alone."

Lexi nodded. "Let's go and check on him later at his house. We can take him over some food."

"Good idea. I'll have a look for something nice in our food stash," suggested Hadley, pushing herself up from the floor to go into the kitchen to look through their supplies.

"Er, wait a second Hadley. Listen, guys. I've got something I want to say to you." Braydon stood in front of the others, nervously fumbling with a wooden bead tied around his neck on a leather cord. They all turned to face him wondering what he was going to say. He looked very uncomfortable.

"What's wrong?" asked Lexi.

"Oh, it's nothing like that. Nothing's wrong," he said awkwardly, shuffling his feet as if unable to stand still. "I just wanted to say thank you for letting me stay with you. I'm sorry I didn't stand up to Broc earlier when he was attacking you girls." He looked down at his feet. "I feel horrible about it."

"Well, that's alright, I guess. Thanks for saying so," said Lexi, smiling slightly at him. She hadn't forgiven him for his part in the home invasion, but at least he felt guilty about it and was trying to do the right thing now.

"Yes. It must have been difficult to stand up against Broc with him being your cousin and everything," agreed Hadley, nudging his foot with her shoe.

Braydon looked at her and nodded. "Yes, it was, Hadley. I should have done it sooner, though. He's not a particularly nice guy, and I shouldn't have gone along with what he was doing. It's just that, he's the only family I have left, so it was hard for me to leave. I just had enough, though. I couldn't stand by and watch him hurt people anymore. It's not what I'm about."

"Well, if you want to stay in this town, you'd better go see the farm kids and do some major sucking up. They had a much rougher time with Broc than we did," suggested Lexi raising her eyebrows.

"Yes, I know, I was there." Braydon looked embarrassed. "I'll go and see them now." He got up to leave. "Thanks again, guys." He gave them a small wave.

"No problem," said Jason. "Good luck at the farm."

Jason looked at Lexi and Hadley. "He's going to need it," he whispered as Braydon walked out the door. "I doubt Lilly and Zac are going to be very forgiving for being beaten and having half their farm burnt down, even if he is sorry."

Jason stood and closed the front door making sure Braydon had left. He turned to face Lexi. "Do you think we can trust him? He's not a Broc spy or something, is he?"

"Don't know. He seems alright?" said Lexi looking towards the door. "He did take a beating from Broc."

"Hmm, you never know though, hey?" Jason said thoughtfully.

"No. You never know," said Lexi bending down to pat Polo. "We'd better keep an eye on him just in case. Agreed?"

"Agreed," said Hadley and Jason together.

"Now. What have we got to eat?" said Jason, walking into the kitchen.

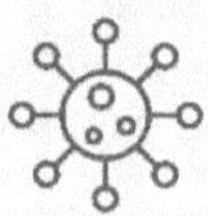

CHAPTER TWENTY-FOUR

The next morning felt like it was going to be another sweltering hot summer's day. The breeze hadn't yet arrived, and the warm air was close and intense. It was like your body was slowly roasting in a huge oven and even though it was early morning, any form of exercise brought out beads of sweat, adding a thin sheen to your skin. Lexi wiped her damp brow with the back of her hand and stared unenthusiastically at the two boxes of her things sitting on her bedroom floor. She had carried them in from the car a few days ago, but with everything going on with first Broc, then Elisha, she hadn't got around to unpacking them.

Lexi got up from the bed and pushed open the white wooden windows. Not a hint of breeze filtered through the flywire shielding the room from other insects. She looked out at the back garden and spotted Polo asleep under a big fig tree in the corner of the yard. Picking up a magazine from the small desk in the room, Lexi fanned her hot face and closed her eyes. But it didn't really help. The sounds of Hadley, Jason and Braydon, arguing about some computer game they'd played drifted in from the front room. They were extremely rowdy, and Lexi was beginning to feel stifled in the close confines of the house. She had to get out for a while. Grabbing her white sun hat, she decided to go down to Bryer's Creek. It wouldn't take too long to walk to as it ran directly along the back of their house and dipping her feet in the cold water was going to be sweet relief. As she sat down under a tree and peeled off her shoes, Lexi noticed that Braydon had followed her down to the stream. She felt a little surprised and frowned at him, raising her hand to her face to shield her eyes from the glare of the sun. *So much for being alone*, she thought to herself slightly irritated.

Braydon stood completely still with his hands hanging loosely by his sides. He peered out at the water. After a while, he said cautiously, "You don't like me very much, do you? Is it the red hair?"

"No!" laughed Lexi. "Actually, I kinda like red hair. My mum had red hair." She smiled remembering her mum's lovely long red hair. "It was the same colour red as yours." Lexi finished taking off her shoes and placed them neatly next to her on the ground.

Braydon gave a slight smile.

She glanced up at him again not quite sure how to proceed. Lexi cleared her throat. "Look, it's not that I don't like you. It's just that… well, it's difficult not to associate you with Broc. He's not exactly a nice guy, and you *were* part of that gang."

Braydon flopped down onto the ground to sit next to her. He picked up a stick and started poking the ground with it. "Hell, look I know, and I'd probably feel exactly the same way if I was you." He threw the stick into the water and looked beseechingly at Lexi. "The thing is, I really want to leave all that behind me, Lexi. You have no idea how much I hate Broc. Yes, he's my cousin, but that doesn't mean I'm like him. In fact, we are nothing alike, and I bet I hate him as much as anyone here does!"

"Hmmm I think Lilly and Zac hate him more," she tilted her head to the side and peered closely at Braydon's face trying to judge whether he was telling the truth or not. He looked so miserable she thought he probably was. No one could fake that sadness. She nodded her head at him to show that she understood.

"I just want to find somewhere to live my life without too much drama," Braydon continued. "And if Broc doesn't want that, then I guess I'll just have to do it without any family." He looked down at the ground sadly. "I guess that saying, *you can pick your friends, but you can't pick your family*, is true."

Lexi continued to watch at him. "Why were you with him, anyway? I know he's your family, but surely if you hate him that much?"

Braydon didn't say anything. He stood back up and wandered down to the creek, bent over and picked up a flat grey stone. Lexi didn't think he was going to answer her, then he began. "Well, you see, I thought he might have changed. It's a long story but basically, he's the only family I have left, and I kinda just followed him out of the city. I hadn't seen him since we were younger kids. I should have known he'd still be a complete dick. He was a bully when we were younger, and he's still a bully now." Braydon examined the stone for a few moments, turning its smooth edges over in his fingers, then threw it angrily across the water, watching it skim across the surface before sinking to the bottom. He bent down and picked up another.

Lexi watched him for a while, his arm muscles flexing as he released each rock. She was surprised at how muscular he was. Lexi hadn't seen him in short sleeves before, only big bulky sweaters, even in the heat.

She pushed herself up from her spot under the tree, wondering why he liked wearing such bulky clothes in summer. *He looked much better in a t-shirt*, she thought to herself with a smile as she wandered down to the water's edge. Wiggling her toes in the coarse sand of the creek bed for a moment, Lexi enjoyed the cool sensation on her feet before carefully wading further into the water. The cold water soon reached her ankles. The change in temperature felt wonderful, and if Braydon hadn't been there, she would have been tempted to strip to her underwear and jump right in.

She waded in a bit farther until the water reached her thighs, the bottom of her denim shorts just getting wet. Looking down at her shorts, Lexi wondered if any of the clothing stores in town had bathing suits. She hadn't thought to pack her own pair when they'd left the city.

The water was flowing quite quickly, and Lexi pondered if it ever flooded in winter. She looked down at her feet. The water was crystal clear and sparkling in the sun. She noticed that the floor of the creek bed was covered in slippery stones, smoothed by the current of the water continuously running over them. Once or twice, Lexi almost fell and had to steady herself by holding her arms out wide, like a toddler learning to walk on shaky ground.

The cold water felt magnificent. Lexi closed her eyes and turned her face upwards towards the sky breathing in the fresh air. Her hair shimmered in the sun's rays, and she looked intensely happy.

Braydon stood watching Lexi as she balanced precariously on the rocks, the pleasure obvious on her face. She looked lovely. He bent down and started taking off his shoes, as though he meant to join Lexi in the water. "I wonder what her lips taste like?" he said quietly to himself. "Mint, strawberry?" He shook his head and relaced his Converse sneakers. He'd only just started to break down the barrier between them. As much as he wanted to kiss her, he didn't want to jeopardise things.

Feeling his eyes on her, Lexi opened her own eyes and spun around. Braydon was staring at her, as though he wanted to grab her or something. "What are you…?" She began to say before Braydon saw the look on her face and quickly backed away up to the tree where Lexi's shoes lay. Lexi thought he looked embarrassed.

"Er… I'm just going back to the house," he stammered loudly, wondering why he felt so confused around this girl.

Lexi felt confused herself. "Um, okay." She nodded before turning back to face the water.

Braydon took a deep breath, "I just want to make things right with you. And Hadley and the rest of the town," he added quickly. "I want to make things work here." His voice was once again calm.

Lexi nodded her head and gazed down the stream, wondering absently how far it flowed. He sounded genuine. When she turned back around to talk to him, he was already walking away. She watched his back retreating up the path that led to the house, wondering if she could trust him. She wanted to; there was something about him that enticed her. In her old life, she would have said, *yes, why not.* But in this new world, she wasn't so sure.

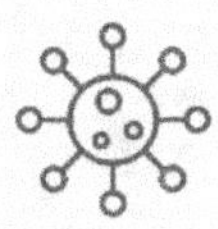

CHAPTER TWENTY-FIVE

Over the next couple of days, things were quiet in town. After their meeting at the creek, both Braydon and Lexi felt a little awkward around each other. There was definitely a connection or attraction between them, but Lexi was in no way ready for it or willing to even admit it. Most of the town kids still saw Braydon as one of the *bad* guys, and even Lexi continued to feel unsure about him. On the one hand, he'd been relatively passive in both the attacks on the farm and their house, but he hadn't exactly done anything to stop them either. On the other hand, he had eventually stood up to Broc in the town square and copped a beating for it. And then there was the lure she felt towards him. She couldn't pinpoint what it was. The more time she spent with him, the greater she could feel it. There was something about him she felt an attraction to. Perhaps it was his honesty. She couldn't stand liars and cheats. Maybe it was the stupid jokes he always made; she found them quite funny. Or maybe it was just his red curls and intense blue eyes. Whatever it was, she was keeping it to herself. She didn't want anyone else, and especially not Braydon, to know the way she felt. Especially when she wasn't even sure herself just how she felt. There had been little sign of Elisha, or Broc and his gang, and some of the kids began to wonder if they had moved on to another town. Lexi wasn't so sure.

"Do you think Broc will move on to another town?' Asked Lexi as she sat with Braydon on the porch at Rosewood Avenue. She brushed the red dust from her pants before tucking her hands under her thighs. Lexi glanced at him awkwardly.

"I doubt it," replied Braydon watching Lexi's hair shimmer in the sunlight. "Especially now I've decided to stay in town." He tenderly felt under his eye where the flesh was still swollen and bruised. "I'm probably putting you in danger. I really should leave." He swallowed.

Lexi stretched her arms up above her head, enjoying the stillness of the morning. It wouldn't be long before the sun became too hot and uncomfortable to sit outside. "No. I think you should stay," she said, looking up at him through her eyelashes. Lexi could feel her cheeks reddening, so she quickly stood and walked to the edge of the porch hoping Braydon didn't notice. She raised her hand to her eyes to shield them from the glare of the sun and peered down the street. She could hear the sound of cicadas in the bushes and white cockatoos screeching in the nearby trees; however, no other people were about.

"Don't let Broc dictate where you can and can't live. If he can't handle you moving on, that's his problem. Not yours."

"Hmm. It was a very toxic friendship if you can even call it a friendship." Braydon tapped his foot.

"Yes, more like a dictatorship, with the emphasis on *dick*," Lexi grinned playfully.

Braydon let out a big belly laugh. The awkwardness between them was broken. He stood and went to stand by Lexi, leaning casually on the porch post. "Talking of friends, have you seen your friend Ethan about?"

Lexi turned to face him, her face serious again. "Actually, I have. I saw him last night. He was hanging with a bunch of the younger kids. Fuse, Angel and Harvey I think their names are. They all looked totally drunk." Lexi shrugged. "I was surprised as Ethan always seemed so mature. I was going to say something but what right do I have. I'm not their mother, and they don't know me very well. They'd probably tell me to *piss off*."

Lexi plucked at her top in agitation. She hadn't been happy seeing Ethan in such a state. "Zac told me that Fuse, one of the twelve-year old's father was an alcoholic. That's probably where they got the alcohol from." She tapped her foot on the porch step, her brow furrowed. "I think I should go and see Ethan later today when he's sober, just to make sure he's doing alright. I want him to know he can come and talk if he wants to."

Braydon put his arm around Lexi's shoulders. "I can come with you if you like, though I don't know if Ethan would like that. The kids are probably just bored. Without school or their parents around its easy for them to get into mischief. What the town needs is something for them to do. Something to get involved in." he scratched his chin thoughtfully.

"I have an idea," said Lexi heading back into the house. "It's something we can all be involved in, and it might just help with the Broc problem too." She smiled turning her head to glance back at Braydon. "Come on. Let's get Hadley and Jason together. I want to discuss it with them too."

Ollie

Somewhere in the bushland surrounding the town. Ollie was out among the tall eucalyptus and marri trees, just past the boundary of cars the kids had set up a few days ago. He knew he wasn't supposed to be out there, and his older brother Levi would rant at him if he knew he had gone out past the boundary, but he'd been chasing a rabbit through the bush, and this is where it had led him. He'd seen it scoot under one of the parked cars and he'd been small enough to squeeze under there, too. Unfortunately, he'd lost it on the other side of the car and had been patiently looking for it the rest of the morning. It must have disappeared down a burrow nearby because he couldn't see it anywhere. He'd willed himself to sit still and calm on a big grey rock, trying to spot any movement or rustling in the undergrowth, but the only movement he'd seen was from a blue-tongued lizard making its way slowly across the ground looking for a patch of sun to warm up in. The rabbit was gone.

Ollie bent his leg up and rested his chin on his knee. He gazed out towards the tall trees with their shiny green leaves and dark pink blossoms. The honeyeaters and wattle birds would soon be out, flitting between the flowers, looking for food. Ollie got up and stretched his arms over his head, yawning tiredly as he did so. He could never keep still for long. Ollie had woken up early that morning before the sun had made its full appearance in the sky and snuck out of the house he shared with his older brother. He just loved being out in the bush in the early hours of the morning when everything was still and quiet, and the animals were waking up. It made him feel happy. He also loved to hunt rabbits, and the best time to catch them was early in the morning. Another reason he loved to get up at dawn.

Ollie's older brother, Levi, who was nine and his father, who had died from the virus within weeks of it hitting the town, usually went camping with him every school holiday. His father had told them that it was important for Aboriginal people to stay connected to the land, that it was part of their culture. He taught both boys how to snare and catch rabbits, how to skin and prepare them, and how to make a stew out of them. Sometimes, if they managed to catch a few, they would bring some home to their mother, and she would make a rabbit and vegetable pie out of them. She made the best pies. How he would love to be able to make one of those pies. Both boys had tried a couple of times without much success. They just couldn't get the pastry right. It always turned out sticky and dense when they made it. Not light and flaky like their mother's.

Ollie sat back down on his rock and thought about his mother. Thinking about her pies had made him remember just how much he missed her. He was only six, and even though his older brother told him he had to be a *'man'*, and he tried really hard to be, he still wished his mum was here. She had been an art teacher at the primary school, so he got to see a lot of her during the day, even when she was at work and he missed that.

As Ollie sat alone on the rock thinking, he suddenly heard voices off to the right of him. He slowly stood, crouching over so he couldn't be seen and peered through the bushes to see who the voices belonged to. "I wonder who's out here in the bush?" he murmured.

Ollie moved the bushes aside so he could see more clearly. At first, he couldn't see anybody, and then Ollie spotted Kevin, one of the older boys from the Bailey farm. *He must be out here with his brother,* thought Ollie as he stood straight and was just about to call out *'hello'* when he noticed that Kevin was not with his brother at all. In fact, he wasn't with anyone from town. He was with a bunch of kids that Ollie had never seen before, and it looked like he was leading them somewhere.

"That's weird," said Ollie under his breath as he continued to watch them from behind the bushes.

The group was following along after Kevin, as though he was the Pied Piper. All in single file, smashing their way through the bush and undergrowth as they went. A boy with large muscles was walking closely behind Kevin, swearing and hitting bushes with a baseball bat as he went. He had a scowl on his face and looked angry. The others were less vocal, but still loud enough to scare away any wildlife. Ollie watched them file past. *Was this the gang his brother had been telling him about?* He stood as still and as quiet as he could, willing them not to look in his direction. He didn't want to be seen.

As the gang trudged past, Ollie wondered where Kevin was leading them. They were moving away from the town, but Ollie was sure they were up to no good wherever they were going. Having lost all chance of catching the rabbit with all the noise the gang had been making, Ollie decided to follow them and see what they were up to.

As soon as they moved past him, he crouched back down and let them get a little way ahead of him before he carefully followed behind. They were easy to follow with all the noise they were making, plus the girl at the back had on a bright pink shirt, which Ollie could see easily through the greens and browns of the bush. Whatever they were up to they obviously didn't think there was anyone out here to see them.

After about twenty minutes of walking, Ollie saw that the group had stopped on a small hill. The older boy was arguing with Kevin, who was pointing to a fenced-off area not far from where they had stopped. The boy turned to look at where Kevin was pointing before storming off in that direction. The others all followed. Kevin stood for a moment watching them go before he too, followed in the same direction.

Ollie quickly scrambled up the hill, not wanting to lose sight of where the gang was going. Once he reached the top, he looked down and noticed a fenced off area surrounding a cleared section of bushland.

He raised his right hand to shield his eyes from the bright sun, which had now risen into the sky and tried to see what was in the cleared area. He hadn't been this far into the bush before and hoped he would be able to find his way back into town.

"What are *they* doing this far out of town?' he muttered quietly, his eyes narrowing.

"I better find out what they're up to," said Ollie scratching the end of his nose. "I bet nobody else knows they're out here" *It was up to him find out and report back to the older kids.*

Before he started down the hill behind the gang, Ollie briefly turned to look behind him, back towards the bush and the rabbit he'd been hunting. There were butterflies in his stomach, and his legs were trembling a little. The kids in the gang were all a lot older than he was, and he didn't think that Kevin would help him if he got caught by them.

"I'd better make sure they don't see me watching them," he said quietly nodding to himself. Ollie thought of his older brother; he knew that if he were here with him, he'd probably tell him 'to man up'. He closed his eyes, took a deep breath and then quickly followed the gang down the hill towards the fenced-off area.

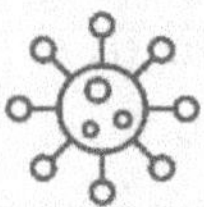

CHAPTER TWENTY-SIX

Once Ollie had reached the fence, he couldn't immediately see the older kids, but he could hear them. They obviously thought no one was around because they were making a lot of noise. A sharp metallic banging sound filled the air followed by laughing and cheering. The earlier peaceful sounds of the bushland were drowned out by the intrusive noise of the gang.

Suddenly, there was a loud noise of glass breaking, and it sounded very much as though something was being smashed. Ollie instinctively crouched down, wondering what the sound was.

All he could see in front of him were a couple of red brick buildings. They weren't large, probably maintenance sheds or offices, however, he didn't think the noise was coming from there. It sounded farther off.

"I'm going to have to get closer," he said his eyes darting to the side. "I need to see what they're up to."

Ollie made his way closer to the wire fence and crept slowly along the boundary until he came to a hole in the line. Peering closely at the wire, Ollie noticed that the strands looked as though they had been cut, and a section of the wire folded back to make a hole in the fence. *This is obviously where the gang climbed through.*

Ollie gripped onto the fence with his fingers, wondering if he should climb through, too. Standing high on his tip-toes and peering through the fence, he still could not see past the buildings to where the gang had gone. He knew if he were going to have any chance of seeing what they were up to, he would have to get closer.

Ollie took a deep, shaky breath and climbed through the hole, being careful not to catch his shirt on the sharp wire strands. As he moved forward, the sound of breaking glass and metal hitting metal was growing louder, and Ollie knew he was getting close to the gang. He now had his back to one of the building's and was slowly inching his way along its perimeter as he tried to get a better viewpoint. Ollie knew that once he reached the corner of the building, he would be able to poke his head around and see the gang. He would finally be able to discover what they were up to. However, that also meant they would have a chance of seeing him.

Ollie's hands shook. The gang kids were a lot bigger than he was, and there were quite a few of them. He knew he was a quick runner; his teacher Mrs Frost had told him so at school, but he didn't know if he'd be fast enough to run from them if he had to. Ollie suddenly needed to pee.

Wiping his clammy hands on the sides of his pants, Ollie slowly crept forward, taking one step at a time, making each foot go in front of the other. He closed his eyes for a brief moment and tried to imagine his dad was right there beside him. Just a couple of metres away, around the corner, if he just kept going a little farther, he would see him when he reached the edge. Of course, he knew it wasn't true, but the thought that his father was there waiting for him helped him move his feet just a few more steps so he could reach the edge of the building.

The sounds of raised voices and malicious laughter were extremely loud now, and Ollie knew the gang were only a few steps away from him. Every instinct in his body told him to turn around. Turn around and run. Go back to the quiet and peacefulness of the bush, away from the violence that was happening just around the corner from where he stood. His body rocked uncertainly. Ollie knew that the safest thing to do would be to go back home, back to his brother. But he also knew that he would feel ashamed if he just turned and fled. Finding out what the gang was doing might be important to the town and all the other kids who lived there. He was sure no one else knew that the gang was out here, apart from Kevin, and Kevin seemed to be with the gang now. If Ollie didn't stay and find out what the group were doing, then they would *get away with it*. He didn't want that to happen.

Crouching down on his haunches, Ollie took a slow breath in. Then carefully, just like a little mouse peeping out of its hole, he poked his head around the corner of the building. At first, he wasn't sure what he was looking at. There were pieces of broken glass, and jagged pieces of silver and black metal lying scattered all over the place. "What is that stuff?' he whispered under his breath.

Ollie narrowed his eyes. He could see Kevin's back. His hands were hanging loosely by his sides as though he hadn't been participating in the destruction. Ollie's eyes flicked to the next person. Next to Kevin was a skinny boy with light brown hair cut Justin Bieber style. He didn't look as though he were doing much either, just watching whatever was going on.

Ollie turned his head a little, being careful to keep his breathing quiet. Just off to one side, Ollie noticed the short, stocky boy he had seen earlier. The boy was leaning on a metal baseball bat balanced on the ground and looked pleased with himself. He was laughing and joking with a black-haired Asian girl with a bright pink streak in her hair. She also held a baseball bat; hers was resting on her left shoulder.

From his crouched position, Ollie couldn't quite see what was going on. The gang's bodies masked whatever they were doing. *He needed to see more.* It was apparent the gang had been having *a lot of fun* smashing something, but with all the bodies in the way, he just couldn't see what it was. Ollie leaned farther to the side, trying to see through the legs that stood like the tree trunks of a forest in front of him. There was something there, however, but from his position down on the ground he couldn't make out what it was.

I'm going to have to stand! Ollie knew it would make his position more vulnerable, but he had come this far and had to know what they were doing. The two kids with the baseball bats were smirking and looking extremely pleased, so it had to be something important, didn't it? Something worth risking being seen for?

Before he could change his mind, Ollie stood up. He kept his eyes fixed firmly on the guy with the baseball bat, ready to run if he had to. Stretching up onto his tiptoes, Ollie could see rectangular shaped objects that stood on metal legs and looked like they were covered in shiny black glass. The rectangular structures were all tilted to one side, angled to face the sun. *They seemed familiar.* As Ollie peered past the gang, he noticed rows and rows of the shiny metal and glass objects, and more than half of them were smashed.

Ollie put his hand to his eyes to shield the sun trying to get a clearer view. The objects looked almost alien, and he wondered why the gang were destroying them. He stared intently at the black glass panels with their repetitious pattern of grids and circles trying to remember where he had seen them before. It seemed important. Ollie knew he had never been to this part of town before; however, the objects sparked a memory. He just couldn't grasp what it was.

As Ollie stared at the smooth black glass, he wondered what it would feel like to run his hand across the shiny surface.

His fingers twitched, and for some reason, he suddenly thought of his teacher, Mrs Frost, on Earth Day. Ollie could picture her talking about something. *What was it?* He remembered she had been showing the class a film on the big TV at school. He'd been excited as it was the first time his year one class had been allowed to sit in the media room with the older kids at school. His brother Levi had been there with his year four class, and he'd waved enthusiastically at him. *What had they been watching?* Ollie closed his eyes for a moment and tried to remember. It was something important. Something to do with the panels the gang were smashing to pieces.

Suddenly, like a flash, it came to him. They had been watching a show on energy, and their town had featured in it. *Why had Jasper's Bay featured in it?* Ollie tried to remember back to that day. It had been Earth Day, and they'd been talking about energy and conservation. He remembered looking at Mrs Frost as she spoke about Jasper's Bay, she'd seemed very proud. Her eyes had been shining bright, and her cheeks were rosy.

Then he remembered. Solar energy! They'd been talking about solar energy! Ollie almost clapped his hands but caught himself just in time. He took a peek at the gang. No one had noticed him.

Ollie closed his eyes and again remembered back to that day at school. He saw himself watching the show. The television program had been all about their town because Jasper's Bay was one of the only towns in Western Australia to be run solely on power from the sun. He remembered now. Mrs Frost had explained it to them as they all sat cross-legged on the floor looking up at her with interest. The way Jasper's Bay got its power from the sun, was by using its solar power plant!

Ollie opened his eyes wide and stared at the shiny black rectangles. Solar panels! He gasped as he realised what the gang had been up to. They were smashing all the town's solar panels. Without the solar panels, the town would be without power! They'd be helpless against the dark. Broc and his gang would be able to sneak into the town without anyone seeing. He had to get back into town and tell his brother and the other kids.

As he quickly turned to go, Ollie heard the distinctive sound of someone chuckling and froze on the spot.

"Hahaha, well…what have we got here? A nasty little spy. He's not with you, is he, Kevin?" Broc turned his head to glare at Kevin. "You said no one came out here! You said we wouldn't be disturbed." Broc's eyes narrowed meanly.

Kevin stammered nervously. "No …no he's not with me. He's just some little kid, Broc. He's probably just playing or something. Don't worry about it."

"Don't worry about it!" exploded Broc, spittle flying from his mouth as he yelled. "Don't worry about it!"

Kevin looked over at Ollie frowning, wondering who the kid was. He didn't know his name. Probably one of the younger brats from town. Kevin sneered at him. Whoever he was, he was spoiling things with Broc. "Hey, you," he yelled nastily. "Get out of here you little brat. Go and stick your ugly nose somewhere else!" Kevin looked over at Broc as if for approval.

Broc didn't even glance Kevin's way. His focus was elsewhere. Round and round he swung his baseball bat his wrist turning faster and faster as it spun. Broc' eyes were locked onto the young boy in front of him. He ran his tongue over his lips and stared at Ollie as though he were a deer on the African savannah and Broc was the lion waiting for its prey to move.

When Ollie didn't say a word, Broc's face became cruel. His mouth turned up in a snarl. "He can't leave," he said in a low voice full of menace. "He's seen us, and *I* haven't finished yet." Broc swivelled his head towards Kevin. "I want every one of those stupid panels destroyed except one. And that one will be for me and me alone. The only person with power in this crappy little town will be me. Got it!" His voice rose loudly as he screamed out his demands.

Ollie's legs shook violently, and his knees almost buckled beneath him. His eyes were wide with fear. *This boy did not look nice, and he didn't think he was going to be very kind to him.* Ollie quickly glanced at the other gang members. Not one of them had a friendly look in their eyes, not even Kevin. He could see from the looks on their faces that they meant to do him harm, especially the tough boy who was yelling and screaming. Ollie knew he was on his own; no one was going to help him. He licked his lips nervously. *I'm a quick runner*, he thought to himself. *I'm the fastest in my class; maybe I can outrun them.*

When Broc turned to scream at Kevin, Ollie took his chance. He sprinted back toward the hole in the fence. His heart hammered in his chest. If he could make it to the fence and through the gap, he was sure that he could get away.

Behind him, Ollie could hear the gang chasing him. Someone was whooping and hollering in excitement, and the girl was laughing in a high-pitched giggle. Their pounding footsteps sounded loud on the ground behind him, and he felt as if he were being hunted. Up ahead, a few metres from him, Ollie suddenly spotted the gap in the wire fence. His heart lifted, and he willed his legs to run just a little faster.

Within a few moments, Ollie reached the fence, his fingers clinging on to the wire in desperation. He quickly bent down to clamber through the hole in the wire. He could see the bush beyond and his way back to his home and his brother. Ollie stretched his head forward, about to thrust it through the gap when he was suddenly jerked backward off his feet. A rough hand was grasping onto his t-shirt pulling him violently back.

Ollie was dragged backwards by his shirt, with his legs splayed out in front of him. He was pulled along the ground, away from the fence, and away from freedom. A pleased voice yelled in his ear. "Where do you think you're going, you little brat? Someone ought to teach you a lesson for spying on people." Broc grinned down at the squirming kid he held roughly by his yellow t-shirt "Luckily for you. I'm an excellent teacher." Broc laughed loudly. "This might turn out to be a good day after all!"

Ollie's heart sank. He stared up at the older boy with the mean eyes and hoped he would change his mind. The boy started back with a nasty grin on his face. His eyes were dark and full of hate. Ollie looked into those dark callous eyes, and he knew then, that the boy would not change his mind. This boy was uncaring, and he liked to be cruel.

I'm in trouble thought Ollie, tears springing to his eyes.

CHAPTER TWENTY-SEVEN

Ollie was lying on his right side on hard concrete. He could feel its coldness against his thin yellow t-shirt, slowly seeping into his skin. He wondered miserably where he was. Not in the bush; there were no concrete floors in the bush. He felt ensnared, just like one of the rabbits he liked to catch. His hands were bound together behind his back with grey packing tape as were his feet, which were also bare. Broc had ripped his shoes from his feet before he had taped his legs together and thrown them into the bush somewhere. *They were my only sneakers,* he thought miserably, tears forming in his eyes again.

Ollie shifted his position on the ground slightly; his body felt sore. His eyes and mouth were covered with the same thick tape that bound his limbs, and the right side of his body was smattered with scrapes and abrasions from when Broc had roughly thrown him into this place. His small body had skidded across the concrete floor like a bowling ball hurtling towards the pins. With his hands tied, he hadn't been able to stop himself from falling, and it had hurt when he'd tumbled to the ground. Broc and the others had laughed at his pain and warned him to "stay put and be quiet." As if he could say anything anyway with his mouth covered in tape.

Ollie gingerly sat up feeling bruised and tender. He listened quietly, but could not hear anything except his own breathing, which sounded loud. The tape covering his eyes was thick and wide, so Ollie couldn't see anything either. He once again wondered where he was and if he were alone. He knew he was sitting on a concrete floor, and he could feel a solid wall behind him when he stretched out his fingers, however, other than that, he was unsure. Broc had covered his eyes and mouth and bound him before he had dragged him to his current location, so Ollie hadn't seen where the gang had put him. Ollie had heard a door being shut and bolted, so he knew he was in a building; however, he didn't know if he were alone. *Maybe someone was in there with him, watching him, waiting for him to move so they could pounce on him.* Ollie's stomach clenched. He sat frozen to the spot and his heart beat fast. Tilting his head to the side, Ollie tried to listen to his surroundings. *Could he hear someone breathing, or was that just his own anxious breath?*

Sweat ran in little rivulets down his spine and his t-shirt stuck to his back like a wet cloth. The air inside the room smelt musty and old as if the space hadn't been open to fresh air for a while. Ollie could feel his face growing warm, and he started to squirm. It was getting hot. *It must be near mid-day, and his brother would be wondering where Ollie was. Maybe Levi would come looking for him?* Ollie thought with a little spike of hope. Then he remembered miserably that he hadn't told Levi where he was going. He hadn't even left a note. Ollie had snuck off into the bush while his brother was asleep.

He groaned, and his shoulders slumped. *I should have left a note. No one knows where I am. Nobody knows I'm trapped, and no one is coming to help me.* He was going to have to get out of this predicament himself.

Ollie wriggled around, his arms were hurting, and his feet were starting to tingle. *He had to somehow get out of these bindings.* Ollie again tilted his head to the side; however, he couldn't hear a thing. I *must be alone.*

Ollie made a decision; he would just have to take a chance. If he didn't move his arms now, they were going to become numb all over and then they'd be no good to him. He had to try an escape now before the others came back.

Ollie shifted into a more comfortable position, and although his arms were bound behind his back, Ollie knew he was nimble and flexible. *I might be able to slip my legs through my arms and bring my bound hands towards my front.* Slowly standing being careful not to lose his balance, Ollie leant back against the brick wall. Then, bending forward at the waist, he slowly stretched and maneuvered his hands past his backside and down towards his feet, before squatting and bending his knees up to his chest. With his body in a scrunched position, Ollie was then able to feel for his feet and slowly move his hands forward in front of him. He wriggled his fingers. It felt so much better having his arms in their more natural position, even if they were still bound. He rolled his shoulders and jiggled his arms up and down, trying to get the blood flowing back into them to regain some feeling. His fingers tingled as though a hundred tiny needles were pricking them, and he opened and closed his fists.

Once the feeling had come back into his hands, Ollie stopped moving. In the pleasure of getting his arms somewhat free, he'd momentarily forgotten that someone might be in the room with him, silently watching what he was doing. Ollie became still, squatting quietly by the wall waiting for his captor to start yelling at him or hitting him for moving his arms to the front. He waited as still as a statue, his heart hammering in his chest like a wild animal. Sweat ran down the side of his face and dripped onto his shoulder. He could smell its pungent, sour stench. Ollie bowed his head and wished he could see. He hated not being able to see.

He waited in his quiet, crouched position. Slowly the minutes ticked by, but no tirade came. He gave a small smile and stretched his arms above his head. He must be on his own in here, and that was a good thing. That was an excellent thing!

Feeling a lot more comfortable now that his arms were no longer constrained behind his back and he knew that no one was watching him, Ollie quickly reached his bound hands up to his face and felt around with his fingers for the edge of the tape covering his eyes. He needed to find out where he was being held captive. His probing fingers felt a frayed piece of tape near the corner of his left eyebrow, and he gently tried to pick at the edge so that he could pull it off. It took a while as the tape was stuck securely onto his skin, but gradually, Ollie managed to work an edge of it free. Slipping his fingers under the frayed edge, Ollie took a deep breath. This was going to hurt, especially when the tape ripped off his eyebrows and eyelashes.

Slowly he pulled the tape free, one little piece at a time, like trying to remove a Band-Aid from a cut. He knew he should probably rip it off quickly, but he couldn't bring himself to do it. Slowly, he pulled the tape from his skin, trying to be as gentle as he could. The packing tape on his mouth muffled his groans as some of the hair from his eyebrows ripped out in the process. He angrily scrunched up the tape, throwing it across the room and heard it bounce off a wall at the far end. *The enclosed space he was in must not be large,* he thought to himself.

Ollie waited a few moments for his eyes to adjust, then cautiously looked around him. It was still dark inside, but as far as he could tell, he was alone. He breathed a sigh of relief. At least no one was in here with him to give him trouble and being alone he could look for a way out and escape before Broc came back. Ollie looked around him. Through the darkness, he could make out the shapes of four walls close together, like a square box. He thought he must be in some type of shed. He could hear Broc yelling somewhere and others talking, but he didn't think they were close to him. They didn't sound loud enough.

He looked up. There was no blue sky, so he must be inside somewhere. Ollie noticed little slivers of light shining through the corners of the roof where the walls weren't exactly square, and he knew that at least it was still light outside. He could also tell from the heat in the room that it was still daytime.

His whole shirt, both front and back, were now covered in sweat and the air in the room seemed to be getting heavier, making it more difficult to breathe. Reaching his fingers up to his mouth, Ollie quickly pulled the constricting tape away. His mouth stung as the tape pulled away some of the skin from his lips, and tears immediately sprung to his eyes. He covered his sore mouth with his fingers and rested his back against the tin wall of the shed behind him.

Ollie carefully ran his tongue over his tender lips. If only he had some cold water to drink. *Why hadn't I brought water and food with me,* he thought to himself. His dad had always brought water with him when they'd go hunting together. He'd just been so keen to get out into the bush to look for rabbits, that he hadn't thought about it. He realised dismally that it probably didn't matter anyway because he doubted very much that Broc would have let him keep any supplies he'd had with him. At that moment, Ollie felt quite glad that he hadn't caught that rabbit after all. He would have hated seeing Broc take it away from him.

Once his mouth stopped stinging so much, Ollie tried to get the tape off his wrists with his teeth. He pulled and gnawed at the tape until it eventually came free. Shaking his arms up and down and rotating his wrists around in circles, finally free from their bonds. Next, he unwound the tape from his ankles which took some time as the girl in the gang, Cindy, he thought her name was, had wound the tape around and around his legs tightly. Eventually, he removed it all, with a lot of his leg hairs stuck to it and flung it angrily to the floor. He'd had enough of being stuck in this hot box. It was time to find the door and get out of here.

As his eyes adjusted to the darkness, he could see the wall next to him and slowly he slid his right palm along it, in the direction he thought the door might be. He took one small step after another, not wanting to bang into anything in the darkness. Suddenly, the loud sound of smashing glass made him jump. He stopped feeling for the door and froze on the spot trying to hear what the noise was.

Ollie could hear what sounded like breaking glass followed by laughing and cheering. It was the gang. He realised with dismay that Broc must have resumed his destruction of the town's solar panels. At least with the gang being distracted with their vandalism, it would give him time to escape. If only he could find the door and somehow open it because he very much doubted Broc would have left it unlocked, then he could make a run for it. He looked down at his feet. He couldn't see them in the darkness, but they felt sore. He had cut them on the debris from the solar panels that were scattered all over the ground when Broc had taken his shoes. He wriggled his toes. His feet were sore, his side was scraped, and his lips felt swollen like a supermodel's, but that wouldn't stop him. Nothing was going to stop him getting out of here and running away from this place. He wanted to be back home. Back home with Levi.

Gradually feeling his way around the wall, Ollie found the door of the shed. His eyes had adjusted quite well to the darkness now, and he could see quite a lot. Reaching out his small hand to the metal door handle, he quickly turned the knob. It wasn't locked! The handle twisted easily in his hand. He pulled the handle downwards as far as it would go and yanked on the door. It didn't budge. It didn't even move a tiny bit. *Maybe the door opens outward,* he chuckled to himself as he once again turned the handle, but this time tried to push the door outwards. Once again, the door didn't budge. The handle twisted in his hand without any problem, but for some reason when he pushed or pulled on the door, it wouldn't open. Stepping back from the door he frowned in frustration. Why wouldn't it open? It was clearly unlocked, or the handle wouldn't move, and yet, it still held him trapped.

Ollie brought his leg up to the door and kicked at it in frustration, crying out in pain as his bare cut feet impacted with the solid metal door. He slumped to the ground and held his bruised feet in his hands. He had to think. It was no good getting frustrated. That wouldn't get him out of here, and he was sure that once Broc got tired of smashing the solar panels, he was probably going to smash something else. Ollie did not want to be around when that happened. He closed his eyes and tried to remember what he had heard when they had thrown him in this shed. They'd been laughing and jeering at him, and Broc had yelled at him to 'be quiet', then it had been silent, and he'd heard another noise. He tried to remember what it was. Ollie opened his eyes suddenly and looked at the metal door. It had been the sound of a bolt being slid across. The door was locked, but not by a key or latch. It was by a deadbolt attached to the door.

Quickly standing, Ollie looked up at the top of the door. Maybe the bolt was on the inside of the door? Then, he felt foolish. How could Broc lock the door if the bolt was on the inside? It would have to be on the outside, and that meant Ollie couldn't get to it. He groaned in frustration, he wanted to kick the door again but remembered his bruised feet and restrained himself. He would have to find another way.

The sound of his stomach grumbling filled the quiet room. He didn't know what time it was, but it must be past lunchtime, and he was feeling ravenously hungry and thirsty. All he'd had to eat that day was some Coco Pops and milk for breakfast, and now he was starving. He sat back down facing the door and thought of food. He couldn't help himself. He knew it wouldn't do him any good, but all he could think about was grilled cheese sandwiches. The golden melted cheese running down the sides like molten lava. He could almost taste it in his mouth, and his stomach growled loudly again in anticipation of a meal that was not coming.

A sudden loud banging on the door made him jump and scoot backwards toward the wall. One of the gang members was outside. He could hear them laughing. It sounded like the girl.

"Hey, you in there. You want some food? We're just gonna take a break from our redecorating and have some lunch. If you want some, just come on out and join us." Cindy laughed at the closed door. "Oh, wait, your mouth is taped shut. Oh, well, never mind then," she giggled meanly as she sauntered off toward Broc, who was sitting waiting for her in the shade of one of the buildings.

Ollie could feel himself starting to cry. He couldn't help it. The tears welled up in his eyes like the water busting loose from a dam. He bent his legs up and rested his head on his knees letting the tears flow. They rolled down his face and dripped onto the floor next to his feet in little droplets. He'd been brave all morning. Even when Broc had been shoving him around and yelling in his face, and the other older kids had all been laughing and jeering at him, he'd been brave. He hadn't cried even though he had wanted to. Now it had all become too much. Ollie looked at the locked door in front of him. He was never going to get out of here! He was going to starve to death! Ollie couldn't think of what to do; he squinted his eyes and rubbed his small fists on his forehead until it was red, trying to make himself think. What could he do?

It was no good. All Ollie could think about was toasted cheese sandwiches on white bread with the melted cheese all yellow and gooey. His mouth started to salivate at the thought; he couldn't focus on anything else. Loud gurgles and groans from his stomach filled the air like some weird musical instrument, except this one didn't make you want to dance. This one just made you feel even more hungry. Ollie turned his head slightly to the side and started to weep again.

When he felt a tiny bit better, he wiped the back of his hand across his nose and opened his eyes a fraction. As his eyes widened, a little flicker of light suddenly caught his attention. He immediately stopped crying and sat up tall, looking towards the door.

He couldn't see anything. *That was strange*, Ollie thought, *maybe I just imagined it*. Frowning, he slowly lowered his head back towards his knees again, still looking towards the door as he did so. There it was. A sliver of light coming from the direction of the door. He hadn't imagined it! The light looked as though it was coming from the bottom of the door. He hadn't seen it before because he'd been standing. Now with his head bent down low towards his knees, Ollie could definitely see it. He quickly scurried on his hands and knees over to the door, his spirits suddenly lifted. Placing his little fingers at the bottom of the door and running them along the edge, he could feel a small gap between the door and the floor of the shed, and even better yet, he could feel dirt. There was a gap of sand about 20 cm on the floor from the edge of the door to where the concrete started. Ollie smiled happily. If he could dig enough of that dirt away, maybe he could squeeze under the door? Perhaps he could escape, after all.

Ollie didn't waste any time. His heart was hammering fiercely in his chest; he knew he had to hurry. The gang members might be back at any time now, so he quickly started scraping away at the dirt under the door frame with his bare hands. There was nothing else in the shed that he could use as a tool, so his hands would have to do. He wasn't very big, so he didn't think he would need a large space under the door. Any space he could squeeze his body under would be fine.

Luckily, the sand under the door frame wasn't compacted or hard, as there hadn't been the slightest bit of rain for a few weeks. The dirt was loose and crumbly just like beach sand, and Ollie was able to dig and scoop the sand out from under the door with his fingers quite easily. *It was just like he was digging a tunnel in the sandpit at school,* he thought to himself happily.

After a while, Ollie sat back on his haunches and looked at what he'd done. There was now quite a nice hole under the door and into the shed. It was time to see if he could squeeze underneath and make his escape. He looked tentatively at the hole. Which way should he go through? Head first or feet first? He decided on feet first; that way he could protect his head as it went under the bottom of the door. His face was already sore from the tape, and he didn't want to add to it by scraping his head on the metal door.

Sticking his bare feet into the hole, Ollie made himself pause for a moment. His whole body wanted to quickly squeeze into that wonderful hole and make a run for it, but a small part of himself was warning him to be cautious. As hard as it was, Ollie made himself wait for a few moments.

It was torturous trying to listen out for any signs that might mean that the gang was nearby, but he couldn't afford for any of them to see him. That would be disastrous.

Ollie tried to slow his thumping heart and listen carefully. He could hear the sounds of Broc and the others laughing and smashing the panels, but they sounded as though they were far away, not at all close to him. Good. Now was the time to leave. He was ready. Ollie took a deep breath in, reminded himself to be brave, and pushed his sand covered legs farther into the hole. He lay on his back and started to wiggle his body farther and farther into the hole and under the door. The space he had dug in the dirt was only about 30cm deep, but it was enough for Ollie to maneuver his thin body under the door. He squirmed and moved just like a snake until all that was left to fit under the door was his head. Ollie turned his head to the side to protect his face from the metal and inched his way forward. He used his hands to grip the dirt outside and move onward.

Finally, Ollie's head popped out from under the door, and he was free.

Taking a big gasp in, Ollie was surprised at how nice it felt to breathe fresh air again. Standing, Ollie looked down at his body and noticed he was covered in dirt from head to foot, like some sort of mud monster. He had bits of sticks and tree roots from the ground stuck to his legs and face where the tape had left sticky residue on his skin, and his hair was matted with sweat and dirt. Ollie didn't care. He was just glad to be free. Well, free of the shed at least. He still had to find his way back home.

Quickly looking around, Ollie tried to work out exactly where he was. It looked as if he was still behind the fence in the complex where the solar panels were. Over to his right, he could see the main buildings where he had been hiding and watching the gang earlier, and he knew that just beyond those were the solar panels. That's where the gang would be. He definitely did not want to head in that direction. Turning his head to look behind him, Ollie stared at the small building he had been captured in. It looked like a storage shed of some kind. There were three of the exact buildings all in a row. *They must have been used by the workers who tended to the solar panels,* he thought to himself.

Ollie turned to look to his left. There was nothing in that direction except the fence line and bare concrete. Ollie nodded, that was precisely where he wanted to go. He would follow the fence line back to the hole in the wire, and then he could escape into the bush. Once he was in the bush, Ollie was sure he would be able to find his way back home. At least he would be away from the gang. He just had to make sure they didn't spot him, or he would be dragged straight back into that dark, hot shed again, or worse.

Ollie crouched over to try to make himself less visible and ran straight for the fence. It didn't take him long to get there, his fingers reaching out to grab onto the wires as if they were a safety line. He clung to the fence for a moment, the metal strands leaving deep red indents in his fingers as he listened for any shouts of discovery. Slowly, Ollie turned around fully expecting to see Broc standing there ready to pound him into the dirt. His heart was hammering in his chest, and he felt like he was going to throw up. *Please, let no one see me,* he whispered to himself as he raised his eyes from the ground to look around him.

No one was around. Ollie was all alone. The sounds of the gang members yelling and laughing still filled the air, but they were some distance away. Ollie knew he was safe. For the moment anyway but he must move now while the gang was still occupied. As soon as they lost interest in what they were doing, he knew their attention would turn back to him. Crouching over again like an old man with a stooped back, Ollie jogged along the fence line. All the while, his eyes darted from side to side on high alert watching for any sign that he'd been spotted.

Just when he started to worry that he might have run past it, Ollie saw the hole in the fence. He felt instant jubilation and wanted to cheer out loud, but he knew better than that. Gripping onto the sides of the cut wire and poking his head through the hole, Ollie smiled to himself. The gang had underestimated him. They hadn't even contemplated that he would be able to escape from their makeshift prison. Broc thought he was just some dumb little kid. Well, he'd shown them! Ollie climbed through the fence and started running as fast as he could. As much as he loved his shoes, he would have to come back and look for them another time. Right now, he had a job to do. This 'dumb kid' was going to warn the other kids of Jasper's Bay just what was going on out here. Ollie started to laugh. By the time the gang realised he had escaped, Ollie would be back in town with a pretty good story to tell. *A story that deserved a reward of a second serving of toasted cheese sandwiches,* he thought to himself and ran a little bit faster.

CHAPTER TWENTY-EIGHT

Meanwhile, back in the central part of town, the effects of Broc's destruction of the solar panels were being felt.

"What do you mean nothings working in the house?" asked Jason, sitting at the kitchen table.

"Look." Lexi flicked the light switch on and off. Nothing happened. "Nothing's working. Nothing is working in any of the houses. The power is off, and my guess is, it's staying off."

"Fantastic." He slumped down in his chair. "No more laptop."

"Don't you start! I've had kids coming in all morning whining because they can't charge their iPod or watch a DVD," complained Lexi. "I don't know why they're coming to me. There's nothing I can do. I just had to send them away and tell them to find something else to do." She shrugged her shoulders.

Just at that moment, Hadley came charging in through the front door, letting it bang loudly behind her. "I just rode over to the farmhouse," she said breathing hard. "Katie says the farm generator is still working, so they've got power. Hi Jason," she waved at him, and he nodded his head in greeting. "Apparently, they're not connected to the main town electricity supply, though, because they're too far out of town or something."

Hadley had become good friends with Katie and rode a bike they had found tucked away in a shed at the back of the house over to the farm quite often to play. "She doesn't think they've got much fuel left for the generator, though, so I don't know how long it will last, maybe another week."

Jason and Lexi had been having a meeting in their kitchen, discussing what needed to be done over the next few days. The discovery that the town was now without power was not a good one. A lot of things relied on electricity to function, and the kids relied on those things to survive. Air-conditioning, heating, lights, stoves for cooking, washing machines for washing, refrigerators for cooling. Without the electricity, they had all grown up with and were used to, life would be a lot more complicated.

Hadley dropped her pink backpack onto the table and went to get a drink from the fridge.

"You'd better not open that too often," advised Lexi, pointing at the fridge.

"Why?" asked Hadley, closing the fridge door.

"She's right. With the power out, food is going to go bad quickly," agreed Jason, nodding his head.

Lexi stared off into space thinking. "Hmmm, that's going to be a real problem, lots of rotten food. Things are going to get very smelly around here pretty quickly." She brushed her hair out of her eyes. "I wonder how much ice they have at the shops. There was no power on in there either by the way."

"Right. Well, the ice is a great idea. Let's get some and put it in the esky. At least it will help keep the food fresh for a little while longer," suggested Jason, getting up from his chair.

Hadley nodded. "We should tell everyone else too. We can share out the ice.

Might as well use it before it melts." The others agreed.

Lexi walked over to the table. "Okay. Here's the plan. Let's get everyone to put as much food as they can in their eskies or their bathtubs and fill them with ice from the shop. Things like meat, milk, cheese, anything that will go bad should go in the ice. That should help for a few days. I'm not sure about the rest, though." She rested her chin on her fist and stared out into space deep in thought.

"I have an idea," said Lexi rubbing her chin. "Why don't we cook up any food we can't put on ice, plus any in the supermarket. That will stop it going rotten, and we can all have a big feast in town? I'm sure everyone would be happy with that. What do you think?" Lexi looked enquiringly at the other two, tilting her head slightly to one side.

"Mmm, that sounds great. I'm hungry already!" said Hadley, licking her lips. "It's only going to go bad, anyway, might as well eat it," she grinned cheekily.

Lexi laughed at her. "Yeah, that's what I thought, might as well eat it." She grabbed her sister's hand. "Come on then, let's go spread the word. We're gonna have a town party. That'll raise everyone's spirits!"

Jason got up from his chair. "Cool, sounds excellent! I'll get us some ice," he offered as he walked out the door, singing as he went.

Later that afternoon, the town's children lit a large bonfire in the town square, and the wonderful smells of roasting chicken and beef were making Broc's mouth water. He was pacing back and forth, repeatedly glancing towards the bonfire and the town kids feasting around it. He was hovering on the other side of the barrier of cars, watching them through the car windows. His eyes were steely hard, and he smacked his fist into his palm impatiently.

Although destroying the town's solar panels had been a bit of relief from the boredom he felt, Broc had expected to come back into the town and find all children running around in a panic. Instead, it looked as though they were getting ready to have a celebration and Broc could feel his anger starting to build. He pouted like a toddler who couldn't get his way.

"Where's that bloody Kevin?" Broc muttered indignantly to himself. "He said he'd be here. He'd better hurry up." Broc petulantly kicked a stone that was in his way. "Smashing those bloody solar things was supposed to stuff this town up, not give 'em a party! Where the hell is Kevin? This was his idea in the first place!"

Showing Broc the location of the town's solar panels was not the only thing Kevin had been doing to help the gang. After the incident in the town square, Kevin had volunteered to be the gang's spy, and Broc had been ecstatic at the suggestion. When Broc thought about the look on Lilly and Zac's face when they found out their younger brother had been spying on them, he had laughed heartily.

Broc stared at the kids throwing wood and sticks into the bonfire with distaste. His lip curled up in a snarl. He hated the way they were enjoying themselves. His hands balled into fists by his side, and his anger grew as Kevin kept him waiting.

"I can't wait to take over this town and start taking revenge on certain kids," Broc sneered, kicking his foot out at one of the black car tyres. "Especially that bitch who dared to hit me!" He grabbed his groin in painful memory. "She's going to get more than just a haircut!" Broc grinned, cracking his knuckles.

Not seeing any sign of Kevin, he started to pace again. Back and forth, back and forth.

*
* *

Meanwhile, Kevin who had stolen a whole lot of food from the feast was trying to find a way over the barbed wire that had recently been placed on top of the ring of cars surrounding the central part of town. Every time he tried to climb over, the wire cut his hands and got caught on his pants or shirt. Kevin sighed in frustration.

"This wasn't here this morning," he grumbled. "I would have noticed it. The kids had obviously put it up that afternoon. Just my luck!" Kevin jumped down from the roof of the car and peered underneath. There was no way under either as there were now boards of plywood dug into the earth under the car closing any gaps. "Those losers have been busy," he muttered scratching his cheek and staring at the wire. "I'm going to have to cut it." It would mean the others would find out someone was getting through the town's defences, but he couldn't think of any other way over.

Carefully hiding the food under the car as best he could in the small space, Kevin raced over to the hardware store to find some wire cutters. He was going to have to be quick as Broc would be getting impatient.

Luckily all the town kids were at the bonfire, and no one saw Kevin enter the hardware store where he was able to steal a pair of wire cutters and a couple of lighters. Not waiting around, he scampered back to the car, retrieved the food he had hidden and hoisted himself onto one of the car's rooves.

While the rest of the town was enjoying the feast, Kevin was busily trying to cut through the barbed wire without ripping his fingers to shreds on the sharp barbed bits. He had to work carefully. Whenever he cut a piece of the wire, it would spring back like a slinky and almost got him in the face once or twice. Wouldn't do him any good getting cut. He paused and looked down at his bag of stolen items. Not only was there food inside, but also stolen cigarettes, a bomber jacket and even a kid's iPod that had been left lying around. Kevin smirked. He had been smuggling food and other items out of the town for the gang for a couple of days now, and nobody had noticed.

"What a bunch of dumbasses!" he exclaimed as he cut another piece of wire. He was almost through the barrier.

Kevin looked up at the darkening sky. It wouldn't be long before it was night and Jasper's Bay would be in darkness. He chuckled and ran his tongue over his parched lips. Kevin had been the one to suggest smashing the solar cells that supplied the whole of the town's electricity. Broc hadn't even known they were there. The solar cells were located a little way out of the main part of town where none of the town kids ventured, so the gang had been able to get to them easily. Apart from the little Aboriginal kid spying on them, then somehow getting away, and Broc threatening to smash Kevin's nose just like the solar panels they'd been destroying, everything had gone to plan.

Kevin tapped the wire cutters on the final strands of wire and chuckled. It wouldn't be long before Jasper's Bay was plunged into darkness.

*
* *

Back by the bonfire, the Bailey family were looking for Kevin. "Have you seen him?" Katie asked, giving baby Sarah a beef bone to chew on. "He's going to miss out on his share of meat." Sarah made a happy, contented gurgle as she sucked on the beef bone.

Zac shook his head. "No, I haven't seen him for a while, actually. Come on. I'll help you look for him. Grab that plastic plate, and we'll take some meat for him." He pointed to a spare plate sitting on a fold-up table Lexi had set up by the bonfire.

"I'll come too," said Lilly, getting up from her seat by the fire and taking the baby. "I want to stretch my legs. I'm so deliciously full," she exclaimed, patting her stomach happily. "I think I've got a food baby!" It was the most they had eaten for a while.

"Hmm, me too," smiled Katie in delight. "This feast was a great idea. I feel like I'm going to burst."

Zac tousled Katie's messy hair. "Come on then, piggy, let's go find Kevin, it's starting to get dark."

The four siblings trundled off to look for their brother unaware that he had been betraying them or was involved in smashing the solar cells. In his relief at escaping the gang and being back safe at home, young Ollie had forgotten to mention Kevin's involvement with the gang.

"Logan said he saw him head this way," mentioned Katie as she swung her torch around in a wide arc trying to spot Kevin. She suddenly froze mid-step. "Is that a person up there?" she asked quietly. That didn't seem right. Katie swung the torch again, this time more slowly, stopping once she got to the car. Surprisingly, there actually was a person kneeling on the roof of the vehicle. How strange. She went closer to have a look.

"What is it, Katie?" Lilly asked, following closely behind her.

"I'm not sure," whispered Katie, hesitating. She squinted trying to see better in the growing darkness. "I think it's…" She stopped and started waving. "Oh, hey, Kevin! We've been looking for you. What are you doing up there?" She laughed. "We've brought you some roasted meat. It's really yummy!"

Lilly and Zac stopped walking and looked to see where Katie was waving.

"Kevin?" said Zac frowning. "What are you doing up on top of that car?" He grabbed Katie's torch and shone it towards his brother.

"Look! He's cutting the wire," said Lilly sadly, her voice full of emotion. Zac and Katie turned to look at her, their faces confused.

Lilly nodded and pointed to Kevin. "He's got wire cutters."

Zac turned back to look at Kevin, who had managed to cut a large hole in the wire barricade. He was standing on the car roof giving his siblings the bird. Katie looked horrified.

"You little shit!" Zac started to yell before Lilly grabbed his arm.

"Just leave it," Lilly said shaking her head. "He just wants you to react."

"But what's he doing?" asked Katie with a tremor in her voice. "Why's he cutting the wire? Is he leaving town? The gang's still out there!"

Zac put his arm around his little sister's shoulders and pulled her towards him. "Katie, I think that's where he's going."

"What? Why?" Katie's eyes flicked from Zac to Kevin. Her face looked as though she'd just lost her favourite toy. Kevin might be a pain sometimes, but he was still her brother.

"I don't know why Katie. I guess he just doesn't want to be with *us* anymore," said Lilly, peering up at Kevin as he balanced on top of the car.

Kevin laughed at his siblings staring up at him forlornly. They had the same gloomy look on their faces as they had when their parents had died. "See ya, losers!" He said condescendingly as he jumped from the car with his bags of goodies and ran to find the gang.

Lilly and Zac shook their heads in dismay before slowly wandering back to the bonfire. They tried to pull Katie with them, but she refused to go. She stood quietly in the dark for ages, staring out into the blackness. Now and then she would call Kevin's name hoping he would come back.

He didn't.

CHAPTER TWENTY-NINE

With the re-emergence of Broc and his mob, the discovery that they were the ones responsible for the loss of power to the town, plus, the added insult of Kevin aiding the gang, resulted in a lot of anger, resentment and fear amongst the children of Jasper's Bay.

Some of the other kids glared at the farm children with looks of mistrust as if they were somehow involved. Or that it was their fault that their brother Kevin had betrayed the town. Many of the kids stood in groups on the streets, huddled together whispering and gossiping. There was a general air of mistrust and an underlying current of anger in the town.

Kevin had done more than steal the children's belongings and food. He had taken some of their camaraderie and trust. With the power now permanently off, there would be a lot of work that needed to be done to keep the town running and the children who lived there, safe. This was the first time Jasper's Bay had been without permanent power since the KV17 virus spread and the children were afraid.

Lexi stood and watched the small groups of children pointing fingers and gossiping. She knew with the way things were at present, with everyone fighting and mistrusting each other; it was going to be impossible for them to work together effectively. And that's what the town needed if they were going to survive. Be a unified town, not a divided one. Otherwise, Broc would just walk in and take over. Something had to be done and quickly.

Lexi suggested a town meeting be held before things got out of hand. Fighting among themselves would not help their problem with the gang at all. Braydon, Hadley, Jason, Logan and Harry all helped her spread the word of the meeting around the town. It was to be at 1 pm that day.

The children of Jasper's Bay crowded into the small church, anxious to hear what was going to be said. Many gave Lilly and Zac a wide berth as they sat perched at the end of a pew looking anxious and alone. Luckily, Katie had stayed back at the farm along with Hadley and Sarah, so she didn't have to experience the hostility. She bit her bottom lip and held her brother's hand tightly. Tension and unanswered questions hung in the air. *Why had Kevin helped smash the solar cells? And why was he helping the gang at all?* It made it worse that the farm was the only place in town that still had power. It looked highly suspicious.

One boy wearing a dirty blue hoodie stood and pointed an accusing finger at Zac. "Maybe the farm still has power on, because they've done a deal with the gang!" He yelled accusingly.

Others also stood up and started to yell out nasty comments, and the meeting soon escalated into a tirade of name-calling and verbal abuse. The town wanted someone to blame for their loss, and without Kevin or the gang around, they were going to blame it all on the remaining farm kids.

Lexi went to sit by Lilly and Zac. She put her arm around Lilly's shoulders. As the noise level in the small church rose higher and higher, Zac and Lilly sat quietly their eyes defiant as they stared at their attackers. Unhappy with their silence the other children began to crowd around Zac and Lilly pushing into them and yelling in their faces.

"Hey!" shouted Lexi. "Get off them!" She tried to shove them away. The other children ignored her and continued to yell and scream abuse, spit flying from their mouths.

Logan and Harry quickly moved from the front of the church to stand behind Zac, Lilly and Lexi. They glared at the other kids in disbelief.

"What the hell is wrong with them?". Yelled Logan trying to make himself heard above the turmoil. "I know they're upset, but this is bloody ridiculous!"

The children's voices were high and shrill as they screamed their insults. Others, even some who were usually quiet and shy, were waving their fists in the air as if they wanted a fight. Logan stared at them and shook his head in dismay.

Some of the younger children had their hands over their ears trying to block out the noise as they crouched down in terror at the crowd that was quickly becoming a rabble around them. Quite a few started to cry in fright. Their tiny fingers clutched at their heads as they became more and more afraid, glancing around them at the older kids yelling and screaming.

Harry took one look at the younger kids cowering in fright and decided that enough was enough. "This is disgusting," he spat. "You're supposed to be our friends and neighbours!" Holding onto Logan's shoulder for support, Harry stood on one of the church pews and cupped his hands around his mouth. He yelled out in a loud, strong voice. "Everyone be quiet!"

Nothing happened. The noise in the church was too loud for him to be heard. Logan pointed to the front of the church where the minister usually delivered his sermon. There was a raised platform at the front where Harry could stand.

Climbing back down from the wooden pew, Harry started to push his way through the yelling kids towards the front of the church. Logan joined him, shoving kids out of his way if they wouldn't move.

Lexi continued to stand in front of Lilly and Zac with her arms stretched wide trying to shield them from the verbal abuse. Her eyes were narrow, and her mouth set in a thin line as she stared grimly at the hostile children in front of her.

Meanwhile, Harry and Logan reached the front of the church. Harry stood upon the small raised platform, and Logan went over to a table of candles set nearby. Harry nodded to him that he was ready. Logan took the matches that were also on the table, and one by one lit the long white candles. There were about twenty of them. When they were all lit, Logan took two of them in his hands and walked over to join Harry. He started waving them in the air back and forth trying to gain the crowd's attention. Some of the children closest to him stopped screaming and turned slowly to look in his direction. They stared at him for a moment before sitting down in one of the pews.

Harry again cupped his hands around his mouth and yelled out as loud as he could. "Everyone shut up! Be quiet!" A couple of kids turned to look at him, but most of them continued to yell at Zac and Lilly.

Lexi put two fingers in her mouth and whistled shrilly before pointing in the direction of Harry. A few children in front of her slowly turned around to look. As they turned, it was like a chain reaction. Slowly more children stopped yelling and turned to see what everyone else was looking at.

Logan continued to wave the candles back and forth.

One by one, the children ceased their hollering and eventually sat back down in their seats. The room fell silent. No one looked at each other; most of the children dropped their eyes to the floor. Their faces were flushed and sweaty.

Logan glanced to the back of the church where Zac, Lilly and Lexi stood. They looked stunned at what had just transpired. Zac's face was bright red as if he wanted to explode in anger, and he glared at the backs of the children's heads sitting in front of him.

Logan waved the trio to the front of the church.

The small church stayed quiet and numb as Lilly and Zac walked forward past their accusers. They held their heads high as they stood by Logan on the platform and stared out at the children below. Zac stood rigid and stiff, and Lilly held her arms across her chest, her hands were clenched in tight fists.

Lexi watched her friends in dismay. How had the town dissolved into such hatred so quickly?

When no one said anything, Lexi walked to stand by Logan on the platform and turned to face the children down below. Even though she was an outsider, she felt as though she had to say something. She had always hated public speaking and just for a moment wondered what possessed her to come up here to speak. Then she saw Lilly out of the corner of her eye, and she knew why. Lilly and Zac were her friends, and they needed defending.

Lexi cleared her throat and stood tall. "Wow, that was disgusting," she said slowly shaking her head. "I could maybe understand if you turned on myself or Jason because were outsiders and you don't really know us," she said with a sad voice. Lexi peered out at the crowd as she spoke. Not many children held her gaze as she looked at them, most stared at the floor or their hands. "But as far as I know, the Bailey family have lived in this town for generations. A lot of you have gone to school with Lilly, Zac and Katie. You know them, and you're supposed to be their friends. Is this how you treat your friends?!"

Lilly reached forward and took Lexi's hand in hers. It was trembling a little, and Lexi turned to her and gave her an encouraging smile. Lilly gave her a small nod in return, so she continued speaking.

"Lilly, Zac and Katie are good people, they help to feed you, and they don't deserve to be blamed for something over which they had no control. Just because their brother was involved with the gang doesn't mean *they* were too." A few of the children sitting quietly in the pews raised their heads and nodded.

Braydon and Jason made their way to the front of the church to stand beside Zac and Lilly. The eight supporters all stood together at the front of the little church, staring down at the other children of Jasper's Bay in front of them. They wanted to present a united front and show the other kids that Zac and Lilly still had friends that trusted them.

"Okay. So now everyone has calmed down a bit," Lexi said in a slightly sarcastic tone. "We can hopefully have a *normal* discussion about the situation were *all* in and what we can *all* do about it. It's no good blaming Lilly and Zac for something their brother did." She paused for a moment and glared at the boy in the blue hoody who had stood and looked like he was about to say something, once more. He sat back down. "I'm sure most of you have brothers and sisters. You wouldn't want to be blamed for something they did wrong, would you?" Many of the kids started shaking their heads. Most of them had siblings, and they didn't always do the right thing.

Lexi continued. "The real enemy is not in this town. The real enemy is Broc and his gang! They're the ones causing trouble, and now it looks like Kevin has joined them." She glanced sideways at Lilly and Zac, who nodded their heads in agreement. "Well, that's his choice; however, that means he's not welcome in Jasper's Bay anymore, just like the rest of the gang. We don't want trouble-makers here, and they're a whole lot of trouble. What we need to do is come together to work out how to keep them out of town and keep ourselves safe. Fighting amongst ourselves is just going to make us weak."

The other kids were now nodding to each other in agreement. They all wanted to help protect the town.

"I came up with an idea a few days ago, and I think things have gotten to the point where we need to implement it," said Lexi as she glanced back at Braydon who nodded at her encouragingly. "I know it's extra work," began Lexi. Some of the children groaned loudly, so she paused and held up her hand to quieten them. When the room settled, she began again. "As I said, I know it's extra work, but I think we need to start foot patrols to walk the boundaries of the barricade. If Kevin can get through the wire using cutters, then so can Broc."

Some of the children looked up at Lexi with wide, frightened eyes. She knew all this talk of defence and fighting was a new concept to most of them; however, it was something they were *all* going to have to get used to.

When Lexi stopped talking, Lilly whispered in her ear. Lexi nodded and stepped back. She felt relieved that someone else wanted to speak; she only hoped the others wouldn't start hurling abuse at Lilly again.

Lilly moved her hand to brush her hair behind her ears before remembering all her lovely long blonde hair had been shorn off by Broc and Cindy. She self-consciously rubbed the stubble on the top of her head instead. Lilly looked out at the crowd of children, some still eyeballing her suspiciously.

"I know you're all upset," Lilly began, her voice strong. "Zac, Katie and me, are upset too. How do you think *you* would feel if you found out your own brother was a dirtbag who not only betrayed this town but his own family as well!" She looked out at the crowd, her eyes bright with emotion.

Zac moved to stand right next to her. Lilly felt his body heat next to her and glanced at him thankfully. "Have you all seen our farm lately? Its half burnt down because of that pig

Broc, and we've got no dry food left to feed our cows or chickens. All we've got is what's in the paddock." Lilly paused and turned to point at Zac. "Plus, Zac was beaten up by Broc the other night, and he did this to me!" She rubbed her bald head with her hand. "Do you really think after everything he's done to our family, we would make a deal with him! You've got to be joking!" She stared at the children seated below her in defiance. They stared back at her, most of them looking shamefaced and regretful at what they had said earlier.

"Yeah, but what about the power?" questioned the boy in the blue hoody.

"Shut up, why don't you!" yelled someone from the crowd of children and a few kids laughed.

Zac gestured with his hands for the kids to be quiet before they started up again, and nothing got resolved. "It's alright. He just wants to know how come we've still got power, and no one else has, right?" Zac looked over at the kid asking the question.

The boy nodded.

"Right, well, it's simple. Out at the farm were not on the same power grid as you guys in town. We are too far out for it to reach us, so we've always had our own power. We're not connected to the solar plant. We've got a big generator that runs off diesel fuel, and that generates electricity for us." Zac studied the kids in front of him to see if they understood. He wasn't sure if they did, but they were nodding their heads, so he continued. "The problem is, Dad used to get the diesel for the generator delivered to the farm from Albany. Obviously, there are no more deliveries now, and we're almost out of fuel. We've probably got about a week's worth left, and then unless we find some more from somewhere, we will be without electricity too."

A lot of the kids in the crowd looked frightened, and an anxious murmuring started up among them.

Zac once again spoke up. "Look, I know the idea of not having any electricity is scary. It's not something we've had to deal with before. Our parents have always been here to sort it out, right? Well, now *we* have to deal with it. We'll work something out, but right now, I think the most important thing is to protect our town from Broc and the gang. We don't want them creeping into town and trying to take over."

Zac pointed to a group of younger children huddled together in the corner of the church. "Make sure you've all got candles, torches and lanterns that work, and look around your homes for any spare batteries. I'll go to the supermarket and gather together all the batteries and candles from there and bring them back here." He pointed to the church altar.

"Let's work together and keep Broc and that lot out of our town! Okay?" Zac pumped his fist in the air, his eyes shining with enthusiasm.

"Okay!" everyone yelled.

"Right then, let's get on with it!" Zac stepped back down off the platform, and the older kids crowded around him. Now the immediate situation had been diffused and the younger children's focus back on survival, they needed to come up with a solid plan to defend the town and get rid of Broc.

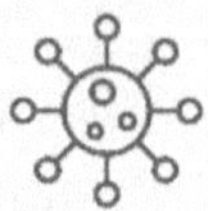

CHAPTER THIRTY

The children of Jasper's Bay had decided to go on the offensive and set up patrols around the perimeter of the town. Four kids patrolled at a time. Two at one end of town and two at the other, walking the boundary looking out for any signs of trouble. It probably wasn't hugely effective; they knew that Broc could get in if he really wanted to. However, being proactive and doing something, made them feel a whole lot better than just waiting around for him to attack.

Each pair of boundary walkers had a whistle. Three sharp bursts on the whistle meant they'd spotted trouble. Every kid in town apart from the toddlers, of course, had to take a turn at walking the boundary day and night. Though, the older kids usually took the night shifts.

This late afternoon Braydon and Lexi were at one end of town, and Jason and Logan were at the other.

After some thought, Lexi had decided to forgive Braydon for his part in terrorising Hadley and herself. She wasn't sure why, but Lexi felt quite intrigued by him. She liked his red curly hair; it looked just like tiny little springs. She was tempted whenever she saw him to run her fingers through it to see what it felt like. And she liked the way his kind eyes made her spine tingle whenever he gazed at her intently as though she was the only person in the room. But more than that, Lexi wanted to know more about him. He seemed conflicted.

As they walked along the boundary of cars, the wind rustled the dried leaves scattered on the ground and blew them against Lexi's feet. She stepped on them making a satisfying crunching sound beneath her shoes. Turning her head to look at Braydon she decided to try to find out more about him. They were alone together so now was the perfect time to talk. She just wasn't quite sure what to say. Braydon was quite a bit taller than she was, so Lexi had to look up at him as they walked along. His eyes were darting back and forth along the row of cars glancing everywhere, except at her. He seemed jumpy, and Lexi wondered if it was the threat of Broc or her, that was making Braydon nervous. She decided to try making conversation about the town, then maybe he would relax.

"My sister, Hadley, and I have only been here a few days. It seems like a nice little town, doesn't it?"

"Uh huh, it does." Braydon continued to gaze at the barrier of cars.

"I'm hoping we can stay and make a home here. What about you?"

Braydon didn't say anything, he just shrugged and kept walking. Lexi wondered if he was cross with her for some reason.

"Do you think Broc will really attack us? What does he want anyway?" Lexi probed as they walked the town boundary line. Having had a close-up encounter with Broc already, she wasn't too happy about the situation.

Braydon stopped walking and looked at her, his eyes serious. "Yes, Lexi, I think he will and for no other reason than to piss people off. He enjoys it, and he won't be happy until he's made a lot of people miserable. Plus, I can guarantee he's not happy with me. I'm sure he'd love to *teach me a lesson,* as he would put it."

"Great," sighed Lexi.

"Look, it doesn't mean we have to take it. We can do things like we are now, keeping a watch out for him. And we can fight back. He needs to learn that he can't always have it his way. Ever since we were young, he's been bossing me around, and it's got to stop."

Lexi looked up at him quizzically, a slight frown on her face. "Oh, yes, sorry. I forgot you two are cousins. This must be even more difficult for you." She gave him a small smile.

"Mmm, unfortunately, yes, and I feel partly responsible for him attacking the town. If I moved on somewhere else, he probably would too. The thing is I like it here; I'm not ready to leave." Braydon looked down at his shoes feeling despondent. "Broc is the only living family member I have left, and I hate him. I always have!"

Grabbing his arm, Lexi pulled him towards her. "You don't know for sure that he won't go. Like you said, Broc seems like the kind of person who would destroy things for fun. He'll probably get tired of being here and leave after a while."

Braydon looked at Lexi, his eyes examining her face. "Hmm, maybe. I think he won't stop unless I either leave Jasper's Bay or go back to him, all sorry and ashamed like a naughty boy. And that's not going to happen. I'm never going back to the gang."

"But why does it matter to him what you do?" She didn't understand.

"Because Lexi. He won't want to see me happy." Braydon stared out at the row of cars in front of them. "When I was ten my parents gave me a new BMX bike for my birthday. I'd been thrilled. I had broken the frame of my old bike a year before doing a jump, and I hadn't been able to ride since, so as you can imagine, I was pretty excited," he said his voice happy.

"Bet you loved riding it." Lexi punched Braydon lightly on the arm.

"Hmm, I did. Except that I didn't *actually* get to ride it until weeks later."

Lexi frowned. "Why not?"

"Well, as I was unwrapping the present, I noticed Broc glaring at me across the room with an angry scowl on his face. I'd been so involved in the joy of unwrapping my gift that I originally didn't think anything of it, until later that day." Braydon stopped walking and rubbed his eyes. He peered up at the blue sky for a moment before continuing. "I'd gone outside to ride on my new bike for the first time, only to find the tyres had been slashed to ribbons. I was devastated. Broc had followed me outside, and smugly suggested I must have run over some glass. Well, I obviously knew this wasn't true as I hadn't even ridden the bike yet. Plus, I remembered seeing Broc playing with a red pocket knife earlier that day."

Lexi stood shaking her head. "What did you do?" she asked wondering where Braydon's story was going.

"I confronted him about it." Braydon laughed. "And can you believe it, he threatened me with his knife saying he would cut up the seat too if I told my parents! By the way, he was only nine at this point, so you can see he was already turning into a bully."

Lexi stood with her mouth hanging open. "Nine. That's pretty young to have a knife!"

Braydon rubbed the back of his neck and gave Lexi a half-smile. "Yeah, well his dad was a bit of an asshole too. I remember Broc told me once he had found a wild mouse when he was four and wanted to keep it as a pet. His dad had made him flush the poor thing down the toilet and then beat Broc with his belt when he cried."

"Well that explains how Broc turned out," said Lexi looking up at Braydon. His shoulders were slumped, and he looked sad. She wanted to hug him but held back.

"It didn't make him easy to have around that's for sure, and because he was my cousin, I always had to invite him to my birthday parties. When I was eleven, I tried to get out of having him over, but my mum had insisted telling me I had to learn to be more welcoming," Braydon rolled his eyes. "I knew he would be a problem, and he was."

"What happened?" asked Lexi chewing on the edge of her fingernail. She could tell by the look on Braydon's face that it wasn't going to be anything good.

Braydon sighed looking at the row of cars as if in deep thought. "That year my parents had given me a little red Siamese fighting fish in a round glass fish bowl with coloured rocks and a little rock cave for the fish to hide in." Braydon smiled. "I called him Ollie and put him up in my room on my desk by the window. It was a lovely sunny spot, and I thought he would enjoy it up there. Anyway, after my birthday party was over, I went up to my room to look at Ollie, and I found my fishbowl lying on its side. The water and rocks were spilled all over my desk, and Ollie lay on his side, dead." Braydon's voice broke at the memory, and his mouth stretched downwards.

"I rushed to my desk and scooped Ollie up in my fingers, but his little fins lay limp in my hand; he was definitely dead. I hadn't known what to do and had raced down the stairs to find my parents." Braydon clenched his fists his body tense as he told his story. He sighed before continuing. "I found Broc instead. He was waiting for me at the bottom of the stairs, and I immediately knew he had done it. I can still remember the smug look on his face."

Braydon bent down to pick up a stone from the path. He looked at it for a moment before flinging it forcefully towards the barrier of cars. "He's such an asshole. We got into a massive fistfight, and I didn't speak to him for years. That was until he suddenly turned up on my doorstep a couple of months ago."

Braydon shrugged. "With both of our parent's dead from the KV17 virus, Broc suggested we team up. I hadn't known what else to do, so I agreed. I was hoping he had changed in the years since I'd last seen him. Obviously, I was bloody wrong, wasn't I?!" Braydon kicked at the ground sending red dust and pebbles into the air.

Lexi placed her hand lightly on Braydon's back. He was staring at his feet and seemed a million miles away. His brow was deeply furrowed, and he looked irate. Lexi tried to lighten the mood and change the subject.

"Well, listen. Let's forget about all this for a few minutes." She waved her arms around gesturing at the boundary of cars circling the town. "I want to know what you like doing in your spare time. You know, before all this happened?" Lexi gazed at him expectantly, a big friendly smile on her face.

Braydon looked down at Lexi's happy face, her big green eyes watching him intently. He cleared his throat nervously. It had been a blistering hot summer day, and even though it was now mid-afternoon, the sun was still blazing fiercely. It felt just like the inside of an oven. Braydon's shirt was sticking to his shoulder blades and sweat was trickling down his spine.

Impulsively he grabbed Lexi's hand. "Let's go sit in the shade for a minute. I'm melting out here. Wouldn't be too good to get sunstroke."

Lexi went along with him, and they sat in the shade of an old knotted tree, its branches all bent and withered like an old man. It felt good to get out of the sun for a while.

"You still haven't answered my question," Lexi persisted. "What did you like doing back home?" She wanted to know more about this boy. Something about him fascinated her.

"Umm, well, you're going to laugh," replied Braydon, still feeling unsure of himself. He could feel his face turning red.

"Come on, it can't be that bad," coaxed Lexi, smiling at him.

Braydon laughed. "No, it's not bad. It's just that, well…" He hesitated and then blurted out in a rush. "I like drawing mythical creatures." He paused to see if she was laughing at him. She wasn't, but she was grinning.

"What, like mermaids and unicorns?" Lexi asked teasingly.

Braydon laughed. "No! Like vampires and werewolves."

Lexi was still grinning. "Oh, like Twilight?" she joked pulling her knees in towards her.

"No!" Braydon's face went red, and he shoved her playfully. "More like the ones on True Blood and Vampire Diaries. Have you ever watched those shows? My older sister used to love them."

Lexi nodded vigorously grabbing his arm excitedly. "Hell, yes. I love Vampire Diaries! Great characters. Well, except Bonnie the witch girl. I'm not too keen on her," Lexi screwed up her nose in distaste. "I used to wait all week for the next episode."

Braydon laughed and nodded in agreement leaning in close to her. "Yeah, so did my sister. She would go on about it all week," he grinned, happily remembering. "She had posters of the shows on her wall, and I used to like drawing the characters on them."

"Your sister, what happened to her?" Lexi asked, resting her hand lightly on his arm, expecting bad news.

"Well, I'm not too sure. She's actually my step-sister. My mum remarried. Anyway, she's a year older than me and is on, or should I say *was* on, a school exchange trip to France." He gazed into the distance, a worried look on his face. "I haven't been able to contact her since the phones and Internet went down. I hope she's alright. I'm not really sure how to reach her."

Lexi rested her head on her knees for a moment. "That sucks," she said sympathetically. She felt relieved that her own sister, Hadley, was here with her. She placed her hands behind her head and lay back on the ground staring up at the sky. There were a few clouds making shapes across the endless expanse of blue sky, and she watched them for a moment. It looked so peaceful.

After a while, Lexi turned her head to glance at Braydon, and she noticed him staring intently at her. "What?" she said shaking her head slightly. "Why are you looking at me like that?"

Braydon smiled. "I'm just looking at your eyes. They're beautiful."

Lexi coughed. "Er, thanks." She sat back up rubbing her cheek which had flamed bright pink.

"Sorry. I didn't mean to embarrass you," said Braydon, his own face turning red. "They *are* beautiful, though. I know I sound like a creep or something, but it's true. I'd love to draw them." Braydon cleared his throat and looked away.

Lexi looked down at her shoes sneaking glances at him through her eyelashes. She wasn't sure what to say, so they both sat quietly.

After a while, Braydon stood. He grabbed Lexi's hand and pulled her up with him. "I know what you mean about that girl Bonnie," he said, trying to get the conversation going again. "My sister was always saying she's so judgmental."

Lexi laughed. "I like the sound of your sister. I hope I get to meet her someday." She kept hold of Braydon's hand in hers. It felt warm and secure. She leaned her body in towards him, the awkwardness she felt moments before now gone.

Braydon smiled at her. With all the stuff that was going on in the town, it was great to be able to talk to someone about the things they used to enjoy. The two of them walked together for a while, hand-in-hand, chatting about characters from TV shows. Just for a moment, they completely forgot about the time and why they were there and just enjoyed each other's company.

On the other side of town, Jason and Logan grabbed a pair of fold-out deck chairs and put them on the roof of one of the cars marking the town's boundary, making a lookout. Logan had a pair of binoculars glued to his eyes and was scanning the surroundings intently. Dust was blowing around in whirl-winds, making it difficult to see. The landscape looked dry, barren, and uninhabitable.

"Man, it's so hot and desolate out there. I don't know how Broc and his lot have been surviving."

Jason agreed. "Well, don't forget Kevin's been giving them our food and stuff."

"Oh, yeah, that's right. What's wrong with that guy? I mean, who would want to join up with Broc and that lot?"

"Yeah, right. Definitely a bit crazy," said Jason, tapping his head with his finger. "You wouldn't catch me joining up with him."

"Nope, even his cousin Braydon didn't want to stay with him," agreed Logan wiggling his eyebrows. Both boys laughed.

Actually, I went to school with Kevin," said Logan his face growing serious. "He never seemed particularly happy, but I never thought he would do something like this." Logan picked at the fabric on his shorts distractedly.

"What were *you* like at school?" asked Jason watching Logan.

"Me?" Logan laughed. "Oh, well, I had my best friend Harry with me, so I enjoyed school. We've been friends since kindergarten. We used to love making forts in the sandpit," he grinned at Jason. "I always loved getting home from school though. My dad was the town vet, and I usually worked in the clinic after school." Logan chuckled. "I love animals; they never judge you. I wanted to be a vet too when I got older. Guess that's not going to happen now."

"Yeah, things have certainly changed," agreed Jason looking out across the spinifex strewn landscape. "Only six months ago I was trying to work out if I wanted to go to university and look at me now. I'm on sentry duty here with you." Jason winked at Logan and pulled two lolly pops from his pocket. He offered one to Logan. "Strawberry or watermelon?"

"Where did you find those?!" asked Logan his face lighting up as he smiled.

"I have my ways," grinned Jason wiggling his eyebrows. "Actually, Lexi gave them to me!"

Logan looked at the lollypops in Jason's outstretched hand. "You took them from her stash, didn't you?"

"Yeah, I did," blushed Jason.

Both boys looked at each other for a moment before bursting out laughing, each enjoying the other's company.

Sucking on his watermelon lolly, Jason used his hand to shield his eyes from the brightness of the sun. He peered out into the rocky landscape continuing their surveillance of the area. "What's that?" he asked pointing his finger towards a patch of nearby trees.

Logan raised his binoculars to his eyes and quickly scanned the clump of vegetation. He thought he saw the glint of metal reflecting in the intense sunlight and stood to get a better look. He breathed in sharply and handed the binoculars to Jason. Something wasn't right.

Back on the other side of town, Lexi and Braydon continued to chat as they walked the town's perimeter. "Well, you're lucky. It's a great skill. I wish I could draw," Lexi said admiringly rubbing her fingers together.

Braydon smiled at her, obviously pleased with her comments. His arms swung loosely at his sides as he walked. "I suppose I could take it up again once things have settled down here. I could teach *you* if you want," he offered casually.

Lexi laughed. "Hmm, not sure about that. You'd really have your work cut out for you. I'm terrible at drawing."

Braydon looked at her and grinned. "You can't be that bad."

"Oh, yes I am! I think a three-year-old could draw better than I can."

Braydon laughed heartily, taking her hand in his again.

They both felt happy to be talking about something that didn't involve food, electricity, or Broc.

Lexi glanced at Braydon laughing. She loved the sound of his laugh; it was deep and contagious. Just hearing it made her want to laugh too. As she stared up at him, she was surprised to feel her heart flutter in her chest like a bird trying to escape its cage. Lexi realised she was starting to feel an attraction to this boy. His face radiated a real warmth whenever he talked to her, and it made her feel happy. Something she hadn't felt since her parents had died.

Lexi covertly studied his features when he wasn't looking and noticed that he had quite a defined chin with a little cleft at its base. She suddenly had an intense desire to touch it and wondered what it would feel like to run her fingers along its ridge. As she was thinking about it, Lexi felt her hand unconsciously move towards his face before she realised what she was doing and quickly drew it back, thrusting her hand behind her back.

Braydon, who had been gazing off into the distance, turned and smiled at her. Lexi wound a stray piece of hair that had escaped from its bonds around her finger nervously. She hoped he hadn't seen her trying to touch his face. She didn't really want to explain why she was trying to feel his chin!

Luckily, Braydon didn't seem to notice her awkwardness, so they continued their patrol, slowly walking past the old school and around the corner. Lexi swung her arms as she walked. She was just about to ask Braydon about his home back in Perth when she heard the distinctive sound of a whistle being blown three times. That meant trouble. Lexi's gaze locked onto Braydon's for one fleeting moment. The peace and tranquillity of the afternoon were about to be shattered. The sharp trill of the whistle blew again, an urgent call for help. They both started to run.

Lexi could hear a lot of yelling and booing going on as she and Braydon rushed to where Logan and Jason had been stationed. She saw Hadley there with Lilly and Zac, and she waved to them frantically. They waved back to her, their faces looking serious. Something was definitely going on. She saw that Ethan and his crew of drinkers were there, along with quite a few other kids. Everyone was milling around looking unsure of what was happening.

Braydon ran up to Jason and Logan. "What's going on? Did you blow your whistle?"

"Yeah, I did." Logan pointed to a spot just beyond the line of cars.

Braydon squinted to see what Logan was pointing at. It was Broc! He was standing on top of a tower of crates, one hand on his hip in a cocky pose and the other holding a megaphone.

"Where the heck did Broc get a megaphone from," Braydon asked, his voice on edge. "Probably Kevin."

Lexi stood next to Braydon. She put her hand in his, her body tense. "What's he doing?" she asked standing on her tiptoes and whispering in Braydon's ear.

Braydon squeezed her hand affectionately. "My guess is he's trying to get attention."

As if on cue, Broc suddenly spoke up. The megaphone screeched as he brought it to his mouth. He moved it away a bit and started his speech. "Ahem, people. I need your attention here! Your attention. Look this way!"

The crowd reluctantly turned to look at him. No one really wanted to hear what he had to say, but they couldn't look away, either. It was like being summoned by the headmaster at a school assembly.

Broc puffed his chest out like he was some great military leader. He looked as though he was enjoying the attention of everyone gazing up at him. He gave a fake smile and began his speech.

"I have decided that when I take over the running of your pathetic little town, I will be the president." Broc gestured to the smug gang members standing around him. "And my friends will be my council members. We will be making all the rules and decisions for you to abide by. Including rewards and punishments."

Harvey, one of the younger kids, spoke up. "Er, this is Australia you dumb ass. We don't have a president here!" Harvey's friends gave him a thumbs-up and snickered.

Broc turned to face him, his hand twitching in anger. He took a deep controlling breath. "You have to be patient with these children," he told himself under his breath. "You have to *educate* them in your ways." Broc smiled forcefully and brought the megaphone back to his lips. "Yes, well. I will be the *first* president then, won't I? You would do well to learn to accept it," he added snidely.

Harvey, Shawn, and Fuse all sprang up together as if standing to attention in the army. They held their bodies stiff and erect.

Broc smiled feeling satisfied. "That's more like it."

The crew turned to him and yelled, "Sir, yes sir!" They slowly brought their hands to their heads as if they were going to salute him as you would in the army and at the last minute, gave him 'the bird' instead.

Everyone started howling with laughter and cheering wildly. That is, everyone except Broc. Broc was not laughing. He wasn't even smiling. His eyes had narrowed in anger as he stared at the defiant little group. Slowly turning his back on them, Broc clicked his fingers at Kevin. Kevin quickly ran up to him, carrying a tall glass bottle. The bottle was filled with a dark liquid substance and had a limp piece of rag dangling from its neck. A Molotov cocktail.

"Let the education begin," said Broc in a cold hard voice as he lit the rag and sent the flaming bottle sailing over the wall of cars and into the group of children below.

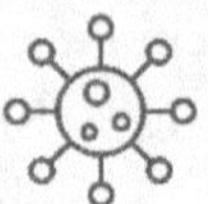

CHAPTER THIRTY-ONE

The glass bottle shattered as soon as it hit the hard ground, directly at the feet of the unsuspecting twelve-year-old Fuse. The overwhelming smell of petrol was immediate and intense. As if by magic, his shoes and blue nylon tracksuit pants instantly ignited in bright orange flames. Fuse screamed in terror as he frantically tried to slap at the flames with his bare hands. He looked like a puppet dancing around on a string, and Broc laughed out loud in delight. He snapped his fingers again, and obediently his gang members stepped forward, all with their own glass bottles in their hands. Cindy was grinning enthusiastically, bouncing from one foot to the other in excitement. Broc raised his hand in the air, held it there for a few seconds, and then brought it down quickly. The bottles went flying through the air like missiles, straight towards the town kids.

The acrid smell of petrol filled the air making it difficult to breathe. Bits of ash and embers floated around, threatening to catch hair and clothing on fire as children scrambled to find safety away from the danger.

Lexi felt panic starting to rise inside her as she frantically looked through the crowd trying to locate her sister. *Where was she?* Everywhere she looked, there was a maze of kids running and screaming in terror. Glass was shattering all over the place as more bottles hit the ground and small fires started up. Everything from car seats, to small bushes, caught fire. The thick grey smoke invaded her senses, making it difficult to see, difficult to breathe. She tried calling Hadley's name, but with all the screaming and yelling going on it was impossible to hear.

Crouching low, trying to find some clear air to breathe among the smoke haze that covered the town square, she stumbled forward through the crowd. Pushing others out of the way as she moved, Lexi eventually found her sister kneeling by a blue car over in the corner of the square. She was with a small group of frightened younger children. They were huddled around her like a mother hen, clinging onto her arms in terror as all around them the bottles continued to smash and burn, spewing forth their liquid contents and catching fire.

Hugging her sister tightly, feeling a tremendous amount of relief, Lexi spoke rapidly in her ear. "Listen, Hadley. Things are getting bad here. I want you to get to the farmhouse. You can stay there with Katie and baby Sarah." She tried to pull her away from the others.

Hadley resisted and took her sister's face in her hands. Looking Lexi in the eyes, she argued, "I know you're scared. I am too but, there is no way that I'm leaving. You can't make me. I'm staying here. We are going to need all the people we can get." She sounded determined. "Anyway, I can help the younger kids." She gestured to the huddle of frightened children still grouped around her.

Angel's younger sister Amy was there, along with the two brothers Levi and Ollie.

They all looked terrified.

Lexi sighed reluctantly, nodding in agreement. Hadley was probably right. If they were going to have any chance against Broc, they were going to need everyone. "Come on then, I'll find some of the other older kids. *You* find somewhere safe for these young ones to hide."

Hadley nodded her head and quickly started to herd the younger kids away from the car and away from the immediate danger. *Where could she take them,* she wondered to herself, not knowing the town well. The library was nearby; however, Hadley didn't think that was a very good idea just in case the fires got out of control and spread. Books and flames don't mix that well. She paused for a moment wiping the soot off her face, trying to think what to do. With all the screaming and crying going on around her, she couldn't think straight. Hadley felt a tugging at her coat sleeve and looked down to see Levi staring up at her.

"I know, honey. I'm trying to think where to go. I don't know your town very well. Just give me a minute."

Levi continued to pull on Hadley's sleeve. He looked as though he wanted to say something to her, so she bent down closer to him.

"What about The Magic Lantern?" Levi whispered. Hadley could hardly hear him. She looked at the little kids all clustered around her, looking up at her, their eyes wide with fright. She tried to be patient.

"What's the Magic Lantern?"

"It's a gift store," said Amy, pointing with her finger in the direction of the shop. "They sell board games and figurines and stuff."

Hadley nodded with enthusiasm and started to pull the kids in the direction Amy had pointed. "Board games, great idea. You guys can play a board game in the shop. You'll be safe there, and I can come back here and help out." The little group made their way out of the turmoil and headed straight to the safety of the shop.

Back at the conflict site, the smoke and ash were getting thick and heavy in the air. Everywhere kids were yelling and crying in confusion. Ethan had Fuse on the ground and was trying to smother the flames with his jacket as he was writhing around in pain. There was a genuine panic in the air. Behind all the screaming and crying, Lexi could distinctly hear Broc and his gang laughing in glee at all the turmoil they were causing. It made her blood boil in anger. *How could someone be such a dick,* she thought to herself.

Suddenly, through all the anguish and confusion, someone made three sharp blows on a whistle. Lexi turned towards the sound trying to locate the source. She spotted Braydon standing by one of the cars with a whistle in his mouth. He had three fire extinguishers, a couple of baseball bats and a tyre leaver lying by his feet. His face was serious and in control.

"Listen, people," he spoke calmly and with strength. "Things just went up a level. We need to put out these fires and protect ourselves. We are not going to let those bastards through the barriers. Right?!"

"Right!" Yelled a few others near him. At the sound of the whistle the children had stopped running in a panic and had gathered in front of Braydon. Eager to listen to what he had to say.

"And, we won't be needing any so-called president in this town. Right?"

"Right"! Yelled more kids, their fists held high in the air in defiance.

"I can't hear you!?" Braydon cupped his right hand around his ear.

"Right!!" the crowd yelled more loudly as they stared up at Braydon, eager for someone to give them direction.

"Okay. Then let's do this!" Braydon turned towards a group of middle-grade children. "Angel, I want you to find Hadley and grab these fire extinguishers. You two are on official fire duty," he said nodding to a young dark-haired girl. "Go and put out any fires you see but be careful not to get too close." Braydon handed one of the fire hydrants to Angel who promptly ran to find Hadley.

"Everyone else, find a weapon and watch out for those fireballs. We don't want anyone else getting burnt." Braydon's eyes drifted over to Fuse who was sitting propped up against a tree moaning in agony. "Shawn and Harvey. You two take Fuse back to your house and put him in a cool bath. He's going to be in even more pain once the alcohol wears off. Just leave his clothes on, don't try and take them off or you'll take his skin off too, okay?"

The two boys nodded grimly and grabbed Fuse under the arms. He moaned in pain, gritting his teeth as they helped him limp away to safety. The hair on one side of his head had been burnt, and his face was red with nasty-looking blisters. His hands where he had tried to put out the flames were even worse. Braydon shook his head in dismay as he watched them leave. What Fuse really needed was a hospital. Unfortunately, the nearest one was in Albany, and there was no way to get him there.

Ethan went to follow Shawn, Harvey, and Fuse. Braydon noticed and quickly called out after him. "Ethan don't go. I'm going to need you here."

Ethan hesitated, watching Shawn and Harvey move away from the group.

He sighed and reluctantly walked back to Braydon.

"Come on, mate," said Braydon, looking him in the eye. "We need you with us and, besides, don't you think Elisha would have wanted you to help protect the town?"

Ethan looked up at him feeling ashamed at his drunkenness. "Yes," he said quietly. "Yes, you're right. She would have." Slowly picking up a baseball bat, he looked at it for a moment before making his way over to stand by the barrier of cars with a bunch of other kids. He dragged the bat along the ground behind him as he went. "Time to fight back," he called to Braydon. His voice sounded determined.

Soon after, Logan came running up to Braydon with several others following behind him. They looked like a bunch of kids from the Lord of the Flies novel. Their faces and clothing were covered in sweat and soot, and they all held an assortment of weapons in their hands. A couple of others carried heavy buckets of water to help put out the small fires that had started up around the place. All their eyes were shining brightly, full of adrenalin and bravado.

"I've got this!" Logan said with a grin. He had his father's electric cattle prod in his hands. "If he gets through the barrier, I'll let him have it." A cheer went up from the group of kids assembled behind him.

Braydon took a step back. "Jeez, I forgot you said you had that! Keep it away from me. I don't fancy being toast!"

Logan grinned and released a few static charges into the air, much to the delight of the crowd gathering around him. Braydon gave him the thumbs-up and backed away smiling.

"And I found this." Jason had a slingshot in his hand. "It's not much, but I also found these." He held out his hand and in it were about twenty small metal balls about the size of a ten-cent piece and thirty or so marbles. "They're small, but I reckon they'd really sting if they hit your arm or leg."

Logan gave him a high five. "Come on then, let's go and station ourselves over by that red car. You can have a few practice shots, and I'll perfect my aim." He let off a few zaps of electric charge as they ran off to position themselves at the blockade.

All around the place, kids were arming themselves with baseball and cricket bats they had found in the school sports shed. A few had pitchforks with rubbish bin lids for shields, and one even had a mean looking machete. It looked like a scene from a horror movie.

After talking to Angel about putting out the fires, Hadley sent all the younger kids she could find, to The Magic Lantern Gift shop to hide, hoping that it was far enough away to keep them safe. Then, with Angel's help, they'd put out as many fires as they could and were now standing by on the lookout for any more.

Everyone else stood quietly behind the barrier of cars, ready with their weapons and shields. Determination and pride were set on their faces, ready to battle Broc and his gang and defend the town.

Braydon looked over at the crowd of town kids. Some were young, some were older, some were athletic, and some were not, yet here they all were, ready to do battle. Well, he thought to himself, smiling happily, if Broc wanted some attention, he was sure going to get it.

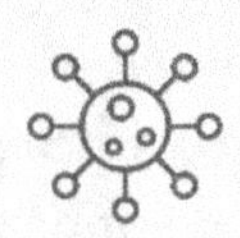

CHAPTER THIRTY-TWO

The sounds of children crying, and screaming had started to die down. Broc knew that now the shock of his surprise attack had worn off, the town kids were probably getting ready to launch a counter-attack. He'd watched enough war movies to know that's how things go in a battle. Attack defend and counter-attack. He'd have to be ready.

Broc put his fingers to his mouth and gave a sharp whistle. He could smell and taste fuel from the bottles on his hands. Cindy, Aaron, and Kevin came running over. He smiled. They were good little soldiers, not like his bloody cousin Braydon. When he got past these damn cars, he was really going to damn well enjoy kicking Braydon's backstabbing arse.

Broc rubbed his chin thoughtfully. "How many bottles have you got left, Aaron?"

"I've got one, Broc," replied Aaron, raising his bottle in the air.

Broc turned to Cindy.

"None."

"You?" Broc pointed at Kevin who hesitated.

"Umm, four."

Broc glared at him. "Not been throwing too many, huh?" His voice was thick with contempt as he prodded his finger roughly into Kevin's chest. Kevin looked down at the ground. Disgusted, Broc turned his back on him.

"Right, I've got one, so that leaves us with six. We can't do much damage from out here with six bottles." Broc looked over at the barrier again. "We're gonna have to get through those cars."

The others agreed. Cindy was particularly eager and sidled up to Broc, grabbing his hand. She wanted to get close to him. Broc shook her off, irritated at her clinginess.

Scanning the perimeter of cars, Aaron scratched his head in wonder. He pointed to a spot in the wire. "Well, looks like they've fixed the wire you cut, Kevin."

Kevin looked over at the barricade, then back to Broc, who was staring at him with a nasty look on his face. Kevin swallowed nervously as if he knew what was coming.

So did Cindy. She sidled up close to Kevin, putting her face right next to his, invading his personal space. "I'll go get the pliers for you, honey," she offered, smiling sweetly.

Kevin pulled a face at her and then turned towards Broc. "You want me to climb up there and cut the wire? In front of everyone!"

Broc nodded.

Kevin's face turned pale, and he looked as though he were going to be sick. "But then the whole town will know I'm a traitor! They'll know it was *me* stealing their stuff." He looked at Broc in horror with his mouth turned down. He knew Broc was going to make him do it.

Broc smirked and put his arm tightly around Kevin's shoulders. Kevin flinched. "Aww, don't worry, mate. I think they might have already worked that out. I'm sure your lovely sister has already been on a rant about it to the whole town. She probably couldn't wait to tell them what a traitorous bastard her brother is." Broc winked at Cindy, who grinned back at him. Kevin's face fell. He licked his lips, looking at the wire on the car in front of him.

Broc handed him the pliers and pushed him forward. "Go on then, little man. Remember, you're either with us or against us, and you don't want to be against us, do you? Not when you're all by yourself out here." Broc looked at him meaningfully. "Go show the town just how much of a traitor you really are." Broc shoved Kevin again.

Kevin stumbled forward with the pliers clutched limply in his hand. He looked back at Broc, who was standing threateningly with his hands on his hips, glaring at him with his eyes narrowed, daring Kevin to defy him.

Kevin sighed and stared at the ground. "This sucks," he muttered through clenched teeth, as he reluctantly took a step forward towards the barrier of cars.

As Kevin reached the first vehicle and put his hand upon the cold metal to pull himself up, he could see through to the kids on the other side. They were all standing and staring at him, their faces slack with wonder. There were kids Kevin had gone to school with, kids who lived down the street and kids he'd played basketball with. He wiped his forehead, wet with sweat.

Taking a deep breath to steady himself, Kevin pulled himself up onto the car bonnet and clambered onto the roof. His hand trembled. He ran his fingertips over the sharp blades. Kevin again wiped the sweat forming on his brow and snuck a glance at the kids below. Their faces had quickly changed from looks of surprise to ones of anger as they realised what he meant to do.

"What the hell are you doing, Kevin?" Yelled Logan, who was holding a baseball bat in his hand. "Why are you doing this? You're supposed to be our friend! You don't want to join with that asshole!" He was obviously upset, and his voice quivered in anger.

Broc who was listening jeered back; "OOOOO, nasty."

As Kevin stood on the top of the car roof, it buckled slightly under his weight. He took another deep breath and showed Logan the pliers. "Look. I'm with *them,* now, and I'm staying. You'd better watch out Logan, and all the rest of you lot, cause we're coming through!" He waved the pliers around. "And you're not going to like it when we do!"

"How can you, Kevin? You grew up in this town. Your family and friends live here!" Logan stared at him incredulously.

Kevin shrugged indifferently. "I don't care what happens to my family or any of you," he remarked rolling his eyes.

"Traitor!" someone from the crowd yelled loudly. Quite a few kids had gathered around Logan, anxious to see what was going on.

"Yeah, you're a traitor, Kevin, you belong with that scumbag Broc. If you hate our town so much, why don't you just leave?"

Another voice joined in. "Yeah, why don't you and Broc find a nice pig sty to go live in with all the other pigs? I'm sure you'll be very happy together. Just leave us alone!"

Katie had pushed her way to the front of the group and stood staring at Kevin with her mouth open in horror. "Why are you doing this Kevin? I don't understand." Her small face was screwed up in confusion.

Kevin remained standing stiffly on the car, staring down at Katie and the other kids below. He had a little smile on his face. All around him the insults kept flowing.

"Broc's just a dick, Kevin. He's going to wreck our town. You can't help him!"

"Come on. You don't want to end up like him Kevin. A jackass with everyone hating you!"

Broc laughed at the insults. They didn't bother him in the slightest. "Hurry up, Kevin. I haven't got all day!" he snapped.

Kevin glanced back over his shoulder at Broc. They nodded at each other, and he squatted down to again start cutting the wire. The sharp blades of the pliers cut through the first strand easily, and it recoiled back like a spring.

"Stop!" A strong voice from the crowd cut through the air. "Stop right now, Kevin. I can't let you do that. Broc is not coming back into this town."

Kevin paused, looking up for a moment not recognising the voice calling to him.

On the other side of the barrier, Broc tried to peer past the cars to see who was causing the hold-up. He saw Jason standing there, a slingshot aimed at Kevin. Next to him stood Logan with some type of pole. Broc snorted loudly before bending over and laughing hysterically. He thought that they looked like a couple of Boy Scouts. Definitely no match for him. He couldn't wait to have a little educating chat with them when he started ruling this pathetic town and its pathetic kids.

Ignoring Jason, Kevin positioned the pliers back on the wire and cut another strand. He looked down at Jason in defiance.

Jason raised his eyebrows and looked over at Logan shaking his head. Logan shrugged his shoulders. "Looks like he wants a fight," he said, his voice sad.

Jason looked back at Kevin in dismay. "Well, let's give it to him then," Jason exclaimed as he carefully loaded his slingshot with one of the metal balls.

Pulling the rubber cord of the slingshot back until it was taut, Jason held it for a brief moment, then let it go.

The metal ball flew at tremendous speed, like the snitch in a game of Quidditch. In the silence, you could hear it make a slight whizzing sound as it flew. As it reached its target, the little silver ball dramatically smashed into the window of the car Kevin was kneeling on. The glass shattered instantly.

The ball's speed was so great that it kept going through to the window on the other side of the car before finally wedging itself into a tree. As the glass shattered loudly into thousands of pieces, Kevin let out a yelp of surprise. He dropped the pliers and covered his head with his hands. The town kids watching below let out a triumphant cheer.

"What are you doing? I told you to hurry up, Kevin!" demanded Broc in frustration.

Kevin tentatively picked up the pliers, glancing nervously at Jason. Kevin started to cut the wire again, his hand now trembling. A thin layer of sweat had formed on his upper lip, and he licked it away. He focused on the wire.

"Unbelievable," muttered Jason looking at Logan who was standing next to him. "Well, he asked for it." He turned another little silver ball over in his fingers. The metal was cold and smooth. Letting out a sigh, Jason again loaded the slingshot and carefully took aim.

At the same time, Logan raised the cattle prod he was holding and ran towards Kevin. "Just make sure you don't hit *me*!" Logan yelled back at Jason as he ran.

Jason took careful aim. He took a breath in and let it out slowly. Then just as Logan reached the car, he let his second ball fly.

The little metal ball spun through the air just like the first one. This one's trajectory, however, was a lot closer to Kevin. Kevin raised his head to look at Logan, whom he saw with alarm was coming at him with a cattle prod. At that same moment, Jason's little silver ball flew past. It hit Kevin on the top of his ear, making a slight buzzing sound as it whizzed away. The metal ball was travelling so fast it took a little piece of Kevin's ear with it as it sped past. Kevin instantly cried out and grabbed his ear in pain as blood ran down his fingers in bright red droplets.

Logan reached up with the cattle prod and activated the high voltage electric current. It made an ominous buzzing sound. Kevin yelped in alarm at the sight of the electricity. Clutching his bleeding ear, he quickly jumped back off the car. Everyone below cheered.

"Stay away from the barriers, Kevin! yelled Jason, waving his slingshot in the air.

On the other side of the barrier, Broc stomped forward, screaming furiously at Kevin. "What the hell do you think you're doing? Get back up there now and finish cutting those wires!" Broc's face had turned red, and his eyes blazed in fury.

Kevin shook his head and backed away. Blood was starting to run from his ear and down his arm. He stumbled clumsily over to a tree and sat down with a thump, woozy and light-headed.

Broc looked at him in disgust. "Pathetic! He yelled in frustration, kicking sand at Kevin, who cowered away from him. Broc laughed before scanning the surrounding area looking for ideas. He spotted a bottle sitting half-buried in the sand, went to it and picked it up with glee. Lighting the fuel-soaked rag with his lighter, he grinned as it immediately caught fire. The orange flames burned through the cloth more quickly than he expected, scorching his fingers and he hurtled the bottle over the barrier in anger. It smashed straight through one of the barrier cars windows lighting up the interior of the car like a Christmas tree, only not so lovely. Broc and Cindy cheered and laughed with excitement.

No one was cheering on the other side of the barrier. There was a deathly silence as the town kids watched the car catch fire and burn. They felt the heat of the blaze on their faces and watched as the flames burnt and devour the cloth covered seats like a hungry animal. No one moved or said anything. It was if they were caught in a spell. They stood that way for several minutes until the awful silence was suddenly broken by the sound of someone in the crowd letting out an anguished scream. Then all hell broke loose.

CHAPTER THIRTY-THREE

As soon as Broc and the gang started throwing their flaming bottles of destruction, Braydon, Zack, Lilly and Harry huddled together and started planning their attack. They wanted to sneak in behind Broc and take him by surprise. Everyone knew that if they just waited inside the barrier of cars Broc would never give the town any peace. He would continue to torment them day and night. They had to force him to leave. What they needed first, though, was a distraction.

Lilly raised her hand. "*I'll* do it. He hates me. I'll stay here and distract Broc. I can keep him focused on me, while you guys get around behind him."

Zac patted her on the back protectively. "Well, watch out for those flaming bottles, sis. I'm sure he'd love to set you on fire."

"Yep. I'm sure he would too. Luckily I haven't got any hair left to catch on fire." She rubbed the coarse stubble on her head with her hand. It felt strange to her touch as though she was rubbing someone else's head.

Zac smiled at her fondly. "Yeah, lucky. Just remember what happened to Fuse. Listen, why don't you get a couple of other kids to help you, alright?"

Lilly nodded and winked. "Ethan can help me."

"Okay. Just make sure Broc can see that it's you and make sure you're really annoying. We want him to be completely focused on you."

Lilly smiled at her brother. "Oh, don't worry. I think I can be annoying enough."

"Jeez, don't I know it!" Zac rolled his eyes at her. "You're the *queen* of annoying."

Lilly started to laugh, then took a big gulp of air as out of the corner of her eye, she saw a bottle thrown by Broc come flying through the air like a blazing comet in the night sky. It sailed over the barrier in an arc, hitting one of the cars as it fell, instantly igniting the fabric seats as the fuel and flames rapidly spread across the cloth. She stared at the fireball. It was amazing how quickly the car had caught on fire.

Suddenly, a loud noise filled the air as the car windows shattered from the intense heat generated by the fire inside. Shards of sharp glass flew outwards, sending glass everywhere. Lilly instinctively ducked her head at the sound.

In the background, Broc and Cindy could be heard cheering.

"The sooner you are gone from our town, the better," hollered Lilly, her face full of loathing. She held her arms tightly across her chest as she watched the car burning. Thick, black choking smoke began to fill the air.

Just as Lilly was about to race towards the car to help put out the flames, she heard a sickening scream. She immediately swivelled her body and saw Harry collapse to his knees. A large piece of glass from the burning car's windshield had wedged itself into his throat. Harry had his hands pressed to his neck desperately trying to stop the blood flowing from the wound. He was making a kind of gurgling noise, and his face had gone deathly pale. He looked terrified.

Hadley and Angel raced to the lit car with their fire extinguishers, squirting foam onto the wreckage to try to stop the spread of the flames. The heat felt intense as it burned through the fabric of the seats, and it seemed to take ages to put it out.

At the same moment, Logan was walking over to Jason. He was happy that they had dislodged Kevin from the car and stopped him from cutting the wire. Logan hummed a little to himself as he walked feeling quite relieved that things hadn't gone too badly. He had almost caught up to Jason when just ahead of him he suddenly saw his best friend, Harry, slowly fall to his knees and collapse in the dirt.

"Harry, no!" Logan yelled, dropping the cattle prod and racing to his buddy. His feet pounded the dirt as he tried to quickly bridge the gap between them. Logan skidded and dropped to his knees as soon as he reached him. "God, Harry, what happened?" he whispered as he knelt beside him, looking at his friend in shock. The wound looked horrific. Logan quickly took off his shirt and held it to Harry's neck. It immediately soaked through with blood turning a bright crimson red.

Logan looked up at Lilly in alarm. She shook her head, and her mouth turned downwards. "He's got a piece of glass stuck in his neck from the car window. It's huge."

"Yeah, I can see it. Can't we pull it out?" Zac asked squatting beside Harry, his arm around his shoulder trying to steady him. Harry was starting to shiver violently as his body went into shock.

"I don't know. I don't think so. I think the glass might have hit an artery. Look how much blood he's losing," Lilly's voice shook with emotion, her face had turned pale. "What would your dad do, Logan?"

Logan looked at her with wide eyes and shook his head. He was feeling frantic. "I don't know. I've never seen him deal with anything like this! We've got to stop the bleeding, but if we pull the glass out it might kill him!" His voice trembled.

They could hear Broc whooping and laughing in the background, and the smell of smoke and burning material filled the air with terror. Lilly's face flushed with anger and her eyes turned steely hard with hate. She opened and closed her fists as though she wanted to hit someone. Closing her eyes for a moment, Lilly began to breathe hard. "Harry needs you. Stay in control," she whispered through clenched teeth.

Another bottle came flying over the barrier landing extremely close to them, smashing on the rubble. Flames erupted as the fuel in the broken bottle seeped along the ground. Lexi quickly kicked dirt onto the fire trying to extinguish the flames before they spread.

Harry grimaced at the sound of the bottle smashing near him and grabbed Zac's hand. "Go and get that bloody bastard before someone else gets hurt," he said through gritted teeth.

"What about you?" Zac squeezed Harry's hand tightly. Harry smiled feebly. "I'll be fine. Just go." He slumped over to one side. Blood now soaked the whole right side of his shirt.

Logan looked at Zac and nodded grimly. "You guys get going. I'm staying here with Harry." His voice was quiet, almost a whisper as he gently pushed Harry back up into a sitting position.

Zac hesitated, he didn't want to go either. Harry was his friend too. "No. I'm staying too." The wind was swirling around blowing eddies of smoke and ash around the clearing in little whirl-winds. "I wish we had some adult here to help us!" Zac cried, his voice full of frustration. He wrung his hands obviously unsure about what to do.

Lilly, Zac, Ethan and Logan all sat around Harry trying to comfort him.

Even though he had told them to go, he was kind of relieved that they had stayed. He didn't want to be alone. He looked at all the blood that had soaked through his shirt. It looked as though someone had thrown a tin of tomato soup at him; there was so much red. *How could there be so much red?* He was beginning to feel scared. He wasn't ready for what came next.

Lexi, Braydon and Jason stood off to the side, unsure of how to help. They wanted to stay, but they didn't want to intrude on the others' grief. They decided that Broc and the gang could wait a little while longer. No one wanted to leave.

Harry was starting to feel very cold and tired. More tired than he had ever felt before. He just wanted to close his eyes and fall asleep, but the others wouldn't let him. They just kept shaking him and talking to him, saying strange things like, "remember when we did this, and remember when we did that?" Harry tried to listen, but he couldn't focus on what they were saying. Their words kept drifting in and out of his mind. The wound in his neck had been excruciating at first, and he'd lost so much blood. He could see it pooling on the ground around him. Gradually he had felt the pain go away and where his heart had been racing in terror a few minutes before, he now felt much more at peace. He let his eyelids slowly close. They felt so heavy, and it felt so nice to rest them. Suddenly, he was startled awake by movement. Harry could feel someone shaking his shoulders. Reluctantly, he opened his eyes again. It was Logan. His best friend Logan, and his face looked worried.

Harry reached up and placed his hand on Logan's shoulder. His skin felt hot under Harry's cold fingers. "You are the best mate anyone could have."

Logan looked upset as if he was trying not to cry. He shook his head. "Aww, Harry, please don't…"

Harry interrupted him. "It's alright, I'm not in pain anymore," he murmured taking a shallow breath. "I just wished I could have started that mechanics business like I wanted to." His voice sounded tired.

Logan nodded his head and smiled at his friend. "Yeah, mate. It would have been great." His voice cracked with emotion, and he had to look away for a moment.

Harry's fingers tightened on Logan's shoulder. His breathing was becoming ragged and strained. Logan looked back at his friend, his eyes full of concern.

Leaning in close to Logan, Harry put his mouth to his ear. "Logan don't let Broc take over the town. And thanks for being my friend all these years." Harry's voice was quiet, almost a whisper, however, he knew his friend had heard, so he slowly closed his eyes once more, giving into the sweet relief. It was time to let go.

As Harry closed his eyes, his hand fell from Logan's shoulder with a thump, and he slipped over to one side, his body falling into the dust.

Logan couldn't hold in his anguish any longer and his face crumpled in pain. Slowly placing his hands over his eyes, he started to weep in loud wretched sobs.

Lilly took one look at Harry laying in a pool of his blood, and Logan weeping in utter distress before raising her face to the sky and screaming in fury.

"Broc you bastard!"

CHAPTER THIRTY-FOUR

Lexi watched Lilly's face turn from sadness to one of fury. Her eyes were dark, and her lips pressed together firmly. She stood with her hands on her hips glaring at the patch of blood on the ground staining the earth crimson.

"Harry never hurt anyone! He didn't deserve to die out here on the filthy ground, his blood spilling uselessly among the dust and rubble!" Lilly's voice shook with emotion as she spoke. "He'd had his whole life ahead of him, and now it's gone. Wasted. And all because of that gang of idiots out there!" She pointed her finger towards the gang's direction.

Lexi noticed Lilly's hands were shaking. She could hear the gang laughing and cheering in the background, oblivious to the pain they were causing.

"Are you alright Lilly?" asked Lexi going to her friend's side to comfort her.

"I feel like I'm going to explode!" exclaimed Lilly, banging her hands on her thighs. "It's like I've got an itch inside me that I can't scratch." The anger and frustration burned inside her like a festering wound ready to infect her whole body. "I just want to storm past the barrier and confront Broc, my damn brother and that bitch Cindy, right now!" Lilly held her hands clenched in tight fists of anger, rigid by her sides as she tried to maintain control.

Lexi gently placed her arm around Lilly's shoulders; she could feel her body was hot and sweaty. Lilly turned to face Lexi. There were tears in her eyes. "All I can think about is clawing Broc's face and slapping Cindy's," she gave a small unhappy snort. "that would stop them laughing!"

"Don't worry, we all feel the same," said Lexi wrapping her arms around Lilly hugging her. Both girls stood in silence for a moment.

Lilly ran her fingers through her hair. "I just can't believe Harry's dead," she whispered, her shoulders slumped. "And, I can't believe my scumbag brother! Arrrg. How could Kevin turn against us, his own family and his own town?" She slowly closed her hand into a tight fist, the knuckles going white. "What have we ever done to him?" Lilly's voice rose again, and she began pacing up and down beating her fists against her thighs, her anger returning. "I should go and confront them," she was muttering under her breath, her voice on edge.

Lexi watched Lilly taking big angry strides across the ground, thumping her feet as she walked. Her face had become a ball of rage and pain, and she looked as though she were about to explode. Lexi hated seeing her friend so furious but what could she say? *Lilly had a right to be angry; they all did. What Broc and the gang had done was diabolical. To take an innocent person's life for no reason at all, it was shocking!*

Lexi walked to catch up to Lilly and grabbed her by the shoulders. She forced Lilly to stop pacing and calm down. Lilly seemed surprised to see her there as if she hadn't even noticed Lexi walking beside her. Gradually, her face started to lose its hostile look, and her shoulders slumped. Lexi really felt for her. *Seeing someone die like that right in front of you and not being able to do something about it, really sucked.*

"Lilly, look at me," she said calmly, taking Lilly's face in both her hands and looking her in the eye. "I know you want to punish those bastards, we all do. But if we rush into this, someone else will get hurt." Lexi dropped her hands from Lilly's face. Her eyes flicked towards the barrier. "We have to play it smart, outthink him, something he's not good at, right? He's not exactly the brightest crayon in the box."

Lilly slowly unclenched her fists. She straightened her shoulders and reluctantly smiled, the anger dissipating. "Damn straight," she agreed, her voice steady. "Outthink him, got it. That shouldn't be too hard." She crossed her arms and stared out beyond the row of cars, "and then we'll get the bastard."

Lexi nodded. "Yes, then we'll get the bastard."

Feeling enraged at Harry's death and the burning of Fuse, the group decided to go ahead with the plan to go beyond the barrier and confront the gang. Lilly, Ethan, and a few other kids positioned themselves near the ring of cars, ready to act as decoys. Close enough so Broc could see them, but out of range of his flaming bottles.

The plan was to get Broc to agree to leave the town and go somewhere else. It was Braydon's job to try to talk to Broc rationally and convince him to leave peacefully.

Braydon glanced up at the sky. There were only a few wispy white clouds in an otherwise blue sky, and it looked so peaceful up there. Much more peaceful than down below.

"God, how I detest my cousin," Braydon whispered to Lexi as they sat close together discussing the plan. His leg was jiggling up and down, and he was talking quickly. "He always makes things so difficult."

"What if he wants to fight with you again?" asked Lexi taking his hand, linking her fingers through his. She was thinking back to a few days ago in the town square when Broc had given Braydon a beating.

Braydon looked at Lexi sadly and shrugged. "I guess I'll have to fight him. He's a lot stronger than me though, and he won't fight fair." He glanced at the others anxiously waiting to carry out the plan. Jason was talking to Logan and Zac to Lilly. Everyone looked edgy.

"I know everyone wants to help protect the town, but I can't ask anyone else to go up against Broc. I know Broc the best, and besides, I feel responsible for him hanging around the town." Braydon stood and pulled Lexi up with him. He turned to face her, tenderly tucking a stray piece of hair behind her ear.

"It's up to me to make Broc and the rest of the gang leave, and it has to be now," declared Braydon, his voice was no longer uneasy. "Enough damage has already been done. It's time for them to go."

The two of them walked to join the others. Everyone looked jumpy but ready to go.

"Be careful," called Logan looking up at Jason. He was still sitting next to Harry and had placed his jacket over his friend's face.

"And say *hello* to our traitorous brother!" Lilly whispered to Zac, slinging her arm around his shoulders.

"You guys just watch out for those flaming bottles," Zac replied solemnly, walking towards the boundary. "We don't want any more injuries." His eyes flicked to Harry for a moment before he turned to go.

Making their way over to the cars, Lexi, Braydon, Zac and Jason slipped through one of the vehicles on the right-hand side of the barrier. Ready to sneak behind Broc as soon as Lilly started her distraction. All the cars had their side windows boarded with sheets of wood, their doors locked, and barbed wire strung across from one car to the next hoping to deter anyone getting past the barrier. To go through themselves, the group used the keys to the car to quietly unlocked the door, climb through to the other side and then lock the car door again. Braydon put the keys in his jeans pocket for safe keeping. They'd need them to get back through later.

Zac went first, followed by Jason, then Lexi, and Braydon last. When it was her turn, Lexi quickly scuttled along the back seat of the car and through the door on the other side. She crouched down beside the car, waiting for Lilly to draw Broc's attention. She was finding it hard to sit still. Her hands felt jittery, and she tapped them restlessly against her thigh, her stomach quivering in anxiety. *Why did she always feel like she was going to throw up when she was nervous?*

Lexi craned her head to the side, stretching her neck past Jason and Zac so she could see what was going on. She spied Broc standing smugly with his hands on his hips and his chin jutting forward. He was talking to Kevin, and although Lexi couldn't hear what Broc was saying, from the look on Kevin's face and the smirk on Cindy's, Lexi guessed that it wasn't pleasant. She almost felt sorry for Kevin. Almost. It was his choice to join the gang, after all so, whatever he had to suffer at the hands of Broc, it was his own doing.

As they squatted by the car waiting for the right time, Lexi hoped and prayed that Broc wouldn't turn around in their direction. There was absolutely no cover for them, and he would spot them for sure. Adrenaline coursed through her body making her heart beat fast and her palms sweaty. The others all seemed as nervous as she was. Jason's eyes were wide, and he was fidgeting anxiously. Zac was cracking his knuckles, his mouth set in a thin line as he peered ahead. Only Braydon looked calm.

As Lexi watched Braydon, he smiled at her and nodded reassuringly. For some reason, it made her feel calmer. She took a deep breath, then breathed out slowly attempting to control her nerves. *Lexi wondered how Braydon could seem so relaxed when he knew exactly how unpredictable his cousin was?*

Everyone was crouched down silently by the car, each thinking their own thoughts, waiting for Lilly to start her distraction ploy so that they could all move up on the gang. Braydon glanced over his shoulder back at Lexi resignedly and hoped they'd all get through this alright. He made a pact with himself that by the end of this day, he would pluck up the courage and kiss her. He only hoped that Broc didn't beat him up too much before he could do it.

The stillness was suddenly broken by the sound of a loud, clear voice. "How are you going over there, Mr President, with all your tin soldiers?" Lilly yelled in as condescending voice as she could put on. "Must be lonely only having trained rats for friends!" She jeered sassily, hoping to get Broc's attention. She needn't have worried. Broc sprang to his feet as soon as he heard Lilly's voice. A look of anger past over his face briefly before he managed to control it.

"Is that the lovely farm girl? It's such a pity Facebook is no longer working. You'd have to change your profile picture," Broc jeered back at her. "Don't think you'd get too many boyfriends, though, with that flat chest and lovely boy's haircut," he laughed.

Cindy stood up and joined in. "Yes, she's *very* sexy now. You'd have to change your status to permanently single. And ugly."

Lilly blushed. Ethan, who was standing next to her, grabbed her hand and squeezed it in support. He whispered for her to keep going. The distraction was working.

Nodding her head and clearing her throat, Lilly continued her taunting. "Well, Broc, Perhaps I could steal one of your boyfriends. I'm sure you've got plenty to spare."

Cindy looked highly offended by this comment and huffed, "He doesn't have boyfriends. He has me!"

Ethan laughed and yelled out sarcastically in response. "Oh, well, I'm sure he's sooo pleased about that."

"Shut up! What would you know?" Cindy screamed back at him as she picked up the bottle that was sitting by her feet and threw it against a nearby car. It wasn't even lit. The bottle smashed harmlessly on her side of the barrier, the liquid inside spilling all over the ground leaving a pink puddle.

Broc exploded in a fury. "What the hell, Cindy! That was our last bottle, you stupid bitch! God, I'm surrounded by morons!" He ranted for several minutes, screwing up his face in anger and waving his arms around dramatically. Kevin, Cindy and Aaron all watched him in alarm, not sure what he would do.

"Er, sorry to interrupt!" yelled Lilly, starting to enjoy herself. "I think your pet monkeys, I mean, council members, need a bit of discipline over there."

Broc glared at Cindy, his eyes narrowing in anger. She stormed away from him and sat down in a huff next to Kevin, putting her arm across his shoulders looking for some sympathy. He ignored her.

"I hope you plan on running the town a lot better," Lilly continued to taunt Broc. Like most bullies, getting a reaction from Broc, was easy.

Hearing Lilly's voice once again, Broc angrily turned towards her and hissed like a viper. "Oh, don't worry, love. I'll be showing the town some discipline alright, and you'll be the first to get some." Grinning menacingly, he cracked his knuckles loudly one by one. "I can't wait to get my hands on that farm girl again; she's far too sassy for my liking," he grumbled hitting his fist into his palm.

Back by the cars, the sun was beating down relentlessly baking the soil until it was dry and brittle. A few tiny lizards and ants braved the afternoon sun on their search for food, but mostly all was still. While Lilly was busily distracting Broc,

Braydon and the others had silently crept forward. They were slowly inching their way closer and closer towards him, step by step.

The group moved forward in single file trying to make their progress harder to see. The dust from the dry ground was stirred up as they crouched low and scuttled along the ground like crabs along the shore. Lexi was trying desperately not to cough as the dust particles tickled her throat. She put her hand over her mouth trying not to breathe in too deeply. She didn't want to be the one that gave them away.

Broc remained with his back to them and was now waving his arms around in an animated fashion as he returned insults back and forth with Lilly. She was doing an excellent job of keeping him occupied. He was fuming at Lilly's taunts.

Every now and then, Broc would begin to turn around, and the group would freeze thinking he would spot them sneaking up on him. Luckily, Lilly's taunting words always brought him back to face her again.

With Zac in the lead, the group gradually made it right up-close to the gang without being spotted. Cautiously and quietly they inched forward, closer and closer like a cat hunting its prey. Lexi was beginning to think that this plan might just work when Kevin glanced towards the group and instantly spotted Zac.

Zac instinctively froze like a deer in headlights, then slowly raised his finger to his mouth hoping Kevin would stay silent. They only needed a couple more metres, and they would be able to take Broc by surprise.

Kevin gazed happily at the little group and nodded his head in recognition. They could see what looked like blood smeared down one side of his face and shirt. Turning his head slightly, Kevin glanced at Broc, who was still occupied with Lilly.

Placing his hands on the ground next to his feet to steady himself, Kevin stood slowly. Taking his time, he stretched his arms over his head, then motioned for the group to come forward. Zac breathed a sigh of relief and gave his brother a happy nod. The group got ready to tiptoe forward again.

Then, before Zac could take one single step, Kevin's face abruptly turned hard and mean. He gave Zac and the others a nasty smile, and without warning, he turned towards Broc and yelled out dramatically, "Broc, look out, we're under attack!"

Broc immediately spun around with a look of pure excitement on his face. "At last a bit of action," he crowed happily.

Zac looked gutted. His own brother had just coldheartedly betrayed him. Zac stood motionless. His hand, which only moments before had been raised in a friendly wave, now hung limply by his side.

"You're such a wanker, Kevin!" yelled Lexi, shaking her head at him, frustration written all over her face.

Kevin stared at her blankly, a dull look on his face. "I don't care what you think," he mumbled. "I'm sick of the lot of you." He turned his back on Lexi and looked towards Broc.

Broc was clapping his hands in glee like a little child at Christmas, excitement welling up inside of him. "Well, well, well. Hello girly, so nice to see you again. And so nice of you to come over to this side of the barrier." Broc laughed heartily. "It makes things so much easier. I do believe I owe you for a certain injury you caused me last time we met."

Lexi smirked at him. "Oh, yes, how are they?" She pointed towards his groin.

"Better than you're going to be," he threatened, taking a step towards her, a fake smile plastered on his face. Braydon quickly moved in front of Lexi shielding her with his arm.

Broc snorted and laughed nastily, "Well, I see you now have a protector, hey, love? That's going to make things *very* interesting." He cracked his knuckles again, making loud popping sounds and glared at Braydon. His eyes were full of malice. "*Very* interesting."

Cindy quickly stood wanting to join in the action. Brushing her hair out of her eyes, she glanced at Lexi as though trying to work out who she was.

Watching Lexi talk to Broc, Cindy suddenly took a sharp breath in. "You're that bitch who smashed my leg with the bat!" she shrieked her voice full of hate. "I can't wait to see you face down in the dirt crying like a baby." Cindy's eyes narrowed into slits, and a nasty smile spread across her face. She stomped towards Lexi.

Zac, who was standing close to Cindy noticed her scowling at Lexi with what looked like pure hatred. Her fingers had contorted into claws as if she wanted to scratch Lexi's eyes out.

Alarmed, Zac quickly moved to cut Cindy off before she could cause any trouble. He grabbed her by the arms and held her tight. "I don't think so. You stay right where you are." Zac's voice was calm and resolute.

Cindy squirmed and thrashed around in Zac's grip furiously. She bent her body to the side trying to reach behind and hit him with her fist. Zac held her tighter.

"Oww, Broc, he's hurting me," she complained in a childish tone, her lips pouting as she aimed hard kicks at Zac's shins. Twisting her body back and forth, she tried to break free.

However, Zac was used to handling cows and held her in a vice-like grip. "You're not going anywhere," he warned through gritted teeth.

Broc glanced over at her. "Oh, shut up, Cindy." His focus was purely on Braydon and Lexi.

Scowling at Broc's lack of interest, Cindy turned to Aaron. "Aaron, a little help. Now!" she demanded petulantly.

Aaron looked at Cindy struggling in Zac's arms and moved towards her. Jason saw him move and put his arms up to stop him. He rested one hand on Aaron's chest. "You'd better stay where you are, pal. I don't want to have to go all ninja on your ass."

Aaron peered anxiously at Jason for a moment deciding what to do. Jason was scowling as though he meant business.

Aaron held up his hands and took a step back. "Sorry Cindy, you're on your own," he muttered looking at the ground.

Braydon quickly took a step towards Broc and put his hand out in front of him trying to make peace. "Listen, cousin. No one needs to get hurt here. We've just come to talk with you guys," he said looking at the gang members hopefully. Although Braydon's face appeared calm, a single drop of perspiration ran down the side of his head betraying his anxiety.

Broc folded his arms across his chest and stared at Braydon with a bored look on his face. He picked a piece of food from between his teeth, flicking it at Braydon. "Go on then. Talk."

Braydon swallowed. If he could reason with Broc, maybe they wouldn't have to fight, and no one would get hurt. He glanced at Lexi and cleared his throat apprehensively. "Well, okay. Look, you've had some fun here with this town and these kids." He gestured towards the town with his hand.

Broc nodded as he took his knife from his pocket and began cleaning his fingernails with its shiny blade. "Go on."

Braydon looked at him, trying to gauge his mood. "Don't you think it's time to move on and find another town? Aren't you getting bored here?"

"Oh, don't worry about me, I'll move on, cousin. I'll move on today. But only if you come with us," Broc smirked, looking between Lexi and Braydon. He winked at Lexi. "I'd be happy to take my coward of a cousin back. But there's no way I'm leaving this town while he stays and plays happy families." He turned his head and spat on the ground. Cindy laughed.

Braydon sighed. Broc was obviously trying to provoke him. "Broc. I'm sorry, but I just don't want to go around causing trouble anymore. I'm sick of it," said Braydon keeping his voice steady and calm. "I want to stay here and make a life." He looked Broc in the eyes, hoping he would understand.

Broc just snorted. "Well, you're no fun anymore," he jeered, and in one swift movement, he took the blade of his knife and viciously plunged the cold hard steel straight into the muscle of Braydon's thigh. "Looks like I'm going to have to teach you a lesson before we drag your sorry ass away with us, cousin."

As the hard metal blade sank deep into Braydon's thigh muscle, the pain was instant. His face twisted and he cried out dropping to his knees. A bright red pool of blood quickly began to form through the fabric of his pants. It looked like a child's painting as it started to spread out in a red pattern, slowly growing in size.

Jason and Zac stared at Broc, stunned by what just happened. His eyes were wild with excitement and an evil grin spread across his face like a possessed clown. He started laughing gleefully, having no remorse for what he had just done. He obviously didn't care who he hurt. Family or not.

Lexi let out a gasp of surprise and horror as she watched Braydon grab his leg and collapse to his knees in pain. She couldn't believe it; Broc had actually stabbed his own cousin. *What sort of person did that?* Lexi stared at the knife protruding from an awkward angle in Braydon's thigh and the bright red blood patch spreading from the wound. Feeling a wave of revulsion spread over her, Lexi turned to glare at Broc. He had both his hands on his hips and was happily grinning at everyone as if he had just won a prize in a competition.

Lexi was horrified at this guy and his crappy attitude. The way he thought he could do anything he damn well liked. "Well, not this time," said Lexi under her breath. She wasn't going to let him get away with this. Marching up to Broc, she stood bravely in front of him, her own eyes glaring fiercely.

"Braydon has made his decision. He is staying in this town where *he* is welcome. You and your gang are *not* welcome, and you are bloody well leaving. Today."

Broc abruptly stopped laughing. It was if a switch had been flicked off and his eyes were drawn to her face. They were full of hate and disdain. Lexi expected him to say something snide to her, and she got ready to say something straight back.

Instead, Broc remained silent. He stared at her without blinking. A slight tremor flickered above his right eyebrow.

Lexi felt unnerved at the silence. She was about to repeat herself, when, without warning, Broc raised his right hand and slapped her hard across the face. The stinging blow made a loud cracking noise as Broc's hard calloused hand made contact with her soft skin.

Lexi instantly saw stars and stumbled backwards, reeling away from him. The force of the slap sent her flailing, her arms pin-wheeling around like a giant wind turbine, trying to stop her fall. Unable to stop the momentum, she felt herself tumbling back towards the ground as gravity took hold. As she stumbled backward, her head hit the trunk of a tree with a loud thwacking sound. Crying out in pain and confusion, Lexi's knees buckled under her, and she slumped to the ground unconscious.

"You shouldn't have interfered, you stupid bitch," Broc said in a cold hard voice, devoid of emotion. "Braydon was fine before he clapped eyes on you. Now he's all soft and gooey like a marshmallow," he sneered tauntingly at Braydon.

Braydon, who had been clutching his bleeding leg, looked over at Lexi folded on the ground, motionless like a discarded rag doll. Her legs were crumpled up where she had fallen against the tree, and her head was slumped to the side. He breathed in sharply. His eyes flicked from Lexi to Broc standing above her with his hands planted firmly on his hips, laughing and boasting about who he was going to hurt next. Again, Broc was showing no remorse for his actions. He was revelling in it all like some deranged dictator.

Braydon's eyes flashed wildly as though a white-hot rage was bubbling inside of him, burning his insides like a smouldering furnace. The years of torment at the hands of his cousin filling his body and his mind. The memory of all the bullying Braydon had to endure came rushing through him in a torrent. The feelings of hate and betrayal from his early childhood washed over him like a wave.

Braydon's jaw hardened. His hands clenched into tight fists, the veins sticking out on his forearms. Braydon's eyes whipped to where Lexi lay still and unconscious. Then, without hesitation he grabbed the shaft of the knife protruding from his leg and pulled the bloody blade from his thigh, the pain was momentarily forgotten. Awkwardly pushing himself to his feet, Braydon staggered forward lunging at Broc, the deadly, blood-soaked blade held out in front of him. "You fucking bastard!"

Broc's eyes suddenly widened in surprise, and his gloating face turned to one of shock. His mouth formed a perfect O shape as his own knife plunged deep into his chest, directly piercing his heart.

Broc looked down at his shirt in alarm. A bright red pattern, like a flower, had started to form on the blue checked fabric, rapidly growing larger with every passing second. Raising his eyes to meet Braydon's, Broc nodded his head ever so slightly as if in respect, before his eyes slowly closed, and he tumbled to the ground. It had all happened in an instant.

Braydon let out a loud moan of anguish and shock, covering his face with his hands. He was mortified. His anger now completely dissolved. Dropping to his knees beside his cousin, Braydon placed his right hand gently on Broc's chest. There was no movement. Not a single breath passed through Broc's lungs.

"No!" Yelled Braydon his voice full of emotion. "This was not what I wanted. It didn't have to be like this!" He looked around at the others in dismay before crumpling forward, his forehead coming to rest on Broc's motionless chest. Silence filled the air as everyone stood in shock staring at the morbid scene in front of them. *What the hell, had just happened?*

Cindy looked over at Broc lying motionless on the ground. She stared at his body, waiting for him to move, to get up and punish Braydon for his disloyalty. When he remained motionless, she glanced from Braydon to Broc, her face a picture of uncertainty. As she realised at last that Broc had not moved an inch and was not going to move ever again, she let forth a terrible scream. She screamed in a high-pitched wail, like a siren going on and on relentlessly. Her face contorted in misery.

Kevin, who had been quietly watching events from under the safety of his tree, suddenly started laughing uncontrollably. Tears and snot ran down his face as he saw his idol lying in the dirt, covered in blood. "What just happened? What just happened?" he kept repeating over and over, his voice full of disbelief. No one answered him, so he just kept asking the same question.

Aaron, standing close by, went to hide behind a tree. He took one look at Cindy and Kevin, who were still crying and babbling and ran off into the bush. "I don't want any part of this!" he cried out, his voice shaky.

Jason watched Aaron go, then quickly ran to Lexi. She had regained consciousness and was gingerly raising herself to a sitting position, her back resting awkwardly against the tree. She could feel its rough bark digging into her skin through her thin shirt. Her head pounded in pain, and blood had started to stream down her face in long red streaks from a nasty cut on the right side of her head.

Squatting down beside her, Jason quickly pulled off his shirt and pressed it carefully to her scalp. "Here, hold this on your head. Got to stop that bleeding."

Lexi's face had turned a shade of white, and she grimaced. The cut stung, her head felt woozy, and her cheek hurt where Broc had hit her. Tilting her head slightly to the side, she could hear a piercing noise in her ears, though her head still felt quite muffled. Slowly looking around, Lexi wondered if the sound was coming from her own ears or somewhere around them. Then, she saw Cindy, her body rigid, screaming. Feeling alarmed, Lexi quickly looked for Braydon. *What had happened?*

Lexi spotted Braydon kneeling on the ground a few meters away from her. He was bent over and completely still. *What was he doing?* Then, she noticed Broc. He was lying on the ground beside Braydon, his face as white and as cold as snow. Lexi swallowed and glanced up at Jason, wanting answers. He nodded gravely. Broc wasn't going to be giving them, or anyone else, any more trouble.

Cindy's screams had now dissolved into wretched sobs, and Zac slowly lowered her to the ground. She sat there staring mournfully at Broc. Her mascara ran down her face in long black streaks, as her tears fell unchecked. Zac left her where she was and wandered over to his brother, Kevin.

Kevin was standing slumped against a tree. He had stopped laughing and now glared at Zac as he walked towards him. His eyes were thin and mean.

Zac stopped in front of Kevin. Neither brother said a word. It was like a standoff in an old Western movie.

After a few moments, Zac shrugged his shoulders. He grabbed Kevin's arm and tried to drag his brother behind him. "Come on, Kevin, come home and see your sisters," he urged.

Kevin resisted, digging his feet into the dirt. He forcibly wrenched his arm back away from Zac, leaving deep scratches on his arm from Zac's fingernails.

"No way. That pissy town is not my home, and you're not my pissy family. I'm never going back. Do you hear me? Never!" Kevin screamed at Zac in sudden fury, spit flying from his mouth as he yelled.

Zac took a step back and stared at him in astonishment, his eyebrows raised in concern. "What are you talking about? Of course, it's your home!"

"No, it's not!" Kevin screamed in anger, his face right up close to Zac's their noses almost touching.

Zac just looked at him. His arms were hanging loosely by his side.

Slowly Kevin started to calm down. "Look. I'm leaving, Zac, and I'm not coming back. You'd better get used to it. I'm going to try and make it to the city."

"What? Why? You won't know anyone there."

Kevin looked at his brother with hard eyes; his mouth turned up on one side as he smirked at him. "Exactly and no family."

Zac stared at Kevin for a moment, before wiping his hand across his forehead and slowly shaking his head. When Kevin remained silent, Zac turned to join the others. His head drooped, and his shoulders slumped.

Kevin sneered at him.

"Don't you at least want to say goodbye to your sisters?" asked Zac twisting back around. "You might not ever see them again."

Kevin turned his back on Zac and started to walk off. "Nope."

As Kevin walked away, Cindy walked over to join him. Her usual swagger gone. Kevin looked sideways at her before grabbing her hand and pulling her along with him. "Let's find Aaron," he suggested looking around. "Then we need a car and some fuel. It's time to get the hell out of this dump!"

Zac stood still and quiet as he watched Kevin leave. "I hope he's not going to be a problem," he said quietly. Kevin obviously didn't care about his family or the town. Zac only hoped he hadn't picked up Broc's penchant for causing trouble.

He shrugged and turned around. Jason was helping Lexi, and he noticed that Braydon was still crouching over Broc. Blood was still flowing freely from the knife wound in his leg. He would need stitches. Quickly taking off his shirt, Zac ran over to help.

Braydon looked mortified at what he had done to Broc. His face was pale, and his hands were shaking.

Zac quickly tied his shirt around Braydon's thigh, trying to stop the flow of blood. He wasn't quite sure what else he could do, so he rested his hand reassuringly on Braydon's shoulder. Braydon glanced up at him and nodded thanks. His eyes were full of turmoil. Jason had helped Lexi struggle to her feet, and they made their way over to where Broc lay. She put her arm comfortingly around Braydon's shoulders. She knew he must be feeling terrible remorse. They had wanted Broc gone, not dead. After all, he was Braydon's cousin and only family.

"Come on, let's find some branches to cover his body," she suggested tactfully as Zac and Jason pulled Braydon to his feet. Braydon's hands were shaking. Beads of sweat had formed on his forehead, and his stomach churned with acid. He did not feel well at all. Bending over he rested his hands on his knees and took in deep breaths, trying to stop himself from vomiting. He sat back down on the ground with a thump.

Lexi dropped the branch she was carrying and rubbed his back soothingly with her hand. Braydon wondered what she thought of him now. A murderer. Glancing up at her, he noticed the slight breeze had caught a few wisps of her hair that always seemed to escape from her ponytail and blew them around her face. He wanted to tuck them back behind her ear, but he dared not touch her. She might not welcome his touch. He looked back down at the ground in misery.

"I'm a murderer! How can I live with that? No one's going to want a murderer around."

Lexi surprised him by grabbing his hand and pulling him towards her. She looked him straight in the eye, her gaze unwavering. "I do," she said firmly. "And besides, we all know it was an accident." She squeezed his hand. "You must be feeling pretty shitty right now. Just remember, you did try to talk to him. He just wouldn't listen. You know he wouldn't have stopped until he had hurt a lot of people. Something had to be done."

Braydon stood up gingerly, putting weight on his injured leg. He was starting to feel light-headed from losing so much blood. "I know. But it doesn't make me feel any better. It wasn't how things were supposed to turn out. He was just supposed to leave. I just felt rage when I saw him there laughing and gloating after he hit you. I didn't mean…" Braydon's voice drifted off, and his face twisted in fierce emotion.

Lexi swiftly pulled him into her arms and hugged him tightly. She held onto him until she felt his rigid body slowly relax and hug her back. Lexi felt emotional herself, and as she looked around at the others, they all looked much the same way. It was time to head back into town. The others would be waiting anxiously for them, unaware of the events that had just unfolded. Braydon's leg badly needed stitching before he lost any more blood. Lexi had a fierce headache and Jason and Zac both seemed to be in a state of shock.

After they had covered Broc's body with branches and Braydon had said his goodbyes, the victorious group staggered back into town, content, but sombre. They were battered, bloody and two of them were shirtless, but they were alive and safe. Now they just had to go back and tell the others what happened. The battle was over.

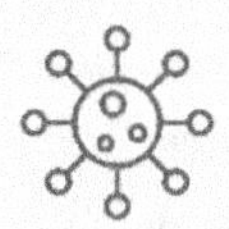

CHAPTER THIRTY-FIVE

The campfire popped and crackled as the dry wood caught in the smouldering flames. Even though it had been a fiercely hot day, it was a comforting sound, and the town kids were automatically drawn to it. They were scattered around haphazardly, some standing, some lying and some sitting chatting quietly amongst themselves. Everyone was feeling a mixture of relief and horror at what had just happened. Their tormentors had finally been stopped, but it had taken murder on both sides to make it happen. Kids felt confused about whether they should be feeling happy or upset by this. It wasn't something they'd had to deal with before.

"Okay, you lot. Look what *I've* found!" Lilly came staggering up to the group laden with cans of soft drink. She handed out the sweet fizzy drinks and kids grabbed them eagerly. "In times of stress, I always say a sugar fix is the best solution," she laughed, her eyes twinkling.

"Where on earth did you find those?" Lexi asked her, taking a Fanta.

Lilly grinned at her and whispered, "I had them hidden. For a special occasion, and you can't get more special than this one." Lilly winked.

"Guess not," said Lexi, sipping the sweet drink. The bubbles felt wonderful in her mouth. She grabbed one for Braydon and wandered over to where he was sitting by himself, gazing hypnotically at the fire. Lexi sat down cross-legged next to him, their bodies touching. She could feel the heat of his thigh next to hers. Lexi's head had been patched up, and Logan had managed to do a passable job of stitching up Braydon's leg over at his Father's vet centre, managing to stop the bleeding. It hadn't been an easy thing for Logan, who was still feeling devastated at his friend Harry's death. However, he had done the best he could under the circumstances. Braydon would probably have a nasty scar on his thigh, but that didn't really matter. Nobody cared about scars and blemishes so much anymore.

Lexi pulled the can of Coke from her jacket pocket and handed it to Braydon. He glanced at the drink for a moment but didn't take it. Instead, Braydon gave Lexi a strange long look before turning to stare back at the fire. He didn't utter a single word.

Lexi looked quizzically at him for a while. *Guess he didn't feel like talking right now.* That was understandable; he was probably still feeling upset about what had happened on the other side of the barrier. He hadn't talked about what he'd done, and she didn't feel like asking him. Lexi was happy to just sit quietly next to him for a while. If he wanted to talk, she'd be there.

They gazed at the fire for a while watching the flames flicker and burn. It had been an emotional and physical day, and they both felt totally worn out. After a while, Braydon seemed to relax a little. He pulled his eyes away from the fire, leant over towards Lexi, wrapped his arm around her waist and gave her a huge hug. Lexi hugged him back, turning her head towards him with a big happy smile on her face. She was surprised to see that Braydon did not have a smile on his face too. In fact, he actually looked angry. *What was his problem? Why was he angry at her?*

Feeling confused, Lexi moved to pull away from him; however, Braydon wouldn't let her. He roughly grabbed her face with both his hands and quickly kissed her on the mouth before standing and walking to the centre of the group. Lexi stared at him with her brow furrowed. She didn't know what to think of his strange behaviour. She knew he was upset about Broc, but his manner had changed entirely from earlier in the afternoon when they had walked together hand in hand. Then, he had been all relaxed and playful. Now, he was aggressive and sour.

Walking over to one of the cars at the barrier, Braydon banged loudly on the door with a golf club he'd found lying abandoned on the ground. The sound made a harsh metallic clanging noise like a gong being rung, and it drew everyone's attention to him. Braydon reluctantly raised his eyes and turned to face them. He didn't look at all comfortable with what he was about to say.

"Um, everyone, I've got an announcement to make, and it's not good." He rubbed his hand over his bloodshot eyes and a hush fell over the group as kids stopped talking and looked up at Braydon, waiting for him to continue.

"Listen, I don't want to upset you." He paused and looked directly at Lexi, who was staring back at him, her eyes full of concern. "But, well, there's no other way to say this." He again stopped and looked over at Lexi. A grimace crossed his face as if he was in pain.

Taking a slow breath, Braydon continued. "The thing is, I think I might be starting to mutate. You know, with this virus thing."

Lexi jumped up and started shouting. "What? No, you can't say that! What happened with Broc, that was just self-defence; it's not the virus!"

"Come on, Braydon, you didn't have a choice, man," argued Jason who was standing with Logan, his arm around his shoulder. "Come and sit by the fire and join us. I know it's not easy, but you've got to try to forget about what happened."

"I'll never be able to forget," Braydon whispered. The image of Broc lying cold and lifeless with the bloody knife protruding from his chest wasn't something Braydon was likely to forget.

Braydon looked around him at all the faces staring up at him. Everyone was talking over the top of each other. A lot of them looked scared and confused. They had taken him into their town and given him refuge, even though he had been one of their tormentors and now he was saying he was a threat again. Swallowing hard, Braydon once again banged on the car door calling for silence. "Listen, guys. I know you think it was just the fight with Broc, but it isn't. Yes, it started there, but I can still feel this kind of rage coursing through me like fire, even now. It's taking all my effort to control it!" As if confirming this, Braydon's face was covered in sweat. He looked exceedingly uncomfortable and agitated.

"Come on, Braydon. It's just the adrenaline from the fight. I feel it, too." Zac walked up to Braydon trying to reassure him. "You'll be fine in a couple of hours." Zac made a move to pat Braydon on the back.

Braydon suddenly yelled out in anguish. "No, stay back! Look," he said, quickly pulling up his shirt sleeves. Even in the dull orange glow of the campfire, the others could see the bright red welts of a rash running along Braydon's forearms and on the backs of his hands.

With the memory of Elisha's meltdown fresh in their minds, the younger children began scrambling to get away from Braydon, falling over each other and kicking up dirt in their haste.

Braydon watched the other children scurry away from him, like mice running away from a cat. His face fell in sadness, and he looked down at his outstretched arms.

Refusing to move, Lexi stood her ground feeling completely numb. She stared at Braydon standing mutely with his arms outstretched and bare like some mummy from a late-night movie. Only hours before he had saved the town and now kids were running from him in terror as if he were a monster. After all the town had been through lately, she didn't blame them, but at the same time her heart went out to Braydon. He must be feeling miserable.

Braydon slowly pushed his shirt sleeves back down and once again spoke. "Listen, it's going to be alright. You don't have to worry. I'm leaving town." His voice was loud and clear, and the children stopped and stared at their fallen hero. "I'm putting myself into voluntary exile before I can cause any trouble."

Lexi could see Braydon flexing his hands into fists as he struggled to keep control. She couldn't stand by and watch him suffer any longer. It made her feel terrible. Running to him, she desperately wanted to wrap her arms around his waist and tell him it was going to be alright. He could stay and teach her to draw, and they could chat about the movies and TV shows they'd watched. They'd find an abandoned house for him to live in and everything would be fine. It would all be okay.

As Lexi got closer to Braydon and looked up into his face, she knew that it wasn't going to be true. She could already see the madness forming in his eyes. They were getting that same wild feral look in them that Elisha had in hers. The look of a wild beast. A beast that you couldn't talk to, you couldn't reason with. It scared her.

Braydon quickly put up his hand to stop her from getting any closer. He didn't want to hurt her. Lexi stopped where she was, a single tear running down her cheek. *It just wasn't fair*, she thought bitterly.

"Lexi, you're going to be alright." He called out to her. "You're one of the oldest kids here now, so you know you're going to have to help run this town?" Lexi looked at him and nodded, swiftly wiping the tear from her face.

"You just have to…" he started to say something before closing his eyes tightly and grimacing. Braydon was obviously beginning to struggle. He began hitting his leg with his fist and let out a strange murmuring sound, as he fought to maintain control of his anguished mind. Sweat was now dripping from his face in rivulets onto the ground. Jason, Zac and Ethan all stood anxiously nearby, glancing at each other as they watched and waited to see what would happen next.

Lexi had blocked everyone else out of her mind and completely focused on Braydon, knowing that he could lose control at any moment and hurt her. She stood still and cautious. Ready to run if she had to but wanting to stay and hear what he had to say. She knew it might be the last time she got to speak to him.

Braydon licked his bottom lip with his tongue as he watched Lexi. He rubbed his chin as if thinking, before suddenly stepping forward broaching the distance to Lexi and quickly taking her in his arms for one last kiss.

Lexi's body tensed for a moment before kissing Braydon back. He felt good in her arms, and she could have stayed there all day. If only things had been different. Breaking the kiss and bending his lips to her ear, Braydon whispered, "If you want to survive, you're going to have to learn to be more ruthless."

Lexi nodded to show she understood, before quickly kissing him again. She could feel the stubble of a moustache starting on his upper lip, and his breath felt hot against her mouth. After a few precious moments, he pulled away, tenderly brushing a strand of stray hair from her face before stepping back.

"I have to go, Lexi, I'm beginning to lose it, and I don't want to do that in front of you,' he whispered, his voice cracking. Braydon's arms were starting to shake and tremble. "It's like being in a dream where your body isn't your own," he said emotionally.

Braydon tried to smile at Lexi but ended up grimacing at her instead. "I wanted to say so much more to you about how I feel," he said as his voice caught in his throat. "If only there had been more time," he whispered sadly, tears forming in the corner of his bloodshot eyes.

Braydon looked around at the friends he had made. He ran his hand over his eyes, obviously in distress. "I wish I could stay and be part of the town," he shouted. "But I just don't want to risk hurting anyone. I'd better go." Braydon took one last glance at Lexi before swiftly turning away and fleeing down Millers Road, directly out of town.

"We'll leave you some food and water!" Lexi called out after him, holding back the tears that threatened to burst forth like a dam breaking. Her arms were trembling with the emotion building inside her. Lexi's feelings were ragged. In only a matter of hours, she had gone from happiness and joy earlier in the day to complete sadness and misery now.

Hadley crept up and wrapped her arms around her sister's waist holding her tight. It was *her* turn to do the comforting for a change. Lexi certainly looked as if she needed it and Hadley wanted to be there for her. The two sisters hugged for a while, staring out in the direction Braydon had run. It looked barren and harsh out there. Not a great place to be on your own. Hadley gently pulled Lexi away and back towards the group. It was time to re-join the others.

The wind blew softly, sending the remnants of ash and cinders from the bonfire into the air. Everyone was looking around at each other in astonishment at what had just happened. Shock and dismay were written all over their faces. No one had seen that coming. Some had witnessed the fight with Broc, and some had heard about it. However, no one thought it meant Braydon had the virus. It had all happened so quickly, just like it had with Elisha. Maybe an uncontrolled burst of anger or aggression triggered the change? No one really knew. Without any scientists left to study the virus, all they could do was guess.

As night started to fall in the town, it began to get quite cold. People were drawn to the heat and comforting light of the bonfire that had been relit in the centre of the clearing, but no one felt completely comfortable. Every now and then they would cast anxious glances behind them, reassuring themselves that Braydon wasn't coming back. There was an unsettled feeling in the air, and everyone seemed restless, yet no one wanted to leave. The camaraderie of the fire drew them all together. It had been a horror-ridden day with the deaths of Harry and Broc, the burning of Fuse, and now the unexpected departure of Braydon. No one wanted to be alone.

The sky had now turned an inky black, broken up by a mass of twinkling stars. On any other night, it would have been beautiful but not this night. Zac, who had been chatting quietly with Ethan, strolled up to Lilly to see how she was handling things. "Good idea with the drinks," he smiled good-naturedly as he opened another one.

Lilly gave him a forced smile.

Zac leaned in and looked at her closely. He could tell she was upset. "You alright? Is it Kevin?".

Lilly shook her head and quickly grabbed Zac's hand bringing him closer to her. "No, it's not Kevin. It's something else." Lilly paused and looked at her brother in the eyes. Her face was determined. "You're not going to like this, Zac, but I've decided to go into exile with Braydon."

Zac looked at her sharply. "What!? What for? No, you can't! He'll be alright on his own. You don't need to go with him."

Lilly spoke quickly, her voice quiet but resolute. "No, Zac, listen to me. It's not that. I think I'm changing, too." There were tears in her eyes. "I can feel the anger bubbling up inside. It's like a volcano ready to burst out of me. It's just like Braydon described." She rubbed her hand over her shaved head; her fingers were trembling. "I feel like I'm on the verge of losing it, big time."

"This day is just getting better and better!" complained Zac bitterly as he reached over and grabbed Lilly's other hand, holding them, warm between his. "That's normal! It's just because of the fight and Harry's death, and the stuff that happened at the farm." He pointed to her shorn head. "You're just angry at that; it's been a pretty rough couple of days." His voice was desperate.

Lilly looked at him sadly, wishing it were true. "That's what I thought too at first, but I can still feel the rage gaining strength. I can't turn it off no matter what I do. I don't want to risk hurting you, Katie or Sarah. Or anyone else for that matter. I have to go. It's the only option." She turned abruptly away pulling her hands free from his. Her eyes were full of hot tears.

Zac pulled her back. "Wait. I don't get it. That can't be right, Lilly. How come I don't feel any of that? We're twins, so shouldn't we both be feeling it?" Zac looked at his sister pleadingly.

Lilly turned back to face him. "I don't know, brother, I only know how I feel," she shrugged. "I'm sorry. Maybe I'm wrong, and if I am, I'll come back into town. Right now, though, I'd feel better if I stayed away from people. At least until I know for sure that I'm safe. All our friends are here, and I don't want to hurt anyone. Can you imagine how I'd feel if I hurt Katie, or baby Sarah, or you?" Lilly's face looked fierce as though she had already made up her mind to leave.

Zac grabbed Lilly's hands again. "Wait, Lilly. What about Katie and Sarah, they're going to need...." he paused abruptly, turning her hands over in his. His eyes widened in shock. There was a raised angry red rash creeping up the skin on both of them. It looked sore and itchy. Zac blinked his eyes and closed his mouth, not sure what to say.

Lilly quickly pulled her hands away from him and hugged them under her armpits. She smiled at him weakly. "It's alright, Zac. I'll be okay," she sniffed as tears ran down her face.

Zac stepped back away from Lilly. His face fell, and he looked deflated. Zac's legs suddenly buckled underneath him, and he sat down on the ground with a heavy thud. "No, it won't be okay, Lilly. Nothing's going to be okay!"

Lilly bent down and hugged him tightly. "Aww, come on, Zac, don't give up. I always annoyed you anyway. Remember?" She ruffled his hair with her hand and then wiped the tears from her eyes.

Lilly peered out into the darkness, as she twisted her fingers in her hands. It looked inky black out beyond the glow of the fire. Lilly swallowed hard. She grabbed Zac's hand once more. "I'm frightened Zac," she said, her eyes growing wide. "I don't know what's going to happen to me. I don't want to end up like Elisha."

Zac squeezed Lilly's hand. "Then stay. I'll help you," his voice trembled with emotion. "We can find a way to control it!"

"I can't," Lilly said, her voice barely a whisper. "What if I kill someone like Elisha!" Lilly shook her head. Her hands were shaking badly. "I have to go, Zac. Tell Katie and Sarah that I love them," she sobbed. "And look after our farm." Her voice cracked, and she quickly backed away, stumbling into the night.

Zac stood quickly. "Lilly wait!" he called after her, his hand reaching towards her. It was too late. She had already disappeared into the darkness.

Letting his hand drop to his side Zac flopped to the ground in dismay. He stared bleakly at the dirt at his feet. His face looked stunned, as though someone had just slapped him hard across the face.

Large black bull ants scurried about near Zac's feet, carrying specs of food and rubble with them across the dirt. He watched them go about their work, his face blank.

Seeing Zac sitting on his own away from the others, Lexi and Jason sat down on either side of him. "Hey, bro, what's up?" inquired Jason. "You look unhappy. What are you looking at?"

Zac shrugged. "The black ants." He pointed to a line of Bull ants that were trying to make their way up his leg.

"Oh," said Lexi, raising her eyebrows at Jason in concern and putting her arm around Zac's shoulders. "Zac, are you alright? Where's Lilly by the way? I wanted to ask her about…"

Zac interrupted her. "She's gone. She has the virus. She's exiled herself like Braydon, so she doesn't hurt anyone," Zac said bitterly, looking over at Lexi with sad eyes.

"What?! Are you sure?" Lexi asked, putting her other arm around him.

Zac nodded. "Yes, I saw the red rash all over her hands and arms. She said that she felt like a volcano ready to explode." His voice became emotional as he explained.

"Lilly said she's been getting intense rushes of rage for the last couple of days as if she wants to scream and scream. At first, she thought it was just her anger against Broc. Then, she saw the blotchy red rashes on her skin and understood it was the first stages of the virus in her body." Zac abruptly stopped speaking and dropped his head into his hands in anguish.

"Jeezus!" Yelled Jason angrily, picking up a rock and throwing it at a nearby tree. "First Elisha, then Braydon, now Lilly. When will this ever end?" He put an arm around Zac's shoulders, and the trio hugged for a while.

"Well, this turned out to be a pretty crappy kind of day!" fumed Jason, throwing another rock at the tree and missing.

Lexi looked at both boys. They looked utterly wiped out. Slowly standing she brushed the dirt off her pants. She felt both emotionally and physically exhausted herself. "Right," she said, grabbing Jason's arm and pulling him up. "I think we should wrap this up. Everyone is exhausted and strung out. Let's put out that bonfire and get all the kids back to their homes. We need to have a meeting in the morning at the church to talk about what's happened here today. Jason, can you let everyone know?" she looked at him hopefully, and he nodded as she knew he would. He was someone she could rely on, and that was good because she was going to need help to hold this town together.

Lexi helped Zac up from the ground too. Turning him to face her, she looked him in the eye. He looked a wreck. "How about you, Katie and Sarah, come live with us? You'd be closer to town and everyone," she asked him in a kind voice hoping that he would agree.

Zac looked at her and half smiled. "Aw, no it's alright. The farm's our home, and anyway, someone needs to look after the animals."

Lexi smiled at back at him. "Uh huh, okay. Well, let's get some kids to help you out there. You can't do it all on your own, and Katie's got to look after Sarah. We'll organise it tomorrow at the meeting." She leant over and gave him another hug. "Want to at least stay with us tonight? It's a long way back to the farm."

Zac nodded. "Yeah, alright. I just need to find Katie and tell her about Lilly. She's going to be really upset; first Kevin and now Lilly. Our family's falling apart." He gave a big sigh. His heart felt as though it had been kicked around, and he had a pounding headache.

"Of course, Zac. Come over when you're ready. Hadley will be there so Katie can talk with her if she wants to." Giving him a tired wave, she started to walk away back to the main group.

Zac called after her. "Hey, Lexi." She stopped and turned back to face him.

"You're going to do a great job running this town," he smiled encouragingly before turning away. Zac pulled his black plastic spider from his shirt pocket and stared at it numbly for a few moments before walking off to find his younger sisters.

Lexi thought about what Zac had said. She wasn't so sure. Gazing into the distance, she listened to the sounds of chatter drifting in the breeze. These kids didn't even know her. She'd only been in the town a few days. Why would they listen to anything she had to say? Then Lexi thought of Braydon and remembered his last words to her. *I suppose I don't have to be 'liked'. Just the occasional bitch, to get things done.* Lexi grinned, she was sure she could do that.

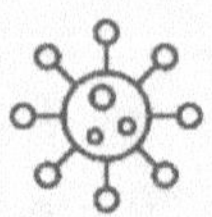

CHAPTER THIRTY-SIX

Lexi looked down from the precipice. Her toes balanced precariously on the brink as her weight caused little flurries of sand and pebbles to tumble over the edge. Plucking up her courage, she leaned forward slightly and peered downwards. The sheer cliff face plunged straight down in a vertical drop. Lexi flinched. Her first instinct was to shy away from the descending wall of rock. She wasn't a big fan of heights.

Feeling the warmth of the sunlight on her cheeks, Lexi took a slow, steady breath in. After a few moments, she once again tentatively peered over the edge, her toes gripping the ground beneath her feet for balance. Looking down to the bottom, Lexi was surprised to see two figures standing at the base of the cliff, on a little stretch of white sand. They seemed to be beckoning her to join them, and she wondered how on earth they could have got down there. The cliff face was sheer vertical rock with no hint of stairs anywhere.

Squinting her eyes so that she could see a little more clearly, she noticed that the two figures looked vaguely familiar. One had a bright shock of flaming red hair, and she soon realised that it was Braydon. Next to him stood Lilly. Lexi frowned. Why were Braydon and Lilly standing at the bottom of a cliff, and for that matter, what was she doing there?

Standing straight, Lexi peered around her in confusion. *What was going on?* There was no one else in sight at the top of the cliff, just a sparse landscape stretching out to the horizon on one side and a calm blue sea on the other. There was no wind, and everything was still. Not even a hint of a breeze rippled the surface of the water. The sea looked flat and smooth like a polished stone.

Far below, Braydon and Lilly continued to beckon to her, their arms moving in a continuous *come-hither* motion. Lexi felt herself inexplicitly drawn to them; however, something was holding her back. In her mind, Lexi knew it was dangerous to step off the cliff, and yet, she could not look away. Raising one heel slowly from the ground with her toes clinging resolutely to the ground, Lexi felt herself move steadily forward, drawn to the figures below.

At the moment her toes left the ground, Lexi felt her body violently jolt, and she wondered if she had hit the rocks. In her confused state she sat up hastily, her body moving sideways and her head hitting the wall with a thud. She groaned in pain and realised she hadn't jumped at all. The intense sunlight was gone. It was dark, and she was lying in her bed with the four walls of the bedroom surrounding her. No cliff face, and no Braydon or Lilly. She'd been dreaming.

Using the back of her hand, Lexi wiped away a thin layer of sweat that had formed on her upper lip. The room felt hot and claustrophobic. Quickly swinging her legs from the bed and going to the window, she pulled the curtains aside and peered through. It was early morning, and a slight hint of pink light was forming on the horizon, signalling the start of a new day.

Lexi fanned her face with her hand. "I need to get out of this room for a bit," she whispered, turning from the window. "I need some fresh morning air for a while.

The intense realness of the dream and its ambiguous message had startled her, leaving her feeling unsettled. *Did it mean something or was it just her subconsciousness playing with her mind?* It had been an awful, disturbing day yesterday. Perhaps she was just missing her friends.

Lexi shook her head a little to help clear her mind. As she walked around to the front of the house, her feet crunched loudly on the gravel. There was an old camping chair leaning against the wall of the house, so Lexi slowly unfolded it and carefully looked-for any spiders underneath. Getting bitten by a redback spider would be the last thing she needed right now! As she positioned the chair on the front porch, Lexi flopped down into it to think. The chair was a lot more comfortable than it looked and she brought her knees up to her chest and hugged them lightly. It was peaceful without anyone around, and Lexi gave a satisfied sigh, enjoying the solitude.

Without the sun's hot rays, the land had not yet started to heat up, and the air felt quite cool for summertime.

As she looked out beyond their front garden, Lexi could see the flickering of candlelight in a few of the distant house windows. In the darkness of the early morning, the candles looked quite magical. She rested her chin on her knees and watched them for a while. All around the garden, crickets were chirping, and birds were tweeting as the wildlife around their home started to stir in the beginnings of a new day.

Lexi thought about what needed to be done that day and hoped she would be up for it. Rubbing her tired eyes, Lexi again found herself thinking about her dream. She wished that Braydon and Lilly were here to help her. Being from the city and new to Jasper's Bay Lexi hoped that the town kids would listen to her. She bit her bottom lip. Lexi didn't want to make a fool of herself. Public speaking was not really her forte. She hated it!

Feeling movement by her side, Lexi flinched and looked down to see what it was. *It was only Polo!* He had appeared from wherever he'd been sleeping, shook himself and flopped down by Lexi's side. She smiled at him, patting his head. *He was a good dog, and she was glad that they'd rescued him from the Robertson's' garden and brought him with them.* He looked up at her before resting his head on his paws in front of him and going to sleep.

"How can you fall asleep so quickly! I wish I were like you," Lexi said quietly stroking Polo's back.

Lexi watched Polo sleeping peacefully for a while, before turning her eyes to look at the horizon. The sun was now starting to rise, and Lexi watched it peep gradually over the horizon. It was a beautiful orange and pink colour, and she gazed at it for a few minutes taking in its wondrous beauty. Lexi leaned back in her chair, stretching her arms above her head and yawning. Whatever happened today, she would do her best to help the kids of the town. It was up to them if they wanted to accept her help or not. Lexi had no control over that. She would be tough but fair. With Lilly, Braydon, and Elisha gone, Lexi was now the oldest in the town.

The loss of power and the battle with Broc, not to mention the exile of Braydon, Lilly and Elisha had been a massive shock to everyone. The town was going to need someone to make decisions.

"If the others help me, this could work." Lexi nodded her head slightly and smiled. The town needed to get back on its feet.

After a while of sitting in the same spot, Lexi started to feel restless. Pushing herself out of the comfy chair, she strolled back into the house and through to the kitchen. It was time to start planning the meeting at the church. There was a lot to be done, and it was starting to get light. First, though, Lexi would have loved a cappuccino coffee and a toasted bagel. If only the coffee shop were still running! "Oh well," she smiled to herself picking up a jar of instant coffee. "At least I can still boil water; instant coffee will have to do." She began humming a tune to herself. Lexi hoped today would be a better day than yesterday.

The meeting in the town church started quite late. After the emotional dramas of the day before, Lexi had decided to let everyone sleep in and recharge. There wasn't any rush, anyway. Inside the church, it was beautiful. The sun shone through the stained-glass windows making an intricate pattern of colours and shapes on the floor, and the room felt warm and inviting. Lexi gazed at it in wonder for a few moments, gathering herself for her speech.

The kids sat in the church pews chatting quietly to each other. Every now and then, they glanced at Lexi expectantly. Jason, Ethan, Hadley, Zac, and Logan all stood by her side. They were now the oldest kids in town and, as such, had decided to take control of the situation.

Lexi glanced sideways at Jason, and he nodded at her reassuringly. It was time to begin. Clearing her throat, she stepped forward to face the crowd. She felt nervous, unused to speaking in front of people, even if they were just a bunch of kids like her. They were strangers, and she wasn't sure if they would listen to her. After all, she'd only been in town for a few days, and now she was going to tell them how to run it! They'd probably tell her to piss off back to the city! She peered out at the sea of faces, all looking at her waiting to hear what she had to say. She had to give it a go. At least then she would know that she had tried.

Lexi's voice trembled slightly as she spoke. "Well, every-one. I called a meeting this morning because we need to organise ourselves to keep this town running. Thankfully, Broc and his gang are no longer a threat." Kids started cheering and clapping happily at this remark.

Lexi smiled and nodded at them putting up her hands for quiet. "We still have things that need to be done. Obviously, with all the solar cells damaged, there's no electricity anymore. You've probably also realised by now that we are on our own. No adults are coming to help us." Her voice sounded stronger, more confident. Pausing, she looked at the faces peering up at her, all looking very young. Some of them looked frightened too, and she tried to give them comfort by smiling warmly at them. "I know it seems scary without the adults but remember, you've basically been handling things on your own already. It's just going to be a little bit more difficult without any electricity or running water. We can do it, though. We just need a plan, and we…" she motioned to Jason and the other kids standing beside her, "have come up with one."

Lexi again glanced nervously at the crowd of younger children to see if she still had their attention. She did. They were all sitting there like kids in a school room waiting to be told what to do. Maybe this would work out all right, she thought, before continuing. "It's not a complicated plan. We've decided to have a roster of things that need to be done around town and the farm, and we are *all* going to help." Lexi looked at them meaningfully as she swept her hand across the crowd. "Anyone who doesn't want to be part of this, or doesn't pull their weight, can leave town. And I mean today."

A rumble of voices went through the crowd as the kids absorbed her words. Lexi glanced back at Jason and Hadley, feeling unsure. They nodded to her encouraging her to go on. She raised her voice to be heard over the escalating noise in the church. "I know that may seem harsh. But think about it. Because there's only a few of us here; it wouldn't be fair for some to be burdened with all the work while others slacked off."

A lot of the kids in the crowd were now nodding their heads in agreement. Lexi continued, "If we are going to make this work, everyone has to do their share. Everyone will have a job to do. It's the only way to make it fair."

Jason stepped up beside Lexi. "Yes, and later today, we will be putting up a roster of the jobs that need doing. Like planting and watering crops, harvesting and collecting food, distributing food evenly, burning rubbish and medical needs. We all need to start planning for the future." Jason swept his hand across the crowd to include them all.

Jason and Lexi looked warily at the crowd. If they didn't accept the plan, it would make things difficult. More kids were nodding their heads in approval, so Jason took this as a good sign and kept going. "Everyone in their own house will be responsible for keeping that house clean, cooking their own food, getting their own water from Bryer's Creek. Plus, digging their own toilet pit out the back of their house."

"Ewww," shouted Angel. "I'm not digging Fuse or Harvey's toilet". Angel and her sister had moved in to help Fuse who was continuing to suffer with his burns. He was still in a lot of pain, and his friends had decided to take care of him.

Angel called out again in a joking voice. "Have you seen how many cans of baked beans they've been eating lately?!" Everyone laughed, breaking the seriousness of the mood in the church.

"I think everyone can dig their own toilet hole, Angel. You won't have to dig Harvey or Fuse's," Jason laughed, smiling at her.

"What about food?" one of the younger kids in the crowd called out.

Lexi again stepped forward. "That's an important question," she nodded to the young boy who asked it. "Over on the farm Zac and Ethan are going to plant more crops, so we will need volunteers to help." A few eager hands shot up from the crowd and Lexi smiled at them, happy that they were willing to volunteer. It made things easier. She continued, "it's going to take quite a while for any food we manage to grow to be ready. We do have supplies of tinned and dried food, but that will only last a short while. So, we had better start rationing what food we have. Hadley is going to use one of the old rooms at the school for a storeroom, and she will make an inventory of what goods we have. Don't worry we won't let anyone starve!" Lexi stepped back from the front hoping she wouldn't regret those words.

All around, kids started talking positively about the roster and how they could help. Lexi felt a wave of relief wash over her. It looked like most of the kids in town would accept the group's plan, and with a lot of hard work and a bit of good old luck, she thought they could make it work.

Hadley came over and hugged her, grabbing her around the waist and pulling her close. "Well done," she whispered in her ear. "I think they'll be okay with it."

Lexi nodded. Feeling encouraged, she spoke up again. "We will put up each week's roster on the noticeboard here in the church." She pointed towards the rear of the church where a corkboard sat pinned to the back wall. "That way, you can find your name and see what needs to be done. Also, we're putting a suggestion box next to it for any ideas on how to improve things. If you're finding things tough or you're a bit lonely, some of you younger ones might want to think about moving in with some of the older kids. You can come and see us about that or organise it yourself. It's up to you." No one looked too upset or angered by this initial plan, so Lexi stepped back and let Logan step up and take his turn at the front of the group.

Logan had been standing quietly at the back of the group of older children, watching them speak. He looked over at Jason and whispered, "You guys got the easy part. Now let's see what they think about what *I've* got to say." He raised his eyebrows meaningfully.

As he stood waiting to speak, Logan noticed some kids stand up to leave, so he quickly moved forward to say his piece. Being the vet's son, he had somehow become the person everyone now went to for medical advice. Though he didn't really know why, because watching his dad help a cow give birth and stitching up the arm of some kid who has fallen from his bike wasn't exactly the same thing. Still, he was who they looked to now, so he was just going to have to roll with it.

Logan spoke up. "Hey, guys, one more thing before you leave. I know we have all been through a lot in the last few days, but we have one more thing to talk about." He rubbed his hand across his chin and cleared his throat. "We need to talk about the virus mutating."

The chatter in the church stopped abruptly, and the whole place fell silent. Kids sat staring up at Logan with apprehension and fear on their faces like a bunch of school kids waiting to sit their final exams. Nobody really wanted to think about it, let alone talk about it. However, Logan continued anyway.

"Us older kids have talked about the situation amongst ourselves. Plus, we've had discussions with some of the kids we know in Albany. They are having the same problems as us." Logan paused for a moment and looked about the room. Everyone was looking at him wide-eyed.

"Anyway, the thing is, nobody understands exactly what is happening with this sickness. It seems as though the virus is now starting to affect older kids, not just adults." Logan noticed one little girl had her hands firmly over her ears, determined not to listen. He cleared his throat again. "So, from what we can work out, the virus must have mutated. Apparently, it doesn't kill children as it did with the adults, otherwise Lilly, Elisha and Braydon would all be dead." Logan coughed and glanced at Ethan and Zac as if in apology. They nodded to him to keep going.

Logan shrugged. "Anyway, it seems as though when a person nears the age of seventeen or older, instead of killing them, the virus changes them instead. Well, you've seen it. The virus makes them have uncontrollable rage and anger. It seems to affect their emotions."

Lexi stepped back up beside Logan. She patted his shoulder. "Yes, you've all seen it in Elisha, Braydon, and maybe Lilly." Kids started nodding their heads vigorously, looking uncertain and wary. Lexi could see the mood changing to one of panic. "Look, we don't want to scare you, we just want you to be informed. As we said, it's not just happening here, it's been happening in Albany too, and I'm sure it's been happening in the city as well, if not worldwide."

The church fell silent again as the children inside absorbed what they had been told. The morning wind could be heard whistling eerily outside and through the rafters of the church's steep roof. When a large piece of debris blew against the church doors making a loud banging noise, one of the younger girls screamed in fright before crouching down under the pews, her fingers over her eyes.

Lexi spoke quickly, her hands out in front of her for reassurance before anyone started to panic. "You don't have to worry. If any of us older kids feel the symptoms coming on, we have all decided that we will exile ourselves from the town. Just like Braydon and Lilly did. That way, there won't be any trouble, and you can all keep running the town and following the plan."

Lexi could see the younger kids giving each other sideways glances. They were obviously feeling uneasy about the whole situation, and she didn't blame them. They needed something to reassure and distract them. Lexi spoke up again. "Listen, the good news is we don't think that everyone gets affected by the virus. Look at Zac. He's seventeen, just like Lilly and he feels perfectly fine." Lexi turned and pointed to Zac, who quickly stood and waved animatedly at the younger kids before flumping down in a spare seat. They weren't really sure that he was fine, but they didn't need to point that out right now. As far as Lexi was concerned, she was going to use any piece of good news that she had.

"The second piece of good news is that we are not going to start the roster until tomorrow because we've still got a whole lot of thawed chickens, sausages and hamburgers that need eating. So, let's get that bonfire started again!"

Kids started cheering and racing around the church enthusiastically, like children at a theme park. Lexi looked at Hadley in surprise. "Jeez," she said. "At least I know how to keep them happy. Food! Now if only I could get that old movie theatre working, we'd be set!"

Jason scratched his head and muttered to himself thoughtfully. "Now, there's an idea. I wonder if I could get the projector running from car batteries?" He smiled happily doing a little celebratory dance. Jason loved a good technological challenge. "Back in a moment," he called over his shoulder cheerfully as he ran out of the church to find himself a spanner and a spare car battery.

Lexi, Hadley, and Logan all looked at each other and burst out laughing. At least they knew how to keep *Jason* happy.

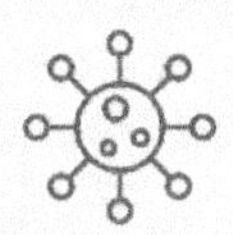

CHAPTER THIRTY-EIGHT

Lexi chewed on the end of her pen as she stared into the distance deep in thought. She had started a diary a couple of days ago as she wanted to keep a record of what had happened to her family and friends. It had been a traumatic few weeks, and she needed to get it all straight in her head. Someone should tell the story of what had happened in Jasper's Bay. Lexi took up her pen and started to write.

Three weeks have passed since the night of the bonfire, and so far, Zac hasn't felt any changes. Maybe he won't. Perhaps it's just as we thought, and some people are immune to this new mutation of the KV17 virus. I hope so. That would mean there is a chance at survival for the human race. Not all of us are going to change into aggressive lunatics. Although in Broc's case, he didn't really need a virus, he was already like that!

After the banishment of Elisha, Ethan has sobered up and moved out to the farm to help Zac and the girls with the work. It gives them, and himself, some much-needed company. I think he likes it out there and it keeps him busy. He says that he just can't stay in his old house anymore now that Elisha has gone, and that he'd rather be out in the open spaces. Anyway, I'm sure Zac is more than happy to have another guy around to talk to besides his two younger sisters.

A good piece of news is that Zac has managed to make a rudimentary hand plough! Using the farm horses and the plough, he has sown one of the paddocks with corn seeds, which is fantastic! It will take a while for the corn to grow, however, as long as we keep them watered, we have a good chance of having the beginnings of a new food supply for the future!

Lexi stopped writing for a moment and twirled the pen around in her fingers. She stared out into space lost in thought. A little Willy Wagtail bird flew up to the car bonnet and perched on the edge. Its tail wagged back and forth, and its tiny black eyes watched her with curiosity. Lexi smiled, her eyes crinkling at the sides. "I wonder what we can make with corn. Maybe soup, bread or corn fritters," she said quietly to the bird. "Guess I'd better learn how to cook."

Tapping the pen on her book, Lexi soon began writing again.

Everyone seems to have accepted Jason, Hadley and myself into the town and I actually feel like a real country-kid.

"Well, almost!" Lexi laughed to herself. "I still can't ride a horse," she said raising her eyebrow at the Willy Wagtail.

So far, the other kids are all following my suggestion of a roster to help around the town. I think most people like order in their lives and are happy for someone to take charge and show them the way. Elisha had been doing a great job before, but I think deep down she was always expecting the adults to come and take over again. We're all certain now that's not going to happen. We haven't heard from any adults for months, so I guess we are definitely on our own in this. So far, we seem to be handling things alright by ourselves, anyway.

Of course, we have had a few minor problems as everyone adjusts to the new routine. Nothing major, just kids trying to skip out on doing their jobs or taking someone else's water, that type of thing. Nothing we can't handle. Occasionally, I have had to become the bitch from hell, nagging people to get things done, but thankfully, that doesn't seem to be happening as much anymore! I think everyone wants to make this work so we're all trying hard to get along.

I must admit I've become used to being a leader, and I'm finding the whole experience quite fulfilling. Yes, it's a lot of responsibility and worry at times, but at least I get to have a significant influence on what gets done around the town, and that is cool. I've found out that without doubt, I'm more of a leader than a follower, and have become quite good at keeping people positive and on-task. Who'd have thought it would take a worldwide epidemic for me to find out my strengths? I'm not the same girl who left the city, so unsure and conflicted. I suppose life is strange like that.

Amazingly, Hadley and I are getting along reasonably well. We haven't been having too many arguments or 'little disagreements', as we like to call them. I think she has actually found some of her strengths too. I know Hadley has been a terrific help at organising the weekly rosters, and I'm really proud of her. It's her job to make sure the work-load around town is evenly distributed. Zac told me she's very thorough and is quite fair about it.

Overall, I think we make a good team for two sisters from the city. Especially considering we'd never been to the country before. We've even started teaching the younger kids how to play some of the old games, like hopscotch and elastics. It's been great fun for us, and they seem to be enjoying it too.

I know Hadley still misses her PSV though, and I absolutely miss the internet, not to mention the radio and music. Actually, I really miss the music.

Lexi stopped writing for a moment and peered down at the Willy Wagtail. He continued to watch her as he pecked at little insects caught in the gully of the car's front window. "Do you think any of those pop stars survived the virus?" Lexi asked the small bird. "Maybe the very young ones like Billy Eilish?" She wondered out loud.

Doodling a few music notes on the top of her book, Lexi started to hum a tune. After a while, she began writing again. *Jason and Logan are officially an item, though Jason still lives with us. They make a great couple, each with a crazy sense of humour and they're always making us laugh, which is a good thing when it's been a long hard day trying to grow your own food or dig your own toilet trench! I know Logan really misses his best friend, Harry, so I'm sure that Jason has been a great comfort to him.*

Little Polo has settled nicely into our new home too. He's marked a place under one of the shady trees out the back of the house. He lays there watching the little finches as they flit back and forth amongst the bushes. He's a friendly dog, and a lot of the younger children come and visit our house so they can play with him. He seems to enjoy all the attention, and I'm glad we didn't leave him behind in Perth. Who knows what would have become of him there?

As for Cindy, Aaron and Kevin, well, we haven't seen or heard from them since the night of the fight and to be honest, no one cares. I'm sure that if they didn't head to the city as Kevin wanted, they might just plan on giving us trouble at some point, but I know we can handle them. Without Broc as their leader, they seem relatively harmless. We shall have to wait and see what the future holds. Either way, I know we can all band together and defend the town again if we have to. We did it once before, and we can do it again. As long as we stick together, we can be strong."

The tiny Willy Wagtail having exhausted the supply of bugs on the window, suddenly flew away.

"Bye, then," called Lexi laughing as she watched him go. She dropped her diary beside her and stretched her arms out in front, releasing the tension in her shoulders. It felt good. The sun was already beating down on her back, and little beads of sweat were forming on her upper lip. It was going to be another hot day.

She was sitting on one of the chairs at the makeshift lookout Logan and Jason had set up on one of the cars. Not only was it a great lookout spot, but it was also a quiet, peaceful place to get away from the other children for a while, and Lexi needed that.

Getting up from her chair, she reached into a canvas bag sitting by her feet and pulled out three apples and a couple of bottles of water. Lexi then placed them into a wicker basket sitting beside her, ready to be left outside the wall of cars still encircling the town. The children had decided to leave the barricade in place around the central part of town for continued security. It may not be a solid wall, but at least it made them feel a little safer.

Lexi turned one of the apples over in her hand and frowned. "I hope this is going to be enough." With the town's own food supplies running low it was all they could spare. She raised the apple to her nose and breathed in the lovely fresh smell before dropping the fruit into the basket. Each morning she left a small amount of food for her exiled friends, and by evening without fail, it had all been taken.

Lexi peered out into the bush, her eyes squinting in the sunlight. "Where are you guys?" she asked quietly, her voice full of questions. "It must be so tough out there." She raised her hand to her face trying to shade her eyes from the sun's bright glare while looking across the sand hoping to spot a tuft of Braydon's red hair. Once, when she was sitting alone, Lexi thought she had caught a glimpse of Braydon in the sand dunes watching the town from a distance. She tried calling to him, however; he was too far away to hear her.

As she looked out at the barren land around her, Lexi hoped they were all okay out there. All she could see were sand, dry yellow spinifex bushes, and bare trees. The wind swirled the sand around in little eddies, and it looked quiet out there. No one was around. Feeling disappointed, Lexi glanced at her watch to see what time it was. She had promised Hadley she would be back at ten o'clock to help her with some project she had going on.

As Lexi glanced absently at the time, she noticed the date on her watch. The sixteenth of March. She raised her eyebrows. "Huh," she said in surprise. "That means it's only a few days until my birthday. My seventeenth birthday!" It suddenly dawned on her exactly what that meant. She'd be turning seventeen. *Seventeen!*

Staring at the date on her watch as if she could erase it, Lexi chewed on the end of her thumbnail. *Would she change like the others or be immune like Zac?*

Reaching down, Lexi scratched at her feet restlessly. They felt itchy. As she pulled one of her socks down, Lexi noticed little red spots! She quickly pulled off both socks and shoes. They both had red spots on them running all the way from her toes to her ankles!

Lexi stared at the marks in disbelief, her brow furrowed in concern. She shook her head. *They were probably just sand fly bites from helping at the farm paddocks yesterday.* "I won't think about that now," Lexi told herself, swallowing hard. "I have too many other things to worry about at the moment."

She quickly pulled on her socks and shoes, covering the red spots. She refused to look at them a moment longer. Pushing herself up, Lexi picked up the food basket and carefully walked to the edge of the car roof. She attached the basket to a rope, and slowly lowered it over the side of the barrier being careful not to snag the rope or basket on the barbed wire. Then, she dropped her diary onto the ground below and slid from the roof to the car bonnet, and onto the ground, tying the end of the rope onto the door handle so she could pull it back up later.

Wiping the sweat from her brow, she pulled her damp shirt away from her body and gazed at her arms. All this time out in the sun had turned her skin brown. At least *I'm not sunburnt anymore,* she grinned. *I always wanted a tan!*

Turning to leave her peaceful spot, Lexi suddenly heard voices in the stillness. Glancing up, she noticed Hadley and Katie skipping down the road towards her.

I must be late. Lexi squinted her eyes to look at Hadley. She was swinging her arms as she walked and singing along with Katie, so she mustn't be too angry. Lexi waved to them.

Hadley cupped her hands around her mouth and called out in a loud voice. "Hey, Lexi, guess what?" She didn't wait for a reply from Lexi. "Katie found two big family sized blocks of chocolate!" She clapped her hands and jumped up and down on the spot excitedly. "Don't worry, we didn't eat it yet, 'cause I said, you'd want some!" Hadley started laughing.

"Damn straight!" Lexi yelled back, laughing too. She took one last look over her shoulder toward the barren bushland. There were still no signs of Braydon, Lilly or Elisha, so she scooped up her diary and eagerly ran down the road towards Katie and Hadley. Organising the town could wait. For now, she had nothing but sugar and chocolate on her mind!

The End

The story of Lexi, Hadley and the children of Jasper's Bay continues in book two of the Seventeen Series

Rage

Author Page

I was born in Perth Western Australia, and as a young adult, I grew up in the small country town of Tom Price situated in the outback of Western Australia. Travelling extensively throughout Australia, I loved seeing the diverse landscapes and animals of the country. My current home is in Perth with my husband, two daughters and our cat Abby.

I have a Bachelor of Science Degree, majoring in Sports Science. My interests include watching movies, especially Sci-Fi and horror, travelling, photography and reading. I also enjoy going to the occasional comic book convention!

Like the young women in my stories, I have had the opportunity to experience many exciting adventures in my life so far, including being part of the Australian Army Reserves, climbing to Mt Everest base camp, descending into one of the pyramids at Giza in Egypt, flying in a hot air balloon over the Valley of the Kings, parachuting from a plane at 12000 feet and sitting on the edge of an active volcano on Tanna island in Vanuatu.

I am a member of the Society of Children's Book Writers and Illustrators and the Australian Society of Authors.

My first novel *Seventeen*, is a YA dystopian adventure story that follows two sisters, Lexi and Hadley as they try to survive in the harsh Australian outback after the KV17 virus kills every adult on Earth.

Rage is the sequel in the *Seventeen Series* where Lexi, Hadley and the children of Jasper's Bay encounter more challenges as they learn to live without the help of adults or modern society.

The Pirate Princess and the Golden Locket is a children's pirate adventure story about a young orphan named Lotty and her cheeky dog, Mr Jacks.

My author website is www.Suzanneloweauthor.com

My Facebook page www.facebook.com/suzanneloweauthor/

My Instagram Page www.instagram.com/seventeentheseries/

WHY I WROTE THIS BOOK

Seventeen is the first book in the *Seventeen Series* about Lexi and her sister Hadley, two teenagers who are trying to survive in a post-apocalyptic Australia without the benefit of adults to help them.

I decided to write ***Seventeen,*** as I wanted to write a story for young adults, about children and teenagers having to survive in a world suddenly vastly different from one they had grown up in. One without adults, computers or any of the luxuries we are used to. Without adult influence, would the rules of society change? This was a scenario I would often discuss and theorise about with my own young adult daughters at the dinner table.

I love reading dystopian and post-apocalyptic stories myself, and I wanted to set my story in Australia, somewhere that is quite isolated and a unique setting for most dystopian stories. I think that the rugged and often harsh landscape of Australia would add to the hardship of the survivors.

The story of Lexi and Hadley and their friends in Jasper's Bay continues in the second novel of the *Seventeen Series*, called **Rage**.

If you as the reader have any questions you would like answered about the Seventeen Series or the characters in the story, please email me at **suzannelowe.author@gmail.com** and I will endeavour to answer your questions.

If you enjoyed this book. I'd be grateful if you'd post a short review on Goodreads, Amazon or wherever you purchased your copy. Your support really does make a difference, I read all reviews personally so I can get your feedback and make this book even better.

Thank you for taking the time to read my stories

Suzanne Lowe

RAGE

BOOK TWO IN THE
SEVENTEEN SERIES

Find out what happens to Lexi, Hadley and the other children of Jasper's Bay in the second book of the Seventeen Series.

As the children of Jasper's Bay realise no adults will be coming to help them, they must band together in order to survive.

With the KV17 virus now in its mutated form, the lives of Lexi and the older children are under threat. As they fight to find a solution, Lexi is unexpectantly caught up in a cowardly attack. The resulting chain of events leave her shocked and humiliated. Will the rage and fury she feels change her forever leading to disastrous consequences, or will her friends rescue her in time? How can they fight an enemy that is too small to be seen?

The exciting and compelling YA series set in the harsh Australian outback.

www.suzanneloweauthor.com

www.silvergumpublishing.com

THE PIRATE PRINCESS AND THE GOLDEN LOCKET

Book one in the **Pirate Princess** series.

The first thrilling tale of adventure, friendship and mystery in the Pirate Princess series.

The Pirate Princess and the Golden Locket is an exciting adventure story for 6-11-year-old children.

Meet Lotty, the brave young orphan whose life is suddenly about to change forever.

When on her twelfth birthday, Lotty is unexpectantly cast out from the Sevenoaks Home for Children, she befriends a cheeky little dog called Mr Jacks. Her life soon becomes an exciting adventure as together they encounter lazy pirates, hidden treasure and uncover the mystery of Lotty's golden locket!

The Pirate Princess and the Golden Locket is a story full of loveable characters, swashbuckling adventures and ruthless pirates!

www.suzanneloweauthor.com

www.silvergumpublishing.com

www.ingramcontent.com/pod-product-compliance
Lightning Source LLC
Chambersburg PA
CBHW071149100726
47908CB00002B/308